W9-BDR-028

CLOSE YOUR EYES, JESSICA . . .

"Listen to the sound of my voice. Feel my hands."

She obeyed him. His voice was rich, his hands warm.

"Think back, Jessica. Tell me what you remember."

She thought back. This man was a stranger to her eyes but not to her heart, she knew it with certainty. She felt an intense urge to sink back into his chest, to feel his lips upon her skin, to turn in his arms and hold him to her breast.

The feeling terrified her.

"No!" she gasped, pulling out of his grip.

"What is it?" he asked.

Her senses swirled. The present had fallen away, and she stood on a precipice of time, dangerously close to the edge . . .

Also by Patricia Simpson

Whisper of Midnight
Raven in Amber

Available from HarperPaperbacks

Harper
Monogram

The Legacy

PATRICIA SIMPSON

HarperPaperbacks
A Division of HarperCollinsPublishers

Special edition printing: February 1994

This is a work of fiction. The characters, incidents, and
dialogues are products of the author's imagination and are not
to be construed as real. Any resemblance to actual events or
persons, living or dead, is entirely coincidental.

HarperPaperbacks   *A Division of* HarperCollins*Publishers*
                    10 East 53rd Street, New York, N.Y. 10022

Cover photography by Herman Estevez

First printing: October 1992

Printed in the United States of America

HarperPaperbacks, HarperMonogram, and colophon are
trademarks of HarperCollins*Publishers*

❖ 10 9 8 7 6 5 4 3 2 1

To Bruce,
for his encouragement and penchant for realism,
and to Donna,
for her enthusiasm and care

A special thanks to Château Ste. Michelle,
Woodinville, Washington,
for making a great Johannisberg Riesling

The
Legacy

Astronomy compels the soul to look upwards and leads us from this world to another.

—Plato

PROLOGUE

July 1938

Michael Cavanetti took the cardboard box to the side yard where he had set up a workbench. He had been cutting lumber all day, and his hair and clothes were covered with sawdust. He had stopped only long enough to greet the mailman and sign for the package, ignoring the contemptuous look the postal carrier gave his shabby work clothes.

After two months in the United States, Michael was accustomed to such looks. As his strong olive fingers ripped open the carton and pulled away the packing, he grimaced. All these Americans, with their chewing gum and their rude impatience, thought he was a fool for buying the old house. But they didn't know about the plan.

Soon there would be a vineyard, a beautiful vineyard on the south slope by the sea. He had the cuttings from the old stock in the outbuilding behind the house. The run-down mansion would be transformed into a spare but elegant Benedictine monastery, and a chapel would be built, a chapel that would ring with the powerful sweetness of Gregorian chants when the monks arrived to join him. With thirty hardworking men, he would transform the mansion and grounds in a year's time. Then he would see those contemptuous looks fade. Ah, what a sight that would be!

Michael pulled out the last of the packing and looked down at the contents of the carton. What was this? He lifted a black robe. A strand of rosary beads fell from the woolen folds and landed in the sawdust at his feet. Michael bent over and picked up the beads, blowing off the wood powder before exploring the rest of the items in the box. There was a hemp belt, a cowl, and an envelope.

Michael frowned and grabbed the envelope. He opened the letter and scanned the message written in Italian, and for a moment he stared off into space, feeling his knees grow weak with shock. Niccolo was dead. His older brother and the rest of the Benedictine monks had perished at sea. Their ship had foundered off the coast of Italy and sunk, killing everyone aboard.

Michael fell to his knees, heedless of the sawdust beneath him. Then he dropped his face into his hands and wept. His brother was dead. Strong, wise Niccolo was dead.

Now no one would come. No one would join him in America.

He crushed the letter in his hand and held his fist to his lips, knowing a sudden jolt of dread larger than his personal grief for his brother the priest. Without Niccolo, the secret was lost. Without Niccolo there would be no more St. Benedict Riesling. Sure, he had the cuttings safe and sound in the shed out back. And sure, he could till the soil better than any man. But without Niccolo's master hand in the wine-making process, there would be no sweet elixir, no highly sought after Riesling.

More than the elixir was lost, however. Tradition would die with Niccolo, a tradition that had survived unbroken since the Middle Ages. With the death of Niccolo had come the end of the Cavanetti legacy.

It was the end of the world for Michael Cavanetti. What could he do? How could the legacy die like this? Ah, Mother of Mary, what would happen? Michael bent his head and clutched the ball of paper. He knew only one thing to do at a time like this. Pray.

He didn't know how long he prayed. Hours perhaps. He prayed until he had run out of strength and tears. Then, heaving a sigh, he crossed himself and looked up. With a gasp, he fell back on his haunches and stared up at the tall form standing just three feet away.

A monk stood before him, hands hidden in the sleeves of his habit, face hidden by the edge of his cowl.

"Brother Michael," the monk greeted him. His voice was deep, powerful.

"Yes?" Michael felt his heart pounding in his chest as he scrambled to his feet. He was afraid of this dark figure, and he didn't know why.

"You called for me."

"I did?"

The monk nodded solemnly. "I am the answer to your prayers, Brother Michael."

"My prayers?"

"Yes. I have come to help you."

Michael slapped the sawdust from his knees. Was this some kind of miracle? He glanced again at the robed figure. "Who sent you?"

"Who answers prayers, Brother Michael?" the monk countered.

"Oh." Michael brushed the sawdust from his hair, wishing he looked more presentable. If this was a miracle, then this monk was surely an angel, and he didn't want to appear so unkempt to an angel.

"But what can I do?" Michael asked. "The legacy can't go on. My brother is dead."

"The legacy will survive. I am here in your brother's stead."

"You know the secret of the wine?"

"Of course." The monk chuckled. "It is I who first came upon the secret, Brother Michael."

"*Capperi!*" Michael stepped backward, edging around the end of the worktable. He grabbed a chisel to arm himself, but the monk only chuckled again.

"Why are you afraid?" the monk inquired.

"Because I know who you are. I've heard of you. You're the sorcerer monk—Cosimo Cavanetti!"

"I am no sorcerer."

"Then how did you get here? Explain that!"

"I was sent to help you."

"Sent by Satan—not by God—by Satan!" Michael crossed himself and stared at the monk, terrified of the blank shadow beneath the cowl.

"I have come to help you, Brother Michael, not hurt you. I promise you that. Do not be afraid. And do not lose hope. You and I shall bring this vineyard to fruition, until a new priest is born to carry on the tradition."

"But how can that happen? There have always been two Cavanettis—a priest to make the wine and a man to till the soil."

"This is a new country, Brother Michael, and a new way of life. The old ways must change to suit the times. The next priest shall not be just a priest, but a man as well. Only one Cavanetti will be required in the future. And that Cavanetti will be the most powerful priest of all."

"What are you talking about?"

"I am talking about the future, Brother Michael. One of your sons will be this man-priest."

"But I am not even married."

"You will be."

"And I will have a son?"

"You will have two sons."

Michael slowly lowered the chisel to the workbench. "And the legacy will pass on then?"

"Assuredly. When your son becomes a man, he will learn all. The chain will not be broken, Brother Michael."

"Then I shall remain here in America?"

"Yes. All will come to pass. And I will be here to help you. I will be guardian. You will not always see me, but I will surely be here."

1

Seattle, Washington—December 1991

Jessica Ward squinted through the fog, trying to spot the turnoff to Moss Cliff Road. Never well marked, the road was hard to find, particularly since she hadn't visited the area for five years. She had passed the antiques shop a half mile back, and the huge madrona tree. The last landmark would be the pillars marking the entrance to Moss Cliff, a prestigious enclave of private estates belonging to the very rich and the very old families of Seattle. But in this fog, the gray stone pillars would be easy to miss.

After driving a hundred feet, Jessica glimpsed the twin columns shrouded in mist. She passed between them and followed a circuitous route between stands of droopy cedars and tangles of rhododendron. Jessica drove carefully, creeping ever upward on the twisting road. Here and there narrow lanes branched off, leading to secluded estates with magnificent views of Puget Sound. But in the darkness and fog she could see no evidence of civilization, not even a single light.

She had almost gained the top of the cliff when her headlights revealed an impressive sign bordered in gold. St.

BENEDICT WINERY was painted in large ornate letters over the image of a hooded monk. An arrow indicated the left fork in the road. "That's new," Jessica mumbled under her breath. She turned left and glanced again at the sign.

When she looked back to the road ahead, she saw a figure standing in the lane, blinded by her headlights. "God!" she cried, slamming on the brakes. Tires screeched as her rental car fishtailed on the damp asphalt and skidded into a shallow ditch.

Trembling, Jessica looked up, horrified that she might have killed someone. The headlights revealed a dark shape at the side of the road. At least the person was still on his feet. She hadn't hit anyone, but the near accident had shaken her considerably. Jessica scrambled out of the sedan.

"Are you all right?" she called, her voice quavering. The figure turned in her direction. She pulled her coat around her while an eerie sensation crept down her back. What an odd outfit the person wore. In the darkness it looked like some sort of parka with the hood pulled up, but the parka was long and reached to the ground. Or maybe she just couldn't see because of the shadows from the brush on the side of the road.

"Are you okay?" she repeated, stepping forward to see better. Yet she wasn't too eager to leave the security of her car. There were enough incidents these days involving women alone to make her wary of strangers. In fact, she had read a newspaper article at the airport that afternoon telling of a woman murdered not too far from the winery. The prime suspect in the case was a convicted killer who had run away from a work-release program and was still at large. What if this peculiar pedestrian was the convict in disguise?

The figure gave no answer but strode away, crossing through her headlights. Jessica gaped. Could her eyes be deceiving her? She would swear the figure was dressed as a monk, just like the one on the winery sign. Would a murderer dress as a monk?

"Wait!" she cried. "I'm sorry! I didn't see you!" She ran after the figure, but it seemed heedless of her and disappeared into the darkness at the side of the road.

"I'm sorry . . ." Her voice trailed off. She couldn't see a thing in the fog beyond the clumps of bracken. For a moment she stood in front of her car, listening for the footsteps of the retreating figure, but the trees and road lay muffled under a silent blanket of mist.

Perplexed, Jessica pushed back the black curls that had fallen over her brow. What should she do? Should she wait to see if he returned? Certainly not if he was the convict. The man didn't seem hurt. He was probably long gone.

Jessica realized she was still shaking. The best thing she could do was continue to the bungalow and have a cup of tea to calm her nerves. She walked back toward her car, gravel crunching beneath her black leather boots, and collapsed into the driver's seat. Then, with trembling hands, she belted herself in and eased the car back onto the road.

A few minutes later she made the final turn and gained the top of the cliff. At the higher altitude the fog was less thick, allowing the moon to filter through. Jessica saw some lights in the distance and felt considerable relief. She shifted into fourth gear and sped toward the lights, knowing her destination was only minutes away.

The lights belonged to the Cavanetti house. Jessica could make out the long line of the roof and the humps of its dormers. Just beyond was the Wards' summer home, a bungalow designed with all the elegance of the twenties but quite plain in comparison to the Italianate mansion next door.

The Cavanettis owned and operated St. Benedict Winery and had been neighbors for many years, but the disparity in houses had not always been in their favor. Michael Cavanetti had purchased the dilapidated mansion for next to nothing and had lived in the rotting shell until he had enough money and time to begin restoring it. Jessica could remember the way her father's relatives had stared out the bungalow windows at the run-down Cavanetti house, making snide comments about the Italians next door, using terms no one would explain to a young girl of five.

Jessica had always liked the mansion, even when it stood in disrepair, its glory faded by salty winds and incessant winter rain. The unusual architecture had caught her fancy. With its tall windows, curved moldings, and elaborate cornices, it looked more like an intricately decorated cake than a house. As a child she had made up all sorts of stories about the mansion and the millionaire who had built the house for his Italian wife. Her father had fueled her imagination with his own creative tales of the mansion's exotic history. But that had been years ago, when Robert Ward was still a vibrant, happy man, basking in his success on Broadway and content with his family. Life had changed drastically since then.

Jessica reached over with a gloved hand and turned down the heater. She hadn't noticed until that moment that she was uncomfortably warm from the aftereffects of her adrenaline rush. As she drove, she listened to the announcer on the radio finish his news broadcast with a station identification and the time.

"It's seven-thirty, Friday the thirteenth."

Friday the thirteenth. That explained everything. The day had not gone well. The airport had been fogged in, she had gotten caught in rush-hour traffic, and she had nearly run over someone. She should have turned back at the first sign of trouble. She should have stuck to her guns this time and refused to help her father. She should have called and said, "Sorry, Dad. Not this time. I'm tired of rescuing you. I'm tired of bailing you out of trouble. I'm sick and tired, Dad."

But she could never bring herself to say such things to her father. And she didn't know why she still helped him. Was it love, duty, or guilt? She couldn't tell anymore. She loved her dad, but she resented him almost as much, which made her feel guilty and selfish for needing a life of her own. More than anything she wanted a stable life, a predictable planned course that she could count on. Life with her father had been anything but stable.

On the radio, Perry Como sang "There's no place like home for the—" Jessica snapped him off mid-croon.

Home. Jessica's grim smile deepened with bitterness. She had never wanted to rush home for the holidays. She had never been able to relate to the greeting-card version of Christmas in which families gathered around their crackling fires and perfectly decorated Christmas trees. Except for the few years of her very early childhood, her home had never been like that. Was anyone's? She didn't think so. But deep inside she yearned for that image to be true and clung to the hope that somewhere a family could be whole and perfect, if only for one night out of the year.

She didn't know where home was anymore, anyway. Her condominium in Stanford, California, certainly wasn't home. She ate and slept in the sparsely decorated apartment but spent most of her hours at the university, where she was an assistant professor in the astronomy department. Her father had sold the family home in Seattle five years ago when he could no longer afford to live there. Of course, the real reason for the sale of the Ward estate had never been revealed to the public; Jessica had made certain of that. She had told everyone that Robert Ward had decided to locate closer to his work on the New York stage. He planned to live in Connecticut, in a fashionable country farmhouse, like other successful playwrights.

The farmhouse story was pure fabrication, although the Connecticut part was true enough. Jessica managed to check her father into an exclusive detox center in New Haven. Robert was dry for a few months, but soon he slipped back into his old habits, drinking away his days and nights while his typewriter gathered dust. Now he lived in the old summer home at Moss Cliff, the only property remaining to the once-wealthy Ward family.

Things change, people change. Jessica knew that only too well. She drove past the mansion and eased down the driveway to the bungalow. The house was dark. Not even the porch light was lit for her arrival. She felt a moment of disappointment but quickly snuffed out the feeling. She should have outgrown such childish expectations long ago. With a harder jerk than necessary, she set the brake.

The first thing she noticed when she opened the bungalow door was the musty smell of whiskey and cigarettes. She grimaced and fumbled for the lights. The front room was still furnished in the style of the sixties, when Robert Ward's life had ground to an emotional halt. The room was neat and clean but looked uninhabited. A strange, incessant metallic clicking emanated from down the hall. Jessica hurried toward the sound.

In the dim light of the family room she saw the source of the noise: a movie projector sending its blind beam through the smoky haze. The take-up reel turned around and around, flapping the end of film against the machine with a *thwank*, *thwank*, *thwank*. Who knew how long it had flung film against metal? Her father lay in his recliner, asleep beside the projector, unaware of the noise or her presence.

Jessica leaned over and turned off the projector. She pulled off the reel and put it into a metal cannister labeled *Hell's for the Living*, the title of her father's award-winning play. He watched it often, hoping for inspiration. But he found his only inspiration in whiskey and soda.

She set down the cannister and gazed at her father. His outstretched hand loosely clutched an empty tumbler. Jessica plucked it from his grasp and regarded his grizzled face. He hadn't shaved for days. He hadn't changed his clothes, either, by the look of his rumpled shirt and wrinkled pants. His once-handsome face was gaunt and lined, his once-thick brown hair now dull gray and hanging in lank strands around his skull. His socks had holes, and one big toe protruded like an eye, observing the stranger who had entered the house.

He should be in bed, but she wasn't strong enough to move him when he was unconscious. There was nothing she could do but cover him against the chill. Jessica walked to his room and pulled a blanket off his bed. Then she returned to drape the blanket over his lean body, making sure she tucked it around his legs and feet. She noticed numerous cigarette burns in the blanket.

She left her father and went down the hall to the kitchen. She set her purse on the counter and gaped in dismay at the disarray around her. The room was a jumble of dirty glasses and ashtrays and old food containers. A pile of newspapers three feet high leaned against an overflowing wastebasket. Jessica put her hand to her mouth. Disorder always bothered her. This disorder almost made her physically ill. She fled from the kitchen to unload the car.

She brought in the groceries she had purchased in town, lugged her suitcases to the front bedroom, and left the heavy telescope in the hall. She made sure the car was locked for the night and closed the front door securely behind her. Then she tackled the kitchen.

The refrigerator was practically empty, just as she had anticipated. A lone bottle of ketchup stood sentinel on the top shelf, guarding a few dubious leftovers. Jessica opened the freezer. It was frozen solid around a bag of peas. Disgusting. She would defrost it in the morning.

Jessica was planning her attack on the garbage when the doorbell rang. She stiffened in alarm. Who could be calling at this time of night? And how could she keep them from smelling the booze and smoke? Frantically she threw open cupboard doors, searching for a can of air freshener. She found some near the pantry and sprayed her way to the front door, ditching the can in an empty vase on the side table.

The doorbell rang again. Jessica smoothed back her hair and looked through the peephole. She could see the distorted image of a small, squat woman huddling in a black coat with a fur collar. Jessica snatched back the chain and pulled open the door.

"Maria!" she exclaimed, beaming in happiness at the old woman.

Maria held out her arms. "Jessica! *Mia bambina!*" The woman's pudgy arms surrounded Jessica in a warm embrace.

Jessica hugged the woman, closed her eyes, and took a deep, satisfying breath. Not everything had changed after all. Maria di Barbieri still smelled of garlic and flour and yeast. Jessica loved the aroma. It was a smell from her childhood, the smell of Maria's kitchen, a place where Jessica had known happiness.

Maria stepped back. "Look at you!" she exclaimed. "You look so beautiful, so grown up."

Jessica smiled. "I am grown up, Maria. I'm thirty years old."

"Thirty." Maria clapped her chubby hands to her face. "No!"

"Yes."

"And so tall!"

"I've been this tall for a long time, Maria."

Maria shook her head in disbelief.

"Come in, Maria. Come in."

"Only for a moment." She hobbled into the hall, stopping to take off the scarf tied around her head. Her hair had gone completely white, in snowy contrast to her olive complexion. And, in the light, Jessica noticed the troubled look in Maria's eyes.

"What's wrong, Maria?"

"Ah"—she waved—"you would not believe the trouble, you would not believe. I saw you drive past and came over as soon as I could."

"Why? What's the matter?"

"You have not been here for years, *bambina*. You don't know what it's like at the big house. You don't know what's going on."

"Tell me. Come and sit down."

Maria sniffed and looked around, and Jessica worried that she was smelling something other than lavender air freshener. But Maria quietly followed her to the front room, where she sat on the edge of a chair and refused to take off her coat.

"I don't have much time," she explained. "That Mrs. Cavanetti will be home any minute."

Jessica nodded, remembering how, for the longest time, she had assumed Maria was Mrs. Cavanetti. Every day she saw Maria go to the Cavanetti mailbox and then walk back to the house. She never saw any other woman at the mansion. Neither she nor her father ever talked with the Cavanettis. The Cavanettis spoke only Italian and kept strictly to themselves. Jessica's Aunt Edna had forbidden her to have anything to do with the family, saying they were the ruination of the neighborhood, that they pulled the heads off their chickens and let their goats eat grass on their front lawn. Their front lawn. Unthinkable!

When Jessica saw the Cavanetti boy carrying lumber into the house one day and wondered out loud what his name was and how old did Aunt Edna think he was, her aunt shut the drapes and told her to quit spying on the neighbors. She didn't care who the boy was, and neither should Jessica.

Not until Jessica's mother went away did Jessica find out that Maria was the housekeeper and cook at the Cavanetti place. Aunt Edna rarely visited after Jessica's mom left, and Robert was too distraught to pay any attention to the activities of his six-year-old daughter. So one afternoon when Jessica was hungry and lonely, she wandered past the Cavanetti mailbox just as Maria strolled down the walk to get the mail. Jessica stared, wondering what kind of person could pull the head off a chicken.

Maria stared back. But her eyes were full of kindness and humor. She asked Jessica how everything was. Was her father feeding her enough? She looked a little skinny. Sometimes fathers were too busy for lunch. Jessica nodded, her stomach growling. Her father hadn't even got out of bed that day. And there was very little food in the house. When Maria asked her if she liked cookies, she nodded eagerly. At that moment she would have liked cooked turnips.

That day had been her first visit to Maria's kitchen, a sparkling white room full of good smells and laughter and plenty of home-cooked food. Jessica wolfed down a huge lunch of ravioli and grapes and finished it off with a handful of oatmeal cookies still warm from the oven. Then she had spilled out her troubles to Maria—how she missed her mother, how she didn't know what to do. And Maria had surrounded her with flour-dusted arms and comforted her with soothing Italian phrases that Jessica somehow understood in her heart.

"Ah, that Mrs. Cavanetti! She will be so mad. I never should have meddled." Maria's wails snapped Jessica out of her memories. *"Capperi!"*

"How did you meddle?"

"I called Niccolo. I got on the phone and said, 'Nick, you come back. I don't care what your papa said to you, you come back. Your papa's lying sick in the hospital. Time for you to come back.'"

"Mr. Cavanetti is in the hospital?"

Maria nodded. "Stroke. Another one."

"He's had more than one?"

Maria rolled her eyes. "Ah, Jessica. Mr. Cavanetti is very

sick. Very sick! He hasn't talked for five years. He just lays there sick. He can't move his leg or his arm on his left side."

"I didn't know!"

"Who does? That Mrs. Cavanetti just hides him away in his bedroom. Like he doesn't exist! When he went to the hospital again, I said to myself, 'That's it, Maria di Barbieri. You're gonna call Nick.' Nick was a good boy. He was always a good boy. I don't care what that Mrs. Cavanetti says about him. I know Niccolo would help his papa if he knew how that Mrs. Cavanetti was treating him."

"So you called him?"

"Yes. And he came as soon as he could. Ah, he's such a beautiful man, Jessica. I never would have dreamed—"

"So he's here?" Jessica's heart thudded painfully.

"No, not now. He went to the hospital. But he left his bags in the house. I told Niccolo, 'Nick, don't leave your things!' But he said he could handle his stepmama. But I'm afraid she'll be mad about it. She'll be mad at me, too, for calling him. I can't take her anger anymore, Jessica. It's bad for my heart, you know."

"Why don't you bring his luggage over here, Maria? If Isabella won't let him stay at the house, he can come by and get his bags from me."

"I was hoping you would help, Jessica." Maria stood up. "You're such a good girl. And not married? Let me see that hand!"

Jessica held out her left hand. "Don't get any ideas, Maria."

"A good girl like you should be married!" She waved the air as she hobbled toward the door.

"Shall we take the car?" Jessica plucked her keys off the side table.

"Yes, we'll need it. That Niccolo. Six bags. Six big bags!" She tied the scarf under her plump chin. "I should have so much clothes."

2

Niccolo Cavanetti did have a lot of luggage. Jessica heaved each piece out of the trunk of her car and maneuvered them into the bungalow. Once all the suitcases were safely in the house, she noticed that three of the cases were black and three were dark brown. Two sets. Had Niccolo arrived with another person? Maybe he was married now. She hadn't thought of that. Her heart flopped again, and she admonished herself for caring whether Niccolo Cavanetti was married or not.

She hurried down the hall, determined not to be curious about Niccolo's marital status. But she got only as far as the side table where she had left the air freshener can in the vase. There she pivoted, and, before her conscience could remind her of her resolve, she went back to the luggage.

She bent down and lifted one of the ID tags belonging to the black luggage. C. Nichols, 10 Burberry Avenue, St. Louis, Missouri. Who in the world was C. Nichols? She pursed her lips and reached for a brown ID tag. L. Girard, 1601 Linden Street, St. Louis, Missouri. This luggage didn't even belong to Niccolo. Was he aware that he had the wrong bags?

What a mix-up. But there was nothing she could do about

it now. She would have to wait until he arrived to tell him. She shrugged her shoulders and returned to her task in the kitchen, hoping she could make some progress before Niccolo returned. She didn't want anyone to know in what slovenly conditions her father had been living.

By eleven o'clock, Jessica had brought order to chaos. She leaned against the sparkling counter, one sudsy hand on her hip, and surveyed her progress. The tile counters were clear and the dishes clean. The cupboards were spotless and filled with food. The garbage can stood scrubbed and refitted with a clean liner. The breakfast nook table and chairs had been wiped down and set to rights, curtains were tumbling in the dryer down the hall, and the floor shone like new.

Jessica breathed in and smiled. Order and cleanliness were good for the soul. Now all she had to do was shower and change before Niccolo showed up. She wore a pair of her old jeans and one of her father's plaid shirts. She had tied back her hair and stuffed her bangs under a Mariners baseball cap. If anyone saw her now, they'd think she was a bag lady.

Jessica retrieved her robe and headed for the bathroom, only to find it a dirtier mess than the kitchen. She slumped against the doorjamb. She couldn't take a shower in that mildewed cubicle. The thought turned her stomach. She crossed her arms and sighed. Two more hours of cleaning and then maybe she could rest.

She had just returned her robe to the front bedroom when the doorbell rang. Jessica froze. It must be Niccolo. He was here. And she still looked like a bag lady. The doorbell rang again. What if she pretended she was asleep and didn't hear it? That wouldn't work. He could see the front bedroom light from the door. He would know someone was up. Besides, she had to give him the bags, even if they weren't his. Jessica had no choice but to answer his summons.

She strode to the door. Who cared what she looked like anyway? She wasn't trying to make an impression on Niccolo Cavanetti. She was above such nonsense now. Jessica put her eye to the peephole just to make sure it was Niccolo and not some stranger. His tall form filled the fish-eye lens as it had filled her dreams so many times. Her heart lurched. Then she opened the door.

For a moment she gaped at the man standing on the welcome mat. Had she been wrong after all? Was this man truly Niccolo Cavanetti? He had the same dark brown hair, the same Tuscan black eyes, and the same broad shoulders she remembered from years ago, but there the similarity ended. This Niccolo was a polished, gorgeous man, much more cosmopolitan-looking than she ever would have guessed Niccolo could be. The porch light gleamed in his glossy hair, glinted off his wire-framed glasses, dissipated over the dark folds of his cashmere overcoat, and lost itself entirely in his dark corduroy pants and cordovan shoes.

"Jessica?" he inquired.

Jessica's glance vaulted from his shoes back up to his face. Embarrassment immobilized her tongue. She had been staring at him without a thought to her own appearance. What a sight she must make. Self-consciously she raised a hand to the ball cap.

"Hey, how about those Mariners!" he chuckled.

"Nick?"

"Cole."

"Pardon?"

"Cole. It's Cole Nichols." He held out his hand, a tanned, powerful slice of a hand that could easily engulf her own. Confused and blushing, she raised her hand to meet his and noticed that a scum of soap bubbles had dried on her wrist. She whipped back her hand and dragged it across the tail of her overlarge shirt.

"Cleaning," she explained with a sheepish grin. Then she shook his hand, wondering at the name change. Cole was the nickname she had given him when they were both younger. But why the strange last name?

"How've you been, Jessica?"

"Fine. How about you?"

"Fine." He smiled and stood in the doorway as if waiting for her to make a move.

She felt awkward, as if she should have hugged him, as if

the handshake wasn't enough. "Come on in, Cole," she said, motioning toward the bags in the hallway. "I saw the name C. Nichols on those bags and thought you had the wrong luggage."

"Didn't you know I was Cole Nichols, Jess?"

"No. Should I?"

"And you don't know who Cole Nichols is?" He crossed his arms over his chest and grinned at her.

"Well . . . the name sounds vaguely familiar." She looked back up at his smiling face. He had a crease in his forehead that slashed between his brows, right in the center of his glasses, which gave him an attractive expression of constant concentration. Where had she seen that face? On television? In the newspaper? She shrugged and shook her head, stumped.

Cole laughed outright then, a belly laugh that rumbled out of his chest and bubbled up into his eyes. "You've never heard of Cole Nichols?" He made a motion with his left hand, as if throwing something. Jessica raised an eyebrow. "Football?" he added.

Jessica shrugged again, helplessly ignorant.

"St. Louis Bulls? The team most favored to win the Superbowl this year?" He seemed so certain that she should recognize him that she felt a twinge of guilt.

"I don't follow sports, Cole. Especially football."

"Unbelievable," he chuckled. "Someone who doesn't know Cole Nichols."

Jessica bristled at his laugh. Did he think he was so famous that everyone should recognize him? What an ego. He hadn't changed a bit in thirteen years. She scowled. She disliked being toyed with, especially by a man, especially by Cole. And to be laughed at made her even angrier.

"Is this some sort of joke?" she asked in a constricted voice.

"No." Cole's smile faded immediately. "Hell, no."

"You seem to think it's pretty amusing!"

"Wait a minute!" He held up his hands in protest. "I didn't mean to make you—"

"You might have introduced yourself as Niccolo."

"I thought it was obvious—"

"Maybe to you and your football fans. But how was I supposed to know? The luggage tags don't say anything about Niccolo Cavanetti."

"That's because I changed my name."

"Why?"

The smile completely faded from his mouth and his eyes. "I think you can guess, Jessica."

"Guess?" She crossed her arms and glared at him. "What is this—a game show?" She was still angry, and when she was angry or nervous she had a bad habit of making sarcastic remarks that she sometimes regretted. "What do I win for getting the right answer? A refrigerator?"

His eyes glittered, and she felt a stab of guilt. She could certainly guess the reason for his name change and knew it wasn't a subject for sarcasm. Yet he had no right to make fun of her like that. She wasn't a skinny teenager trailing after him anymore. She was a grown woman. Jessica opened her mouth to tell him what she thought of his ego just as someone honked a car horn outside.

Cole turned in the doorway. Jessica looked around him and saw a sleek black Jaguar parked next to her rental sedan. Cole waved off the person who had honked.

"L. Girard?" Jessica questioned.

Cole turned back to her. His manner was considerably cooler. "Yes. L. Girard. A very tired, very cranky L. Girard." He strode over to the bags and picked up four of them as if they were no heavier than pillows. Jessica grabbed the remaining smaller ones and followed him out the door.

"Nice car," she commented as he opened the trunk.

"Thanks." He stowed away the bags. When he closed the trunk, Jessica caught a glimpse of a blonde in the passenger seat.

"L. Girard didn't like my stepmother."

"Oh?"

"Especially since the witch wouldn't let us in the house."

"She wouldn't?"

Cole shook his head. "That's okay. I've made reservations at a hotel near the hospital. I'll be closer to Pop that way." He held out his hand. "Hey, thanks, Jessica, for helping out."

"Sure." She marveled at the warmth of his skin as he took her hand. She felt cold and stiff in comparison—her usual uptight self. This meeting had ended in the same manner as their last meeting thirteen years ago—awkward and disappointing.

"Sorry about the mix-up, Jess."

"Sure. Bye." She hugged her chest as he sank into the driver's seat of the Jaguar, and waited in the dark as he started the engine. Then, with a wave and a flash of lights on the bushes, Cole Nichols roared off into the night.

She watched him drive down the lane. So he called himself Cole now. The whole world knew him by the nickname she had given him years ago. *Cole.* It was flattering in a way, his use of the name. And oddly fitting. Nick was appropriate for a rebellious, shaggy-haired young man. But the man who had just touched her was definitely no longer a Nick.

Jessica walked back to the bungalow and switched off the porch light. Then she tackled the dirty bathroom, scrubbing mildew with an intensity that matched her racing thoughts. All the while she cleaned she thought about Cole and how he had changed.

He had always been tall, and the hours he spent working in the vineyard had laid a fine foundation of muscle over his olive shoulders and arms. He had grown taller and more powerful than she would have thought possible, coming from the short Italian stock of his father and mother. Neither Michael nor Theophilia Cavanetti had grown over five and a half feet tall. Cole must be six foot three.

Jessica sprayed down the shower. She could remember Cole's old-fashioned clothes, his conservative haircuts and courtly mannerisms. He certainly dressed differently now. His clothes bore the unmistakable stamp of hand-tailored elegance. But it wasn't just his clothes that were different. He had changed everything—even his name—to separate himself from the family, business, and heritage that had burdened him with far more responsibilities and restrictions than a young man should have to bear.

She wondered what Maria thought of all this. And what

would Michael Cavanetti say when he found out his son had forsaken the family name? Maybe he wouldn't be surprised. Michael Cavanetti had disowned Cole years ago. Perhaps he would think it natural that Cole had turned his back on his Italian heritage and cut himself off from a father who had been a harsh and unforgiving taskmaster.

The situation made Jessica sad. She had known the Cavanettis in happier days, when father and son loved each other. She found it hard to believe that Michael Cavanetti could have been so hard on Cole, blaming him for things Cole had not done, punishing him for trouble Cole had tried to avert. But Isabella, the new wife, had come between father and son, poisoning Michael against his own boy.

Jessica bit her lip and sprayed cleaner on the mirror. She polished the surface until every speck was wiped away. It was as if Niccolo Cavanetti had vanished, as if he had died, and in his place a stranger had returned. She grimaced at herself in the glass. What was so bad about that? She had wished Niccolo Cavanetti dead at one time and had vowed never to think about him again. And here she was, brooding over him as if she still were a mooning adolescent.

Jessica turned off her thoughts and finished cleaning the bathroom. When she was done she looked around. The fixtures gleamed, the porcelain gleamed, the ceramic tile gleamed. She could take a shower at last.

She closed her eyes in luxurious fatigue when she got into the shower. She raised her face, feeling the glorious jets of hot water spray away the grime of the day. She pushed her hair back with both hands and shampooed it, while thoughts of Cole and the past rushed back unbidden.

Jessica had spent each summer vacation at the bungalow, happy to escape to its solitude. At Moss Cliff she didn't have to make up excuses to explain to her friends why they couldn't drop by after school. At Moss Cliff there were no boyfriends expecting to come in and meet her father. She would have been devastated if any of her friends had seen her father drunk. They all thought he was a successful playwright, too busy in New York to attend his daughter's school functions. Jessica had duped everyone, even her teachers and the school officials.

At Moss Cliff, she didn't have to pretend quite so much. She and her father spent their days quietly—he drinking and reading and she writing, playing her guitar, and taking care of the house. Every summer she looked forward to seeing Maria and Cole and Mr. Cavanetti and sharing evening dinners with them on the piazza of the mansion. But she noticed that as she became older, it seemed harder each year to break the ice with Cole. He was five years her senior and thought of her as a silly girl most of the time.

Then, when she was thirteen, Cole went off to college. He and his father had heated arguments about which university he should attend. Cole wanted to go to Notre Dame. His father wanted him to go to the University of Washington so he could live at home and help with the vineyard and winery. Cole wanted more than anything to leave the slave labor and his stepmother behind. Isabella wanted Cole to be as far away as possible. So Cole went to Notre Dame and came back only for the summers.

Jessica remembered those three summers with a smile. She was gradually becoming a young woman, and each succeeding summer she thought for sure that Cole would take some notice of her. But he seemed indifferent to her nascent charms, and his father kept him busy from sunrise to sundown anyway. Most of the time Cole turned in early after a grueling day in the fields.

Then came Cole's college graduation. Michael Cavanetti threw a party for him, complete with barrels of wine and a hired orchestra. People from all over the area came to celebrate.

Cole looked so handsome and mature in his rented tuxedo that Jessica couldn't take her eyes off him. Her girlfriends would laugh if they knew how she worshipped him. They would say he was just an Italian boy with little money and a dim future. But Cole had always fascinated her. He was so different from the boys who went to her high school. Her boyfriends were glib and reckless and insincere. Cole was quiet and confident and serious. All her friends drove cars their parents had bought for them. Cole drove an old truck he had restored in a shed behind the winery. All her boyfriends wanted to do was drive out to the beach and neck. Cole never looked at her twice.

Maria fussed over Cole at the party, beaming and crying. She was so proud of him. He had graduated summa cum laude from Notre Dame, as well as quarterbacking the football team, breaking records right and left. Maria kept weeping and lamenting the fact that his mother had missed this moment. Jessica knew that Cole barely remembered his mother, who had been an invalid for most of his young life and had died when Cole was five. For both Jessica and Cole, Maria had been a maternal substitute, showering them with love, good food and plenty of laughter, doing her best to make up for the loss of their mothers at such a young age.

Jessica and her father were invited to the party. Jessica wore a new dress with a very low neckline in hopes that Cole would see how womanly she had become at seventeen. She knew it was her last chance. Soon she would leave for college herself, and Cole would go his own way. They might not see each other again. That may not have bothered Cole, but Jessica was desperate to make her feelings known to him. She asked him to meet her at the bungalow so she could give him a special graduation present.

The present she had planned to give Cole was her well-guarded virginity. She had not given herself to any of the silly boys at school. None of them would have taken the event seriously. But she knew Cole would appreciate her sacrifice. Besides, it really wouldn't be much of a sacrifice. She wanted to give herself to him. She had gazed at Cole's bare torso on many occasions and wondered what it would be like to touch him, to embrace him, to feel his skin against her own. She had watched him stack crates upon crates of wine in the warehouse, throw bales of straw off the backs of trucks, and dump mountains of grapes into the crusher-stemmer for hours on end. She knew the texture of his skin by heart, every powerful posture of his back, every ripple of muscle beneath the taut skin of his chest and stomach. She had adored his body as a sculptor might adore a finely polished bronze.

Looking back, she was certain Cole had guessed the nature of her present. He came to the bungalow long past the designated hour, as if avoiding her. By the time he knocked on the door, Jessica was furious. She had spent two hours waiting for him, fussing over her hair, reapplying her lipstick, and making certain that her new diaphragm was inserted properly, all the while afraid to sit down because her dress would get wrinkled. When the doorbell rang, she glared at the door, her feet aching in her high-heeled shoes, her back sore from standing all that time, and her feelings absolutely crushed.

Instead of answering the door immediately, Jessica ran to her bedroom around the corner, threw on her old robe, kicked off her shoes, and mussed up her hair. Then she went to the door and yawned in his face. His present? Oh, she had forgotten he was even coming by! She'd drop the gift off in the morning. Would that be all right? He had accepted her memory lapse with calm equanimity and a damnable slow smile. She remembered shaking his hand. The bastard.

She was petrified that Cole might have seen through the sham. She would rather die than let him know how much his rebuff had hurt her. Why should she be interested in him anyway? She was destined for college, for fraternity boys and a life spent doing charity work. Why even look at that Niccolo Cavanetti?

After her anger cooled, she cried herself to sleep. She was a fraud, a complete fraud. Her entire life was based on ever-increasing lies and deceptions, all interwoven to protect her father and hide the emptiness of her own existence. She could never confide in anyone, never share her fears or dreams. Niccolo had been the one person she had longed to confide in. But she could never let down her guard for fear of being caught in a lie. What if he discovered what her family was truly like? Her loneliness and shame burned in her constantly, an ache that wouldn't go away.

◆   ◆   ◆

Jessica turned down the comforter in the front bedroom. At least the linen was clean. She turned off the lamp, then went to the window to take one last look at the night.

She loved the night. She loved the stars. When she observed the heavens, she no longer had to pretend to be Jessica Ward, the little rich girl who was not quite as rich as everyone thought. She was nameless, ageless, bodiless, just an eye behind a lens. The stars and heavens made her feel tiny and insignificant and her problems infinitesimal. She thought of the heavens as a piece of velvet sprinkled with diamonds, each star and moon a gem waiting for her discovery, and she pursued each one with quiet exuberance.

Jessica drew back the curtain and gazed out, letting her eyes grow accustomed to the dark. She pulled her robe around her, hit by a sudden feeling of unease. Something was not right. She focused on the foreground, her expert eye keyed to the slightest change in her environment. There by the monkey puzzle tree was a dark shape, a shape that did not belong to the familiar landscape. Jessica narrowed her eyes as a pricking sensation crept across her scalp.

Someone was in the yard, looking at the house. With a rush of fear, Jessica realized the figure was staring at her window. Her heart in her throat, she stumbled backward, fumbling for the drapery pull. The drapes slid together, obliterating the vision of the hooded figure.

3

The monk was outside her window. Jessica rushed from the bedroom and checked all the doors and windows to make sure they were locked. There was no telling what kind of lunatics were loose anymore and what they might do. She considered rousing her father but knew he wouldn't be lucid.

Nothing happened. No one tried to break in. No one rattled the doorknobs. After a few hours of sitting nervously by the kitchen phone, lights blazing, she trudged down the hall and fell into bed, exhausted and drained.

When Jessica woke at nine the next morning, she was still tired but knew she should get out of bed. Her father wouldn't be up for hours yet, so she decided to bake a coffee cake and take it to the Cavanettis. She would find out how Mr. Cavanetti was doing in the hospital, and she also intended to inquire about the monk she had seen. If nothing else, she could at least alert the neighbors that someone was loitering around the property.

Jessica pulled on a loose-fitting jumpsuit, belted it with a wide leather thong decorated with dull brass, and tried to ignore the peculiar, uneasy feeling the monk's presence caused her. She did not open her drapes.

An hour and a half later she left the bungalow, the warm coffee cake resting in a plastic container. Jessica closed the door and glanced at the monkey puzzle tree in the yard. Of course no one was there. Could she have been overtired and imagined the monk? Jessica quickened her step. She could not fool herself. She had seen him. Twice.

The morning was overcast and misty, and Jessica shivered under her jacket as she walked up the driveway to the main road. She crested the rise and let out a small whistle through her teeth when she saw the Cavanetti house in the light of day.

She had not seen the metamorphosis when she passed in the night, for the details had been shrouded in darkness. But this was not the same house she had known five years ago. This was a showplace.

Jessica ambled forward, spellbound, never taking her eyes off the mansion. The entire house was painted a beautiful rose color, as delicate and subtle as a light blush wine. The filigrees and moldings around the windows and the deeply sculpted cornice were painted darker shades of rose. A grand marble staircase now curved upward to pass through a columned entrance, a graceful complement to the Italianate mansion.

Even the landscaping was new. Jessica strolled up the walk, marveling at the manicured lawn, cut and trimmed to perfection even in the middle of December. There would be no goats on this lawn. Near the foot of the staircase was a plaque. WINTHROP HOUSE, 1888. Jessica raised an eyebrow. The house was most likely on the National Register of Historic Places now. Good for Mr. Cavanetti.

Jessica rang the buzzer and Maria opened the door.

"Ah, Jessica!" She beamed. "Come in! Come in!"

"Thanks, Maria. Is Mrs. Cavanetti here?"

"Yes. She's in the drawing room. I'll announce you."

Jessica raised another eyebrow. Announce her? That was a new practice. Amused, she followed Maria down the hall to the drawing room, and she couldn't help but gape at the changes in the interior of the house. Everywhere she looked she saw new wallpaper, polished oak, crystal and lace. Even the old house smell was gone.

On cue, Maria motioned her into the drawing room, where Isabella Cavanetti scrutinized wallpaper samples that a man held against the wall.

"I'll be with you in a moment, Jessica," Isabella threw over her shoulder without looking at her.

Jessica watched her tilt her head and flip her hand impatiently. The decorator selected another swatch and held it up.

"That's too blue. The rose has a bit of peach in it. That blue just kills the rose, don't you agree?" Isabella's voice was clipped but musical, as if she had taken voice lessons.

The man surveyed the swatch and the woodwork. "Yes, I think you're right, Mrs. Cavanetti. How about this one?"

Jessica looked at the swatch. That one was definitely too peachy as far as she was concerned. She let her gaze travel back to Isabella, wondering if Mrs. Cavanetti was really that concerned with the wallpaper or just wanted to make her wait. She suspected the latter.

Mrs. Cavanetti was a tall woman with delicate ankles and wrists and excellent legs, which she accentuated with high-heeled pumps and dark stockings. As usual, she was exquisitely dressed, in a navy wool jersey topped off with a navy-and-jade challis scarf. Her red hair shone with burnished highlights that could fool the eye into believing the color was real. But Jessica knew from Maria that Isabella had dyed her hair for years. She was still vigorous, however, even at sixty-five.

Suddenly Isabella turned. "What do you think, Jessica? Does this go well with the carpet and paint?"

Jessica shook herself out of her daydream and regarded the swatch again. "It looks too peachy to—"

"Exactly. Too peachy. Don't you have anything else?" She glared at the decorator.

"Mrs. Cavanetti," the man protested, "we've gone through every sample book I have. This is it. I still think this first swatch would—"

"Oh, that first swatch is horrible, just horrible!" Isabella threw up her hands. "I can't believe you don't have something that will coordinate any better!"

"Of course, Mrs. Cavanetti! We'll find one. I'm sure there's one we've overlooked."

"I swear!" Isabella passed her fingertips across her forehead. "Christmas is what—eleven days away?—and the wallpaper isn't done yet. It's outrageous! That's what it is—outrageous!"

The young man flipped frantically through his books while she hurled abuse at him. Jessica felt sorry for him. He had probably been trapped for hours with Isabella.

"Really, Mrs. Cavanetti," Jessica put in, hoping to ease both of them, "the house looks wonderful!"

"Does it?" Isabella glanced at her. "I've been working so hard to get it finished for the Christmas party, but God knows how much trouble I've had."

"What about this one?" The decorator held up a pattern of muted stripes coordinated with a demure calico print border.

Isabella pursed her lips. "Well, it looks good with the carpet."

"And it picks up the rose in the paint. Look at that. Perfect." He held the swatch against the wall. "This is it, Mrs. Cavanetti. I don't know why we didn't consider this one before."

"When can you have it?"

Jessica glanced at the container she still carried in her hand. Steam had condensed on the top. The coffee cake was probably damp and ruined. She listened idly as Isabella and the man discussed schedules. Then Isabella dismissed him and turned to Jessica.

"Thank goodness that's out of the way!"

Jessica smiled and held out the coffee cake. "I thought you might like a treat to help you through this stressful time."

Isabella took the cake. "How very thoughtful of you." She set it on a side table next to a huge vase of gladioli without even looking inside the container.

"How is Mr. Cavanetti?"

"As well as can be expected, as long as he doesn't have any relapses." Isabella slowly pivoted and faced Jessica. "I must say I have my reservations about Nick showing up. You do know he's back, don't you?"

"Yes."

Isabella compressed her lips into a tight line. "Nick's

presence will make it harder for Michael. You know how they don't get along. Nick will only upset his father." She put a hand to her throat. "He's always had that effect on people."

"He seems to have changed, don't you think?"

"Maybe on the outside." Her eyes narrowed. "But he doesn't fool me. Have you heard that he's gotten into some kind of trouble back East? I'm telling you, Jessica, I don't want his kind here. Trash, that's what he is. I hate to say it—he is my husband's son—but he is trash, pure and simple!"

"What kind of trouble is he in?"

"He assaulted a woman in Philadelphia."

"What?" Jessica gasped. "I don't believe it!"

"Believe it." Isabella adjusted her scarf. "That's trash for you. And he calls himself Cole Nichols. How convenient. He thinks he can change his name and no one will know he's Italian." She laughed coldly. "What will he do now? Change it again so no one will know he's committed a crime?"

"I can't believe Cole would do that."

"You don't know him well, do you? Why, you were a teenager when he left."

"But still—"

"Those football types think they own the world, that they can do anything, that they're above the law. Well, this time Nick is going to get what he deserves."

"Has he gone to trial yet?"

"No, but he will. And I can't wait. I hope they lock him up for years. I just wish it had happened sooner so he wouldn't have had time to come back here and harass my poor husband."

Jessica was confused and shocked by the news of Cole's trouble. He didn't seem the type to assault women. Yet, she didn't really know him. She hadn't even been aware that he played professional football. She had nothing on which to base her belief in him except a certainty deep in the pit of her stomach.

Isabella glanced at her watch. "I hate to cut our visit short, Jessica, but I'm running late this morning, and I have to pick up Frank at the airport."

"Oh, that's all right. I just stopped by to see about Mr. Cavanetti. Which hospital is he in?"

"University of Washington Medical Center, but he really shouldn't see visitors yet."

Jessica walked to the door of the drawing room, and Isabella led her out to the front hall. "Oh, by the way, I'm having a Christmas party Friday night. You're welcome to come. Semiformal. Eight o'clock."

"Thank you. I'd like that."

Isabella held open the door. "Oh, and you might want to go to the open house at the Falls Winery tomorrow night. The Seattle Enological Society is sponsoring a tasting and Christmas party. Some local celebs will be there. You might find it interesting."

"Will you be able to go, with Mr. Cavanetti in the hospital?"

"It's one of those social obligations I simply can't duck. Anyone who's anybody will be there."

Jessica nodded and started to leave.

"If you want to go, just give Maria a call. You can ride out to Woodinville with us if you like. Frank will be going."

"All right. Thanks."

"Bye now." Isabella swept the door closed, and Jessica walked thoughtfully down the marble stairs. On the bottom step, she paused. She had forgotten to inquire about the monk.

Robert Ward sat in the kitchen drinking a Bloody Mary when Jessica got back. She stood in the doorway watching him read the paper for a moment before he became aware of her presence. Finally, he looked up.

"Oh, there you are, Jess." He pulled out a chair. "Sit down."

He didn't even mention the fact that she had cleaned the kitchen and bathroom. She lowered herself into the chair and glanced at the tall glass at his fingertips. She wished she could throw the glass out the window and end his drinking once and for all. But she knew he would simply pour another belt as soon as she left the room.

"How long are you staying? through Christmas?"

"Yes. I'm leaving after Christmas."

"That'll be nice. Haven't had a family Christmas for years."

Jessica looked down. Had the two of them ever had a family Christmas? The bitterness she felt gave her the resolve to be firm with him. She raised her eyes.

"I'm not here for Christmas, Dad, and you know it."

Robert combed his fingers through his lank hair and took a long sip of his drink. His eyes glinted with watery bleariness when he glanced at his daughter.

"So, Wes called you?"

"Yes." She leaned forward, her forearms resting on the table. "Dad, listen. You've got to get a hold of yourself. Wes says you haven't been keeping up with your bills. I had to pay the taxes on the bungalow this year. You could lose the house if you don't pay the taxes."

"Didn't I pay them? I was sure I paid them."

"No, you didn't. And there are other matters you've ignored. Where's all the mail?"

Robert squinted. "The mail?"

"Wes says he's called and written dozens of times and never gets a response from you. Finally he called me. He mentioned some legal matter that must be settled, a lease."

"A lease? We don't have any leases." Robert waved her off. "He must be confused."

"Don't the Cavanettis lease the vineyard property from us?"

Robert shrugged. "Yeah, I guess they do. Seems they've had it so long, it's theirs."

Jessica's lips tightened. "Dad, don't you even know the extent of your assets?"

His eyes shifted away from her, and he raised the glass, talking into it. "I don't like the business end of things. I'm an artist, for chrissake!"

She wanted to tell him that he was a drunk, not an artist, but she bit back the words. Instead she sighed. "Dad, you've got to get your affairs in order. From what Wes says, you're running out of capital." She stood up. "We need to look at the terms of that lease and see what your options are. Maybe you could sell the property, and that would give you what you need."

Robert finished the Bloody Mary while Jessica waited for his response. After a moment, she realized his eyes were on the paper in front of him, and he had no intention of pursuing the lease conversation.

"Well?" she asked, putting a hand on her hip.

"Yeah." Robert waved her off. "I'll go through the mail."

"When?"

"As soon as I read the paper."

"And when will that be?"

"When I'm finished."

Jessica stared at him, fighting to keep her anger under control. Her father was well on his way to oblivion already. She grabbed her purse off the counter, expecting him to ask where she was going, but he didn't even look her way.

Jessica rushed out the door and jumped into her car. In minutes she was halfway down Moss Cliff Road, shifting gears with ruthless precision while her car splashed through the winter rain. She decided to ignore Isabella's advice and see for herself what condition Michael Cavanetti was in.

She pulled up in front of the University of Washington Medical Center, a huge tower of stone and glass. Then she whisked through the automatic doors, asked what room Michael Cavanetti was in, and took the elevator to the eighth floor. As she soared upward, she closed her eyes and lifted her face.

Were all fathers hard to live with? Her father's illness had stunted her own development, perhaps irrevocably. She had always considered Mr. Cavanetti the kind of man she would have wanted for a father—strong and warm, hardworking and steady—yet as Cole had grown older, his father became harsh, intractable, expecting far too much of his teenage son. And then had come the moment when Cole had announced his intention to make his own life apart from St. Benedict Winery. His father had disowned him and had never been the same since.

The elevator doors slid open, and Jessica walked onto Eight North. She went to the desk and inquired about Mr. Cavanetti.

The nurse on duty looked up and took off her huge glasses, revealing a pinched face and cold gray eyes. "I'm sorry, ma'am. No one but family is allowed to see Mr. Cavanetti."

"But why?"

"Mrs. Cavanetti's request." The nurse put her glasses back on her nose as if in dismissal. Jessica stood at the desk for a moment, wondering what she should do. She had driven more than ten miles to see Michael Cavanetti.

"Okay. Thanks." Jessica sighed and dragged her hands from the counter just as a tall man walked into the waiting room.

"Jessica!"

She turned. Cole Nichols strode toward her, a smile on his face. She admired the way he walked, a direct gait full of assurance. His shoes were beautifully molded to his feet, probably custom-made. He was dressed in dark blue slacks, a chambray shirt, and a blue wool crew neck sweater that set off the golden tones of his skin.

"Hi, Cole."

"Are you here to see my father?"

"Well, yes, but they won't let anyone in except family."

"Are you kidding?" He took her elbow as he walked to the desk.

Instantly the nurse jumped up. "Oh, Mr. Nichols! Good afternoon!" Her pinched face bloomed with delight.

"Hi, Norma. How's my father?"

"Better. Much better. He's still awake if you want to pop in."

"Norma, this is Jessica Ward. She's known my father for years. She's like a daughter to him. Any time she wants to see him, you just let her in, all right?"

"Oh." Norma nodded toward Jessica. "I'm sorry. I didn't know."

"That's okay." Jessica smiled at Norma, although the nurse had already turned her attention back to Cole.

"Say, Mr. Nichols . . . uh, may I call you Cole?"

"Sure."

She pushed a tablet across the counter. "Cole, my grandson would just die for your autograph. . . ."

Jessica watched as Cole scribbled a short message and his

name on the paper. Her eyes traced the sharp line of his profile as he wrote. She hadn't realized until that moment that Cole might not simply be a football player, but a football star. She gazed at his hand as he clicked the pen shut and gave it back to the nurse. His hand was tan and well-formed, with long, lean fingers—not too big to be clumsy, and not too slight to be weak. Hands like his were capable of fine dexterity and surprising strength. She remembered how warm his hand had felt the night before.

"Thanks, Cole!" Norma beamed. "Oh, this is so nice of you!"

Cole smiled at Jessica and led her down the hall.

"There are some advantages to being a famous quarterback," he commented. "You can make people happy once in a while, just by writing your name."

"I didn't know you were so famous. What team did you say you play for?"

"The St. Louis Bulls." He chuckled. "I can't believe you've never heard of us. We're on the way to the Super Bowl this year, you know."

He stopped in front of the door to Michael Cavanetti's room, and his grip tightened around her elbow. Jessica looked up in surprise.

"I want to warn you, Jess. He's changed. I don't want you to be shocked."

"What do you mean, changed?"

"He's aged. Considerably. I saw him earlier this morning when he was asleep. It was a good thing he wasn't awake, because his appearance got to me."

"You haven't seen him for thirteen years, Cole."

"I know. But thirteen years couldn't possibly have changed him this much."

He held open the door, and Jessica passed over the threshold. A single bed stood near the window across the room. A slight figure lay in the bed. She could see a pale arm covered with liver spots lying on the sheet, and the beak of Michael Cavanetti's nose in silhouette. Jessica breathed in, called upon her finely honed acting ability, and moved forward with a smile.

4

Jessica waited a moment before she spoke, so she wouldn't startle Mr. Cavanetti. Slowly, he turned his head toward the two young people who stood beside his bed. Jessica forced the smile to remain frozen on her lips while she gazed down at the emaciated man she knew to be Michael Cavanetti.

He had indeed changed. His eighty-year old body was as gnarled and withered as a weathered grapevine. His hair, once black and thick, had thinned to white cobwebs on a liver-spotted skull. His cheekbones jutted out like ledges under his eyes, and his nose and ears seemed oversized in comparison to his narrow, wrinkled face.

"Hello, Mr. Cavanetti," Jessica said in a voice evenly modulated through sheer self-control. She reached out and covered his bony hand.

He blinked and stared at her. Sudden recognition flooded into his face. He knew who she was. She could see it in his eyes. At least his memory was still intact. Michael struggled to say something, but his lips contorted over a swollen tongue. Jessica patted his hand. "It's all right, Mr. Cavanetti. Don't strain yourself. I just wanted to stop in and say hello."

She squeezed his hand. "Look who's here."

She watched Michael's eyes shift upward to take in the tall form of his elder son, the son he had banished thirteen years ago.

She felt Michael's hand twitch beneath hers. "It's Niccolo," she remarked softly.

"Hi, Pop." Cole stepped from behind Jessica and looked down at his father. "Maria told me you were in the hospital."

Again Michael's mouth contorted, and Jessica saw his eyes widen with strong emotion, but she couldn't read his expression. He might have been alarmed, or he might have simply been shocked to see his son towering over him, powerful and handsome and in the prime of life.

"The nurse says you're doing much better," Cole ventured. "Maybe you can go home soon."

Suddenly Michael's hand clutched Jessica's, and she gasped. Michael struggled, trying to lift his head, trying to speak, but all that came out was a guttural noise.

"What's the matter, Mr. Cavanetti?" she asked. His eyes stared intently at her and then at Cole, as if imploring them to do something. He managed to shake his head and then fell back, exhausted. He closed his eyes.

Jessica looked up at Cole. "What do you think he's trying to say?" she asked. "He seems distraught."

"I don't know. I can't make out his mumbling." Cole reached over and touched his father's hand. "Pop, I know you and I have had our differences. I know how disappointed you were in me for giving up the winery. Maybe I deserved to be disowned. But I want to help you now." He watched for a sign that his father heard him. Michael lay unmoving. "Pop, let me help you."

Michael's parchment-lidded eyes opened. He gazed at Cole, his eyes moist and glittering. Cole withstood the scrutiny without saying a word or breaking the gaze.

Once again Michael tried to speak. Then he paused, as if making a great effort at concentration, and pushed forth a single word.

"Bunk?" Cole questioned, puzzled.

"No," Jessica countered. "It sounded like *monk*." Michael squeezed Jessica's hand. She glanced at him. "Did you say 'monk'?"

Michael nodded slightly just as the door opened. A nurse came in with a tray. "Sorry, folks. Time for Mr. Cavanetti to rest now."

Cole leaned closer. "We'll come back soon, Pop. Don't worry."

Jessica slowly rose and released Michael's hand. She followed Cole out to the hallway. "What do you think he meant by that?" she asked.

"You mean 'monk'?"

"Yes."

Cole rubbed the back of his neck. "I don't know. Maybe he's drugged up and talking nonsense."

"No, I don't think so. He squeezed my hand when I asked him if he said 'monk.' I think he was lucid."

"But it doesn't make any sense." Cole slipped a hand around her elbow and strolled with her down the hall. Ordinarily she felt awkward when someone touched her in such a casual, proprietary fashion. But with Cole she felt no unease, perhaps because her mind was focused on Michael Cavanetti.

"Can I get you a cup of coffee at the cafeteria?" he asked.

"No, thanks. I should be getting back."

"Then let me walk you to your car."

She couldn't refuse him. "All right," she answered.

They walked in silence to the elevator. When the doors closed, Jessica leaned against the rail. Cole pushed the button for the lobby and then looked over at her.

"He's old. I never thought he'd look so old," he said.

"I don't think he wants to go home, either, for some reason."

"Why? He always hated being away from the place. Why would he change?"

"I don't know." Jessica shrugged and looked at the light bouncing from number to number as they descended. "But didn't Maria mention that Isabella locks him away upstairs? You don't suppose she's actually abusive to him, do you?"

"You know how Maria exaggerates."

The doors *whooshed* open. Cole let her out first. "Where's your car?" he asked.

"Right outside."

He guided her out of the hospital and lingered as she unlocked her car. She paused when she opened the door.

"Cole, do you know anything about a monk at the winery?"

"What do you mean?"

"Is there someone posing as a monk?"

"Not that I know of. Why?"

"I've seen a monk twice since I've been there. Once on Moss Cliff Road, and last night outside my bedroom window."

Cole smiled, his white teeth flashing against his golden skin. "A monk voyeur? That's a new twist."

"I'm serious!" She found her ignition key and sank into the seat of the car. "Maybe it has something to do with your father. Maybe the monk has frightened him or hurt him or something."

"Not likely. I can't imagine a monk hanging around the winery. Maybe you just thought you saw a monk."

Jessica shook her head and started the car. She was certain of what she had seen.

Cole leaned into the car. "Are you going to the Falls Winery open house tomorrow night?"

"I don't know. Maybe. Are you?"

He nodded. "Lucy wants to try her palate at tasting. And I wouldn't mind seeing old faces again. Maybe we'll see you there."

She gave him a quick smile, and he closed the door, his long fingers lingering on the window frame. For a moment she gazed at his hands and then turned the wheel. In her rearview mirror, she saw him standing in the drizzle, watching her pull into traffic. Jessica gripped the wheel. She couldn't remember the last time anyone had watched her departure from anywhere.

◆ ◆ ◆

Shawn Cavanetti flung open her suitcase and put her hands on her hips. She wore a tight leather skirt, but she didn't think she was showing yet, especially when she let her oversized T-shirt hang over the waistband of the skirt. Shawn glanced at her profile in the mirror on the closet door and sucked in her gut. Then she faced her reflection and gazed at the shirt, smiling, her lips stretching across teeth stained by her dark plum lipstick. On her shirt was a green-and-black screen print of the Better Than Dead Boys, a group of headbangers whose concert she had attended a month ago. She liked the Boys, but she liked even better the look of outrage that had petrified Isabella Cavanetti's face when her daughter-in-law had taken off her fake fur jacket downstairs to reveal the shirt.

What a stick-in-the-mud, her mother-in-law. Shawn fumbled in her purse for her cigarettes and lit up, breathing in deeply. God, it felt good. She hadn't had a smoke on the plane or on the trip from the airport. She exhaled toward the ceiling and smiled again. It would be a shame to smell up that Mercedes or Mrs. C.'s perfectly coiffed hair. She couldn't imagine anything of Isabella Cavanetti's ever smelling of cigarette smoke.

Shawn held out the long, slender cigarette and regarded it solemnly, as a frown pushed her dark red lips into a pout. She really should stop smoking now that she was pregnant. She had heard it wasn't good for babies. Ah, well, she'd finish off her pack and then quit. That was a promise.

She held her cigarette between two short white fingers as she pulled a shirt from her suitcase. She had walked only two steps toward the closet when a short rap on the door stopped her in her tracks.

Isabella swept into the room. "Don't bother unpacking, Shawn."

The icy tones of Isabella Cavanetti did not make Shawn blink. She looked Isabella up and down, giving her one of her best sneers, and then turned to the closet.

"I said"—Isabella stepped closer—"don't bother unpacking."

"I'm not deaf, Mrs. C." Shawn pulled a hanger from the rack.

"And don't call me that horrid name!"

"If we are both called Mrs. Cavanetti," Shawn replied, "people might get confused about who's who."

"Hardly!"

Shawn ignored her and slipped the shirt over the hanger.

"Didn't Frank tell you that I forbid smoking in the house?"

"No." Shawn glanced at the cigarette in mock dismay. "He didn't. But that's Frank for you. Falling down on the job again." She shrugged.

Enraged, Isabella walked to the suitcase and pushed down the lid, snapping the clasps shut.

Shawn turned. "Hey!"

"I want you out of here, Shawn. Frank never informed me that you were coming, and I'm afraid I haven't made arrangements for you to stay."

"Haven't made arrangements?" Shawn put a hand on her hip. "This is Christmas time, for God's sake, Mrs. C. Family time. And I'm part of the family whether you like it or not. What was I supposed to do, stay in Boston like I did when you and Frank went traipsing off to Europe last summer?"

"Frankly, I don't care where you stay." Isabella dropped the suitcase onto the floor. "Had I not been so stunned to see you, I would have suggested you stay at the airport, or book a return flight."

"You think you can keep ignoring the fact that I'm your daughter-in-law? You think you can keep leaving me behind? Well, Mrs. C., I'm sick of being left behind and ignored!"

"I don't like being ignored either. I told you to leave, Shawn. And I want you out of here now."

Shawn took a drag of her cigarette and blew the smoke out of her nostrils, knowing unladylike behavior infuriated Isabella. She squinted at Isabella through the smoke. What a witch. No wonder Frank was such a wimp. With a mother like Isabella, he didn't stand a chance.

"Right now, Shawn!"

"And if I don't go?"

"I'll call the police. I'll have you thrown out. Frank is going to divorce you, you know."

Shawn smiled. "I don't think so, Mrs. C. In fact"—she pulled a paper out of the pocket of her skirt—"I think you and my dear husband are going to start treating me real nice."

"Why should we?"

"Because of this." Shawn dangled the paper between her thumb and index finger and swung it back and forth. She could see a gleam of curiosity flare in Isabella's eyes, but the old lady snuffed it out immediately.

"And what is that, pray tell?"

"Well, first of all . . ." Shawn ground out her cigarette in an African violet plant on the nearby dresser, much to Isabella's disgust. "I bet you don't even know my first name."

"Isn't it Shawn?"

Shawn shook her head smugly. "Nope. That's my middle name. My first name is Iona. Isn't that sick? I don't know why my mom ever gave me such a sick name."

"Perhaps if you knew your mother, you could find that out."

Shawn tried not to let the barb get to her. How had Isabella known she was adopted? Had Frank told her? Frank wasn't supposed to tell anyone that she was adopted. Shawn pressed her lips together, forcing herself to continue.

"Anyway, my real name is Iona Shawn Gilbertson. Now it's Iona Shawn Cavanetti, and I live in Boston with your darling Frank." She crossed her arms. "Didn't you live in Boston once, Mrs. C.?"

She saw Isabella blink quickly. Ah, good. She was getting to the old bitch. This was great! Just like in her favorite soap operas.

Isabella lifted her chin. "What does that have to do with anything?"

"Well, a few weeks ago I got this strange letter in the mail from a man in—" She glanced at the paper to refresh her memory. "In some place called Firenze, Italia."

She leveled her eyes upon Isabella and saw her mother-in-law go pale around the lips.

"Florence?" Isabella murmured. "Italy?"

"Is that it?" Shawn laughed. "I should have guessed."

Isabella was not the least amused. "What did the man want? I can see you are dying to tell me." She tried to affect a bored expression, but Shawn could see an anxious look hovering in her eyes.

Shawn regarded the letter again. "It seems the attorney of a Marcello di Leona is looking for a wife Marcello once had. He claims the wife will be named beneficiary of Marcello's estate if she'll make herself known. It's kind of a penance thing for this guy, I guess. Seems he got religion in his old age."

"Why should I be interested in all this?"

"Why?" Shawn folded the paper and stuffed it into her skirt pocket. "Because the wife's maiden name was Isabella Buccaliero. Isn't that a strange name? Buccaliero?"

"I don't know." Isabella's lips were grim. "It's probably common in Italy."

"Apparently this lawyer found out that Isabella Buccaliero had changed her name to Isabella Cavanetti. I. Cavanetti. They tracked down an I. Cavanetti living in Boston, thinking it might be you. But"—Shawn stepped closer—"they got me instead." She smiled, and Isabella turned away from her.

Shawn followed Isabella to the window. "Now, some people would throw a letter like this right in the trash. I mean, what possible use could it be? Just a simple mistake. But not me. I did some homework, Mrs. C."

"Oh?" Isabella's voice cracked.

"You didn't think girls like me did homework, did you, Mrs. C.?"

Isabella did not turn around or answer her.

Shawn walked back to the bed. "Well, do you want to know what I found out?"

"Do I have a choice?"

Shawn picked up her suitcase and replaced it on the bed. She snapped it open again. "I found out that you were born in Italy, Mrs. C. You were married at a very young age to this Marcello di Leona person. When you were eighteen you fled to the United States with a lover and lived in Boston for a while. Then you came to the Northwest and married Mr. Cavanetti. Only you forgot one thing."

"And what is that, pray tell?" Isabella turned to look at her.

"You never got a divorce."

Isabella stared at her. "You little tramp. Do you think for a moment that anyone is going to believe this silly story of yours? You're ridiculous!"

"Am I?" Shawn pulled out a mini skirt and held it up. "Do you think this skirt would be okay to wear to the open house, Mrs. C.?"

"No!" Isabella snatched it away violently. "You're not going to the open house! You're not going anywhere but the bus station."

"Not when I have a letter proving that you're a bigamist."

"That paper doesn't prove a thing, and you know it!"

"What would your precious friends say if I told them you were living in sin with Michael Cavanetti, and that your dear, darling Frank was a bastard? Well, he is anyway, but I mean a *real* bastard?"

"Your sad little scheme will never work, Shawn."

"Oh, yeah? Try me, Mrs. C." She put her hands on her hips. "Send me away, and I send the letter to the *Seattle Times*. And poor Frank. It could ruin him if he can't inherit St. Benedict Winery. Oh, and that brother of his—what's his name? Niccolo?—would get it after all!"

"He wouldn't. He was disowned."

"Well, think about it, Mrs. C." She slid the skirt out of Isabella's grip. "And just remember. You treat me right, and I'll treat you right. Do unto others as—"

"Spare me, you slut!" Isabella stormed out of the room and slammed the door.

Shawn smiled at the closed door and twirled to the closet, holding the skirt in front of her as if it were a dancing partner. At last she was going to have some fun, and see some of this high society Frank was always talking about. Isabella couldn't keep her away now.

5

Robert Ward was feeling no pain when Jessica got home from the hospital late that afternoon. He met her at the door, drink in hand.

"Hi, Jess." His speech was slightly slurred.

She greeted him and hung up her coat. "Did you know Mr. Cavanetti's in the hospital?" she asked.

"Yes. The old buzzard. How old is he anyway? A hundred?"

"Eighty."

"Jesus. That makes me sixty-eight." His words echoed in his glass before he took a swallow.

"You haven't seen a monk around the bungalow, have you, Dad?"

Robert narrowed his eyes. "A monk? No. Why do you ask?"

"Oh, just wondering." She strolled to the kitchen, and Robert followed her.

"How about the mail? Did you get to it?"

"Well, I found it. Most of it. I made a pile for you on the kitchen table."

"Great." Jessica glanced at the table. Envelopes littered the surface, and a few had fallen to the floor. She stooped to pick them up and then straightened the chairs. "I'll check these after I make you a decent dinner."

"Jess, I'm not that hungry. You don't have to."

"You need to eat, Dad. You're underweight." She opened the cupboard. "Now, what would you like?"

Before he made a choice, the doorbell rang. Jessica glared at her father. "Stay here," she ordered, and then bustled to the front of the house. Maria stood on the porch with a casserole in one hand and an umbrella in the other.

"Maria! Come in!"

"Just for a moment." She smiled and handed the casserole to Jessica and then shook the rain off her umbrella.

Jessica breathed in the aroma that wafted up from the glass lid. "Ah, Maria! What's in here? It smells heavenly!"

"Manicotti. Your favorite." She folded her hands in front of her. "I was making it this afternoon, and I remembered how much you used to like it."

"Manicotti! I can't believe it! And I was just about to make dinner."

"Well, enjoy."

"Thank you, Maria. You spoil me!"

"I must get back. Mrs. Cavanetti is a bundle of nerves today. I think Frank's wife upset her." She picked up her umbrella.

Jessica glanced out the front window at the darkness of early evening. Maria had walked to the bungalow. Considering the strange monk wandering around the property, Jessica didn't think it would be safe to let her walk back alone.

"Let me walk you back, Maria." She put the casserole on the table with the vase.

"No need, *bambina*. No need."

"Then we can talk. Besides, I could use some fresh air."

She pulled her coat out of the closet and found an old black umbrella that was still serviceable. She buttoned her coat and then followed Maria out the door.

"You say Frank brought a wife home?" Jessica asked. "I never even knew he was married."

"Most people don't. That's the way Mrs. Cavanetti wants it."

"Why?"

"Because Frank married a girl without Mrs. Cavanetti's approval. And I must say that Shawn is not the type I would have thought Frank would marry."

"What type is she?"

"Shawn? She's one of those harsh-looking girls, so thin, so much makeup. Like one of those—what do you call them?—punk rockers. She's got dyed black hair with orange streaks in it."

Jessica chuckled. "No wonder Mrs. Cavanetti is upset!"

Maria nodded in agreement.

"Does Frank seem happy with her?"

"Franco?" Maria spread her fingers wide. "You know Franco. He treats her just like he treats his mama. He does everything that Shawn wants. Sometimes I wish Franco would just . . . Ah, well, I talk too much."

They reached the main road and crossed over to the long driveway leading to the Cavanetti mansion. Jessica watched the ground, trying to avoid puddles. "The house has certainly changed since I was here last."

"Ah, the house! Can you believe it? I don't know how much money that Mrs. Cavanetti is spending, or where in the world she's getting it!"

"I just assumed the winery was prospering."

"Not that much!" Maria shook her head. "I'm telling you, Jessica, Mr. Cavanetti would never have stood for this if he wasn't so sick. Never! All that money she's spending on the house when the winery is falling apart. She hires the cheapest migrant labor she can find. I see them tramping through the vineyard, not a care for the age of those plants, leaving the dormitory a dirty mess when they leave. And she doesn't notice. She doesn't care! Not as long as she has her historic home and all her fancy friends and her trips to Europe."

"Mrs. Cavanetti went to Europe?"

"Yes, last summer with Franco."

"When Mr. Cavanetti was sick?"

"Sure. She got a nurse to take care of him." Maria marched

to the side entrance of the house. "I tell you, Jessica, it can't go on like this. I'm afraid of what will happen!"

"Maybe Cole will be able to help."

Maria put her hand on the door latch. "Maybe."

"Isabella mentioned that he was involved in some sort of trouble back East. Did she tell you about that?"

"*Si.*" Maria's eyes hardened. "But I told her I didn't believe Niccolo would do something like that. Then she showed me the newspaper with his picture and everything. I still couldn't believe it."

"Maybe the woman is lying."

"She must be. Still, why would a woman lie about something like that?"

"People are strange, Maria, and they do strange things."

"I suppose they do. Yes." She pulled open the door. "Would you like to come in for some coffee?"

"No, I've got to get back to my father and that manicotti."

Maria's eyes crinkled, and she snapped shut her umbrella. "Well, don't be a stranger, Jessica. I've missed you in my kitchen all this time."

Jessica hugged the small woman and turned to leave. But she pivoted on the walkway and raised her umbrella. "Maria, have you seen a monk hanging around?"

"No. Why do you ask?"

"I saw a monk last night. And Mr. Cavanetti said something about a monk today. That's all he said. Monk."

Maria studied her. "Maybe Mr. Cavanetti was talking about the new advertising campaign they've dreamed up."

"And what is that?"

"Oh, it's basically the same as ever—the secret formula of the St. Benedict Riesling being guarded by a monk. But now they put the ads on television. You should see them. They're really funny."

"Funny?"

"This monk, Jessica, he is a bumbling friar who can't keep out of the cellar. Every time I see it, I start laughing."

A door slammed in the house, and Isabella's voice rang out. "Maria! Where are you!"

"I must go!" She pulled off her scarf. "Good night."

"Good night, Maria. Thanks for the dinner."

Jessica turned up the collar of her coat and walked back toward the bungalow. Without Maria's company the night seemed darker and colder. She clutched the handle of the umbrella with chilled fingers and hurried down the driveway. All the while she shot glances into the shrubbery, looking for the dark shape she half expected to see in the shadows. But the monk did not appear.

She walked over the crest of the road and down the driveway to the bungalow. Thankful she had left the porch light on, she headed for the pool of light with a quickened pace.

Just as she gained the bottom of the driveway, she skidded on some loose gravel and turned her ankle. She nearly toppled over.

"Ow!" Jessica cried. She fought to retain her balance and hobbled a few steps. Her ankle throbbed. She bent over to massage it for a moment, swearing at her slick-soled boots. As she straightened, her breath caught in her throat.

Standing not twenty feet away was the robed figure. Jessica's skin burst into gooseflesh. Speechless and unable to move, she stared at the monk, the umbrella poised at a crazy angle behind her head.

The monk did not approach her. The only movement came from the wind rustling the folds of his habit. He was a large man, over six feet tall. Jessica could see no face in the shadows beneath his hooded cowl.

"Who are you?" she called.

The monk was silent.

"What do you want?"

The monk didn't respond.

"Look, I'm sorry I almost hit you—I just didn't see you!"

She took a step toward the house. He didn't lunge for her. He simply regarded her. His motionless stance gave her the courage to continue. She stumbled sideways toward the porch, never taking her eyes off him until she grabbed the front doorknob and flung herself into the house.

"Dad!" she screamed.

Her father didn't answer. Jessica locked the door and fumbled with the chain. Her hands were icy cold and quaking, and twice she couldn't get the round piece at the end of the chain into the slot.

"Dad!" she screamed again.

Silence.

She hobbled down the hallway, terrified of the figure outside the house. "Dad, where are you?"

She found her father in the recliner again. Jessica sank to the floor beside the arm of the chair and pulled her knees to her chin. Her entire body was shaking.

"Dad," she whispered. "Oh, Dad, he's out there!"

Her father was oblivious to her fear. He was dead drunk.

The next morning Jessica called Isabella to see if she knew anything about the monk. Isabella swore that no one had been hired to dress up like a monk, and she had not seen a monk on the property either. No one but Jessica had seen the robed figure. Jessica thought it quite odd. The man in the monk outfit must be some kind of nut seeking revenge for the incident when she had nearly run him down. He might even be the convict she had read about in the newspaper.

Jessica called the police after talking to Isabella. She gave a description of the "prowler," as the police referred to him, and they promised to come out and look around the bungalow. Jessica hung up the phone feeling less than reassured.

Before her fingers had left the receiver, the phone rang. Isabella needed a favor. Shawn had nothing appropriate to wear to the open house at the Falls Winery, and she didn't know the Seattle area or where to shop. Isabella would have taken Shawn shopping, but she had a migraine and couldn't leave her bed. She wondered if Jessica could possibly take Shawn out this morning and help her select a decent outfit?

Jessica agreed but did not look forward to a shopping

spree with Frank's wife. She doubted Isabella had a headache. The woman just didn't want to spend time with her daughter-in-law. She might not even want to be seen in public with her, judging from Maria's description of the girl.

One look at Shawn later that morning and Jessica knew she was right on both counts.

Shawn strolled down the mansion steps to Jessica's waiting car. She was dressed in a black skirt, black tights, some kind of black lace leggings, and a pair of clumpy shoes topped by violet bobby socks rolled down around her ankles. She had yanked her black-and-orange hair to one side and tied it with a black-and-purple-checked scarf. Huge silver earrings made of crucifixes bounced against the collar of her fake fur coat. Jessica tried not to stare as Shawn approached the car.

"Hi," Shawn greeted her, slumping into the passenger seat.

"Hello. I'm Jessica Ward." She held out her hand. "Nice to meet you."

Shawn shook her hand and inspected Jessica's face and clothing, which was subdued and understated—a teal pullover and long black skirt.

"So, you've known the Cavanettis a long time?"

"Yes." Jessica drove down the circular drive toward the lane. "For many years."

"Bet you didn't know about me, did you?"

"No." Jessica glanced at her. "How long have you and Frank been married?"

"About two years."

"Two years?" Jessica raised an eyebrow. "It's funny, Mrs. Cavanetti never mentioned that Frank was married."

"She hates me. She wishes I'd never married Frank."

"Isabella's a bit of a dragon, but you'll get used to her."

Jessica turned her attention to the road and didn't speak much until they had pulled up to a line of boutiques in downtown Seattle. Shawn had craned her neck to see the sights of Seattle—the ferries, the Space Needle, Pike Place Market, and Pioneer Square—and let her bored expression lapse. Jessica watched in amusement.

They walked into a store that Jessica hoped would carry

something appropriate yet still rebellious enough to suit Shawn. She knew she had a monumental task ahead of her: that of pleasing both Isabella and her daughter-in-law.

A bell tinkled as they stepped into the shop. Jessica walked behind Shawn and noticed that every clerk in the small store came to attention at the appearance of the young woman with the orange-and-black hair. The clerks busied themselves stocking shelves or arranging displays, all the while furtively watching Shawn inspect the merchandise. Jessica felt a prick of anger. Did they expect the girl to shoplift just because she wore outlandish clothes?

No one came to Shawn's assistance. The clerks must have decided that nothing in their shop would appeal to her, and certainly nothing about her appealed to them. Jessica waited for a few minutes to see whether anyone would ask if they needed help. She saw other women receiving immediate service as soon as they stepped in the door. Shawn got no service whatsoever.

Shawn picked up a pair of sunglasses and tried them on, turning to Jessica and grimacing. She left them on, the tags fluttering between her eyebrows, and strolled to a rack of hand-knitted sweaters. A thin male clerk appeared at her elbow.

"Miss, if you aren't going to buy the merchandise, don't carry it about the store."

Shawn slid the glasses down her nose and stared at the clerk over the rims. "What?"

"If you aren't going to buy the glasses, leave them where you found them."

Jessica felt her temper rising. She stepped forward. "Why do you assume she isn't going to buy them?"

The clerk turned to Jessica and seemed surprised to see an ordinary person standing next to Shawn. "Well—I—I assumed—"

"Assumed what?"

"That she was just looking."

"She is now." Jessica took Shawn by the arm. "But she's going to *buy* something next door." Jessica put out her hand for the glasses and Shawn gave them to her. Jessica folded the wings and neatly placed the glasses in the pocket of the clerk's shirt while his face went as pale and flat as a slice of raw potato.

"There you go"—she glanced at his name tag—"Loren, old chap. The merchandise is safe and sound."

She strode out of the store, pulling Shawn behind her. Any form of bigotry infuriated her, since she was a little girl and heard her relatives making derogatory remarks about the Cavanettis.

She slammed the shop door behind them.

"All right, Jessica!" Shawn raised her fist in a victory salute. "Yes!"

Jessica frowned, not certain if Shawn's approval was anything she wished to elicit.

"You were great!" Shawn continued. "You really told him where to get off. What an attitude!"

After that Shawn's facade cracked enough to show some cooperation. Jessica flipped through racks of dresses, trying to find the right look. It was obvious that Shawn liked black. Jessica was also certain that Shawn considered the shock factor in whatever she wore. She suggested a theme, which delighted Shawn.

They left the shop with a dress of satin, sequins, and lace, with monumental shoulder pads, a hat and veil, and pair of hose with seams down the back. She would show up at the open house looking every inch a movie star from the forties, complete with cigarette holder. Shawn was so excited that she could hardly wait to dress for the evening, and she made Jessica promise to help her fix her hair.

Jessica dropped her off at the Cavanetti house. Shawn raced up the front steps and then turned and waved happily. Jessica's mouth turned down in a rueful smile. Surprisingly enough, she had half enjoyed herself with Shawn. She even looked forward to seeing the impression the young Mrs. Cavanetti would make at the party. The evening suddenly promised to be more interesting than she had first supposed.

6

Jessica spent the remainder of the afternoon tackling the mail while her father read the Sunday paper. Soon she came across an item sent by her father's attorney, Wes Haley. She unfolded the document. It concerned the lease between the Cavanettis and the Wards, a decades-old contract that would finally expire on Christmas Day.

Jessica read the document carefully. The lease was renewable and had an option to buy clause, giving the Cavanettis exclusive first rights to purchase the property before anyone else. Jessica put the document in the "to do" pile. She hated the thought of selling the remainder of the Ward property, but she saw no other immediate solution to her father's financial difficulties. He had no income. She made only a modest salary as an assistant professor. They had sold their stock and principal residence years ago. And her father would soon need expensive medical care if he continued to drink.

After an early dinner, which her father scarcely touched, Jessica took a shower and got ready for the open house at the Falls Winery. She dressed in a dark jade silk tunic that hung below her knees, and paired it with matching pants that hugged her long, slender legs. The color was nearly black, which set off the banded tourmaline crystal she draped around her neck. Then she slipped into a pair of high heels and appraised herself in the mirror.

She often wished she might have been petite like her mother. Her aunt Edna had referred to her mother as a gazelle, a fairy queen upon the stage. Why couldn't Jessica have inherited some of that delicacy? In these heels, she would be as tall if not taller than most of the men at the open house.

She fluffed her cloud of ebony hair, running her fingers through the curls, pulling at the widow's peak that dipped into her white forehead. Her hair was almost dry. Good. If she tried to blow dry it, she would end up with a frizzled mess.

Jessica hummed as she walked to the bathroom to put on her makeup. She was looking forward to the evening, happy to get away from her father and the threat of the monk. The police had come earlier in the afternoon and hadn't found a trace of an intruder. Somehow she wasn't surprised.

Leaning forward, Jessica applied mascara, brushed on some blush, and lined her lips with dark red lipstick. She liked the contrast of her snow-white skin and the red of the lipstick, like Beaujolais spilled on a linen tablecloth. She blotted her lips on a tissue and left the bathroom.

Her father was asleep in front of the television. She bid him a silent good-night, grabbed her purse, and left for the Cavanetti house to fulfill her promise to help Shawn with her hair.

Frank drove Shawn and Jessica to the open house. Isabella had decided not to go. She was still suffering from a migraine headache and had gone to bed early. Jessica was slightly disappointed that Isabella hadn't seen Shawn's outfit. Her daughter-in-law looked smashing, and even Frank had stared in surprise when she came down the stairs. Shawn was a bit unsteady in her stiletto high heels, but Jessica knew her balance would come after a few minutes of walking around.

Jessica sat in the back of the Mercedes and idly gazed at Frank's profile as they drove to the winery in Woodinville, a half hour away. Frank had the same coloring as Cole and a similar nose and chin, but his features were rounded and soft in comparison to those of his half-brother. He was not nearly as tall or as well developed. He was twenty-five, ten years younger than Cole, and had recently graduated from Harvard with a law degree.

Frank had been raised in a different environment than Cole. He hadn't known the lean years, he hadn't lost his mother at an early age like Cole, and he had never worked in the vineyard as a common laborer. Isabella had sent him to private schools and made certain he cultivated friendships that would advance his career. Jessica had heard that Frank was a formidable tennis player, but she had never thought of him as much of an athlete. He was outgoing and friendly, though, and had considerable polish. She imagined that Harvard coeds might have found him attractive, but he was almost too charming, as if he didn't really mean the nice things he said.

Frank opened the door for Shawn and helped her out of the car while Jessica fended for herself. She followed them to the Nelson house adjacent to the winery. The Victorian farmhouse was ablaze with light. Festoons of fir lined the porch rail, and Jessica could see a tall Christmas tree twinkling in the bay window. She could hear music drifting over the laughter inside the house. This house approached her idea of a perfect Christmas setting, and she felt as if it held the promise of a wonderful evening. Her spirits rose as she walked up the steps behind Shawn and Frank.

Mrs. Nelson met them at the door. She knew both Frank and Jessica and chatted with them until the doorbell rang again. Jessica stepped to one side and glanced at Shawn. She had to smile. Shawn looked great. The hat and veil hid all traces of her orange hair and concealed her glaring youth. The old-fashioned satin dress set off her slender shape and showed a great deal of her ample cleavage. No wonder

Frank had found her desirable enough to marry.

"Have you ever been to a wine tasting before?" she asked Shawn as Frank disappeared with their wraps.

"No. I'm a beer drinker, myself." Shawn watched the newly arriving guests and did not look at Jessica. "And I enjoy hard liquor once in awhile. But wine? Yuck!"

Jessica wondered if Shawn was expecting someone by the way she surveyed the crowd. But Frank came back before she could ask.

"Can I get you ladies something?"

"Surprise us, Peaches." Shawn reached up and touched the tip of his nose with her cigarette holder. She had enough sense not to light the cigarette in the crowded room. Frank brushed the cigarette holder away.

Suddenly, two arms came around Jessica. She almost squealed in shock.

"And what would *you* like, Peaches?" A familiar voice laughed behind her.

Jessica whirled around. "Greg!" she exclaimed, backing against arms that did not release her.

"Jessica! Wow!" Greg looked her up and down, his blue eyes gleaming with impish delight, both at her appearance and his success in making her jump. "You look like a million bucks!" He let her step back but did not let her go. "What have you done to your hair?"

"I've quit ironing it."

"It looks great!"

She tried to step away again, still breathless from being startled, but he held her fast. She looked at Greg Kessler, wondering what he had done to *his* hair. His hairline had receded considerably since she had seen him last. To compensate he had grown a mustache and beard, much darker than his sandy hair. He had also taken on a little weight around the middle.

"Jess, long time no see!" He embraced her, and she patted his back for old times' sake. Once she had thought herself in love with Greg, unaware that her hormones had overwhelmed her heart at the time. He had helped break in her new diaphragm when she was a college student. They had gone steady for two years, until they drifted apart after she left for graduate school in California. She had never felt a sense of loss at the demise of their relationship.

"Are you back to see your father?" he asked, leading her to the table set out with a line of bottles and carafes.

"Yes. And you? What are you doing these days, Greg?"

"Well, you might say I've been at the right place at the right time—know what I mean?" He reached for a bottle of Merlot and poured himself a goblet. When he began to pour another, Jessica touched his arm.

"No, thanks," she said.

"What? You still don't drink?" He replaced the bottle. "I can't believe it."

"I never acquired the taste." She smiled. She had never admitted to anyone that she was terrified of drinking. She worried constantly that she would end up an alcoholic like her father if she ever tried a drop.

Greg sipped the wine. "Not bad," he commented.

"So what do you do now, Greg?"

"Well, I inherited my father's place, you know, after he died. I sold that and bought a chunk of property out by your summer home."

"You mean at Moss Cliff?"

"Pretty close. Across the river from the St. Benedict vineyard. That hill. I own that hill." Greg took a sip of wine and beamed at her.

"I imagine that property has increased in value the past few years."

"Damned right it has." He took another sip and leaned close. His breath smelled musky. "I'm making a killing, Jessica, a real killing. I'm putting in a community on that hill, an elite community with a view of the river and the vineyard. Do you know how much people will pay for a three-bedroom house with a view like that?"

Jessica raised her eyebrows.

"Lots." Greg smiled smugly. "Lots and lots. More than I ever dreamed. It's crazy."

They talked over old times, and then he asked her to dance. She felt awkward dancing because her high heels made her slightly taller than Greg. He didn't seem concerned, however, and Jessica realized he might be feeling the effects of the wine.

After the third dance they walked back to the parlor to get something to drink. Just as they passed through the hall, someone shouted, "Hey, it's Cole Nichols!"

Jessica turned and saw Cole coming through the front door with Lucy Girard on his arm. Her glance lingered upon Lucy, who was short and stocky and dressed in a black suit and gold lamé tank top. Next to Cole she did not look glamorous or elegant, just ordinary, which surprised Jessica. She would have thought Cole's taste in women would be more exotic. But Lucy did have kind eyes and a cheerful face, which heartened Jessica somewhat. Perhaps Cole looked past the exterior.

"Cole Nichols!" exclaimed a man near her elbow. "What's he doing here?"

"Cole Nichols?" Greg repeated.

"Do you know who he is?" Jessica asked, wondering if he would recognize an acquaintance from his high-school days.

"Sure! Everybody knows Cole Nichols! He's the hottest quarterback since Joe Namath!"

At that moment Cole caught Jessica's eye and nodded to her. She smiled back.

"Do you know him?" Greg stared at her, awed. "God, introduce me, would you?"

Jessica couldn't resist playing a little joke on Greg. She touched his arm. "Sure. Come on." She led the way through the throng that had gathered around Cole. He stood a head taller than the rest of them, while Lucy's short figure was engulfed by the crowd.

Most of the men and some of the women were firing questions at Cole, asking him about Sunday's game and if he would be back from injured reserve. Jessica turned to Greg.

"Has Cole been hurt?"

"Haven't you heard?" Greg jostled forward. "He's been

taken from the field twice now. Just collapsed. No one even sacked him. Some say he's lost his nerve. The coach pulled him from last Sunday's game. And this Sunday's."

Jessica stared at Cole, who was smiling and vigorous, patiently answering questions while he tried to make headway into the parlor. He didn't look ill. Far from it. He wasn't wearing his glasses, and his face looked warm and golden, his eyes black and sparkling.

"You mean to say he just fell down on the playing field?"

"You got it. The ball hadn't even been snapped. And *whomp!* He falls backward like a big old pine tree."

Finally Cole made his way to Jessica, waving off his admirers with a good-natured smile of protest, but she could see the weariness in his eyes when he finally broke free of the crowd.

"They're worse than reporters!" Cole remarked as he came abreast of Jessica and Greg.

"Does this happen wherever you go?" Jessica inquired.

"Yep." Lucy gave a pert grimace. "Wherever he goes— restaurants, hospitals, taxis—probably even the men's room!"

Cole nodded and chuckled. "This is Lucy Girard, my physical therapist."

Lucy stuck out her hand. "Hi," she said, shaking Jessica's hand. Her grip was firm and her gaze direct. Jessica was surprised to discover an instant, if somewhat grudging, liking for her. "You must be Jessica Ward."

"Yes. It's a pleasure to meet you." She motioned toward Greg. "This is a friend of mine, Greg Kessler."

"Hi, Greg." Lucy shook his hand as well.

"Physical therapist, eh?" Greg looked her up and down.

Jessica suspected that Lucy might be more to Cole than just a physical therapist. Apparently Greg suspected the same thing, but he had lost his manners and his tongue to a bottle of Merlot. Jessica wondered what else Lucy did for Cole besides give his knees a workout. Was she his lover? his significant other?

"Greg." Cole shook his hand. "I remember you."

"You do?" Greg stared at the famous quarterback, still not aware of his true identity.

"You played for the Ridgemont Raiders in high school, didn't you?"

"Yeah." Greg narrowed his eyes and studied the tall man in front of him. "How did you know?"

"We used to beat the crap out of the Ridgemont Raiders. I remember a particular game in 1973 when—"

"Jesus Christ!" Greg blurted. "You're Nick Cavanetti! You're Nick Cavanetti, aren't you!" He looked up at the ceiling. "Jesus! Nick Cavanetti! Why did you change your name?"

"Too hard to pronounce," he said easily. "Besides, Cavanetti doesn't fit well on the back of a jersey."

"Nick Cavanetti!" Greg shook his head. "I never would have guessed!"

Lucy wrapped her arms around Cole's elbow. Her head did not even reach the breast pocket of his suit jacket. Jessica often wondered how tall men and short women like Cole and Lucy managed to kiss without painful body contortions.

"Listen, guys," Lucy put in. "We can talk football and old times all night long. But I came here to learn about Northwest wines. Can we conduct old home week over there?" She indicated the tasting table with a nod and then rolled her eyes at Jessica, as if to comment on the hopeless combination of men and football.

Jessica smiled.

Cole led the way to the table. Jessica noticed many people turn and watch as he passed by. She wondered what it would be like to be Cole, always in the public eye. She didn't think she'd like it.

"All right, Lucy." Cole surveyed the table. "Let's start with something light." He picked up a slender green bottle with the Falls Winery label. "Our host's own."

"What kind is it?" Lucy asked.

"Chenin Blanc." Cole carefully poured a third of a goblet and handed it to Lucy. "Jessica?" he asked, reaching for another goblet. When she shook her head, he asked Greg.

"Don't mind if I do." Greg obviously enjoyed being waited on by Cole Nichols. Cole poured the wine into a clean glass and gave it to Greg.

"How about sparkling water?" he asked Jessica. He seemed concerned that she had nothing to drink.

"That sounds good."

Cole reached into a bowl full of ice and got her a bottle, which he opened and poured for her. She accepted with thanks, grateful for his thoughtfulness.

Finally Cole poured Chenin Blanc for himself. He held up the glass, just above eye level.

"Now, Lucy, the first thing you want to look at is the color of the wine—its robe. A good wine will look clear, with overtones of other colors."

"It looks . . . um . . . ." Lucy pursed her lips. "Well, light yellow."

Jessica tilted her head in order to look through Cole's glass. "Like chiffon," she commented.

"Exactly. Now swirl the wine in the glass. See how the wine clings to the sides? A good wine will linger on the sides in fingers or tears."

Both Greg and Lucy nodded. Jessica noticed an older man watching them from the side of the room.

"Swirling the wine also releases its aroma, or bouquet. Now sniff it."

Lucy wrinkled her nose. "Sniff it?"

"Yes." Cole put the tip of his straight nose into the mouth of the goblet. "Take sharp, short sniffs." He offered the goblet to Jessica, and she copied him.

"What do you smell?"

"Flowers!" Lucy exclaimed in delight.

"Fresh," Greg added. "Very fresh."

"I smell melon," Jessica put in. Cole smiled at her.

"All right, step four is to sip the wine. Just take a small sip. About a tablespoon. You want to spread it over your entire mouth. Even under your tongue, so that all taste buds can be involved. Don't swallow that, Lucy." He chuckled. "Now tilt your head forward and suck in some air through your lips. Exhale through your nose. Did you feel a burst of taste? Don't swallow yet."

Lucy smiled.

"Now chew the wine. Just move your jaws around and taste it. Explore the nuances. You can swallow now."

"Goodness!" Lucy gasped.

"What's your verdict?" Cole inquired.

"It tastes great." Lucy beamed, taking another sip.

"Smooth," Greg added.

"What do you think?" Jessica turned to Cole.

"I find it a light-hearted wine, delicate, even lively, with a melon aroma. Spritzy. A tint of flintiness. But on the whole a well-balanced wine."

"This is fun!" Lucy turned to the wide array of wines on the table. "Let's try another."

"You should clear your palate first. Have a cracker. Also, one of those hazelnuts will stimulate your taste buds."

"I like stimulation," Greg declared. He popped two hazelnuts into his mouth and ogled Jessica. Jessica looked away.

Lucy reached for a carafe. "Shall we try this next?"

Just then the older man who had been observing them stepped forward. "Excuse me. Mr. Nichols?"

Cole turned to the man. He had black hair that was silvering at the temples and a small silver mustache.

"Yes?"

"I couldn't help overhearing your little lesson there. For a football player, you seem to know a bit about wine."

"A bit."

"Allow me to introduce myself." He held out his hand. "Miles Davidson, columnist for the *Seattle Review*."

Jessica saw Cole pause for an instant before he forced a smile. "Nice to meet you, Miles. What can I do for you?"

"Well, I was wondering—would you be interested in a blind tasting? I'd like your opinion on a certain wine."

Cole shrugged. "Sure. Why not?"

"Good! This will make a great column!" Miles strode to the table. "Turn your back, and I'll make my selection."

Cole turned his back. Jessica drank her sparkling water,

marveling that Cole could keep his good humor with the constant interruptions he endured at the party.

"Ready!" The columnist gave a goblet to Cole.

Cole inspected the color and performed all the steps he had outlined for Lucy, except he did each step with deliberate thoughtfulness. Jessica watched, fascinated, as he spit the wine into one of the earthenware spittoons provided for the occasion.

"Good appearance, but on the watery side," Cole said. "Thin, dull, weak. Unremarkable. Practically undrinkable. I wouldn't recommend this wine. I can't say that I can identify the vintner either." He turned to the columnist. "Who makes this stuff?"

The columnist rotated the bottle so that the label faced Cole. For a moment Cole said nothing. Jessica glanced at him, wondering why he was silent. Cole's face had hardened, all warmth vanished. His eyes were as black and flat as basalt.

"Is this some sort of trick?" he growled.

The columnist shook his head. "Exactly what I've been asking myself. What do these people think they're doing? They've taken the best Johannisberg Riesling in the country and turned it into pap."

Jessica looked at the label on the wine bottle and was surprised to see the familiar logo of the hooded monk.

Cole had just pronounced the pride of St. Benedict Winery undrinkable.

7

Cole turned on his heel and, without a word to anybody, strode out of the parlor. Greg watched him go, his mouth gaping, while Lucy called after him. Evidently she knew better than to follow him, however, and Jessica took her cue from Lucy.

"What's the matter with him?" Miles asked, still holding the bottle of Johannisberg Riesling. "What's he so angry about?"

Greg gulped down the rest of his Chenin Blanc. "Don't you know? Cole Nichols is related to the owners of St. Benedict."

"He is? I wasn't aware of that."

"He's the son of Michael Cavanetti."

"But his name—"

"He changed it."

Miles Davidson paused in thought, while his gaze lingered in the direction Cole had gone. Jessica had a sick feeling deep in the pit of her stomach. She wished Greg had not volunteered the information. Cole might have wanted to guard his true identity from the press. Her fears were compounded when she heard Miles ask Mrs. Nelson if he could use her phone. Why would Miles suddenly need to make a call, if not about Cole?

"Excuse me," Lucy said. "I'll try to find Cole and calm him down."

Jessica caught a glimpse of movement outside the window and saw Cole stride out to the parking lot and down the lane toward the Nelson outbuildings. He walked swiftly into the twilight, his hands deep in the pockets of his slacks, his tie flapping over his shoulder. Jessica was surprised that after all these years he would be so upset with the failure of the winery to produce a prize product. Then she reminded herself that she didn't know Cole all that well anymore. Perhaps there was more to him than good looks and charisma. Perhaps he possessed a darker side seldom shown to others. Jessica felt a deep swell of empathy for him. She knew about hiding the darker side. She knew only too well.

After Cole's exit, Jessica didn't feel like dancing. She and Greg mingled with the other guests, talking quietly in pockets throughout the house. Lucy was unsuccessful at finding Cole, and Jessica didn't tell her where he had gone. Lucy admitted that Cole had quite a temper and was better off alone anyway. She walked away in the company of Miles Davidson to sample other wines. Miles was more than delighted to step in as her teacher.

By eleven o'clock, Greg was dangerously close to being drunk, and the wine had made him amorous. His hand kept sliding down Jessica's back to her rump, and she kept moving away to make it clear that she did not appreciate his pawing. Then he leaned closer and propositioned her, suggesting that they drive to his condo in downtown Seattle and see how much they had really changed—inside and out.

Jessica told him no thanks and walked out of the drawing room and down the hall to the kitchen, looking for a glass of water and a respite from Greg's attentions. She breezed through the doorway of the kitchen and was surprised to see Cole leaning against the wall, drinking coffee. His tie was loosened at the neck, and his hair was unruly from being out in the wind. He looked tired, and the crow's-feet at the corners of his eyes were accentuated by the fluorescent lights of the kitchen.

Jessica stopped in midstride. "Sorry," she said. "I didn't mean to barge in."

"I'm just having a cup of coffee."

"You look like a man who doesn't want company."

"I don't consider you company." He sipped his coffee and appraised her over the rim of the cup. He had never looked at her like that before, certainly not when she had been seventeen and dying for such an appraisal. She felt a hot blush spread over her cheeks while she fumbled for a glass in the cabinet above the counter.

"I guess I'll take that as a compliment," she said, stepping to the sink and filling the glass with tap water.

"What I mean is, I don't feel compelled to entertain you. I get tired of entertaining." He sighed. "Always being onstage. Sometimes I wish I could tell them all to go to hell."

"You're very patient. More so than I could ever hope to be."

"Thanks." He smiled. "Want a cup of coffee? It's Starbucks Christmas Blend."

"No, thanks. I'd never be able to get to sleep if I drank any coffee now."

"You're just like a little priestess, aren't you?"

"What do you mean by that?" Jessica raised her glass to her lips.

"Your outfit, no alcohol, no coffee after seven, bedtime at what"—he looked at his watch—"ten? I have you pegged as a ten o'clocker."

"Well, you've pegged wrong, Mr. Nichols." She crossed her arms, holding the goblet with two slender white fingers and her thumb. "Sometimes I stay up all night."

"You do, do you?" His eyes flickered again, the flatness replaced by an attractive sparkle. "Doing what?"

"Now, now, Mr. Nichols, a girl must have her secrets."

"Girl? From what I see, Jessica, you aren't a girl anymore."

His words sent a jolt of fire through her face and chest. She felt her cheeks glowing as she struggled to maintain a grip on her good sense. This man had rebuffed her years ago. She was not about to act the fool with him again.

"How can you tell what I look like?" She took a drink of water. "You can't see that much under this priestess outfit."

"I have a vivid imagination." He put down his coffee cup. "And I appreciate a good mystery now and then."

"What mystery is that?"

"The mystery of what's under all that silk." His gaze lingered on her as he straightened. "And why you feel compelled to hide it away."

"I'm not hiding anything. I just don't like being cold."

He chuckled. "I recall a dress you once wore that could have caused you pneumonia."

"Dresses like that are for hot-blooded teenagers with more hormones than brains."

"So your hormones are under control now, are they?"

"I should hope so." The way she was reacting inside, though, made her out a liar. Cole was giving her hot and cold flashes, and her heart felt as if it might pound out of her chest. She prayed he couldn't detect any physical manifestations of her reaction to him.

"The unflappable Jessica Ward. The same old Jessica. I bet you married an orthodontist and have two children and a cat."

"Not quite."

"A dog then?"

"You're way off, Mr. Nichols." She set her glass on the counter. "How about rejoining your fans and proving to me that you can dance." Where had she found the nerve, she wondered.

"I can dance."

"Then prove it."

He narrowed his eyes and smiled at her. "All right. Come on." He took her elbow and strolled out of the kitchen, a smile playing at the corners of his mouth. Jessica stole a glance at his face. He was amused. She had brought a real smile to his face, and for some reason that gave her pleasure.

As soon as they reached the dance floor, the music slowed to a love song. Jessica hesitated, but Cole only smiled at her, knowing she hadn't expected to dance in his arms. He took her hand in his left one and pulled her close to him with his right.

Jessica stared at his neck, trying to ignore the way her body thrilled at the mere touch of his hand on her back. But staring at his neck didn't help either, because she found herself watching the tendons move in his throat. She surveyed the tight skin at his sharp jawline, examining the way his face flared out near his ear, all the while imagining what it would feel like to touch such a firm jaw. Cautiously, she eased her hand across the wide expanse of his shoulder, slow enough so the movement could not be mistaken for a caress. Then she let her fingertips graze his hair near his collar. She had wished to touch his thick, glossy hair for as long as she could remember.

She didn't realize until Cole spoke that she had closed her eyes.

"Like the music?" he asked. She could hear amusement in his voice.

She opened her eyes. "As a matter of fact, I do."

"I haven't stepped on your toes once, I hope you've noticed."

"I have noticed. You've proved yourself."

"You're as stiff as a board, though, Jessica." He squeezed her hand. "Dancing can be lots of fun if you just relax."

"I am relaxed."

"No, you aren't. Just relax." He urged her closer by pressing on the small of her back. "I learned from a woman once how to enjoy dancing. Just relax and let yourself be close enough to me so that we can feel each other's body move." He pulled her closer, so that her breasts touched his chest and her thigh brushed his. "Imagine that we're connected, that we are one."

Jessica swallowed, trying not to make more of his words than he intended, trying to ignore the way his body felt against her breasts and hips.

"And loosen up!" Cole chuckled. "Let me take you. Just trust me."

Did he realize what he was saying? Jessica tried to relax, but the closeness of his body destroyed all concentration.

"Listen to the music, Jess. Just enjoy it."

He swirled her around, and she did her best to let him swirl her. She tried to relax. She tried to enjoy the music. But all she felt was his warm hand enfolding her cold fingers, his long fingers splayed along her spine, and his thigh moving against hers.

Jessica closed her eyes against the flood of desire she felt for him. She couldn't allow him to transport her back to her childhood and all those old yearnings and dreams. She was no longer a seventeen-year-old virgin, and he was no longer a twenty-two-year-old college student. They were both different people now.

Cole's hand slid up her back, and he bent to her ear. The touch of his breath on her jaw sent another thrill through her. "You're relaxing beautifully," he murmured.

She battled the urge to tense up. "I'm a quick learner," she replied, turning toward his face. Their cheeks touched briefly, and Jessica felt a surge of longing so great that she pulled away. Fortunately, the song ended at the very same moment.

Cole held her hand and did not let her escape. "One more, Jessica." His eyes glittered at her. "For practice."

The music started again. Another ballad. She breathed in and stepped toward him, uncertain whether or not she could endure another song pressed against him.

"You're just the right height," Cole commented as he drew her toward him. "I didn't think you were so tall."

"We never got close enough to find out."

"I guess we never did." He squeezed her hand, and Jessica let him take her across the dance floor.

After the dance ended they walked from the floor together and were met by Frank and Shawn. Frank draped his arm around Shawn's shoulders as Cole approached them, whether to protect her from his brother or hold her back, Jessica wasn't sure. Shawn's face lit up as Cole held out his hand to her. Her blue eyes flashed over Cole's physique, and when she spoke to him, she kept her head tilted while her gaze slyly roved over him. Suddenly Jessica wished she hadn't helped Shawn look so good.

Shawn remained cool on the outside, yet Jessica could see two patches of color behind the veil of netting that draped across the young woman's cheeks. Maybe Shawn was surprised by Cole's warmth and magnetism. Maybe she was simply impressed by his athletic figure and dark Italian good looks.

"I've been wondering when I'd ever get to meet Frank's famous older brother!" she declared, leaving her hand in Cole's grasp longer than necessary.

"Half-brother," Frank put in.

Shawn ignored Frank's comment. "I'm a big fan of yours, Cole," she said. "I watch the Bulls every chance I get."

"Well, thank you, Mrs. Cavanetti."

"Shawn, please."

"Shawn." He nodded. "So you're a fan of the game?"

"Well, I don't know that much about it, but I really enjoy watching men in tight shiny pants and big hulking shoulder pads." She giggled and inched closer to him. "I don't know what it is about football uniforms that make men look like such hunks. Don't you agree, Jessica?"

"I never thought that much about it."

"Really? That's the best part of a game!"

"So you like a man in a uniform, eh?" Cole asked. "Maybe you can talk Frank into joining the Marines."

"Oh, God!" Frank rolled his eyes.

"I can't even get Frank to dance." Shawn pouted.

"No dancing, Frank?" Cole chided. "You drag this beautiful woman to a stuffy old party and won't even dance with her?"

"I hate dancing," Frank grumbled into his wine.

"Then allow me, Shawn." Cole held out his arm. She draped herself over it, affording Cole a private showing of her cleavage. Jessica felt a wave of jealousy so strong and foreign to her that she gasped from the sheer force of it.

"Sorry," Frank said, moving back. "Did I step on your foot?"

"No," Jessica replied hastily, blushing when she realized her gasp had been audible. She stood beside Frank and watched Cole and Shawn gyrating on the floor together. Shawn was evidently enjoying herself as Cole chatted to her. Obviously he didn't have to tell her to relax or teach her to enjoy the music. Jessica doubted that Cole would have to teach Shawn anything.

"Isn't my brother a saint?" Frank observed, his voice full of sarcasm and venom. "Don't you just want to puke?"

Jessica glanced at Frank. His eyes were hard with malice, his lips curled in disdain. Frank took another sip of wine and blinked. Jessica was accustomed to the various stages of drunkenness and caught the small nuance of bleariness in his eyes. Frank was getting looped and allowing his hidden feelings about Cole to surface.

She would never drink. Sometimes her hidden feelings terrified her, and she would rather die than let anyone know them. If wine allowed suave, polished Frank to slip, she couldn't imagine what it would induce her to do. No, she would never, ever allow herself to taste a lively, well-balanced Chenin Blanc or any of its intoxicating relatives.

By midnight the party wound down, as did Frank, Greg, and Lucy. Frank stood silent and brooding as he watched Shawn flirt with Cole. Jessica finally told Greg that she wasn't going to dance with him if he didn't stop nuzzling her neck. Lucy simply sat in a chair near the Christmas tree and stared happily at the sparkling lights and ornaments. She had tasted a variety of wines and had not spit a mouthful out the entire evening.

Frank retrieved Jessica's coat and Shawn's wrap. As he held the wrap out to his wife, he nearly lost his balance.

"Let's go, Shawn," he declared. "I'm bored stiff."

"Can't we stay a while longer?" She pouted at him and then smiled at Cole. "I'm having so much fun."

"We can go somewhere else and get a decent drink."

Cole helped Jessica with her coat. "Frank, you look like you've had enough for the evening."

"Oh, lay off!" Frank retorted. "I know my own limits. And I've had enough of you. Come on, Shawn." He grabbed her hand.

"Bye, Cole!" She waved. "Are you coming, Jessica?"

Jessica took a step toward her, but Cole touched her arm.

"Let me give you a lift back, Jess," he said. "Frank's drunk. I don't want you riding with him."

"Well, if it's okay with Lucy . . ."

"It'll be fine with her. Don't worry about that."

Frank turned and glared at Jessica. "I'm not drunk. I am perfectly able to drive. My big brother has a hero complex, that's all."

"Oh, Frank!" Shawn patted Frank's cheek and laughed at him. "You're jealous! How cute!"

Frank glared at Shawn, his annoyance directed at her now instead of Jessica.

"You go on ahead, Frank," Jessica urged. "You two need some time alone. You don't want to drag me along."

"Right." Frank put his hand on the back of Shawn's neck. "We'll see you later, then."

Greg toasted their departure with his wineglass while Cole went off to get Lucy. "Sure you don't want me to drive you home, Jessica?" Greg wiggled his eyebrows.

"Thanks, Greg. Maybe some other time."

"I'll come out and see you tomorrow, okay?"

"Sure. Just give me a call first."

"Nice to meet you again, Cole." He shook Cole's hand. "You too, Lucy."

Lucy gave him a sleepy smile and clung to Cole's arm as if he were the only thing keeping her on her feet. "Good night, Greg." She sighed. "Wasn't it a wonderful party?"

Cole chuckled and guided her out the door with Jessica trailing beside her to help her down the steps. Just as they reached the parking lot, two men ran up.

"Can we take your picture, Mr. Nichols?" one asked. Before Cole could answer, a brilliant flash went off, blinding them all.

"Damn!" Cole swore, shading his eyes.

"Mr. Nichols, is it true that you're the son of Michael Cavanetti, owner of St. Benedict Winery?"

Cole dragged Lucy past the reporters, his mouth grim.

"Mr. Nichols, is it true you've changed your name to hide your Italian descent?"

Jessica glanced around. Where was that Miles Davidson? She'd like to kick his shins. He must have called these reporters and arranged for an ambush as soon as Cole left the party.

Another flash burst in their faces.

"Mr. Nichols, is it true that you're in the area to take over the management of the winery?"

At that moment Frank stumbled toward them.

"No, he isn't!" He grabbed the microphone out of the reporter's hands. "Cole Nichols has no claim on St. Benedict. No legal claim!"

"Is it true that Michael Cavanetti disowned him thirteen years ago?"

"Yes! My brother made his choice to leave St. Benedict a long time ago. And no one, especially him"—Frank pointed at Cole—"has any right to butt in on the family business. Or my wife!"

The reporter grimaced at Frank's last words and retrieved his microphone.

Frank stumbled toward Cole. "You think you're so great you can just have anything you want, don't you?"

Cole stared at his half-brother but did not answer. A videotape recorder perched on a reporter's shoulder whirred away, documenting everything.

"Well, you're not getting St. Benedict!" He jabbed his finger at Cole's chest. "Do you hear me? No matter how much money you have, no matter how many fans you have, you're not getting St. Benedict!"

"Frank, shut up."

"Go to hell!" Frank took a swing at Cole. The reporters stepped backward, and Jessica grabbed Lucy, who swayed against her.

Cole fended off Frank's attack but did not strike back.

Frank lunged for Cole, but Cole grabbed him around the torso and easily pulled him off his feet. His strength only made Frank angrier.

"Goddamn you!" He wriggled free and was about to lunge again, when Shawn reached for him.

"Frank!" she exclaimed. "Come on, Peaches. He can't have the winery. He knows it."

"Yeah, but he'd like to think he can get it!" He allowed Shawn to straighten his coat. "Well, we don't want you here, Mr. Goddamn Football Hero. We don't want you here! You understand that?"

Jessica glanced at Cole. She admired him for not striking back at his smaller brother. It would have been easy to do, especially when Frank's words were so vicious. It took considerable self-control simply to stand there and take the verbal abuse. Yet Cole's self-control took its own toll. Suddenly his eyes flickered, and, to Jessica's horror, she saw his legs crumple. Without a word, he toppled to the ground.

"Cole!" Jessica screamed. Lucy stared at him, her hands to her mouth, her eyes wide above her fingertips.

Jessica dropped to her knees beside Cole's head. He was unconscious and limp. Frantically she patted his cheek. "Cole!" she urged. "Wake up! Are you all right? Cole!"

8

Cole swirled into limbo again, nauseated and frightened, while darkness clouded his vision. Twice this had happened to him on the playing field, and it scared him more than he cared to admit. He struggled to sit up, to open his eyes. His arms felt heavy; his feet were like dead weights. And for some reason he couldn't catch his breath.

All of a sudden his vision cleared. He glanced around him. He had never been able to see anything during his other blackouts. Yet this time he saw something so bright that he had to squint against the glare.

The glare was sunlight flashing off a metal blade poised to strike. Goddamn! Some maniac with a curved sword was about to hack off his head! Cole rolled to the side to avoid the blow and scrambled to his feet. Instinctively he swung his left hand and brandished a huge sword, slicing first through the air and then through the maniac's arm. His opponent howled in agony and dropped to his knees. Cole swung again, with both hands this time, and cleft through the man's turban—all the way to his breastbone. Cole pulled out his sword, and the man collapsed at his feet like a sack of barley.

Panting, Cole raised his sword again. The chain mail and gauntlet on his left arm was bloody up to his elbow, his hauberk was flecked with blood and sweat, and rivulets of moisture ran from the hair under his coif and helmet into his eyes. But he had no time to rest. Another Saracen was running up to engage him.

Cole looked around wildly. He and a dozen others were defending a bridge across a river. All around him were slain soldiers—French, English, German, and Saracen. Cole glanced down at the river, which was littered with shields and lances and with horses and men, drowning and perishing. In front of him were scores of Saracens, some on foot and some on horseback, trying to force the Christians from the bridge.

A hail of Saracen darts rained down on him. Cole caught most of them on his shield. Then with a howl of bloodlust and rage, he swung his sword and met the enemy. Until William of Doon arrived with reinforcements, he would fight to the death to hold this bridge.

Cole's face was white beneath his tan, and his eyes rolled wildly beneath their lids. Jessica patted his cheek, desperately worried that he had hit his head and suffered a concussion. She cradled his head with her arm and checked his pupils. They looked normal. The reporters hovered about snapping pictures while Frank and Shawn stood near his feet, staring at him.

"Can't you leave him alone?" Jessica shouted, turning on them. "Get away! Go on!"

"What's wrong with him?" Shawn exclaimed.

Before Jessica could answer, she heard Cole moan and felt him stir. Her heart leapt with relief.

"Get back! Give him room!" She waved her free arm. "He needs air."

The reporters stood their ground, determined to get a good story on the famous quarterback. Frank and Shawn moved back, however, as Cole sat up, squinting and rubbing the back of his head.

"What happened?" he murmured.

"You fainted." Jessica put a hand on his shoulder. "Are you all right?"

"Yeah." Cole rubbed his neck and then shook his head, as if to shake off his wooziness. "Yeah."

Jessica glared over her shoulder at the reporters. "Leave us alone or I'll sue your station for harassment."

One of the reporters snickered at her threat, but he realized that the story was over. He turned to go, and his fellows turned with him.

Cole extended his arm. "Give me a hand, would you, Jessica?"

She grabbed his hands and helped him to his feet. Cole brushed off his coat.

"Is he going to be okay?" Shawn asked.

"Yes. He'll be fine. Go on."

Jessica did not even look at Shawn and Frank. She put her arm around Cole and walked with him to the black Jaguar in the parking lot. Lucy trailed at their heels, seemingly stunned by Cole's sudden collapse.

At the passenger's side, Cole stopped. "I can drive," he said. "I feel all right now."

"I don't know—"

"He can," Lucy put in with a slur. "He never falls down twice in a row." She stifled a hiccup.

"How reassuring," Jessica murmured. "Is that an expert opinion?"

"She's right," Cole said. "I just collapse, and then I'm fine. No aftereffects. Believe me." He unlocked the door. "Lucy, why don't you get in the back. By the looks of it, you're going to fall asleep anyway."

Jessica marveled at the way Lucy complied. Had Cole been *her* boyfriend or lover, she wouldn't have given up the front seat for another woman. Cole motioned for Jessica to sit in the passenger's seat. She sank into the fine leather, and he closed the door.

Cole got in and started the engine. He reached over and put his hand upon Jessica's, which were folded in her lap.

"Thanks, Jessica," he said. Then his warm hand left her and returned to the gear shift.

They drove in silence to north Seattle. The silence was not oppressive or tense but companionable. Jessica looked at Cole's profile every once in awhile, wondering what had made him fall. He seemed perfectly healthy. Cole, preoccupied, kept his attention on the road and sped to the University District.

"Where are we going?" Jessica asked, noticing that he was not taking her home.

"I'm going to drop Lucy off at the hotel. She's out."

Jessica looked back. Lucy was propped in the corner, her head resting on the window, her mouth slightly open, deep in sleep.

When they arrived at the hotel, Jessica helped get Lucy out of the car and then opened doors for Cole as they walked into the hotel and then to the elevator. The elevator ride was short. Cole half carried Lucy to her room, which adjoined his—probably for propriety's sake, Jessica mused. She sat in a chair by the television while Cole carried Lucy to her bed.

A few minutes later he stuck his head around the corner. "I've got to take out my contacts," he said. "I'll be right there."

Jessica nodded at him. Then she looked at the mess in the room. Cole's bed was made, but his clothes were scattered on every chair. A suitcase was open and brimmed with a pile of underwear and socks. Several magazines, including *Sports Illustrated* and the *Wine Spectator* lay on the floor beside the bed, along with an empty box of Milk Duds. A jumble of shoes lay at her feet. It took all Jessica's self-control to remain seated in the chair and not bend over to align the shoes in a neat row.

When Cole came out of the bathroom, he was wearing the wire-framed glasses made of a metal nearly the same color as his dark brown hair. Jessica glanced at him. The glasses lent him an endearing air of vulnerability that was at odds with his athletic figure. She liked the contrast.

"What are you looking at?" he asked. "My slovenly mess?"

"Yes." Jessica rose, smiling. "You know, you really shouldn't eat Milk Duds in bed."

Cole pulled off his tie and threw it onto the nearest chair. Then he unbuttoned his cuffs. "I can eat anything I want in bed, Miss Ward. I'm a big boy."

Jessica blushed and was thankful that Cole turned his attention to the closet. He stripped off his shirt while his back was turned, leaving his T-shirt on. Jessica watched him disrobe, feeling as if she should avert her gaze but ignoring the tweak of conscience. Cole shouldered on a thick cabled sweater and pulled it over his head.

"That feels much better. I hate ties," he commented. "A woman must have invented them."

Jessica crossed her arms. "Then men must have invented high heels. And bras."

"Bras? No way. They're too hard to deal with."

"But women are the ones who have to wear them."

"Yes." Cole unbuckled his belt. "But men have to fumble with them in the dark. I don't know what's worse."

He pulled out his belt, and Jessica stared at him, wondering what he was going to do and worrying that the topic of conversation was growing far too dangerous for her taste. He looked at her, and a smile crinkled the corners of his eyes.

"I'm going to slip into some jeans, Jessica. You can watch, or turn your back."

Jessica spun around. She heard him chuckle as he pulled off his slacks. Then she heard the metallic clink of another belt as he stepped into his jeans.

"Throw me that pair of Dock-Sides, would you?" he asked.

Jessica reached down, found a pair of brown loafers, and tossed them behind her. Then she ventured a glimpse.

Cole sat in the chair, slipping on his shoes. She turned.

"You're certainly not shy about dressing in front of people," she commented.

"I've dressed in locker rooms too many times to be shy." He glanced up at her and flashed her a smile. "I bet you're the type that likes to get undressed with all the lights turned off." He stood up. "I bet you're the type that wears those pajamas with the little feet in them."

"Priestesses do not wear pajamas."

"Oh?" Cole laughed. "What do they wear, then?"

"You'll never know until you're initiated." She breezed to the door, acting more cocky than she felt. All this talk about dressing and undressing made her nervous.

Cole sauntered up behind her. "And how do I get initiated, Mother Superior?"

"You take vows, like everyone else." She opened the door, thankful to be out of his room.

Again Cole drove in silence until they reached the top of Moss Cliff.

"That's where I saw the monk," Jessica commented, pointing to the St. Benedict Winery sign. "He walked out into the road right in front of me."

"In the dark?"

"Yes."

"Strange."

They drove past the regimented rows of grapevines, grown mainly for show on the top of the bluff so that tourists would get a feel for a vineyard before arriving at the winery. Moonlight reflected off the pond at the east side of the mansion and traced a silver line on the roof of the Cavanetti house.

"It's beautiful," Jessica murmured. "No matter how many times I drive past, it's still beautiful."

"Damn beautiful." Cole had dug most of the pond by hand and had planted most of the vines on the bluff. His fingers tightened on the steering wheel. Jessica glanced at him. His jaw was set, and his nostrils flared with some emotion she could not define—perhaps love or hatred or a bittersweet mixture of both.

"Why did you give it up, Cole?" she asked quietly.

"I hated it then."

"And now?"

"Does it matter?" He pulled into the bungalow driveway. "You heard what Frank said."

Jessica opened her door when the Jaguar stopped in front of her house, but Cole's voice kept her from climbing out.

"Jess . . ."

She glanced over her shoulder. Cole ran his hand through his short glossy hair. He seemed uneasy for the first time since he had arrived.

"Yes?"

"How about taking a walk with me?"

"You mean now?"

"Yes. Are you too tired?"

Jessica was more awake than she had been for a long time, fired by the emotional roller coaster she had been riding all evening.

"I'm all keyed up," he continued. "And the night is so clear. We could walk down to the river and back. What do you say?"

"Well, sure, but let me change my shoes first."

"Great." Cole shut off the car lights and got out. He followed Jessica into the house. Jessica hoped and prayed her father was still asleep in the family room where she had left him.

"Do you want to wait in the living room?" she asked, motioning toward the right.

"What—I don't get to watch *you* change? That isn't fair."

"I'm not accustomed to locker rooms, Mr. Nichols." She took off her coat and hung it in the closet. "I'll only be a minute."

She slipped out of her tight silk pants and pulled on jeans, socks, and tennis shoes. Then she replaced the jade tunic with a faded University of Washington sweatshirt. All the while she dressed she marveled that Niccolo Cavanetti was waiting for her and they were going to take a walk together.

In earlier days, they had run through the vineyard in breathless games of tag, and on hot summer afternoons they had thrown each other into the Samish Slough, the meandering river at the bottom of the hill. Now the thought of walking through the vineyard in the moonlight with him seemed oddly exotic, even romantic. She hung up her tunic and admonished herself for slipping back into her fantasy. Cole just needed a friend tonight. He was troubled. And he didn't have to entertain her. She was simply the easiest person for him to tolerate.

They left the house and walked around the side, between the guest cottage and the garage, and down a trail that led to the vineyard proper. In the moonlight, Jessica could see the entire expanse stretching down the slope to the slough. Now that winter was here, all the leaves were gone and the vines were twisted wraiths tied to wires with twine.

They could not walk side by side, so Jessica followed Cole. They did not speak until they reached the bottom of the hill, a good mile from the house. There below the vineyard was the silver ribbon of the Samish Slough. They followed a dirt path along the water's edge, stepping over irrigation pipes that Cole had helped his father install years ago. Everywhere she looked, Jessica could see evidence of Cole's hand on this land. His sweat and blood, almost as much as his father's, had built up the vineyard and the winery.

At last they came to a wooden bridge that linked the Cavanetti property to the land on the other side of the slough.

Cole stopped on the bridge and leaned over the wooden rail. He shook the top bar. "This could use a few nails," he said. "It's getting rickety."

"Don't fall in," Jessica warned. "That water's deep. I wouldn't be able to save you."

Cole leaned both forearms on the rail and looked at her. "I think you could save me, Mother Superior."

He remained gazing at her, and she could not break his stare. He seemed so relaxed, so confident. Why was she such a bundle of nerves? She stuffed her hands into her jacket pockets and joined him at the rail.

"I'm a swimmer, but you're a big man, Cole." She felt as if their words had another meaning altogether.

"You're a swimmer, all right."

She glanced at him. His words were cryptic, and his eyes were full of amusement, almost as if he were toying with her again. Jessica straightened.

"If you fell in, I suppose I could just lower my priestess halo to you and pull you out."

Her sarcasm didn't faze him a bit. He laughed. "And if I died, you could say some secret prayer and bring me back." He picked a pebble from a joint in the wood and tossed it into the water. "Yes, I bet you could raise a man from the dead, Miss Jessica Ward. Raise him right up from the dead."

He watched the ripples from the pebble, and his voice died out as the rings disappeared. Jessica surveyed him, wondering what he was talking about. Vibrant, smiling Cole Nichols had turned melancholic and dark. She longed to touch him, put her hands on his shoulders, lay her head upon his back, and embrace him and tell him that she would do anything for him. But she stood rooted to the spot, mute and afraid to make a move.

Cole tossed another pebble. "This bridge was always a symbol for me," he said after a while.

"How so?"

He glanced at the vineyard and then to the other side of the river, where a jogging trail wound through a bog and a park that sloped to the salty waters of Puget Sound.

"Every day I worked the vineyard for my father and looked across the bridge. I could see people in the park, people with their picnic baskets and their dogs, families with a mother and father and pampered children, people with nice clothes and expensive cars." He threw a stone. "My father never had time to take me anywhere. My mother was too sick to even read to me. And I never got a free afternoon except on Sunday, and then they wouldn't let me go anywhere. They were afraid that an Italian kid might get beaten up in the park." He laughed bitterly. "I got beaten up at school—I don't know why getting beaten up at the park would have been any different."

"So you never got to cross the bridge?"

He shook his head. "Not until I learned to play football. Football was my ticket out of slavery. With football, I gained acceptance. I could go to any park I wanted, in the fanciest car I could find. And you know what?"

"What?"

Cole straightened and dusted his hands on his pants. "I found that going to parks isn't that great after all."

"Maybe it's because you forgot to take along a dog and a picnic basket." She raised one eyebrow.

He looked at her, and his melancholy slipped behind a grin. "You're a nut," he chuckled. "Come on. Let's go back."

Jessica walked up the path ahead of Cole and was conscious of his eyes on her most of the way up the hill. By the time she reached the top, her breath came fast and heavy. Cole was barely winded. He laughed and swept her off her feet, slinging her over his shoulder and striding with her past the guesthouse while she kicked and squirmed and demanded to be put down.

"Wimp!" Cole laughed as he deposited her on the front porch.

"Bully!" She wriggled out of his grip. But she couldn't keep a smile from her lips as she brushed back her hair and put the key in the lock. Cole stood beside her. She was afraid to ask him in for coffee or hot chocolate. Her father might be lying on the floor in the kitchen or stumbling around half naked in the bathroom. Even though she had no desire to end the evening, she couldn't take the chance that Cole would see her father drunk.

Cole put his hand on the woodwork of the doorway. "I've got to be getting back." He regarded her face and then her hair, as if deciding whether or not he should say anything more.

"Well, good night then, Cole." Jessica held out her hand. "Thanks for bringing me back."

"No trouble." He smiled when he took her hand, as if amused by her formal dismissal. "Jessica . . ."

She let her hand remain in his. "Yes?"

"I just want to tell you that I'm glad you're here. I didn't know—" He broke off and glanced to the side. "I didn't know how much it would mean to me—seeing the place again, seeing my father, seeing you . . ."

A feeling of warmth spread over her at his words. She smiled at him when his gaze returned to her face.

"It's good to see you, too," she said softly. She longed to kiss him and felt that if she could just kiss him she might make him happy again. "Good night, Niccolo."

"Good night."

He turned suddenly and hurried down the walk to his car. Jessica closed the door and leaned upon it, her body humming with hunger and happiness.

Frank stumbled into the bedroom and saw Shawn standing before the closet, still dressed in the outfit she had worn to the open house. He grabbed a pillow from the bed while Shawn watched him, her right hand perched on her hip. Her legs were long and sexy in the black hose and high heels. He wanted to grab a handful of those shapely calves and squeeze until she squealed. Something about the dress made her look sexy without being cheap—a departure from the norm for Shawn. She was just a tramp who had tricked him into marriage by becoming pregnant. He had done his duty by her, as any Cavanetti man would do, even though Shawn had been nothing but a diversion from his usual sorority girlfriends. But Shawn had lost the baby. And now the time had come to quit himself of her. Still, in that dress . . .

"Where are you going, Frank?" Her question hung in the air like a challenge.

Frank straightened, holding the pillow under his arm. "I'm sleeping down the hall."

"Why?" Shawn took a drag on the cigarette in her holder and held the smoke in for a long moment.

"Because I want to."

"Do you?" she asked, exhaling as she sauntered forward. The way she rolled her hips made Frank feel dizzy. "Or are you afraid to screw in your mama's house? Afraid she'll hear the noise?"

"Don't be idiotic."

She kicked off her shoes and walked up to him, taking another drag while her mouth was poised inches from his. Frank arched his head back but did not move away. The dress she was wearing had driven him crazy with jealousy and lust all night. Her breasts looked so white and inviting that all he wanted to do was plunge his nose between them and kiss them. He felt himself respond to the closeness of her body—exactly what she wanted him to do—and he clenched his jaw, disgusted with himself.

He knew she had just ended an affair. She hadn't even tried to hide this one, and to make it worse, the relationship had been with a tennis buddy of his. She hadn't even had the decency to stay away from his friends. His mother was right. Shawn was not the type of woman to help his career. Yet, she was a turn on. There was no doubt about that.

"Do you like my dress?" she asked, running her hand down his tie. Frank breathed in, trying to maintain his fragile hold on his self-control. "You never said how I looked in the dress."

"Yeah, I like the dress."

"Do you want to see what I'm wearing underneath?"

Before he could answer, Shawn pulled up the dress and displayed shapely white thighs, crossed by the tops of the hose and the straps of her black lace garter belt. She wasn't wearing any panties.

Frank groaned. His grip tightened on the pillow while he hardened instantly. He closed his eyes and breathed in. So help him, he wasn't going to fool around with this slut anymore, so help him.

She clutched his crotch while his eyes were closed and sent him over the edge.

"Damn you, Shawn!" Frank flung the pillow to the floor and grabbed her, biting her breasts as he stumbled to the bed with her. This was the last time, the absolute last time. He tore the dress from her and suckled her ivory breasts while he fumbled with his zipper. She writhed beneath him, driving him crazy while he struggled to free himself. His hands were shaking. God, if his mother knew what a weak-willed bastard he was, she'd have a fit.

Frank raised up, panting with desire, running his hands up and down Shawn's thighs and underneath the straps of her garter belt. He was on the verge of bursting just from the thought of her beneath him, a position she hadn't assumed for months.

Shawn reached up for him. "Have you told your mama your news?" she asked.

"What?" Frank croaked. His erection deflated instantly.

"Your news, Peaches." She ran a painted nail down his chest.

Frank knew it was hopeless, over. Shawn had done this to him. She had deliberately turned him on just so she could destroy him.

"What's the matter, Peaches?" Shawn pursed her lips and looked down at his midriff. "Did Little Pokey turn into Little Gumby?"

"Bitch!" Frank flung himself off her. "You little bitch!" He yanked up his pants, his face hot and flushed.

Shawn propped herself up on her elbows without closing her legs. She was smiling. He wanted to hit her. God, how he wanted to hit her.

"What's the matter, Peaches?" Her voice was full of syrupy innocence. "Was it something I said?"

"I want you out of here!" Frank grabbed the pillow he had dropped to the floor. "Tomorrow!"

"But—"

"Tomorrow!" He slammed the door.

After Cole left, Jessica leaned against the door and remembered everything he had said to her, remembered the way he had danced with her, and pulled her off her feet and carried her to the house. She was delirious. She was ecstatic. She knew that she would not be able to sleep for hours.

The night was clear and bright. A beautiful night, perfect for gazing at the stars. She went to her bedroom and lugged her telescope case into the hallway, then hoisted it up the attic stairs and out to a narrow balcony on the roof.

There she went about setting up the elaborate instrument, a practice so familiar she could do it with her eyes closed. All the while she tightened knobs and adjusted the tripod, she thought of Cole. No man she had ever met in her adult life had made her heart flop as madly as it had done this evening. No man had ever made her feel as if she could burst with some feeling that surpassed mere joy.

Her liaisons with men had been so flat and unsatisfying that she had quit pursuing relationships altogether in the past few years. Men who interested her were hard to come by, and once she found one, the interest invariably dulled within a few months. She blamed herself after awhile, thinking she was incapable of finding happiness with a man.

None of them had produced the feelings she had experienced with Cole. She wondered if her reaction to him was merely a residual infatuation from her girlhood, fueled by the fantasies she had invented over the years.

Jessica pulled off the lens cover. Cole was her last hope as far as men were concerned. If he failed her, even her fantasy would fail, and her fantasy was all she had left. She lowered her face to the eyepiece. Maybe she should keep away from Cole. Perhaps fantasy was better than real life and she should leave well enough alone.

For nearly a half hour she calmed herself by studying the sky. She could lose herself so easily to the heavens. After awhile she decided to move her telescope to get a better view of the western sky. A tree was in the way, and she had to move to the edge of the balcony. Carefully Jessica lifted her heavy telescope and walked backward while keeping an eye on the obtrusive fir. Just a few more steps and she thought she would be clear of it. She continued backward and then set down the tripod and leaned against the banister to sight past the tree.

The banister, rotted from years of sun and rain, gave way

with a crack beneath her weight. Jessica screamed and flailed her arms, trying to get her balance while she teetered on one foot. Below her was one and a half stories of house and a steep slope to a tangle of blackberry bushes.

She plunged over the side of the roof, screaming, just as two hands shot out of the shadows and grabbed her.

9

Jessica was pulled to safety and yanked backward so hard that she staggered and fell, knocking her rescuer into the shadow of the eaves. She jumped to her feet and whirled around, shocked that someone had been on the roof with her and she had not even been aware of another presence.

She peered into the darkness, panting and frightened, the sound of her heart pounding in her ears so loud that she thought she would go deaf from the noise.

"Who's there?" she cried. The shadows shifted. "Who are you?" she demanded, her voice quaking.

The monk stepped from the side of the house. Her heart skipped a beat.

"Who are you?" she whispered in a hoarse voice.

"I am Brother Cosimo," came the reply as the monk moved into the moonlight. He was a tall man, with shoulders as wide as Cole's. His height was accentuated by the pointed hood of his cowl, which cast his face in shadow, concealing his features. He put his hands into the bell-shaped sleeves of his black habit and stood before her in silence.

Jessica felt a bit safer. It would take him a moment to get his hands back out, should he decide to do her harm. Yet he had just saved her from falling. Surely he would not save her life only to cause her injury later.

"What do you want?" she asked.

"So you do see me."

What a curious thing to say. Of course she saw him. "Yes, I see you. What do you think you are, invisible?"

He was silent at her sarcasm. Jessica felt a sudden urge to retract her outburst.

"Look, thanks for saving me, Brother Cosimo. I'm grateful. But you startled me."

"I am sorry for that. I had hoped you couldn't see me."

"Well, I do," she replied lamely.

"And you did see me that night by the sign, did you not?"

"Yes. You stepped right out in front of me. You scared me half to death."

"You scared me!" He chuckled. His deep, rich laugh eased her fears somewhat. He didn't sound like the vengeful madman she had supposed him to be. She put her hands on her telescope. Her legs still trembled.

"What are you doing here?" she asked. "Are you the monk from the commercials?"

"Commercials?" he asked. The way he pronounced the word made it seem as if it were foreign to his tongue.

"You know, the St. Benedict commercial with the bumbling monk."

"I do not bumble."

"Oh." Jessica narrowed her eyes. "Then who are you?"

"I am the guardian."

"Of what?"

"The winery." He stepped forward. "And you are Jessica Ward."

"How do you know?" Her grip tightened on the telescope.

"I have seen you in the vineyard and at the Cavanetti house. The last time I saw you was at Niccolo's party."

"You saw me?"

"Yes, but apparently you did not see me."

"That was thirteen years ago!"

"Was it? Time is mysterious, is it not, Miss Ward?"

"You've been around St. Benedict for thirteen years?"

He stepped closer. "Oh, longer than that. Since 1938."

"Since 1938?" Jessica tilted her head, trying to get a look at his face, but she couldn't see a thing in the darkness. "Why haven't I seen you before?"

The monk shrugged. "I do not know. Perhaps it was not time for you to see me. It is rare that anyone does, you know. And I have not spoken to anyone for many years."

"Why were you standing outside my window the other night?"

"As to that"—the monk's hood dipped as he looked at the ground and then back at her—"I must admit that I was spying on you."

"Why?"

"When I saw you by the sign, I did not know who you were. Since then I have come to the conclusion that you are Jessica Ward the child grown to be a woman. But at the sign I did not know that. And you seemed—" He broke off.

Jessica leaned forward. "Yes?"

"You seemed to be someone else."

"Who?"

"It does not matter, Miss Ward. Not now." The monk sighed, and his big shoulders heaved upward, then back down. "It does not matter."

Jessica stared at the monk, no longer afraid that he would harm her. She shoved her cold hands into her pockets. "There have been legends about St. Benedict Winery, that monks guard the secret to the wines, but I always thought that was hype."

"Hype?"

"You know, just something to catch the interest of the public."

"Ah, yes." The monk nodded again. "Yes, it does capture the imagination, does it not?"

"But it's true?"

"Yes."

Jessica stared at him. The legend was true. A monk did

haunt St. Benedict Winery. And this one had been here since 1938. He must be at least as old as Michael Cavanetti—over eighty. Yet his voice and his physique did not belong to a man of eighty years. Perhaps he had been younger than Michael Cavanetti when he took over the job as guardian. If he had been a young monk of twenty, he would be seventy-two. Jessica inspected the broad shoulders and the erect posture of the monk before her. Could he be in his seventies? Somehow she doubted it.

"Could you tell me, Miss Ward, what it is you are doing up here?"

"I'm tracking the stars. Actually, I'm looking for comets, but the moon is too bright."

"And what is this apparatus?" He motioned toward the telescope. Jessica glanced at his hand. His skin was unwrinkled and unblemished—surely not the hand of a man in his seventies.

"This is a telescope."

"A device for looking at the stars?"

"Yes. Haven't you ever seen a telescope?"

"No." Brother Cosimo moved closer to her. "Would you show me how it works?"

Jessica found it hard to believe that he had never seen a telescope. But she played along and showed him how to look through the eyepiece. She focused the lens on Mars, which hung like a big red beacon near the horizon. Brother Cosimo was delighted with the telescope and displayed an almost childlike enthusiasm for stargazing. Before she knew it, Jessica had shown him the moon, Jupiter and its satellites, and myriad constellations. He knew many of the stars in the sky, which impressed her and encouraged her to show him more. Before she was aware of the passage of time, dawn had blossomed on the peaks of the eastern Cascade Mountains.

Jessica looked at her watch. Her eyes felt blurry and scratchy. "Goodness," she said, looking at her watch. "It's seven o'clock in the morning."

"Is it?" Brother Cosimo straightened. "I must go."

Jessica rubbed her eyes. "I didn't realize it was so late."

She grinned. "I mean, so early!"

Brother Cosimo folded his hands together and inclined his head toward her. "Thank you for showing me your telescope. It is a fascinating instrument."

"Well, you may look through it any time you like."

"Just be careful when you are out, Miss Ward," he warned. "The buildings on Moss Cliff are all old. You must exercise caution."

"Yes, I will. And thank you, Brother Cosimo, for saving my life tonight."

He bowed his head once more. "Perhaps we shall talk again soon."

Jessica nodded and bent to pack away her instrument. When she finished and turned to go, she saw no trace of Brother Cosimo. She hadn't even heard his retreating footsteps.

Jessica looked around, then shrugged to herself and returned to the lower level of the bungalow. She fell into bed and slept soundly, no longer afraid of the monk.

At the hotel, Cole lay awake in his bed with his hands locked behind his head. He stared at the ceiling. What had happened to him at the open house? Where had the images of knights in battle come from? He didn't know anything about the Crusades, and yet he knew for certain that in the vision he had been a knight during the Crusades.

He pressed the back of his head with his palms, as if to squeeze some sense into his thoughts. Were his blackouts the first sign of schizophrenia? One of his buddies had teased him that he was turning schizo. Cole didn't think the idea a bit funny. And now that he had experienced a vision during a blackout, he was far from amused.

For the first time in his life he knew real fear—not the fear of a human locomotive in a football jersey charging toward him, rabid for a sack. That was real and something he had learned to expect. He would either scramble out of the way or be driven to the ground. He could deal with that. But these blackouts were a different matter altogether. He had no idea what would happen or when they would occur.

He shut his eyes, trying to distract himself by thinking about Jessica Ward. She'd grown into a gorgeous woman, much more beautiful than he had expected. She had been such a thin, gangling kid. Yet some people as well as wines benefited from aging, deepening in color and character. Cole felt a tired smile tug at the corners of his mouth. Raven-haired Jessica Ward had grown as silky and smooth as an oak-aged Chardonnay, and he'd bet a case of it that she would taste just as sweet, if not sweeter.

His eyelids closed on the vision of her pushing back her hair and smiling at him. He remembered that smile from the old days, the way the corners of her mouth turned down instead of up, as if she could never allow herself to really grin. He knew he had to look into her eyes to see the real smile. Jessica Ward had always been self-contained and unflappable. He wondered what she would be like if she ever let go. Then again, maybe it was not in her nature to let go of her cool reserve.

Cole slept and plunged back into his strange dream.

The night was cool and calm, but Cole was not fooled by the peaceful atmosphere. He expected to be attacked any minute now by the Saracens encamped on the other side of the river. Cole paced the covered walkway spanning the river, his footfalls echoing hollowly in the darkness. During the day the Christian host had made good progress on the earthen dam below the protective planks of the walkway. But now, in the early evening, the construction site was quiet. Far too quiet for Cole's liking.

He turned at the far tower and strolled back. A dozen of his knights kept watch in the tower near the host. Some played dice in the guttering light of a torch, but most of them gazed anxiously toward the other side of the river, waiting and watching.

Rumors flew that the Saracens might use the deadly

Greek fire against them. Cole pressed his lips together. Everyone knew that Greek fire could burn a man to ashes, and there was little defense against it except two good legs and a fast stallion. Honor would most likely send him and his men to their deaths.

The day had been unbearably hot, but now the desert wind blew cool and fragrant over the river. Cole breathed in and rested his right hand on the hilt of his sword. He winced at the movement. His upper arm was still sore from a wound he had suffered two days before.

He thought of home in the foothills of the Alps, where nights were cool and water was sweet. He thought of his castle rising above his village, and the fields and vineyards spreading up the sides of the mountains. He had always loved the look of the vineyards marching up those steep, rocky slopes, as if defying nature.

Taking up the Cross had seemed like a noble idea, yet after months in the Holy Land he was growing weary of the grit of sand on his tongue and the blood on his hands. He revered God and knew the importance of reclaiming Jerusalem from the Arabs so that Christian pilgrims could travel there unmolested. Yet he had never favored killing or slaughter, and to his chagrin he was quickly becoming renowned for his prowess in battle. And now he must defend with his life this stretch of water and sand and this jumble of planks—an idiotic endeavor if one thought about it. He smiled grimly.

"My Lord, they ready their engines!"

Cole turned in the direction his knight was pointing. Sure enough, Saracens swarmed around eight petraries on the riverbank.

"We are in grave peril!" a sergeant exclaimed. "If they hurl Greek fire at us, we shall be burned alive. Flee!"

"Hold!" Cole thundered.

"But, my lord, what will we do then?"

"We shall pray." Cole glanced at the petraries looming in the darkness. "Every time they hurl fire at us, we shall get down on our knees and pray to our Savior to protect our skins." He turned back to his soldiers. "In the meantime, put bolts to those crossbows and we'll see how many infidels we can deliver to Allah."

The crossbows were of small use against the Saracens. From the far tower, the bowmen were out of range to do damage to the enemy line.

Just before midnight the Saracens hurled their first cast of Greek fire. Cole had never seen anything like it, and for a moment he forgot his own advice to lay low. The fire thundered toward them, the ball of flame as big as a barrel and the tail as long as a lance. It looked like a dragon flying toward them, lighting the sky until it was as bright as broad daylight.

With the Greek fire came stones and darts as well, making it nearly impossible to move. Cole called down for archers, and within a half hour a score of archers hurried up the tower. Cole met them. Behind him part of the bridge was aflame. His knights struggled to douse the fires with cloaks and buckets of water. Soldiers ran around on the riverbank dodging missiles while trying to put out flames at the base of the towers. If many more casts were thrown, the span would be destroyed and all would be lost.

Cole and the archers bent low and stole across the bridge. Crossbows hadn't been effective. Too much time was taken up in drawing the powerful bows and setting the bolts. But English longbows would be a different matter altogether. A good archer could set an arrow nearly as soon as he had let the previous one fly. The effect of a constant cloud of arrows was terrifying and disruptive, perhaps enough to make the Saracens desert their engines.

Cole told the archers what he had in mind, and the men took their posts in the tower nearest the Saracens. The archers were excellent marksmen and stout of heart, unafraid of the rocks and fire whistling past. When an archer fell, a victim of a stone to his helmet, Cole took up his bow and stepped into his position. He was a fair bowman himself.

Fewer and fewer casts were made as the Saracen soldiers scrambled to avoid the arrows. His plan was working. With

renewed vigor, Cole reached for an arrow from the quiver
slung over his shoulder. He heard thunder approaching and
saw a burst of light out of the corner of his eye. But he did
not duck his head. He was intent on the battle at hand.

The Greek fire hit him on the side of his helmet, and the
force of the missile threw him across the span. Searing pain
flared in his head and across his shoulders, pain so intense
that his howl went soundless and breathless. He staggered
against the railing, pulling at his helm, wild with pain. Then
he plunged over the side into the water of the river, knowing he was a dead man.

The phone woke Jessica around eleven the next morning.
She fumbled with the receiver. Maria was on the other end,
upset and ranting about Isabella. Could Jessica come quickly? Mrs. Cavanetti wanted to talk to her right away.

Jessica agreed and jumped out of bed. She took a quick
shower, dressed, and hurried over to the Cavanetti house,
wondering what could have disturbed Mrs. Cavanetti. Maria
let her in the side door and ushered her upstairs to Isabella's
private suite, where she reclined on a chaise near the fireplace.

"Jessica!" Isabella sat up and threw off the afghan that
covered her legs. "Have you seen the paper?"

"What paper?" Jessica inquired.

"The *Post-Dispatch*!" She held up a section of the newspaper and shook it at Jessica. "Take a look at this!"

Jessica swept forward and took the paper from Isabella.
Isabella collapsed upon the chaise and flung her arm across
her eyes. "Maria, get my pills. I'm going to have another
migraine, and I simply can't afford to spend the day in bed!"

Maria bustled into her bathroom while Jessica scanned
the newspaper.

"Tell me what you see!" hissed Isabella.

"Japanese developers open golf course in the Samish
Valley?"

"No, no! Not that!"

Jessica glanced lower. "Oh—" She let her breath escape as the headline caught her eye. *Cole Nichols Flees Past*. She skimmed the article while a sick feeling turned her stomach. The reporters had dug up Cole's past, his trouble on the playing field, and his current problem with the woman in Philadelphia, and they'd woven the information around his brawl with Frank outside the Falls Winery. The story made it seem as if Cole were an angry prodigal son with a penchant for violence, an insatiable ego, and a deep-seated hatred for his half-brother.

Jessica looked up from the story, struck by the skewed viewpoint presented by the reporter.

Isabella pressed her lips together. "Exactly," she snapped as Maria appeared with a glass of water and a bottle of pills. Isabella's hands shook as she pried off the lid and slid three pills into her palm. She tossed them into her mouth and followed them with water.

"It couldn't be worse. I told you that Niccolo was trash. Now he's involved my Frank in a brawl. A brawl!" She closed her eyes. "I shudder to think of what people will say when they read this!"

Jessica felt another wave of shock. Isabella found nothing dishonest about the article. In disbelief, she gestured toward the paper. "But Frank—"

"Frank's reputation will be ruined by that half-brother of his! That—that—that scum!" Isabella massaged her temples. "If the Blakes learn about Nick's connection to this family, they'll be shocked, mortified!"

"Who are the Blakes?"

"The Blakes?" Isabella glanced at Jessica in scorn. "As in Blake, Davenport and Asher?" Isabella sighed at Jessica's blank expression. "Ted Blake has the most prestigious law firm in the northwest. Frank is due to join the firm after Christmas. I pulled every string imaginable to get him a position there."

"Don't the Blakes know that Cole is Frank's brother?"

"No. And I don't intend for them to find out. I haven't worked all my life grooming Frank for a place in society just to have Nick ruin it."

Jessica glanced at Maria, who stood by the head of the chaise wringing her hands, her dark eyes deeply troubled.

"Mrs. Cavanetti, Cole had nothing—"

"You were there last night," Isabella interrupted her. "What went on? Was it like the paper said? How many people saw them fighting?"

"I don't know. Hardly anyone was there except reporters. But, Mrs. Cavanetti, I can assure you that what happened outside the winery could hardly be called a brawl!"

"Then how do you account for that photograph?"

Jessica cast a glance at the paper still in her hand. The photograph showed Cole lying on the ground with Frank standing over him.

Isabella sat up and draped her shapely legs over the edge of the chaise. "At least Frank stood up to the brute and showed him what he was made of."

Jessica shook her head and put the paper on the glass table at the head of the lounge chair. Isabella had chosen not to listen to reason or truth and would probably not accept any words in defense of Cole. She wanted to believe that Frank was not to blame and that Cole was the source of all evil, just as she had for years.

"And do you know what else has happened? Have you heard what went on at the warehouse last night?"

"No. What happened?"

"Someone got into the warehouse and destroyed our entire inventory."

Jessica paled.

Isabella breathed in. "Yes. The entire inventory. Luckily we have insurance or we would be ruined. I'm still not certain how we'll fill our orders."

"Who would do such a thing?"

"You ask me? I say Nick did it. And I refuse to stand by and let that football player destroy everything!" She stressed the words *football player* as if they described the most degrading occupation in the world. "Nick is here because of his father. But I've figured out how to get him to leave."

"And how is that?" Jessica inquired, trying to keep the concern out of her voice.

"I'm having Michael discharged from the hospital into my care. I'm bringing him back here where Nick can't see him."

"You'd keep Cole from seeing his father?" Jessica glanced back at Maria. The old woman was shaking her head and looking down at the floor.

"Nick's presence won't do Michael any good. Precisely the opposite. And once Nick discovers that he is barred from his father, he'll leave. And I'll be rid of him." Isabella stood up. "Maria, set out my green wool suit. I'm going to the hospital."

Maria nodded and scurried out of the room.

"Oh, and Jessica," Isabella added. "Thank you for taking Shawn shopping yesterday. Frank tells me that she actually looked presentable."

"She looked great. You should have seen her, Mrs. Cavanetti."

"Well, I do appreciate the trouble you took. Now, if you'll excuse me, I must dress."

Jessica showed herself out of the house. She walked slowly down the steps and ambled past the small chapel that Michael Cavanetti had built years before she was born. Jessica glanced at the building and decided to go in. She was troubled by Isabella's decision to move Michael Cavanetti to the house just to foil Cole. She needed to think and the chapel was the perfect place for contemplation.

She pulled open the heavy wood door and stepped inside the small stucco chapel. At the far end above the altar was a stained glass window depicting St. Benedict writing in a book. She had always liked the kind expression painted on the face of the saint, and as a child had thought he was Jesus until Maria corrected her. Maria had clucked over Jessica's lack of religious education and did her best to fill the gaps in her knowledge.

Michael Cavanetti had built the chapel as a memorial to his brother, who had been a priest in Italy and had lost his life during World War II. Jessica looked at the glass box that held the habit and cowl, hemp belt and rosary of Michael's brother, an icon of shattered dreams and heartbreaking tragedy. The glass reliquary had always meant more to Jessica than any of the other religious paraphernalia in the chapel.

Jessica wandered up the aisle and sat in a pew on the left. She closed her eyes and let the stillness settle over her. How could Isabella be so cruel to Cole? Was there something she could do to help him? Should she meddle in the Cavanetti affairs?

A strange feeling swept through her, strong and sudden, as if telling her that she was right in trying to help. She felt awash with peace and rightness. Never had she experienced such a direct response to a question.

Jessica opened her eyes in wonder and saw that sunlight had burst through the yellow portion of the stained glass window, bathing her in light and warmth. There was her answer. There was her miracle. She smiled at her own foolishness. Her answer had come from the sun, not a higher source.

She got up to leave just as the chapel door opened. Maria hobbled down the aisle toward her and genuflected before the altar.

"There you are, *bambina*! I thought I saw you come in here."

"Has Mrs. Cavanetti left?"

"Yes. That woman!" Maria shook her head.

"We must do something to help Cole."

Maria nodded. "Yes, but what?"

"I don't know. But she's wrong about Cole. That newspaper article was just a bunch of misleading information. And she took it all to heart."

"She wants to believe that Niccolo is bad. She wants to!"

Jessica put her hand on Maria's shoulder. "Maria, if you think of any way I can help, give me a call. But we must be careful not to ruffle Mrs. Cavanetti's feathers. You and I may be Cole's only link to his father."

"Ah, Jessica, my heart is sick." Maria put her hands to her

cheeks and shook her head. "Poor Mr. Cavanetti!"

"We'll work something out. Don't you worry." She guided Maria out of the chapel to the yard.

"And by the way, Maria, there is a monk."

"There is?"

"Yes. Remember when I asked if you had seen a monk hanging around the winery? Well, I actually talked to him last night."

"You did?"

"Yes. His name is Cosimo. Brother Cosimo."

"What?" Maria put her hand over her breast as her brows drew together.

"Cosimo." Jessica zipped up her jacket. "Isn't that an odd name?"

"Very odd. Jessica!" Maria grabbed her forearm with both hands. "You said you talked to him?"

"Yes." Jessica stared at Maria's hands, surprised at the ferocity of her grip. "He seemed very nice. I showed him my telescope. He said he was a guardian."

"Capperi!"

"He actually saved my life. I almost fell off the balcony at the bungalow, but he grabbed me and pulled me back."

"He touched you?" Maria's voice was full of horror.

"Yes. What's so awful about that?" She tilted her head. "What's wrong, Maria? What aren't you telling me?"

Maria's stare slid away, and she looked around, hugging her chest with her plump arms.

"Maria, what do you know about the monk?"

"I know of only one monk by that name, Jessica. I have heard Mr. Cavanetti speak of him."

"What did he say about him? Who is Brother Cosimo?"

"I can't believe that you spoke to him, that he touched you!" Maria rubbed her upper arms. "Ooh, my skin crawls, Jessica!"

"Why?"

"Because the monk you are talking about—Cosimo Cavanetti? He was a sorcerer, a heretic, a man who raised a woman from the dead!"

"What?" Jessica exclaimed, incredulous. She couldn't

believe Maria was spouting such preposterous nonsense. But Maria was serious, and her eyes were full of alarm.

"You couldn't have spoken to him!" Maria went on. "It is not possible!"

"Why?"

"Cosimo Cavanetti was put to death. He was walled up alive by his brethren."

"Maybe he escaped somehow."

Maria gave a short hysterical laugh. "*Bambina*, he could not have escaped. And even if he had, he could not have escaped time."

"What do you mean?"

"Cosimo Cavanetti died long ago, Jessica. Long ago."

"When exactly, Maria?"

"I am not certain. But I think Mr. Cavanetti said once that Cosimo Cavanetti died in the twelfth century."

10

Jessica walked back to the bungalow lost in a daze of disbelief and denial. Maria had to be wrong about the monk. Perhaps the Brother Cosimo she had spoken to had simply been named after the Cosimo of long ago. That would explain everything. Although why someone would be named after a sorcerer and a heretic was another question entirely.

As Jessica hung up her coat, she noticed her father hovering in the hall.

"Someone just called for you, Jessica."

"Oh? Who?"

"Someone named Greg. Said he's coming over."

Jessica frowned. "Oh, great." She had planned to do paperwork for the rest of the morning and then prepare her presentation for the upcoming astronomy conference at Stanford. A presentation for a national conference was not a last-minute affair, and she had allocated her Christmas vacation as her time to get the bulk of the paper written. Already she had lost two days.

She breezed past her father. He trailed after her as she banged around in the kitchen, trying to find something to eat. She hadn't had breakfast yet, and her stomach growled.

"I thought of a great scene last night, Jess," her father said, holding open the cupboard for her.

She'd heard that statement hundreds of times. Her father seemed compelled to justify the time he spent in his recliner, sleeping off the booze. Jessica had learned long ago that nothing ever came of his "great scenes."

"Did you, Dad?" she replied without enthusiasm. She pulled down the peanut butter and unscrewed the lid. Then she got a jar of pickles out of the refrigerator.

"I think I can really work with this idea, Jess." He watched her slather peanut butter over a piece of bread and lay on hamburger dills.

Jessica folded the slice of bread and sighed. She was tired of playing the encouraging parent role while her father continued to play the child. Their roles had been reversed for years, and Jessica was sick to death of the game. She turned to face him, while bitterness and resentment soured her appetite. "That's just great, Dad. What should I do. Send off flares?"

He stepped back, offended by her sarcasm.

Jessica put the sandwich down on the counter, her appetite suddenly gone. She leaned on the counter and stared at the tile beneath her hands. "Dad, I am sick of your big talk, your plans, and your ideas. Do you hear me? I'm sick of all your hot air!" She glared at him, her eyes burning and her cheeks flaming. "Either you sit down at that type-writer and produce something on paper, or I don't even want to hear about it!"

Her father stared at her, his watery left eye ticking uncontrollably.

"How long are you going to use Mom's desertion as an excuse for your alcoholism? How long, Dad?"

He drew himself up. "I am not an alcoholic."

"What are you, then? A social drinker? Where are your drinking buddies, Dad? Where? How long has it been since you've even talked to another human being besides me?"

"I'm a loner. There's nothing wrong with that." He crossed his arms.

"I just can't get through to you, can I? I don't know why I ever come back! Nothing ever changes!" Jessica stormed past him to the hallway, where she whirled to face him once more. "I have a friend coming over, Dad. Do you think you can keep sober until noon?"

"I'm always sober at noon."

"Sure you are." She shook her head and hurried to her room to change, her heart hard and heavy. She pinched her lips together as she undressed, too angry to shed the tears that welled up in her throat. With vicious tugs she French-braided her hair and glared at her white face in the mirror. How she could be so stupid as to think she could help her father when he wouldn't even face the truth?

The doorbell rang twenty minutes later, and Jessica answered the door, surprised to see Cole and Lucy standing on the porch.

"Oh, hi," she said.

Her surprise was not lost on Cole. "Expecting someone?" he asked, pulling off his sunglasses. Lucy gave Jessica a subdued wave and a wan smile. She was obviously feeling the effects of her indulgence of the previous evening.

"Well, yes. Greg Kessler called to say he was coming over."

"Greg?"

"Yes. We used to—" She broke off. Cole did not know of their previous relationship, and she was suddenly reluctant to enlighten him. "We used to know each other in college."

"Ah." Cole nodded and looked past her into the house.

"Excuse me. Won't you come in?" She stepped back and Lucy and Cole walked into the entryway.

"We'll only stay a moment." Cole sauntered into the living room and sat down on the couch, draping his arm across the back of the cushions. Lucy sat beside him, and Jessica was conscious of another wave of jealousy as Lucy leaned back against his arm. Jessica had spent the night with a monk on a roof while Cole had probably spent the night nestled against the curves of his blond girlfriend.

The euphoria she felt from the previous evening shriveled to a hard, cold stone. Why had she thought something had started between Cole and herself? Why had she allowed her imagination to turn his words into more than they were—a simple declaration that it was good to see an old friend. She was an idiot. Nothing had changed in thirteen years. She was still an idiot, and Cole was still not interested in her.

"Can I get you something to drink?" she asked, trying to keep the frost from her voice. Cole looked at Lucy. "Do you want anything, Lucy?"

"Just a new head!" She smiled and closed her eyes. Jessica felt no sympathy for the woman.

"Greg."

Jessica blanched at the sound of her father's voice.

"There you are, young man."

Jessica turned, aghast that her father had chosen this moment to prove he could be sociable. He had actually tucked in his shirt, but his hair fell into his eyes in unkempt strands. Out of the corner of her eye she saw Cole rise to his feet, and she saw the expression of shock pass over his features.

"Mr. Ward!"

"How are you doing, Greg?" Robert walked across the carpet with his hand outstretched. Jessica prayed that he wouldn't trip and fall.

She slipped her hand around his elbow. "Dad, this is Niccolo Cavanetti."

"Who?"

"Nick. You remember Nick, don't you?" Her voice was tight and forced, hiding the dismay she felt as she watched Cole stare at her father in disbelief. Like everyone else, he had been convinced that Robert Ward was a successful playwright who commuted back and forth from the East Coast. But this skinny, sickly man with the lank hair obviously hadn't seen a Broadway stage for quite some time.

Cole did an admirable job of swallowing his shock. "You

remember me, don't you, Mr. Ward? I used to live over at the Cavanetti house."

"Oh!" Robert shook his hand. "Nick! Sorry, son, I don't have my glasses on! Sure, Nick! Nick Cavanetti!"

He kept shaking Cole's hand and staring at him. "Say, you've grown up. How old are you now, Nick?"

"Thirty-five, sir."

"Jesus Christ! Time flies. You know I'm sixty-eight? Do I look sixty-eight to you, Nick?" He leaned closer.

Jessica wished he would quit talking. Her father looked as if he were ninety, and if Cole were honest, he'd say so. But Cole only laughed and pumped his hand.

"You look fine, Mr. Ward."

Jessica glanced at Cole, and he met her gaze with a look so dark and perplexed that Jessica stood awash in shame.

"And who's this?" Robert said, releasing Cole's hand. "Your little wife?"

Cole continued to stare at Jessica even as her father stepped toward Lucy. Jessica raised her chin and stared right back until Cole finally looked away.

"No, sir. She's my physical therapist, Lucy Girard. Lucy, this is Jessica's father, Robert Ward." Cole put his hand on Robert's bony shoulder. "He's a well-known playwright."

Lucy stood up. "Are you, Mr. Ward?" She shook his hand. "I've never met a playwright before!"

"Ever hear of *Hell's for the Living*?" Robert asked.

"No . . ."

He smiled. "Well, maybe that was a bit before your time. You're a young thing, Miss Girard."

Jessica swept forward. "Dad, shouldn't you be getting back to your project?"

"Project?" he repeated.

"Yes, the one you were talking about this morning."

"Oh, yes." He smiled sheepishly. "That scene . . . Sure, I should get back to that right away."

"Before you go, Mr. Ward," Cole interrupted, "I'd like to ask you a favor."

"Oh?"

"I was wondering if I could rent your guest cottage."

"What?" Jessica gasped.

Cole ignored Jessica. "If it's all right with you, Mr. Ward, I'd like to rent the guesthouse."

Robert blinked his eyes. "Well, now, son, that cottage hasn't been used for years."

"That's okay. Lucy and I will air it out. We'll do anything that needs to be done."

Jessica shook her head, trying to catch her father's eye. She didn't want Cole that close to the house. He had seen her father, but he hadn't seen how bad her father could get. If Cole were staying only a few feet away, he couldn't help but learn the seriousness of Robert's condition.

"Well, I don't even know where the key is, Nick."

"I could pay you, sir. I need to be close to the Cavanetti house. You see, my stepmother is bringing my father back from the hospital, and I need to be nearby. And she won't let me into the house."

"She won't?"

Cole shook his head. Then he reached into his jacket and pulled out his billfold. "Listen, Mr. Ward. Here's a thousand dollars. Rent the guesthouse to me for two weeks. That's all I ask."

"No." Jessica snatched away the money before her father could take it. She returned it to Cole. "That cottage needs lots of work. I doubt it's habitable. You couldn't possibly want to stay there."

"Hold on, Jessica," Robert protested. "It can't be that bad. Let me see if I can't find that key."

"Dad!"

He shuffled toward the kitchen. "That's what neighbors are for, Jessica," he said, turning in the doorway. "We're supposed to help each other."

Jessica crossed her arms and scowled at him. He had picked a fine time to join the ranks of the Welcome Wagon committee.

◆ ◆ ◆

"Well, now. This isn't so bad." Robert passed into the living room of the guesthouse and slowly turned around. "Jess, this isn't bad at all."

"It smells musty," she retorted. She hadn't set foot in the guesthouse for twenty-five years, ever since her mother had left.

Jessica tried not to breathe too deeply of the air in the cottage, afraid that she might smell her mother's perfume. Her mother had abandoned her. Left her. Never once looked back. A sharp feeling pressed against Jessica's throat. It hurt to be in the cottage again.

Lucy strolled past her, staring at the walls. "Say, this is neat!" she exclaimed. "Look at all these pictures!" She stared at the clutter of photographs hanging over a zebra-striped sofa, photographs of great actors and actresses from the stage, ranging from Mary Pickford to Marilyn Monroe. Many of the photographs were signed. "Cole, look at these!" She beamed at Robert. "Did you know all these people, Mr. Ward?"

"Some of them. My wife was an actress. She collected those."

"This place is really neat!" She ran her hand over the zebra skin of the sofa and then touched a rattan chair. "It looks like Rudolph Valentino might live here."

"My wife decorated the place. Her stage friends stayed here when they came to visit." Robert stuffed the key into his pocket with a shaking hand. "I, uh—I, uh, never changed a thing after she left. Never came in here, as a matter of fact."

"Lucy, the place is covered with dust." Jessica wiped the glass-covered coffee table with her fingertip and held it up. "Look at this. And I bet the bathroom is molded solid."

"Oh, that's okay!" Lucy waved her off airily. "I simply adore this place. Let's look at the kitchen, Cole!"

Cole raised an eyebrow at Jessica and followed Lucy out of the living room. Jessica wilted. Her job to conceal her father's alcoholism had just increased tenfold.

"Dad," she said between her teeth, "you've really done it this time. I could kill you!"

"Why?" He pushed back his hair. "Nick seems like a nice fellow. And that Lucy is a doll, isn't she?" He lowered his voice. "Do you think they're living together?"

Jessica felt her heart thump painfully, but she ignored it. "What do you think, Dad?" She turned on her heel and nearly ran into Greg Kessler standing in the doorway.

"I was just about to knock," Greg said, grinning. "Hi, Jessica."

"Hello, Greg." She strode to the door and practically pushed him out of the guesthouse.

"Nobody answered at the house," Greg explained. "Then I saw the door open over here. So I thought I'd just stick my head in."

"My father insisted on showing this place to Cole and Lucy."

"Why?"

"Oh, Cole wants to rent it for a few weeks."

"You don't seem too happy about it." Greg peered closely at her face.

"I'm not, but it doesn't matter." She tossed her head. She had decided not to moon over Cole any longer. She was only asking for disappointment. At least with Greg she knew where she stood, and her emotions were out of harm's way.

Jessica turned at the door. "How would you like to go to lunch, Greg?" she asked.

He smiled. "I was hoping I could drag you out for a bite. Then I want to show you my property. Remember that development on the hill I told you about?"

"Yes. I'd like to see it." She stepped into the bungalow and got her jacket and purse out of the closet.

She settled back against the velour bucket seat of Greg's BMW and made herself a vow that she would have fun, no matter how difficult it might be.

Back at the guesthouse, Robert Ward and Lucy pored over scrapbooks from Robert's Broadway days while Cole yawned and tried to feign interest in the conversation. He was tired. He hadn't gotten much sleep the night before, what with his strange dreams disturbing his rest. He excused himself and ambled to the kitchen to get a drink. Cole filled a glass at the kitchen sink and turned off the tap. The bungalow had not been as dirty as Jessica had thought. Within a few hours he and Lucy had aired it, cleaned it, and made the beds. Robert Ward had helped them and stayed for coffee.

Cole drank his water as he strolled to the master bedroom. He was beat, and this would be a good time for a nap. Without even taking off his shoes, he stretched out on his bed, draped an arm over his eyes, and fell asleep.

Cole woke up to the strange sensation of dampness on his face and neck. When he tried to lift his hand to his face, however, someone stopped him.

"Don't, my lord," a soft voice commanded. A woman's voice.

Startled, Cole turned his head toward the voice. Agony gripped him, sheer agony that flamed through his neck and shoulders. Had he not perished in the river after all? Had the Greek fire not killed him?

Or was he in heaven? He tried to open his eyes to see if the soft voice belonged to a woman or an angel, but his eyes were covered with gauze. And moving his left eye even slightly caused his head to buzz with pain.

Surely if he were in heaven he would not be in such torment. Perhaps he was in hell.

Cole tried to speak, to move his lips, but the effort sent him spiraling into a realm of suffering that nearly made him cry out. The dampness on his face was no longer cool. His face felt hot, and pain rolled in waves upon him. He moaned, and his back tensed against the pain.

"Don't try to speak, my lord," the woman urged. She leaned over him. He could hear her breathing. Then he felt her lift the warm cloths from his face and neck. Carefully she draped new cloths over him. They were blessedly cool. Cole swallowed and relaxed. Ah, sweet Jesus, she must be an angel.

He could smell her perfume, a subtle scent of roses completely different from the heavy perfumes worn by Arab women and men alike. He would lay odds that she was a European. And her voice, so quiet and soothing, was bereft of any foreign accent. She had spoken to him in flawless Italian. Who was she? And where was he?

"Try to rest now." She stood up. He could hear the rustle of her gown as she moved away.

Was she leaving? Cole felt a jolt of panic. She mustn't leave him. The pain would drive him mad. He struggled to rise from the pallet on which he lay.

"My lord baron, you must not move!" Her voice was tight with concern. "Lie still!"

Cole sank back. The cloths were warm again. His skin flamed. His shoulder throbbed. He gritted his teeth, wishing he could faint into oblivion.

She must have sensed his discomfort. Once again she replaced the cloths. Cole sighed. He heard her pour something, and then he caught the sound of metal striking metal. Was she stirring something in a basin? Her skirts swished over the floor as she returned to his side.

"Here," she said. "You must drink this. 'T'will ease your pain and make you sleep. No, do not move. I will give it to you with a dropper."

She placed something against his lips, and he felt liquid trickle into his mouth.

"A little more," she added, putting the tube to his mouth again.

He swallowed, careful not to move his head. She hovered over him, and he knew she surveyed him. Then her hand swept across his hair in a light caress.

"Thank God you have finally come back to us, my lord," she said.

Cole wanted to thank her, to take her hand and keep her beside him, but the draught she had given him made his thoughts sluggish and his limbs immobile. He was suddenly exhausted.

"Sleep," she murmured. "You must gather your strength."

◆ ◆ ◆

Jessica and Greg did not return to the bungalow until late afternoon. Greg walked Jessica up to the porch.

"I've got to run," he said. "I have a meeting tonight."

"That was fun, Greg." Jessica turned the key in the lock.

"It was. We used to have great times together, Jessica. Why did we drift apart?"

"We had careers to pursue." Out of the corner of her eye she saw Cole open the door of the guesthouse and walk toward the bungalow.

"I guess," Greg replied. "Well, you think about what I said. If you do decide to sell that vineyard property, I want to be the first to know. I could make you a deal that would blow your mind. You've heard about that golf course that went in up the valley, haven't you?"

"I saw something about it in the paper. Some Japanese firm is involved?"

"Yeah, they're crazy about the sport. And they'll pay big bucks for land. I can just see a green along the slough. It would be perfect!" He glanced to the side. "Hi, Cole, how are you doing?"

"Greg." Cole nodded and stood off to the side, as if waiting for Jessica. Jessica did not greet him. She intended to make him wait as long as possible.

"I'll think about it, Greg. Dad could use the money, that's for sure."

"Good. Well, I have to run." He leaned forward to give her a kiss good-bye. Jessica stepped closer to him, wrapping her hands around his neck and pressing her mouth to his. She would show that Cole Nichols that she had other interests, too. She felt Greg tense in surprise, and then he melted into her, pulling her against him with both hands.

"Good-bye, Greg," she murmured.

Greg scanned her face, his eyes bright. "Good-bye, Jessica. Whoa!" He released her with a laugh and saluted Cole as he jogged to his car.

Jessica turned the doorknob without glancing at Cole, but

she was highly conscious of him hovering behind her.

"Little girls shouldn't play with fire," he declared.

"Fire?" Jessica tossed her head, and her braid flopped against her back. "Whatever do you mean?"

She glanced at his face. His eyes glittered with forced amusement, but she could see something cool and serious behind them, as if he were displeased or jealous. Good.

"You lead on a man like Greg Kessler, and you're going to find yourself in over your head."

"Who said I'm leading him on?"

Cole studied her face for an uncomfortably long moment. Jessica lifted her chin.

"And I want an explanation about your father." He stepped closer. "All this time—"

"My father is none of your business." She flung open the door and went inside. Cole followed at her heels.

"What's the matter, Jess? Are you sore that I'm renting the guesthouse?"

"No, I'm not sore!"

"Then what's wrong?"

She turned on him. "I came here to get away, to work on a paper, and to see my father. I didn't come here to fill you in on the details of my personal life!"

Cole stared at her.

"Or to hear your comments about Greg Kessler!"

"Listen, Jess. Greg Kessler was never a team player. He was always out for his own glory. That's why the Ridgemont Raiders never became champions. Greg always tried to make the big play when he should have concentrated on short passes and looked for holes in the line."

Jessica threw her purse into the closet. "Some of us don't relate to football, Cole. I have no idea what you're talking about."

Cole tried to help her take off her jacket, but she shook free of his hands. He stepped back, his mouth set in a grim line.

"I heard you talking about the vineyard property. You're not selling it, are you? We've got a lease on that land."

"We?" Jessica gave him a scathing look, hoping to wound him with her words. "If you mean the Cavanettis, yes, they do have a lease. But it expires on Christmas Day."

"And you're planning to discontinue the lease and sell the property?"

"My father could use the money to produce his new play."

"Bullshit, Jessica."

She slammed the closet door shut.

Cole stepped closer. "Does Isabella know about your plans to sell?"

"No."

"Don't sell to Greg, Jessica. Just do me a favor and don't sell to him."

"Listen, Cole, I don't owe you any favors!" She whirled to stride down the hall, but he caught her arm.

"Jess!" His hand closed around her upper arm, not enough to hurt her but just enough to keep her from leaving. She glared at him, her chest heaving with anger.

"Let me go!"

He released her immediately. "Just don't sell. Promise me, Jess. You can't let the vineyard go."

"I'll make my own decisions, Cole. I'm a grown woman, in case you haven't noticed."

His eyes raked over her in a raw appraisal full of anger and something she could only define as lust. Her legs turned to jelly.

"I've noticed, Jessica," he growled. "Make no mistake." He left her standing in the hall and strode out of the house, slamming the door behind him.

Jessica stood in the hallway, rubbing her arm. Suddenly she *did* feel as if she had plunged in over her head. Way over her head.

11

Jessica was still fuming when she attacked her father's paperwork in the study. Every minute or so she thought about her words with Cole, and her body ran cold with anger. He had no right to make demands of her, and she had no intention of giving in to his ego. She paid bills and filed away receipts, forcing herself through sheer determination to work when the whole time she felt like bursting into tears. What was the matter with her?

Near dinnertime she saw her father walk past the study with the projector. She jerked to attention.

"Where are you going?" she asked, pushing back her chair.

"Over to the guesthouse. Cole's busy on the phone talking business, and poor Lucy has nothing to do. So I thought I'd take over the film of my play."

Jessica couldn't believe her father was still sober. In fact, he had combed his hair and put on a clean shirt. She rose. "Dad, Lucy might not want to see an old play."

"She does. She asked me to bring it over."

"Have you been over there all afternoon?"

"Well, not all, but I had to help them find things and get

cleaning stuff for them. Then Lucy wanted to look at the scrapbooks, and we got to drinking coffee. You know how it is."

Jessica hesitated. She hadn't seen her father this animated in years. She was almost glad to see him going out, if only next door. She hoped he wouldn't bore Lucy to death or make a fool of himself.

"Well, that's good, Dad. I guess I'll see you later."

He walked down the hall, and she heard the door shut behind him. Then she sank back into the chair and stared at the empty doorway, tapping her pen on the desktop.

Before she resumed her work she got up to close the drapes in the house. Outside it was pitch black, and she didn't like the idea of anyone watching her through the lighted windows. She fixed herself a cup of tea and carried it to the study, ready to begin work on her paper at last.

As she walked through the study doorway, however, she was startled by the sight of the monk standing near the desk. He turned, holding one of her reference books in his hand.

"Good evening, Miss Ward."

How did he get into the house? Had her father failed to lock the door? Jessica hid her initial surprise and swept into the study. "Good evening, Brother Cosimo."

"This book is fascinating. These are actual photographs of the surface of Mars?"

"Yes." She smiled and set down her tea. "They were taken by an unmanned spacecraft named *Galileo*, which is documenting much of our solar system."

"You are interested in the planets?"

"Why, yes. I'm an astronomer, Brother Cosimo."

"You?" His head came up. "A woman?"

"Certainly."

Brother Cosimo put down the book to pick up another. "You also seem to have a great many books on art. Beautiful books, Miss Ward."

"Yes, some of those volumes are quite valuable." She picked up a leatherbound book on Greco-Roman art. "I've collected these over the years. I believe they'll help me find the comet I'm looking for."

"*Aster kométés,* the Greeks called them," Cosimo put in. "Hairy stars."

Jessica glanced at him sharply, surprised at his knowledge. "Why, yes." She tried to catch a glimpse of his face but failed to see anything but shadow. "You seem to know a bit about astronomy yourself, Brother Cosimo."

"I once dabbled in the sciences, Miss Ward, but science was in its infancy at the time." He closed the book and put it down carefully. "In my day men were not interested in the heavens you study. They were interested only in heaven as it pertained to hell. I found it a suffocating and egocentric pursuit."

Jessica hugged her arms. His words sounded dangerously close to heresy, especially coming from a monk. Goose pimples sped down the backs of her arms. Was Maria right after all? Could she be speaking to the sorcerer Cosimo Cavanetti? And if she were, what manner of creature hid behind that black robe? Was he a ghost? A demon? Why did he appear to her and no one else?

"You stare at me, Miss Ward."

"I—I—I'm sorry. I meant no offense." She took a step backward. "I'm just surprised by your sentiments. I thought priests dedicated themselves to spiritual questions regarding heaven and hell."

"But I am not a priest."

"You aren't?"

He shook his head. "I am a lay brother. And I accepted that role only late in my life when I was forced to retire from society."

"You were forced to retire from society?"

"Yes. But that concerns the past, Miss Ward. I am here to talk of the future."

He came around to the front of the desk. "You are planning to sell the vineyard, are you not?"

"Yes, but how did you know?"

He ignored her question. "You must sell only to the Cavanettis."

"Why?"

"Some things are meant to be, Miss Ward. And the

Cavanettis must have the land or you will break a tradition that has spanned centuries."

"What if Isabella Cavanetti doesn't want to buy the property?"

"You must sell only to the Cavanettis. That is all."

The doorbell rang, and he glanced over his shoulder. "Someone comes. I must leave you now." He strode past her to the door.

"Wait!" She ran after him. "Are you Cosimo Cavanetti?" She stopped in the doorway. "Are you the monk who was entombed alive?"

He turned and studied her. "Many of us go to our graves as dead men already, Miss Ward. You must not think my entombment so hideous."

She paused. He *was* Cosimo Cavanetti! She was talking to a man who had been dead for nearly a thousand years. Jessica sank against the doorway of the study, overcome.

"But as Philip Massinger has written," the monk continued, "'Death hath a thousand doors to let out life.'"

"Massinger?" Jessica sputtered. "What would you know of seventeenth-century playwrights?"

"Your father has many volumes written by many different playwrights." Cosimo inclined his head. "I have read all of them. My modern education is spotty, but not without some depth."

She was too stunned to smile at his wry humor.

"Your doorbell rings, Miss Ward."

"So it does," she whispered, still overcome.

He bowed and flowed down the hall toward the back door while Jessica stumbled to the front.

"Hello." A man with a wrinkled trench coat stood at the front door. "My name is John McIntyre. I'm a friend of Cole Nichols."

Jessica inspected the rumpled man. He didn't look like a football player. But Cole's acquaintances were probably not restricted to athletes.

"I heard that Cole is staying out here."

"Well, not here." Jessica put her hand on the edge of the door. "He's staying at the guesthouse over there." She nodded toward the cottage.

"Great!" The man raised his hand. "Thanks!"

She watched him stride toward the guesthouse and then closed the door, wondering if Brother Cosimo would be in the study when she got back. But the study was empty and dark. She felt a momentary flash of disappointment until she reminded herself that she needed to work on her paper anyway.

Jessica hadn't worked more than five minutes when she heard someone yelling at the guesthouse. Then a door slammed. Jessica jumped to her feet and rushed to the window. She peeked through the crack between the drapes and saw someone hustling a man toward the driveway in front of the bungalow.

Jessica hurried to the front door and opened it just in time to see Cole yank open the door of a car and thrust a man into the driver's seat. Then he threw something after the man and slammed the door.

"And you can tell your friends to leave me the hell alone!" Cole shouted.

The man who had come to Jessica's door revved up his car engine and screeched out of the driveway. Lucy and Robert ran down the driveway as Cole straightened and looked toward the bungalow porch, where Jessica stood in shock.

"Cole!" Lucy called, running to his side.

"It's all right. Go back to your movie, Lucy," he replied, brushing the hair out of his eyes.

Robert touched Lucy's arm, and she backed up a pace, making way for Cole as he strode toward the bungalow. Jessica felt her stomach clench. Who had that man been?

"Cole?" she questioned as he stomped across the porch.

"Inside," he answered.

Wordlessly she followed him into the house and into the living room, where he whirled to face her.

"Don't tell anyone else where I'm staying."

"Fine. But who was that?"

"A reporter hungry for a story." His face was flushed with anger. "They never leave me alone. They're always hanging around. They're bloodthirsty, Jessica. Bloodthirsty leeches."

"He said he was a friend of yours."

"They'll say anything." He turned and strode to the picture window. "Did you see the paper this morning? Did you see the lies they wrote about me?"

"Yes, I did." She gazed at his shoulders and back. "I couldn't believe how they twisted the facts of the incident."

"They'll print anything for the sensation they cause, no matter how it may hurt someone." He looked toward the ceiling. "So do me a favor and don't tell them I'm here."

"All right, Cole."

"Tell them I'm staying in Seattle somewhere."

"Sure."

He sighed and turned back to face her. "Have you heard about the incident in Philadelphia?"

"Yes. Isabella told me."

"Oh, fine!" He laughed bitterly. "She's an excellent source of information."

"I can't believe you would do such a thing."

"You can't?" He laughed again, his eyes wild. "Well, you're just about the only one in the United States who thinks that way."

"Maria doesn't think so either."

"Oh, well—Maria!" He crossed his arms. "She thinks I'm a saint."

"Why do they stretch the truth?" she asked.

Cole sighed. "I don't know. Sometimes I think the press has lost the power to believe that people are good. They prey on the negatives of life, the foibles and failures of human beings, looking for character flaws and ulterior motives. They never see anything else, so we never read anything but the dirt and the smut. I don't know." He pinched the bridge of his nose beneath his glasses. "I just don't know anymore."

"But tossing a journalist into his car certainly won't help

you beat the assault charge in Philadelphia."

"You don't think I know that?" He strode to the door.

Jessica watched him, more worried about him than angry with him now. "Cole, have you seen a doctor about your fainting problem?"

"A dozen or more. They all say the same thing."

"Oh?"

"Healthy as a horse." He gave a bitter smile. "Nothing I can do but wait and see what happens. I can't even get a good night's sleep. Lucy thinks I'm stressed out."

"Maybe you are. And this business with your father won't help matters, either."

"If I could just get in to see him. That bitch Isabella won't let me near him."

"I know. She thinks you'll leave if you aren't able to see your father."

"What is she afraid of? That he'll have a miraculous change of heart after thirteen years and rewrite his will?"

Jessica shrugged. "She doesn't want you ruining any of her plans for Frank. She seems particularly concerned that you'll make trouble for Frank and his budding career."

"I wouldn't want to make trouble for dear old Franco," Cole replied sarcastically. "Not after all he and his mother have done for me."

He opened the door. "Do you think you could call Maria tomorrow morning? At least see how my father is doing?"

"I can try."

"Thanks." He put his hands into his pockets. "I'm sorry I yelled at you this afternoon. It could be I am stressed out."

"Don't worry about it."

"But I still think you should take it easy with Greg."

"I'll keep it in mind."

"I just don't want him to take advantage of you."

"I appreciate your concern."

She closed the door as he walked off the porch. For a moment she stood near the door and raked her fingers through her hair. She had contained herself this time. She hadn't once allowed herself to succumb to her attraction for

Cole. She hadn't once thought of kissing away his troubles. Self-congratulations were in order, but Jessica didn't feel like celebrating. In fact, she didn't even feel like smiling.

Cole strode back to the guesthouse, worrying about Jessica and Greg. He didn't know the extent of Jessica's experience with men, but he doubted she could handle Greg. He knew the type—pushy, aggressive, and untiring. He shook his head, wishing Jessica had never kissed Greg the way she had. A man like Greg needed no more invitation than that to make him think he could demand whatever he wanted.

Grimacing, Cole picked up his athletic shoes and strode over to the bed. Before he had taken more than two steps, his vision went dark and sparkling, and a stabbing pain seared through his eyes. He fell to his knees with a gasp, then collapsed on the floor.

Cole woke up and knew something was different. Somehow, after weeks of constant cool compresses and draughts of medicine, he had cheated death. He felt weak and trembly, but was certain he would survive. He moved his legs. His body was stiff and sore. He moved his eyeballs beneath their lids and felt only a residual tingle of pain in his left socket. Perhaps he had finally mended enough to take off the gauze and open his eyes. He longed to see the woman who had taken such great care of him.

He was half in love with her already and had never even seen her. But he knew her voice, husky and soft as a warm breeze. And he had listened for hours to her quiet singing as she tended him. She had probably thought he was asleep, but many times he had merely lain unmoving, listening to her ballads and her lullabies and dreaming of the angelic face that must belong to such a beautiful voice.

He knew her scent, too, always that lovely rose perfume wafting around him, surrounding him in a delicate cloud. He knew the touch of her hands, feathery light and gentle. She had never once caused him pain in all the time she had nursed him. And he knew her patience. She had fed him, bathed him, combed his hair, trimmed his beard, and never once complained or sighed with fatigue.

Cole reached up to his face and gingerly touched the bandage that covered his eyes, feeling for the knot where she had tied the ends together. He fumbled with the knot and then drew off the bandage, his arms shaking from the effort.

At first the light hurt his eyes, and tears spilled down his cheeks, burning his wounds. He squinted and blinked until his eyes grew accustomed to the radiance of early morning. Then he looked around the chamber. He lay in a wide bed draped in netting and brocade. A featherweight cover of miniver was thrown across his nakedness. Cole's eyes traveled from the bed to the walls of stone and the narrow window meant more for an archer's shaft than for view or ventilation. Near the window was a table full of bottles and a brazier. And sitting in a chair by the table was a young woman fast asleep, her head propped upon her hand.

Cole raised himself to get a better look at her, and in so doing he dislodged a small bell that had been lying on the coverlet. The bell fell to the floor with a tinkle, and the woman raised her head, startled.

For a moment they stared at each other. Cole felt his pulse quicken at the sight of her. She was lovely, though not in the accepted beauty of the day. She did not possess a wan complexion, colorless lashes and brows, or golden hair. Her beauty was of another realm altogether. Her hair was black as night and fell in waves of ebony that reached her waist. Her eyes were a startling topaz color ringed with raven lashes set below dark brows that soared upward toward her temples, lending her a feline loveliness. Her skin was white as frost, tinged with an apricot blush that had blossomed upon her cheeks at the sight of him.

As he stared, she slowly stood up. Her rose-colored bliaut fitted snugly around her breasts and slender waist and then cascaded in silken fullness to the stone floor. Cole had never seen a more intoxicating sight than that of her delicate shoulders straightening beneath his gaze, pulling the shimmering fabric taut across her breasts. She raised a hand to her throat, and the wide sleeve of the bliaut fell away to reveal the white linen of her chainse, intricately embroidered with silken threads of rose and lavender.

"My lord! You're awake!" A smile quickly lifted her lips, but not before Cole noticed the shadow that passed through her eyes. He hadn't noticed the way she had been looking at him until the moment she smiled, as if to conceal her thoughts. What had been in her face? Concern? Pity? Was he imagining things?

"You must be dying of thirst!" She swept forward, bending down to retrieve the bell, which she slipped into a pouch that hung from the girdle at her hips. Then she reached for a goblet upon a small table near the bed and held it out to him. "Drink, my lord."

A million questions went unanswered as he succumbed to an intense thirst he hadn't known he possessed until she held the goblet to his lips. He sucked in great gulps of the watered wine until she pulled it away.

"Easy, my lord!" A soft ripple of laughter warbled from her throat. "You must take one sip at a time." She straightened as if to leave the bedside.

Cole caught her wrist in his left hand and marveled at the smallness of her bones. She pulled back, staring at him in alarm. Apparently his show of strength had surprised her.

"Who are you?" Cole breathed.

She relaxed. "I am Giovanna di Montalcino."

"Montalcino?" Cole repeated, releasing her wrist and lying back on the pillow. His show of strength had not lasted more than a few moments. His arms trembled. "Are you related to the Count of Montalcino?"

"He is my father."

Cole surveyed her. She bore little resemblance to the portly man he had seen on the battlefield. "Where am I?"

"Jerusalem."

"What is the daughter of the Count of Montalcino doing in Jerusalem?"

"I am a pilgrim, my lord." She smiled at him and tilted

her head to one side. Sweet Jesus, she was beautiful, more beautiful than he had imagined from the sound of her voice.

"I thought you were an angel," he murmured. "I thought I was in heaven."

Her eyes crinkled with amusement. "You were close to heaven for a long time, my lord, but never quite there. We were so worried about you."

"How long have I been here?"

"Nearly two months, sir. One of your men saw you fall into the river. He rescued you and brought you to me."

"Why to you?"

"Because I requested it. I have spent my time here nursing wounded soldiers and have learned much about the care of wounds. And when I found out what had happened to you—the great baron who fights with his left arm—I knew I had to try to save your life."

"And you have saved my life. I can never thank you enough, Giovanna. Never."

She blushed at the familiar use of her given name but did not correct him. "It was an honor, my lord. I have seen you joust in the lists. I have heard the songs the troubadours sing about your prowess in battle. I have heard the ladies speak of you. I was honored to save such a champion."

"And you were the only one, weren't you? No one else tended to me, did they?"

"No. I could not leave you. I could not bear to think—" She broke off and reached for the goblet. "Here, drink some more, my lord."

He obliged, but as she drew away the empty goblet, he covered her hands with his own and looked into her face. She stared back at him, the color high on her cheekbones.

"Have you had enough, my lord?" she inquired.

"No." Cole reached out and pushed back the filmy veil that covered her hair. "I am still thirsty, Giovanna."

"Still?" she whispered.

"Yes." He touched a lock of her hair. He drew her toward him, and she bent closer, still holding the goblet between her palms. Cole cupped her face in his hands and pulled her to his lips, pressing her soft flesh. His mouth felt tight and stiff, but he forgot everything save the molten sensation that burst inside him. It was a feeling he had never known. He loved this woman. God help him, but he loved her. He closed his eyes and lost himself to the taste of her.

She was so soft, so yielding, so sweet and delicate. Her hair brushed his chest as she sank beside him on the bed. He heard the goblet clatter to the floor and felt her warm palms come to rest on the cool, bare skin of his chest.

"My lord!" she murmured against his lips. Her hands slid up to his shoulders, and she opened her mouth upon his. Cole moaned with pleasure and tasted the raspy saltiness of her tongue with his own.

Ah, she was wrong. This *was* heaven after all. This was heaven, and she was an angel sent to enrapture him. He sank into the pillows, overcome by her kiss and sheer exhaustion. His hands slipped from her face and collapsed upon the coverlet while she leaned forward.

She encircled his head with her arms and caressed his hair as she covered his face with gentle, desperate kisses. He knew she was kissing his wounds, and he sighed with pleasure and disbelief as she touched her lips to his forehead, his eyelids, his cheek and jaw, and then his mouth. No woman had ever shown such boldness to him before, and he found himself becoming fully aroused.

"Giovanna," he breathed, incredulous. Her lips were a stronger drug than the medicine she had given him. His senses swirled, and he was afraid that he might swoon. She continued her kisses from his ear down the side of his neck to his shoulder and then to his breast. She wept as she kissed him, and he didn't know why. He wanted to ask her, but he didn't want to stop the trail of kisses, so he remained silent, mesmerized by the waves of delight that rippled across his skin.

He was weak, so weak he could not even caress her. Yet his body hummed with desire for her. If only he were strong enough. He longed to crush her delicate frame to his and show her his own form of rapture. But his passion would have to wait until he was more recovered.

She pushed down the miniver coverlet and kissed his chest and torso. Cole's breath came short and fast as she edged closer and closer to his midriff, where a line of dark hair feathered its way from his navel to the territory still beneath the coverlet. Her hands followed the powerful contours of his rib cage and glided down the sleek sides of his abdomen. And then she pulled away the coverlet altogether and kissed her way down his belly.

"Ah, Giovanna . . ." Cole's voice trailed off to a sigh. He tried to tell her to stop, but the protest died in his throat.

Cole shuddered and opened his eyes. His cheek lay pressed upon the carpet of the master bedroom in the guesthouse. The scratchy pile burned his face. He raised his head and struggled to one elbow. He must have passed out near the bed. Good thing he hadn't hit his head on the corner of the nightstand. One of these days, he was going to kill himself during a blackout.

Slowly he dragged himself to his hands and knees, wondering why he felt so odd, as if his skin tingled and glowed. He stood up and stumbled to the bathroom. He was as hard as a rock, and it hurt to move. Frowning, he pulled off his jeans. Many times after sleeping he would awake with an erection, but never one as intense as this.

Cole reached for the shower knob. A quick blast of water ought to bring him to his senses. He pulled off his shirt and briefs and stepped into the hard spray. But as he ran his soapy hands over his jaw and down his chest, he experienced an undeniable sense of déjà vu that startled him.

Someone had been touching him. He was certain of it. A woman had been touching him, kissing him. Cole dragged two fingertips across his lower lip and closed his eyes against the flood of desire that surged through him. A woman had kissed him in his dream, and the feeling had been so real and so strong that it lingered in his memory after waking. What was happening to him? Was he going crazy, as everyone thought? And why wasn't the damn shower having any effect?

12

Frank felt miserable. The water he had splashed on his face in the men's room had provided small relief from his pounding headache and nausea. He wasn't certain if he was suffering a hangover from the night before or was uptight about facing his mother. He had thrown up frequently as a kid, and the tendency lingered with him as an adult. Whenever he was nervous or anxious, especially before a tennis match, he threw up. Frank grimaced. His stomach burned, and he worried that he had an ulcer. Yet how could he have an ulcer? He was only twenty-five years old.

At least Shawn hadn't made the situation more difficult by demanding to go to the restaurant with them. She didn't eat breakfast much anymore and was developing a habit of sleeping in. That was okay with Frank. The less he saw of his bitchy wife, the better. Yet, at this moment he would rather have been with Shawn than his mother.

There she sat, ramrod straight in a high-backed chair, sipping her tea and staring out the window, waiting for him. Frank had brought her to this restaurant because he knew it was her favorite, done in a feminine decor of floral upholstery, delicate Queen Anne furniture, and dusty-rose carpeting.

Frank hated the place. It stifled him, and he worried that he would knock something over or spill something. Then his mother would look at him. She wouldn't say a word. She wouldn't have to. She had a way of looking at him with her lips pressed together that made him feel as if he were seven years old again and had just wet the bed.

That's why he'd agreed to bring Shawn home for Christmas. Shawn served as a buffer. He knew his mother would vent most of her anger on Shawn, leaving him free of her displeasure. He hated it when she was upset with him.

He knew Isabella wanted the best for him, wanted him to have a brilliant career and successful life, but sometimes he wondered if he wanted it as much as she did. He knew he should strive for the things his mother had fought for, but somehow he always fell short of the mark. He had never been tall enough, smart enough, or competitive enough for his mother. She had never said so, but he could see the weary compromise in her eyes when she glanced at him.

Who was she comparing him to? Frank's stomach burned again. Cole. Deep in his heart he knew he was compared to Cole, if not by his mother, then by himself and everyone else. Frank yanked the knot of his tie up against his throat. He had lived in the shadow of his brother far too long. Sometimes he felt as if he were drowning in it.

"There you are." Isabella turned to him. "I thought you had gotten lost."

"No." Frank sank into his chair and scooted it forward. "I had to make a phone call." He reached for his menu and quickly changed the subject. "Did you order yet, Mother?"

"Yes. I got you a Florentine omelette with a fruit plate. Doesn't that sound good?"

Frank would have preferred eggs Benedict but decided not to make a big deal about it. He was thankful that she hadn't asked whom he had called; he wasn't good at lying to her. He took a sip of coffee. The way his stomach burned, he shouldn't eat anything anyway. He reached for the cream.

During their brunch, Frank twice attempted to broach the subject that had turned his guts inside out, but twice he

swallowed back his words. His mother was happy and animated, and he didn't want to spoil everything. When they
were finished eating, Isabella bent down for her purse and
produced a small gift. She pushed it across the table.

"For me?" Frank asked.

"Yes." She watched him open it. "It's something you
should have at the law firm."

Frank's hand stopped in midair. "The law firm?"

"Yes." She smiled, impatient. "Go on, open it!"

"But, Mother, there's something I have to tell you—"

"Tell me later. I want you to see what I bought for you."

Frank sighed and pulled the tissue from the box. He
could tell from the size of the box that he should expect
either a watch or a pen and pencil set. He opened the case.
Bingo. A pen and pencil set.

"They're twenty-four carat," Isabella put in. "Very elegant, don't you think?"

"Very elegant, Mother. Thanks."

An uncomfortable stretch of time lapsed as he crushed
the paper and ribbon and put them aside. How could he tell
her the news? How could he tell her? But he couldn't put it
off any longer. He breathed in.

"Mother, there's something we have to talk about." He
started off strong, but when he met her gaze, he faltered,
struggling for words. His courage had deserted him, but he
knew he couldn't back down now.

"What is it, Frank?"

"Mother, I—I've been thinking."

"About what?"

"About the winery. About my career."

"Everything is going splendidly, don't you think? Once
you get a divorce from Shawn, it's clear sailing, Frank. You
can marry Kimberly Blake, and you'll be on your way to the
top."

"The top?" His voice cracked. He hated it when his voice
cracked as if he were a bumbling teenager. "Mother, I've
been thinking a lot lately. I don't think I'm cut out to be a
lawyer. I'm a tennis player."

"Frank, don't be idiotic!"

"I've always wanted to build a tennis club. I could build one on the property. With my inheritance, I could have a sizable chunk of collateral to put down for a loan. I could do it right. First-class all the way." He searched her face for a trace of enthusiasm but saw only shock and censure.

"Frank, what are you talking about? You never once said anything about building a tennis club."

"I did too, Mother. I'm always talking about it."

She pressed her lips together. Frank saw the expression and wilted inside his suit.

"You're talking nonsense, Frank. You've just graduated from Harvard with a law degree. No one in his right mind would turn his back on that and build a—a—a tennis club! What's gotten into you?"

"Nothing. I just don't think—"

"Waiter!" Isabella motioned with her hand. A slender young man approached the table. "Please bring the check," she said. The waiter nodded and left while Frank stared at his mother. She hadn't even let him finish his sentence.

"Mother—"

"That's enough, Frank! I don't want to talk about it right now. You're—you're—not yourself. Shawn must have put you up to this."

"Oh, for chrissakes, Mother."

Isabella rose when the waiter brought her the check on a tray. Instead of waiting for him to take care of the bill, she picked up her purse and hurried to the cash register near the door.

Scowling, Frank grabbed his pen and pencil set. She wouldn't even listen. She never had. And he had found in the long run that going along with her wishes was easier than trying to fight her. He sighed and walked to the door, holding it open for her while he slipped the gift into his jacket pocket.

He opened her car door. Never once did she even look at him, and her face was rigid and expressionless. She folded her hands in her lap while he buckled his seat belt.

"Frank." She lifted her chin. "Don't do this to yourself."

"I just thought I could use my inheritance for something I wanted."

"There is no inheritance, Frank."

His head whipped around. "What?"

"I had to dip into it over the years. Harvard was expensive, you know. Very expensive."

"There's no money left?"

"None to speak of. I considered it an investment in your future."

"My future?" Frank gripped the steering wheel until his knuckles went white. He had counted on that money. That money was going to *be* his future when he finally got out of college. Now there was nothing.

"Frank." Isabella touched his arm. "How else did you think I afforded that nice car of yours, all your clothes, your pocket money?"

"I thought we were rich." He turned the key in the ignition while he blinked away the nausea he felt welling up inside. "I never thought you were using my inheritance money."

"Frank, I had to, don't you see?" She withdrew her hand. "But it will be all right. Everything will work out. We aren't in such bad shape. The lease is coming due on the vineyard property, but we can put a down payment on that using the bonus the Blakes are giving you when you join the law firm."

"Bonus?" Frank pulled out into traffic while his world crumbled around him. "I'm not getting any bonus."

"But you said—"

"I'm not joining Blake, Davenport and Asher."

"Frank, be sensible!"

"I can't join the firm, Mother." Frank blinked away the image of Shawn laughing at him. He stared straight ahead, waiting for the question he knew would come next.

"Why can't you?"

"Because I flunked my bar exam, Mother." He shot a hard glance her way, more courageous now that the truth was out. "That's right, Mother. I flunked the bar."

She gaped at him, her face white beneath her rouge.

"So there won't be any bonus. There won't be any money, Mother."

That morning Jessica called Maria to inquire about Michael Cavanetti and found the perfect opportunity had arisen for Cole to sneak into the Cavanetti house. While workmen hung paper in the drawing room and bath down the hall, Isabella and Frank had gone to brunch, leaving instructions that Maria and the nurse were not to let Cole near the house. The nurse kept her eye out for the famous quarterback, intending to do her job, but Maria had other ideas.

She let Cole and Jessica in the side door. Cole was dressed in the monk's robe taken from the chapel. The robe had been Jessica's idea. The costume not only provided Cole with a disguise but gave him a reason to visit Michael Cavanetti. Everyone knew that Michael was a devout Catholic, who would very likely be visited by a priest. Monks were scarce in the area, but the nurse in attendance didn't seem to think it odd that a robed brother arrived to pray for the recovery of Michael Cavanetti.

Cole did a marvelous job of mimicking monkish gestures and attitudes, and Jessica found it hard to keep a straight face.

"Bless you, Sister," he said, nodding solemnly to the nurse as she rose from her chair.

"Good morning, Father," she stuttered. She brushed the wrinkles from her uniform.

"And how is Michael this morning?"

"He's doing better," she replied, looking down at the old man in the bed. "He slept through the night."

"I've come to read the scripture to him. Perhaps God's Word will reach Michael and lift his spirits."

"That's a good idea." The nurse stepped away from the bed. "Would you like to sit down?"

"Thank you, Sister—" He paused for her name.

"Carol. Carol Banks."

"Thank you, Carol." He gestured toward Jessica. "Perhaps Miss Ward would like a chair as well."

"Oh, yes." She hurried to the door. "I'll see if Maria can find one for you. I'll be right back."

As soon as she left the room, Cole bent toward the bed.

"Pop?" he said. "Pop, it's Niccolo."

The old man stirred, and his eyelids fluttered. Jessica regarded him closely.

"They won't let me see you, Pop. So I've sneaked in using a disguise."

"Niccolo?" Michael breathed. He opened his eyes and blinked.

"Yes, it's me, Nick."

Michael squinted and surveyed the face above him. "No pills," he mumbled. His eyelids fluttered.

"What did he say?" Cole asked, turning to Jessica. "Did you get what he said?"

"No pills," Jessica repeated.

Michael nodded slightly and sighed.

"They're drugging him!" Cole exclaimed.

"Maybe they've just given him something to help him sleep."

"God, if they're drugging him—"

"Shh, Cole." Jessica clutched his arm. "Here comes the nurse."

Cole straightened immediately. "Ah, there you are Sister Carol." He took the chair. "Thank you."

"No trouble, Father." She hovered in back of him as he sat down. Jessica took a seat as well. Cole opened the Bible he had brought and selected a passage to read.

"Excuse me, but do you think I'd have time to get a cup of coffee?" the nurse asked. "Would you mind?"

"Not at all," Cole replied smoothly. "Michael will be in good hands."

"Thank you. I could use the break, Father. I'm stuck in this room for hours, you know. I really appreciate it!"

"It is no trouble, Sister, no trouble at all." He inclined his head toward the nurse, reminding Jessica of the way Brother Cosimo had bent toward her.

When the nurse left, Cole reached for his father's hand and tried to get him to speak, while Jessica watched in concern. She could see Michael struggling for words, but because of his stroke, and perhaps because he was under the influence of some kind of drug, it was difficult for him to form a coherent sentence.

"You mentioned a monk the last time." Jessica leaned closer. "Were you talking about Brother Cosimo?"

Michael squinted at her.

"The guardian?" she added.

She thought she saw a shadow pass through Michael's dark eyes.

"Did Cosimo hurt you?"

Michael shook his head. His right hand trembled, and he struggled to speak. "Help."

Cole grasped his father's hand. "Is Isabella drugging you, Pop?"

Michael sank back, his eyes closing with weariness.

"Damn!" Cole jumped to his feet. "There he goes, back to sleep again!"

"He's ill, Cole. He's an old man."

At that moment the door whisked open and Carol Banks walked in with her coffee.

"Finished, Father?" she asked, putting the cup on the nightstand.

"Yes. He tires."

The nurse looked at her watch. "It's time for his pill. We'd better give him his medication before he nods off completely."

She reached for a bottle in her uniform pocket and took out two blue pills.

"What are those for?" Jessica asked.

"Oh, they calm him down," Carol answered, lifting his head. "His paralysis really frustrates him, you know. Mrs. Cavanetti has told me what an active man he used to be. He can't seem to reconcile himself to the fact that he's an invalid now. I guess he gets himself into fits. It isn't good for him. So we just calm him down with these."

A horrible sinking feeling settled over Jessica. They *were* drugging Michael. He was probably living on a diet of tran-quilizers.

"That's it, Mr. Cavanetti. Open up now."

"He seems relaxed enough," Cole put in. "Why do you have to give him pills now?"

"Oh, he's on a strict schedule, Father. It wouldn't be a good idea to disrupt his medication."

She poured water down Michael's throat, which forced him to swallow the pills. "Good boy, Mr. Cavanetti."

Jessica stood by, seething. Michael Cavanetti was not a child to coddle or a dog to be handled and praised. They must do something to help him before he lost his dignity and his mind altogether. She exchanged a worried glance with Cole. Obviously he was thinking the same thing.

On the floor below she heard Isabella's high-pitched voice. The other Cavanettis were back. Cole nodded to Carol.

"I will return tomorrow, perhaps," he said. "Good-bye, Sister Carol."

"Good-bye, Father. Thank you for coming. I know it doesn't seem like it, but Mr. Cavanetti is probably grateful for your visit."

"I trust he is." He tucked his hands into the sleeves of his habit and followed Jessica out of the bedroom. They went down the servants' stairway that led to the kitchen. Maria met them.

"Hurry!" she urged. "Mrs. Cavanetti has returned!"

"We heard her." Cole strode for the side door.

"Maria." Jessica turned before she left the house. "Try to get your hands on the empty pill bottles they're using upstairs. Maybe look through the trash."

"Why, *bambina*?"

"We need to know what they're giving Mr. Cavanetti and how much."

"Sure. I'll try."

"And call Jess if we can come back tomorrow, Maria."

"I will. Oh, Niccolo!"

He hugged her and hurried out of the house, with Jessica half running to keep up with his long strides.

"I'm going to kidnap him," Cole spat. "I swear I'm going to kidnap him!"

Cole ducked into the chapel while Jessica continued to the bungalow. He watched her stride away. She had helped him as requested but didn't seem interested in spending any more time in his company. It was his own fault, he supposed. He couldn't seem to keep his temper these days, especially around her. No wonder she had cooled toward him.

He stepped up to the altar. Maybe when this was all over, he'd try to rekindle his friendship with Jessica. He'd like that. He untied the hemp cord from around his lean hips. Hell, he'd like to be more than friends, if he were honest about it.

Cole pulled the cowl off his head and shoulders and dragged the heavy woolen habit over his head. The cool air felt good on his bare arms.

"Keep going, why don't you," a voice drawled.

Cole jerked to attention. He had thought the chapel was deserted. Yet sitting at the back near the doors was Shawn Cavanetti, her feet propped up on the pew ahead of her. She lit a cigarette.

"Go on, you big stud." Her feet came down, and she stood up. "Let me see those pecs of yours."

Cole shook out the robe. "What are you doing here?"

"Having a smoke. Mrs. C. doesn't like it when I smoke in the house." She ambled down the aisle, her shoes clicking on the stone floor. Cole folded the robe and didn't look at her.

"Just look at that big bad body of yours." Shawn took a drag on her cigarette. "It's hard to believe you and Frank are brothers."

"Half-brothers," Cole replied, carefully putting the habit back into the glass case.

"Oh, yeah," she laughed. "Half-brothers. And you got the bigger half, I'd say."

Cole's lips turned up in a wry smile. He looked down at her. She was a small woman pretending to be tougher and older than she really was. She might have been pretty, but her harsh makeup and vulgar mannerisms overwhelmed any chance at natural beauty.

She took his smile for an invitation and sidled closer to him. "I bet a man like you needs a lot of exercise." She stroked his forearm and ran her palm up to his biceps. "What do you do for a workout, Brother Cole?"

"Lots of things." He was unaffected by her touch.

"I work out, too," she continued. "You'd be surprised how athletic I am. And creative."

"You sound like an accomplished lady." He picked up his shirt and drew his arm through one sleeve. "Frank must be a lucky man."

Shawn watched him. "You could get lucky, too, Cole. I mean, I could think of things to do with you that—"

"Sounds tempting, Shawn, but you know what they say . . ."

Her brows drew together in confusion. "What?"

"No women before a game."

"You're not playing football. I heard you were on injured reserve."

"I am." He buttoned his shirt. "But not for long. And I can't jeopardize my performance by fooling around with a woman, no matter how tempting." He winked at her.

She narrowed her eyes, as if trying to decide whether he was bullshitting her or telling the truth. He hoped he hadn't hurt her feelings. Over the years he had learned that women were easily hurt, especially when it came to offering themselves. Ironically, the brassy ones like Shawn were brittle underneath and easily wounded, while the quiet, self-contained women like Jessica had skins as thick as armor.

Cole stuffed his shirt into his pants. "Say, why don't you go jogging with me, Shawn?"

"Jogging?"

"Sure. You said you were athletic. There's a great trail along the beach."

"I didn't mean—"

"It'll make you feel like a new person."

"Well—"

"I'll meet you at the old tennis court after lunch—say, one?"

"Okay." She shrugged. "Okay. It might be fun."

Isabella made certain Maria was busy in the kitchen and then walked up the stairs and down the hall to Shawn's room. She slipped into the bedroom, confident that no one would interrupt her. Everyone else was out of the house, except for Nurse Banks, and she wouldn't leave Michael's room except for an emergency.

Isabella walked to the window and carefully peeked through the sheer drapery. On the other side of the chapel she could see Frank returning serves from a machine on the tennis court. For a moment she surveyed the slight form of her son, now crouched, waiting for the ball to sail toward him, and then exploding in a powerful swing. She had never seen him play tennis. Maybe he was good at it. Still, it wasn't something one chose over a law practice.

She could see Shawn and Cole jogging down the hill toward the Samish Slough. Now there was a pair if ever a match was made in heaven. How she wished Shawn would have duped Cole into marriage instead of Frank. Frank was too sensitive and high-strung to cope with a woman like Shawn. She could wrap Frank around her finger and get him to do anything. Cole, on the other hand, probably had most women cowed.

Isabella's disdainful gaze lingered upon Cole's dark hair and broad shoulders while her lips slowly relaxed from their usual tight line. Seeing Cole as an adult reminded her of Michael—or at least what Michael must have been at one time. She could only guess what her husband looked like as a young man. Michael had been well into his fifties when she met him. He had been a kind enough man, and rich enough, but his hair was graying and his handsome physique had begun to slide.

Isabella's eyes narrowed. She had been robbed of his youthful virility. In fact, she had been robbed most of her life. Not until years after Frank had been born and Michael had finally married her, did she realize why Michael had been so interested in her. He hadn't loved her. He'd simply wanted another son. He was just another lousy man, full of Italian machismo, wanting a son as proof that he was still able to bed a woman and get her with child.

She had spent the last twenty years tied to an old man, living the life of a nun, dreaming of the day she could bury the old bastard and finally be free of him. Yet seeing Cole made her wonder what her life might have been like if she had met a younger Michael Cavanetti.

Isabella snorted in contempt at her daydreaming and turned to her task. She pulled out a dresser drawer and pawed through Shawn's lingerie, a medley of puce panties and leopard-print teddies. Her lip curled in distaste. Isabella was certain that Shawn had put the idea into Frank's head that he should build a tennis club. Where else would he get such a fool notion?

She held up a pair of crotchless bikini underwear and stared at them in shock. Then she slammed the drawer shut and pulled open another.

Once she got rid of Shawn, she'd convince Frank to take the bar exam again. She could hire tutors for him, send him someplace peaceful—away from his worthless wife—where he could concentrate. He'd pass the bar. Then everything would get back on track. Not having the bonus money to work with was a setback, but she could handle the disappointment. There were people to turn to and ways of getting a loan for the vineyard property that she hadn't mentioned to Frank. She had arranged that already. All she had to do now was eliminate Shawn and her cheap form of blackmail.

Where *was* that letter?

13

Frank missed another serve. Ever since he had seen Shawn run past the tennis court with Cole, he hadn't been able to keep his mind on his practice. He had never seen Shawn do a stroke of exercise in the entire time they had been married. He hadn't even known she owned a jogging outfit—although her purple lycra suit with the zebra-striped top looked more appropriate for dancing in an aerobics class than jogging through a public park. Still, her breasts looked great bouncing around like that. Frank missed another serve, and the ball whizzed by his head. Was he imagining things, or were Shawn's breasts larger these past few weeks?

Frank saw his wife returning from her run. Cole turned off at the Ward's guesthouse and waved to her. At the gesture, Frank gripped his racquet and strode across the court to meet Shawn as she walked up the rise to the house.

She panted heavily and coughed as he came abreast of her.

"Didn't I tell you I wanted you out of the house?"

"Your mama doesn't want me to go."

"You've got to be joking."

"Ask her."

"Okay," he replied in a hostile tone. "I will." He fingered the strings of his racquet as she walked by. "So why the sudden interest in jogging?"

"Cole asked me to go." Shawn kept walking. "What's it to you?" She coughed behind her hand and hit her chest with her fist. "Goddamn, I can hardly breathe."

"It might help if you quit smoking."

"Don't start in, Frank."

He watched her walk away and tried not to notice the sexy way her rump jiggled in her shiny purple tights. She had a nice little ass. He thought of Cole looking at her ass. Then he thought of Darrell, his tennis buddy, looking at her, touching her. A dark wave of jealousy washed over him.

"Wait a minute!" he called, running up to her.

"What, Frank? I want to take a shower." She stopped and looked at the ground.

"Listen." Frank grabbed her arm. "I don't like this. I don't want you jogging with Cole."

"Why?"

"Because I don't trust him. And I don't trust you."

"Trust?" Shawn snorted and put a hand on her hip. "Since when was trust important to you?"

"Hey, I know about Darrell. I know you two had an affair."

"So what!"

"So you're married to me, that's what. How do you think it makes me look when you're always running around with other guys? Don't you have any decency? Darrell was my friend, for chrissakes!"

"I happen to like athletes." She smirked. "I just can't keep my hands off them. And they can't keep their hands off me."

Frank glowered at her.

"Jealous, Peaches?"

"Of you?" Frank countered. "You make me sick!"

She laughed and turned on her heel. Frank watched her go while he hit the side of his racquet on the flat of his hand.

One of these days she'd say too much, go too far. Then she'd be sorry.

After jogging with Shawn, Cole worked out for another hour and took a shower. He was pulling on a wool shirt when another fainting spell hit him and knocked him senseless. He slumped to the floor of the closet, landing on a pile of shoes.

He opened his eyes to find himself in the brocade bed. Moonlight poured through the slice of window onto the far wall. Cole sat up, too restless and hot to sleep. He stretched. Soon he would be fully recovered, well enough to return home. The battle for the Holy City of Jerusalem was won, and a Christian—one Godfrey of Bouillon—sat upon the throne of a new kingdom in the Holy Land.

Giovanna had fired his desire to mend quickly, holding the promise of her love out to him like a prize. The thought of her sent blood rushing to his loins. He was ready for her now. For weeks he had held himself back, waiting for the day he could take her in his arms and pledge his love to her.

He slipped from the bed, drew on a robe after the fashion of the Arabs, and paced the floor. Then he looked out the window to the white spires and domes of Jerusalem shining in the moonlight and marveled that the city could be so quiet. He was still at the window when his door opened quietly. Cole looked over his shoulder.

Giovanna stood in the doorway wearing a loose gossamer gown that flowed around her like a cloud of mist. He could see the outline of her lithe form beneath the gown, and the slenderness of her thighs sent a bolt of desire through him.

"Giovanna!" he whispered in wonder. She had come to him. Since the first time they had kissed, she had not spent the night in his chamber.

She hung in the doorway for a moment and then turned and closed the door. Without a word, she sank against the door and stared at him, looking suddenly unsure of herself.

"Giovanna!" he repeated, closing the distance between them. Then he saw her eyes, red and swollen. "What is it?"

She covered her face with her hands, and Cole felt his heart lurch. Why was she crying? He drew her to his chest, and she crumpled against him, sobbing and clinging to the folds of his robe. Cole held her and tenderly stroked her hair, powerless to stop her weeping.

"Ah, my Giovanna, my sweet," he murmured, "why do you weep?"

She shook her head and reached up for him, gazing through her tears at his face. Tenderly she took his head in her hands and pulled him down to her lips.

"My lord," she whispered, her voice thick with tears. "My liege lord!" She kissed his mouth, and Cole crushed her to his chest, raising her off her feet. She was as light as a swan, and he was afraid that he might crush her delicate swan wings in his passionate embrace. But she seemed heedless of such fear and wrapped her arms around his neck. Cole sighed and closed his eyes, giving over to his need for this woman. He lowered her, letting her slide over him, and they both felt the hard proof of his desire between them.

Cole bent to her neck and kissed her, pulling down the shoulders of her translucent gown to reveal the tops of her breasts. He had longed to see them for weeks, to touch them, kiss them, taste them. She moaned and her head rolled back as Cole kissed the nipple he had exposed. It hardened between his teeth while she fumbled with the gathered bodice until her other breast came free of the cloth.

Moonlight danced across the generous curves of her breasts and shadowed the rosehips of her nipples. Cole closed his lips upon her. She was warm and firm and fragrant. He wished he could take her entire breast into his mouth. He suckled her desperately, like a babe that has never eaten, making muffled moaning noises that he could not control. She cried out his name and clutched the back of his head, pressing into him.

Cole suckled her other breast, fighting the urge to drag her to the floor and mount her immediately. How much could he possibly endure before he exploded? He clutched her to his loins and held her fast until he could stand to move again.

She slipped her hands beneath his robe and pushed it away from his shoulders. Her fluttering hands sent him spiraling into oblivion. These hands had dressed his wounds, caressed his hair, shaved his face. He wanted them upon him.

Cole guided her hand to his engorged shaft, and she stroked him while he held his lip between his teeth and untied her dress. He pulled off her gown and gazed at the alabaster goddess before him. Then he let his robe fall to the floor and stood before her naked and fully aroused, more aroused than he had ever been in his life.

He touched her, gliding his palms down the curves of her breasts, down the long stretch of her torso, down the gentle angle of her hips and into the warm sweetness between her thighs. Giovanna sighed as he cupped her nest of hair and caressed her moist flesh while his other hand curved around to the graceful slope of her buttocks. Then, with a growl, he pulled her against him and felt the cool fire of her skin upon his own. Her belly was tight and rounded, and he surged uncontrollably against it.

"Ah, Giovanna. You are so beautiful. So soft."

"My lord," she whispered. "Please. Take me to your bed."

Cole needed no further entreaty. He gathered her in his arms and strode to the bed. He lay her upon the coverlet and sank down beside her, caressing her. And then he was on top of her and spreading her legs. He couldn't wait any longer. He knew he should give her pleasure first, arouse her with his hands and mouth. But he had waited weeks and weeks to feel Giovanna engulf him, and he could not help himself.

He pushed against her, gently forcing himself into her tight, sweet opening. Sweet Jesus, he could barely stand the feeling of her soft flesh around him. He sucked in a breath and held it as he pushed inside her. Then he pulled back and sank into her again and again. She let out a little cry and arched into him, closing her eyes.

"Spill your seed in me, my lord," she whispered hoarsely.

Sweet Jesus! Her words vaulted Cole into a world of frenzy. He tried to hold back, tried to extend the ecstasy.

"Spill it, my lord!" Her fingers dug into his back, her legs locked around his. "Give me a child, my lord. Give me your child!"

Cole plunged into her, exploding into glory, into a shimmering, shattering glory he had never known. He cried out and thrust into her as far as he could go.

"Giovanna!" he panted, delirious.

She hugged him as he fell upon her, exhausted and sated beyond his wildest dreams. She stroked his back and moved beneath him, clutching his buttocks so he could not leave her.

He kissed her and found that her cheeks were wet with tears. He ran a trembling finger down her face.

"My love," he murmured. "Why do you cry?"

She shook her head and would not answer.

He brushed the hair from her forehead and gazed at her, still buried deep and warm within her. She moved her hips, and he felt himself respond. He touched his forehead to hers.

"What is wrong, Giovanna?" he said. "Have I hurt you?"

"No!" She kissed him fervently. "Oh, no, my love. You do not hurt me."

"What then?"

"I will tell you when this night is done."

Cole smiled. "It is not done then?"

"Oh, no, my sweet baron, it has just begun."

She reached for him, and her nipples grazed the hair on his chest. He felt himself blossom within her.

Dawn colored the sky when Giovanna at last sank upon his chest and slept. He held her in complete contentment and dozed until a cock crow startled him awake.

Giovanna raised her head and pushed back her veil of raven hair.

"I must go!" she declared and scrambled out of bed.

He watched her pick up her clothes and dress hurriedly.

"The night is done, Giovanna." He rose on one elbow. "You promised to tell me the reason for your tears."

She bent over and kissed his lips and caressed his hair the way she had caressed him a score of times. "I weep because I love you, my lord." Then she rushed to the door and gazed back at him over her shoulder. Her eyes glistened, full of forlorn lights.

"And because today is my wedding day."

"What!" Cole thundered. He vaulted from the bed just in time to hear a bolt slide across the door on the other side. Damnation! She had locked him in. Cole pounded on the door and yelled for her to let him out. He pounded and ranted and tried to pull the door off its hinges, but to no avail. He could not get out of the room.

Exhausted, Cole sank to the floor at the base of the door and wept, his fists throbbing and his heart breaking. How could Giovanna marry someone else? He loved her. He knew she loved him. He had planned to ask for her hand in marriage once he was completely healed. Now all his plans were dashed. Someone else would share vows with her.

Giovanna couldn't possibly be marrying of her own free will. Her father had probably pledged her to a fat old duke with an equally fat purse. And once married, Giovanna would be locked away in a castle somewhere, protected from past suitors, to breed sons and daughters. Cole might never see her again.

"Giovanna!" he wailed. His howl echoed through the tower room and died there.

Late that evening he heard the bolt slide away from the door. Cole leapt to his feet at the sound, but the door opened to admit an old woman, and his hopes withered.

The woman stared at him as if he were going to attack her, so Cole stepped backward, wondering why she would be afraid of him. Her gaze dropped from his face but not, however, before he saw her pale. What had happened that people should avert their gazes from him?

"Where is Giovanna?" he demanded, put off by the woman's odd behavior.

"She is gone, my lord. She and her husband have set out for Acre and will sail home from there."

Cole breathed in, trying to contain the agony he felt upon hearing the word *husband*. He clenched his jaw.

"She asked me to give you this, my lord, and to tell you that your men will be here in the morning."

Cole took the sealed parchment. The old woman stared at him again and then looked down at her feet.

"Whom did she marry?" he inquired, trying to keep the gruffness from his voice and his chin high.

"Count Rondolfo di Brindisi."

"The younger?"

"The older, my lord."

Cole strode away. He knew it. He *knew* it! She had married a fat old man. A cruel fat old man. He knew of Count Rondolfo. His heart surged in his throat at the vision of that fat old lecher embracing delicate Giovanna. But there was nothing he could do about it. Giovanna had married him. The die was cast.

He turned and caught the old woman gawking at him. Her rude behavior, coupled with his powerlessness to help Giovanna, fired his temper.

"Why do you gape at me, old woman?"

"Your pardon, my lord!" She faltered backward, clutching her skirts. "I didn't mean—"

"What is it about me? Am I a spectacle of some kind?"

"It's your face, my lord!"

"What about my face?"

"It's—" she struggled with words and stared at him in confusion, "it's just so—"

"So what?" he bellowed. "Speak plainly, woman!"

"Hideous!" she screamed and skittered out the door.

Thunderstruck, Cole watched her run away. She found him hideous? He had always been passably handsome and had never given a thought to his appearance. He had not even looked at his face since being wounded. Giovanna had seen to his care and never once allowed him to shave. He felt his cheeks, wondering what the old woman had seen.

His fingers told him everything. His skin was patchy, rough, pocked, and uneven around his left eye. Part of his eyebrow was gone, and some of the hair on the left side of his skull. Cole dashed around the chamber, suddenly obsessed with the desire to see his own face.

There was no looking glass, but Cole's desperation provided him with a solution. He grabbed a jug of wine, pulled out the wooden stopper, and poured the red liquid into a basin on the table. His stomach churned while he waited impatiently for the ripples to settle. Then he looked into the basin and learned the truth.

He was a freak.

14

"Good morning, Jess."

Jessica jumped in surprise at the sound of her father's voice. It was only ten o'clock in the morning, and Robert was up and about—showered, dressed, and holding a sheaf of paper in his hand. She couldn't believe her eyes as he walked into the kitchen, where she stood holding the newspaper in her hand.

"Dad!"

"Did I scare you?"

"Well, kind of. I didn't expect you to be up this early."

"Thought I'd get a jump on the day. You know that idea I was telling you about yesterday?"

"Yes." She sipped her coffee, trying to suppress any hint of hope.

"I'm going to start the opening act this morning."

"Are you, Dad?" She smiled. "That's great."

Robert smiled vaguely in return and looked around as if he was missing something. Probably his usual Bloody Mary. Jessica held her breath.

"Want a cup of coffee, Dad?" she asked.

Robert's eye ticked. "Yes. A cup of coffee. That sounds good."

She poured him a cup, biting back the words of encouragement she longed to say. If he chose to start writing and quit drinking, it was up to him. She had learned long ago that her encouragement only put a hex on his good intentions. She held out the cup of steaming coffee.

"Thanks." He curled his bony fingers around the handle of the mug. "Well, I guess I'll sequester myself in the study. I won't be interfering with your work, will I, Jessica?"

"No." She fought to keep her voice level and free from any enthusiasm. "No, go right ahead, Dad. I planned to head over to the Cavanettis anyway this morning to talk about the lease. I want to see what Isabella is considering."

"Good. I'll see you later, then."

She smiled and watched him walk out of the kitchen. She dared not hope that he had turned over a new leaf. Too often his good intentions had crumbled in a matter of hours. She would not set herself up for disappointment again.

At eleven o'clock Jessica took a folder containing the lease documents to the mansion. She saw an unfamiliar black sedan parked in the circular drive and wondered who was visiting the Cavanettis. Maria met her at the door and ushered her into the newly papered drawing room.

Frank stood up as Jessica entered. He wore a pair of black corduroy slacks and a gray wool sweater, and looked very much like a slighter version of his older brother. But, unlike Cole's, Frank's handsome features had no effect on Jessica.

Isabella sat near the coffee table, framed by the lace-covered window behind her, looking regal in a smart navy dress. Two men stood by the fireplace, looking like thugs draped in expensive black suits. Did the black sedan belong to them?

Jessica wondered who they were, but before she could ask, she saw Maria hobble into the room with a tray of coffee and biscotti. Maria avoided eye contact while Jessica sat down in a wing chair to the left of Isabella. She lay the folder on the coffee table near the tray.

"How is your guest?" Isabella asked, pouring coffee.

"You mean Cole? Well, he's a little disappointed that he can't see his father."

"Good."

"I hear old Nick beat up a reporter day before yesterday." Frank picked up a coffee cup.

"I wouldn't say beat—"

"He should keep a better handle on that temper of his. It's going to get him into trouble one of these days." Frank sipped his coffee and sat back, looking smug.

"It already has," Isabella put in meaningfully.

"Everywhere he goes Cole is pursued by reporters. It's incredible," Jessica protested.

"That's the price he pays for being famous." Frank reached for a biscotti. "If he can't take the heat of the limelight, he ought to get into a different line of work."

"Frank." Jessica leaned forward. "You were there at the Falls Winery. You saw how they treated him. Wouldn't you get mad if someone pestered you like that?"

"I'd put up with a lot for his salary. God, it's criminal what quarterbacks get these days. It'll take me years to earn that much."

"Not if you play your cards right, Frank." Isabella touched his wrist. "And remember, your career will last much longer than Nick's, too."

He gulped his coffee.

"Nick's fame is fleeting," Isabella went on. "He's at the end of his career with nowhere to turn. And if I know him, he's probably squandered his entire fortune. I'll bet that's why he's here. He wants the winery now. He thinks his father will give it to him after all this time."

"And we're not letting him have it, are we, Mother?"

"Not a chance."

Jessica shifted uncomfortably in her chair. Had they forgotten the reason she had come? Instead of talking about the lease, they were gloating over Cole's misfortune.

"About the lease, Mrs. Cavanetti. I'm prepared to sell at the right price. And as you know, you have first option to buy."

"How much do you want for it?" Frank asked.

"Two million."

Isabella's coffee cup hung at her lips. "Two million?" she gasped.

"Greg Kessler told me it's worth that much and more. But I'm asking bottom dollar out of respect for our long acquaintance."

"Two million is more than I expected," Isabella replied. "I will have to talk it over with my associate. He'll be right back. He just went down the hall for a moment."

Jessica glanced at the hall that led to a bathroom under the stairs.

"What about Kessler?" Frank asked. "I know he'd like to get his hands on the property."

"His price would be much higher," Jessica answered coolly.

Just then someone shouted in the hallway, and a loud crash shattered the stillness of the big house.

Isabella jumped to her feet. "What's going on?" she cried.

The thugs in the expensive suits trotted toward the commotion while Frank set down his coffee cup and stood.

Sounds of fighting broke out and then a man stumbled backward into the drawing room, falling at the feet of the two thugs.

"Mr. Vincenzo!" Isabella exclaimed in horror.

Mr. Vincenzo scrambled to his feet just as a tall figure in a black robe burst into the drawing room and grabbed him by his lapels.

"Get out!" a familiar voice demanded. Jessica rose from her chair. She recognized Cole's voice at once. "Get out of this house, you sonofabitch!" He shoved Vincenzo away from him.

Vincenzo staggered backward, holding his nose, which bled profusely, while one of his men fumbled for a handkerchief to give him.

"What is the meaning of this?" Isabella rushed to his side. "How dare you hit Mr. Vincenzo!"

"Nick, is that you?" Frank asked, peering up to see into the shadow of the cowl.

"Nick?" Isabella exclaimed.

"Vincenzo!" Cole threw back the hood. His eyes were blazing, and his face was flushed with anger. "My father told you that if you or any member of the corporation ever set foot in this house again, he'd kill you. Just because he can't do it doesn't mean I can't."

"And who the hell are you?" Vincenzo wiped his nose.

"Boss, that's Cole Nichols!" the taller of the thugs put in. "Cole Nichols of the St. Louis Bulls!"

"I'm Michael Cavanetti's son. I was here the last time you offered to help St. Benedict Winery. My father said no then, and I'm saying no now."

"You have no right!" Frank sputtered. "No legal right!"

"And you don't either," Cole retorted. "Not while Pop is still alive. He's the master of this house and president of the company. He'd rather cut off his arm than get into business with the corporation." He turned to his stepmother. "And you know it, Isabella."

Isabella drew herself up straight and glared at Cole. "Frank, call the police," she said.

"Yes, Frank, call the police," Cole interjected. "And I'll just phone my buddies at the *Seattle Times* and have them come out to cover the story. I can see it now. Isabella Cavanetti invites the Mafia to the Northwest. Good career move for Frank, I'd say, Isabella. Give the Cavanetti name a little publicity."

Isabella was as white as a marble statue and held herself just as rigid. "You wouldn't dare!"

"Try me, Isabella."

Vincenzo returned the bloody handkerchief to his tall assistant, who stuffed it unceremoniously into his breast pocket. "We don't want any trouble, Mrs. Cavanetti." He adjusted his tie. "Perhaps you should talk this over with your husband again. And get rid of this goon." He tipped his head toward Cole. "Then we'll talk."

"No, you won't," Cole declared. "Get out. Now!" He took

a step toward Vincenzo. For a moment the man hesitated, but then he turned and stumbled out of the drawing room, gesturing for his men to accompany him.

"Mr. Vincenzo, wait!" Isabella called.

Cole grabbed her arm. "Just calm down, Isabella. You're not going anywhere."

Jessica heard the front door slam, and then someone began to clap. Everyone turned at the sound. Shawn leaned against the doorway, a smile on her face, while she applauded.

"All right, Cole!" she exclaimed and raised her fist in a victory salute.

Jessica stood on the balcony of the bungalow, gazing at the guesthouse. The rotting bannister had been expertly repaired and she leaned against it now with confidence.

More than anything she wanted to talk to Cole and tell him that she understood, that she would stand by him. She clutched her arms, remembering the terrific row that had flared among the Cavanettis after Mr. Vincenzo left the house.

Isabella had raged at Cole. Jessica had never seen anyone so angry. Even Frank, who did not often show his spine, vented his anger at Cole. Their behavior had made her feel embarrassed, worried that she should not be there to witness such discord, but she could not leave without interrupting them. She tried to calm them down, but Isabella only shook her off. Cole had ruined everything. Everything! Afterward, Cole stormed out of the house and roared off in his car, driving away at breakneck speed down the twisting lane.

He returned home late that night. Jessica knew because she had seen him drive up and the light go on in his bedroom. She gazed at the glowing rectangle of light as her heart grew heavier and heavier. What could she do? If she didn't sell the property, her own father would soon be broke. There were limits to her sentimentality and her loyalty to the Cavanettis.

She heaved a sigh. She might as well quit worrying about Cole and set up her telescope. She turned to do just that when she spied a robed figure standing in the shadows.

"Brother Cosimo!" she exclaimed.

He stepped forward. "Good evening, Miss Ward."

"How long have you been standing there?"

"A few moments." He put his hands in his sleeves. "Long enough to see that you are troubled."

Jessica brushed back her hair. She had no desire to talk about her troubles with anyone, especially Cosimo Cavanetti.

"Look," she said instead, sweeping the air behind her. "The railing has been fixed."

"I was concerned that someone might fall."

"You mean you made the repairs?"

"Yes. The job was not difficult."

"Why, thank you, Brother Cosimo. I haven't had the chance to hire a carpenter."

"Now you will not have to, Miss Ward."

"How can I repay you?"

"By calling me Cosimo."

"All right." She shrugged nervously. What was the danger in becoming more friendly with him? He meant her no harm. "And you must call me Jessica."

"Jessica it is, then." She could hear the smile in his voice. "Come with me, Jessica. I would talk to you where it is not so cold."

He turned and disappeared through the dark doorway. Jessica stared in his direction, marveling that he was certain she would obey his request. Yet she was in his debt, and the least she could do was give him a little of her time and attention. She followed him down the stairs and into the study. He motioned for her to sit in a chair. A fire crackled on the grate, throwing light across his dark robe but none upon his face. She sat down.

"Did you build the fire?" she asked, stretching her chilled feet toward the flames.

"I took the liberty."

"It feels nice." She heard the clink of glass as she sank back into the cushioned chair. Cosimo appeared at her elbow with two glasses of ruby-colored wine and handed one to her. His manner was so full of serene gentleness that she hadn't the heart to tell him she didn't drink.

"Thank you," she murmured.

He nodded and sat down in a chair beside her where none of the firelight danced higher than his chest. He raised his glass into the shadow beneath his cowl. Jessica watched him, waiting for him to speak.

"This is an excellent Cabernet Sauvignon," he commented. "The only decent St. Benedict wine left, and that because it is thirteen years old."

She looked at the beautiful liquid in her goblet. She could see overtones of raspberry and amber around the edge of the glass. Truly it was a beautiful wine.

"You do not care for Cabernet?"

"I don't drink spirits."

"Why?"

"I've always thought"—she swirled the wine—"that it wasn't a good idea to drink."

"Ah." She heard the smile in his voice again. "Have you ever heard what Plato said about wine?"

"No."

"He called it God's greatest gift to man."

She looked at the wine askance.

"So Plato doesn't convince you?" He chuckled. "Perhaps you should consider the healthful aspects."

"What healthful aspects?"

"Wine contains vitamins and minerals and a special quality that breaks down fats. A red wine like this Cabernet has tannic acid in it and other acids that destroy bacteria. A good wine has been known to cure people of typhus."

Jessica smiled. "You're pulling my leg."

"Pulling your leg?"

"Joking."

"In truth I am not, Jessica. There is no need to fear wine."

She shook her head. "I've seen how people act when they're drunk and I don't care to be like that."

"Moderation is the key to everything in life, Jessica. One glass of Cabernet will not turn you into a blubbering fool, believe me."

She looked at the wine. She could smell a sweet aroma of raspberries wafting from the glass.

Cosimo chuckled again. "Or are you afraid the wine will loosen your tongue?"

Her head shot up. Either he was more perceptive than most people, or she was more transparent than she supposed. She raised her chin and stared at him, wishing she could penetrate that opaque shadow of his face and see what expression accompanied that rich voice.

"If there is something you are reluctant to divulge," Cosimo continued, "what better drinking companion to have than a priest, eh?"

"You are no priest. You told me so yourself."

She raised the goblet. No one was going to call her a coward. And she would show him that no confessions would be forthcoming at the bottom of her glass. She drank.

The wine went down silky smooth, sweet and surprisingly fresh, tart but not harsh. Jessica was amazed at the honeyed softness of the Cabernet. She had always assumed wine would be strong and sour.

Cosimo laughed outright at her expression of wonder. "You like it!"

"Yes." She smiled back and turned the goblet between her fingers. "It's much different than I had supposed." She took another sip, then another.

He nodded and got up to refill his glass and hers. As she watched him walk to the decanter, a pleasant feeling enveloped her, a warm sensation, a warmth different from the heat of the fire. She relaxed and reached for the glass he held out to her.

"This Cabernet was the last wine I made at St. Benedict," Cosimo began, sitting down. "Since then nothing has been produced that is worth drinking. In fact, I had to destroy all the whites so the winery reputation would not be ruined."

"You were the one who vandalized the warehouse?"

He nodded. "What I found there did not merit the St. Benedict label."

"Is that what you do as guardian? Destroy private property?"

"When need be. I have been away. And in my absence terrible changes took place at the winery, changes that could mean its downfall."

"Why did you leave if you are the guardian?"

"I had no choice in the matter. But now I am back. And I will do whatever it takes to repair the damage wrought by Isabella Cavanetti."

Jessica surveyed his hood while she took a sip of wine. "Cosimo, why is it that I am the only one to see you?"

He rose, and the folds of his habit fell about his sandals. He faced the fire. All she could see was the wide wedge of his back and the slim line of his hips beneath the robe.

"Yes, why do you see me, Jessica? That is the question that haunts me." He turned. "But I must confess that I am glad you are the one who does see me. It gives me pleasure to talk with you."

"I like talking with you, too," she replied. The words slipped out before she could bite them back. Generally, she didn't like talking to people. Idle conversation made her nervous.

She searched the shadow beneath his cowl. "But I would like to see your face."

"Perhaps someday you will. But for now, I must remain shrouded."

"Why?"

"It is not imperative for you to see my face in order to see my heart."

"Your heart?"

"To know that I will not harm you. To know that we all need to talk to someone. You are here for me, Jessica—the only one to see and hear me. I am here for you. And I assure you that you can trust me enough to reveal what is in your heart."

She gazed at the floor. "There is nothing in my heart, Cosimo. That's the trouble with me."

"Ah, I believe there is a great deal in your heart. Perhaps you do not look at it, so you are convinced there is nothing there."

She heard him sit down again. After a moment of silence, she glanced at him.

"*Agnosco veteris vestigia flammae,*" he said softly.

"What does that mean?"

"Something the poet Virgil once paraphrased. 'Having loved once before, I know the symptoms.'"

"What symptoms?"

"Your symptoms. You have a heart full of love for a man, and yet you lock it inside. What good will it do either of you if it remains behind a wall?"

"Love is not very fun when only one person feels it."

"How do you know only one feels it?"

"Because!" Jessica jumped to her feet, frustrated by years of suppressing her feelings. "I love Cole, but he doesn't care a bit about me! Once I even offered myself to him, and he just laughed at me! It was terrible. Humiliating."

"He actually laughed?"

"Well . . ." Jessica stared at the fire. "He smiled, at any rate. I knew then that he didn't want me. I was so ashamed."

"Perhaps he didn't want you under those circumstances."

Jessica thought about that for a moment and then slowly shook her head. "No. I don't think so. He never did want me. And now he has someone else. So it's better that I push aside my feelings for him."

"It is sad. It makes me very sad, Jessica."

"Why?"

"Because love is precious. Many people never know real love. To feel it and deny it is a sad state of affairs." He rose, and she heard him step close behind her. "Love is more important than pride, Jessica. Sometimes even more important than honor. That is what I have learned in my life."

She hung her head but did not step away from him. For some reason his deep voice and his nearness were of great comfort to her. She pressed her lips together and tried to keep from breaking into tears. Then she felt his hands upon her shoulders. He squeezed gently.

"Close your eyes, Jessica. Close your eyes. Listen to the sound of my voice. Concentrate on my voice and nothing else. Do not think about who you are, or what you are, or what I am. Just listen to my voice."

She obeyed him and lifted her face. His hands were warm, his voice rich. She felt adrift in a soothing pool, floating on the sound of his voice. Was it the wine that made her feel this way? Or was he a sorcerer putting her under a spell?

"Listen to my voice. Feel my hands. Think back. Tell me that you remember."

She thought back. He was a stranger to her eyes but not to her heart, which Jessica knew as a sudden certain truth. She felt an intense urge to sink back into his chest, to let herself be enfolded against him, to feel his lips upon her skin, to turn in his arms and hold him to her breast.

The feeling terrified her. How could a monk from the twelfth century know her? How could she know him? He had hypnotized her. That was it. He had hypnotized her, put her under a spell.

"No!" she gasped, pulling out of his grip.

"What is it?" Cosimo asked, stepping toward her. She stared at him, confused and frightened at the way the present had fallen away, making her feel as if she stood on a precipice of time, dangerously close to the edge. Her senses swirled; the wine made her feel dizzy. All she could see was the blackness of his robe. Or was it the frightening blackness of the past that she saw? She blinked and staggered backward.

"Jessica—" He grabbed for her to keep her from falling.

"Don't touch me!" She stumbled away from him, backing toward the study door. "Leave me alone!"

"Ah, Jessica!" His voice sang out, full of yearning.

She didn't care. She skittered out of the study, dropped her wineglass on the table in the hall, and burst through the front door of the bungalow. Her legs pumped as if they had a life of their own, carrying her to the guesthouse, to the only person who could save her.

15

Jessica plunged through the guesthouse door without knocking and careened through the front room. She ran the few steps to the master bedroom and pounded on the door.

"Cole!" she cried, looking over her shoulder to see if Cosimo had followed her. She pounded again. "Cole!"

She heard footsteps, and the door swung open. Cole stood in the doorway, rubbing his eyes.

"Jessica?" He squinted at her.

"Cole!" She was so glad to see him that she flung herself against him and wrapped her arms around his neck.

"Jess! What's the matter?"

She couldn't speak. She simply stood there and clung to him. She was terrified of the feelings the sorcerer monk had evoked and knew that, of all people, Cole could protect her. His arms felt safe and warm, his body solid and real. She pressed her nose into the base of his neck and shut her eyes.

Cole stroked her back. She could feel the palm of his hand sliding up and down her spine as he asked her again what was wrong. She had never known a more comforting touch.

She squeezed his neck. "Oh, Cole!"

He forced her to step backward so he could see her face.

"What the devil is wrong?" he asked.

"The monk—it's the monk!"

"What monk?"

"The monk I told you about. He tried to put a spell on me! He told me to think back, to listen to his voice, to remember—" Jessica broke off, realizing what she must sound like. Cole probably thought she was a raving lunatic. She pushed against his chest, realizing she never should have run to him in the first place.

"Jess, have you been drinking?" Cole asked, a small smile on his lips.

"Yes, but—"

"Come on." He took her elbow and headed down the hall, dragging her with him. "What you need is a good cup of coffee."

She yanked her arm out of his grip. "I'm not drunk!"

"Then what's gotten into you?"

"It's that monk. He got me to drink some wine, and then got me to talking about—" She broke off in confusion.

"About what?"

"About—" Jessica stared at him. She couldn't tell Cole that they had talked about him. She wasn't about to divulge her feelings, no matter what Cosimo had said about love. "About the winery," she improvised. "And then he tried to put a spell on me!"

"Are you sure you saw a monk?" Cole crossed his arms and surveyed her. "No one else has seen him."

"I know that. But I really did see him."

"Doesn't that sound a bit odd to you?"

"It does, but it's the truth. Come on, I'll show you. He's in the study, drinking a bottle of St. Benedict Cabernet."

She dragged him out of the guesthouse and back to the bungalow. But when they got to the study, all that remained of the monk's presence was the dying fire. Jessica looked around the room in dismay, knowing Cole would never believe her now.

"He seems to be gone."

Jessica frowned.

"Something scared you, though. I can see that. Maybe you were dreaming."

"I wasn't dreaming!" she retorted. "I know the difference between dream and reality, Cole. And he was right here, right in this very room, talking to me."

Cole glanced around. "All right. So he was here. He tried to put a spell on you. Why though, Jess?"

"He seems to think I'm someone else. Someone who should know him. But I don't know him. I don't!"

"Well, he's not here now. Maybe he gave up and left." Cole walked up to her. "Jess, why don't I fix you a cup of coffee?"

"You still think I'm drunk, that I made all of this up!"

"I didn't say that."

His calmness irritated her. He didn't believe her. He was merely appeasing her. Jessica strode to the door of the study and turned.

"Thanks for coming over," she said.

Cole put his hands into the front pockets of his jeans and surveyed her. For the first time Jessica noticed that he was fully dressed. He must have been sleeping in his clothes. His hair was boyishly mussed, giving him that vulnerable look she found so attractive.

She reminded herself of her vow to remain unaffected by Cole, tore her gaze from him, and concentrated on the ivory woodwork of the doorway instead.

"I'm sorry I woke you for nothing."

"Am I dismissed then, Miss Ward?"

"Yes. Thanks, Cole. I'll be all right now."

"Okay." As he walked toward her, he gave her a slow, calm smile that infuriated her even more. Behind that smile he was probably laughing at her again. Jessica held her head high as he brushed past her. She had made an utter fool of herself once again. He probably thought she had fabricated the entire story just so she could throw herself at him.

The next morning Jessica had a visitor. She showed the police officer into the living room, all the while hoping that her father would stay in bed until Detective Turner left. Her father had not stuck to his resolution to quit drinking and was sleeping off the indulgence of the previous evening.

Jessica sat down while the detective drew a pad and pen from his chest pocket. His actions were deliberate, as if part of a ritual. Jessica watched him run a hand over his graying brush of hair. Then he flipped to a blank page in his tattered notebook and squinted up at her. His small brown pupils were nearly hidden behind the puffy skin surrounding his eyes. His jowls hung over a rumpled collar and the crooked knot of his tie. He looked very much like the Cowardly Lion in *The Wizard of Oz*, except for his butch haircut.

"Been told you saw a monk a while back."

"Yes." Jessica tried not to tense up. "Last Friday, I believe."

"Any more sightings since, Miss Ward?"

Jessica wondered why they were interested in Cosimo. She had been frightened by him last night, but not enough to betray his presence to the police. Certainly he wouldn't harm anyone. And she did owe him her life.

"Why?" she asked. "What's wrong?"

"Just answer the question, Miss Ward."

She forced herself not to break eye contact. "I haven't seen anyone since. I guess he was just a prowler."

Detective Turner wrote something in his notebook. Jessica watched him scribble with his stubby fingers, wondering if he were writing comments about her behavior. Could he tell that she was nervous, that she was lying?

He squinted at her again. "Saw the monk by the sign down the lane, and then here at the house?"

"That's right."

"Investigating officers found nothing when they came out at your request."

"No, they didn't."

"Mind if I have a look around?"

"Certainly not. But why the sudden interest?"

"Been another murder." Detective Turner rose and peered around the room, as if he might find something suspicious. Then he glanced at her. "Down in the park. Some poor lady jogger was found strangled by her own sweatband."

"Oh, no!"

"Sweatband." The detective scowled. "Last thing you'd consider as a murder weapon."

"That escaped convict . . ." Jessica trailed him out the door. "Did they catch him yet?"

"Nope. Rogers is still at large. Probably out in that bog somewhere. That's my guess."

Frank walloped the tennis ball and felt some of his tension fly across the court. He had spent most of the morning returning serves, even though a light rain fell on the court. His fingers were stiff and his toes cold, but he planned to stay out of the house as long as he could endure the elements. Isabella was still on the warpath, and he wanted to avoid her.

Out of the corner of his eye he saw someone approaching. He hit another ball and grimaced with the effort, hoping whoever was coming would walk on by. Some days he didn't feel like talking to anyone, and today was one of them.

But Cole soon materialized at his elbow, and patiently watched him return serves until Frank realized his half-brother had no intention of leaving. Sighing, Frank stalked to turn off the serving machine and then stood at center court, with his racquet hanging from his right hand.

"What do you want?" he asked.

"I want to talk to you." Cole ambled forward.

"Yeah? About what?"

"About the winery."

"Look, Nick, just butt out. The winery is none of your business. How many times do Mother and I have to tell you that?"

Cole looked at the mansion. Frank watched Cole's jaw move as if he were gritting his teeth. He gripped his racquet tighter, concerned about Cole's temper and what he could do when he was angry. He watched his brother's dark profile, but quickly averted his gaze when Cole turned back to him.

"Frank, forget Isabella for a minute. Forget how you feel

about me. Think about Pop for once."

"Think about Pop?" Frank pushed up his sweat band. "Since when were you interested in him? You were the one who told him to shove the winery."

"I didn't tell him to shove it. I told him I needed to see the world before I took on the winery."

"That's not the story I heard."

"Frank." Cole surveyed him. "Did it ever occur to you that you haven't been told the whole story?"

"What is that supposed to mean? What are you saying?"

"I'm saying that your mother only tells you what she wants you to hear."

Frank felt the blood rush to the tips of his ears. He turned his back, refusing to listen to any more insults, but Cole came up behind him.

"Isabella is ready to kiss off the winery, Frank. You know it, I know it. Poor old Pop might know it, but he can't do a thing about it. If the winery goes, Pop will go, as sure as I'm standing here."

Frank looked at the green surface of the court, listening to every word. He knew Cole was right, but he wasn't about to admit it.

"St. Benedict is Pop's life, his heart. If Isabella sells it, or gives over controlling interest to the mob, Pop will die, Frank. He'll die. Do you want to be responsible for that?"

Frank took a step away, as if he could escape Cole's words, but Cole followed him.

"I've done enough to send the old man to an early grave," Cole continued. "That's why I'm offering you a chance to buy the vineyard property from the Wards."

Frank turned. "What chance?"

"I'll lend you the money, at no interest. I'll be a silent partner, Frank. Isabella won't have to know. No one will have to know but you and me."

Frank stared at his brother. So the great quarterback hadn't spent all his money after all. He had two million to put down for the property. Wait until his mother heard this.

"What do you say, Frank?"

Frank reached over and turned on the automatic server. He straightened and looked Cole in the eye. "Go screw yourself, Nick!"

Cole seemed genuinely surprised.

"Do you think you can buy the Cavanetti name back, just like that?" Frank sneered. "It's not that easy, Mr. Football Hero!"

"Frank, you're making a big mistake. . . ."

"Listen, Nick, who was the one who left? You! Who was the one who stayed? Me! I've been here, doing my best to be a good son to Mother and Pop. Maybe I don't want to be here either, but I stay. Because"—he touched his racquet to his chest—"I care."

"Don't fool yourself, Frank. You've never really been here. You've been at your private schools getting your elite education. You don't know the first thing about a vineyard."

"Yeah, well, I didn't choose a football career over St. Benedict. You know what you did to Pop by leaving?" Frank watched Cole's eyes darken. "You made him an old man. He's never been the same since."

"He'll be even worse if the winery fails or is sold."

Frank surveyed his half-brother with disdain. He would rather die than accept any charity from him. "Fuck off, Nick."

Frank stalked to the end of the court and crouched, waiting for a serve. "And stay away from my wife!" he yelled at Cole's retreating form.

That evening Jessica dressed for the Christmas party at the Cavanettis. Robert had no interest in attending and avoided Jessica, probably because he had fallen off the wagon again and was ashamed of himself. Jessica put on the same jade tunic she had worn at the Falls Winery open house, but this time she paired it with her black skirt and her short black boots for a more feminine look. She fluffed her hair but left it loose, an ebony cloud that fell well below her shoulders. Then she headed out of the bungalow for the party.

Cole was out on the porch, sitting on the bannister. He rose when she closed the door.

"Hi," he greeted her.

"Hi." Jessica fought down the thumping of her heart as he regarded her from her boots to her hair. What was he doing here? He didn't say anything, but his eyes glinted in approval of her appearance.

"Going over to the party?"

"Yes." She dropped her keys into her bag. "You aren't going, are you?"

"Hell, no. Isabella would call the police!"

She smiled sadly as they walked down the steps.

"Mind if I walk you over there?" he asked. "I heard about that murder in the park, and I don't think you should be out alone."

Jessica glanced at him in surprise, touched by his concern for her safety. "I'd appreciate it, Cole. Thanks."

He zipped up his jacket. "You look great, Jessica."

"Thanks." She shot him a glance, but he was not looking at her. Why couldn't she ever say the same thing to him? What would happen if she started to tell the truth, to say what she really felt? Suddenly Jessica wished Cole would be at the party, where she could dance with him and take advantage of the social function to spend the evening in his arms. She looked at the ground, knowing her thoughts had made her blush.

"About last night, Jess, are you still sore?"

"No." She shrugged. "I don't blame you for laughing at me. I must have sounded crazy."

"I wasn't laughing, Jess."

"Well." She shrugged again. "Even so. I could see it in your eyes."

Cole stopped abruptly in the middle of the lane, and Jessica looked back at him, surprised to see anger in his face.

"You assume too much."

"What do you mean?"

"I have never laughed at you. Maybe with you, but never at you. There's a big difference."

"It's all semantics, Cole." She turned to walk away, remembering the way he had smiled at her long ago, but he caught her hand.

"Dammit, Jessica, we used to be friends. And now you're so defensive! What's happened to you?"

"I don't know what you mean." She tried to pull her hand away, but he held her fast and drew her closer to him. "Aren't we friends anymore, Jess?"

"It's been a long time."

"What does time have to do with it?"

Jessica looked away from his face. Time really didn't have anything to do with it. Her memory of Cole was crystal clear, as if he had never left, and his rejection still stung.

Cole sighed. "Do you know how hard it is to make friends when you're in football? Hell, you're the first woman I've met in years who wasn't in love with my image as a star quarterback. You didn't even know I played ball. And that means a lot to me. With you I can be plain old Cole again."

His hands moved up her arms to her shoulders. "You're different than all those others, Jess. You're honest and sincere. You don't know how rare that is."

"I'm not honest!" Jessica struggled to break free of his grip.

He smiled as if her outburst verified what he had just said. Then he squeezed her arms. "Jess, I could use a friend now. Someone to trust. I have no one. No family. Nothing. People think I have everything—fast cars, money, fame—but those things don't mean a tinker's damn to me anymore."

He looked at her, and Jessica's heart went out to him. She relaxed her arms, standing in silence so he could continue to speak without fighting her.

"I've felt this for years—this restlessness, this dissatisfaction. And coming back to St. Benedict made it clear to me what the problem is. I'm Italian. Family is important to me. And no matter how many autographs I sign as Cole Nichols, I'm still Niccolo Cavanetti deep in my heart. I don't have any family anymore, Jessica. And you're about as close as I can come to one."

Jessica concentrated on his mouth as he spoke, afraid that if she responded, her tenuous self-control would snap.

"You're the only one I can share my past with," he went on. "I don't know why, but that's important to me now."

His words touched off an ache deep inside her. She felt exactly the same way. She had no one but her drunken father. And the only past worth remembering was the time she had spent with the Cavanettis.

"I know you've got your own life, Jess, things you have to do. But can't we spend this time together as friends, instead of me yelling and you getting huffy? It's Christmas, for God's sake."

"Sure. We can be friends, Cole." Her voice, which she struggled to keep level, sounded cooler than she had intended. "If that's what you want."

"Good. And I think friends should give each other a hug once in a while, don't you?"

"I've heard it's done between friends."

Smiling, Cole drew her against him. His collar flaps bent into her neck as his arms went around her and his cheek dipped to hers. His breath blew warm and uneven on her throat as he held her against his torso.

Jessica melted. His embrace made her feel as if she were sugar and he were hot water, dissolving her, enveloping her, absorbing her. She grabbed the front of his jacket to keep from clutching his neck and pulling him to her lips. He wanted friendship, old memories, the warm feeling of having someone who cared. Family. If he didn't want a lover, she wasn't going to take the chance of shamelessly offering herself and spoiling their relationship again.

"Jess," Cole breathed. His nose pressed into her hair, and his arms tightened around her, and the hug went over the line of mere friendship. Jessica closed her eyes and gave in to the delight she felt as his lips brushed the skin near her ear. Her scalp and shoulders erupted in goose pimples. She tightened her grip on the crisp fabric of his jacket, fighting the desire to return the pressure of his embrace and to turn her mouth to meet his.

Then Cole's fingers slipped into her hair and crushed a handful of curls at the nape of her neck, easing her head back. Slowly she opened her eyes to look at him. She could feel the heat of her love radiating from her eyes but could not hold it back. He looked at her, his black eyes backlit with fire and surprise. His mouth was so close to hers that she felt physical pain from resisting the impulse to kiss him.

Suddenly a car honked at them, shattering the moment. Jessica pulled back, realizing with a start that they stood in the center of the lane, bathed in headlights.

"Get out of the road!" a man yelled from the car window. "You idiots!" He turned into the Cavanetti drive and sped off, leaving Jessica's fantasy in a shambles of gasoline fumes and mud puddle splatters.

"Bastard!" Cole stepped backward. "Did he get your dress?"

Jessica glanced at her skirt but couldn't see any evidence of mud. "No." Her voice trembled, and her knees shook.

Cole chuckled as he took her elbow. "I didn't realize we were standing in the road."

"Neither did I." She forced a laugh. "I forgot myself altogether."

He didn't reply but guided her to the mansion and up the walk. He stopped at the foot of the marble staircase, where partygoers jostled them on their way to the front door.

"Jess, could you go up to Pop's room at about eleven o'clock?"

"Why?"

"I'm going to try to sneak in and get him out of there."

"What!"

"I called his physician about the tranquilizers. I told him about our suspicions that he's being drugged. The doctor looked in on Pop, but Isabella charmed her way right through his good sense." Cole glared at the mansion. "The only thing I can do now is get Pop out of there."

"You mean kidnap him?"

"Hell, yes."

16

The Christmas party went by in a blur of tinsel and crystal as Jessica waited for eleven o'clock. When the hour arrived, she walked up the stairs, intent on dissuading Cole from his plan. Not only was kidnapping a criminal offense, but the victim was a sick old man who required constant medical care. Did Cole plan to take him to a hospital after the abduction? She wished she had asked more questions.

The noise from downstairs dissipated as she reached the second floor and padded down the hallway toward Michael's room. At the end of the hall she saw a movement, and Cole stepped from the shadows, holding a finger to his lips. Jessica hurried to meet him.

"Cole, listen—"

"All you have to do," he interrupted in a low voice, "is suggest to Carol that she take a break and get herself a plate of goodies. Then I'll slip into the room."

"Cole, I don't think—"

"Quick, somebody's coming!"

Jessica turned and saw a middle-aged lady emerge from the bathroom. Jessica smiled weakly at her and then hurried toward Michael Cavanetti's room, deciding it was safer to argue with Cole where no one could see them. She rapped on the door, and the nurse opened it.

"Hello, Carol."

"Why, Jessica, how are you?"

"Fine, thanks. I've come up to give you a break. There are lots of goodies downstairs, and I thought you might like to fix yourself a plate."

"How thoughtful of you."

Jessica nodded. "The caterer did a marvelous job. You won't believe the spread down there."

Carol looked over her shoulder at her sleeping patient. Then she turned back to Jessica and smiled. "This is so nice of you, Jessica. Really."

"Think nothing of it. And take your time. I'm rather tired and won't mind sitting down for a while."

"All right." Carol grinned and minced out to the hall. "I'll be back in fifteen minutes or so."

Jessica walked into the room, hating herself for lying. Chances were that the nurse would be reprimanded for leaving her patient and mingling with the guests, should Isabella spy her at the buffet tables.

Moments later, Cole slipped into the bedroom and closed the door.

Jessica strode up to him. "Cole, we've got to talk about this."

"What do you mean?"

"You can't kidnap your father."

"Why the hell not?"

"Legally, I think you'd be guilty of a federal offense even though you are his son. Besides that, your father might suffer from the ordeal."

Cole scowled, but before he could reply, they both heard Michael grunt.

Jessica glanced over her shoulder. Michael had turned his head and was staring at them, fully awake. He flopped his right hand over the side of the mattress, beckoning them to come closer.

Cole leaned over his father. "Pop, what is it?"

"Monk," Michael gasped.

"Brother Cosimo?" Jessica asked, hovering at Cole's elbow.

Michael nodded, and his eyes searched her face.

"I've spoken to him," Jessica admitted. She saw genuine surprise light Michael's face. "He says he's the guardian of St. Benedict."

Michael nodded again. Then he looked at Cole and crooked a finger toward Cole's chest. "You. Leg—" But the words ended in a garble, and Michael shut his eyes in frustration.

"Leg what, Pop?"

"Frank," Michael blurted, opening his eyes again. "Not—not chosen!"

"Pop, I don't know what you're trying to say."

Michael pointed to the nightstand, and Jessica saw a tablet and a pen. She picked them up and handed them to Michael. He struggled to write something, but his hand trembled so much that the pen scribbled across the sheet.

Cole craned his neck, trying to decipher the writing.

"Listen to—" he read.

Michael scribbled something else.

"Cosimo!" Jessica exclaimed. "Listen to Cosimo!"

"Who in the hell is this Cosimo?" Cole demanded, confused.

"He's the monk I've been telling you about. The guardian."

"What does he have to do with Pop?"

Michael scribbled intensely, but the pen dragged across the page as he lost the ability to control his muscles. He sighed and fell back on his pillow. Tears squeezed out of the corners of his eyes.

Cole sank onto the bed beside him and took his hand. "Pop, don't cry. I'm going to get you out of here."

At that moment the door burst open and Isabella stormed into the room.

"What is the meaning of this?" she roared.

Cole glanced at her over his shoulder. Jessica turned, her arms stiff at her sides. Isabella must have seen Carol as soon as she got downstairs. Cole's chance to help his father was gone.

Isabella strode forward, severe in her black dress and red metallic corsage, looking as if she wore a military uniform. "What are you doing here?"

"I'm talking to my father," Cole replied quietly.

"I thought I made it clear that you are not welcome in this house."

"Pop wants me here."

"How do you know?" Isabella sniffed in disdain. "The man's a vegetable."

"No, he isn't!" Jessica countered.

Isabella turned on her. "And you—tricking my employees. I thought better of you, Jessica."

"I was only trying to help."

"Help who? Nick? Now I know where your loyalties lie. And I'm deeply disappointed in you, Jessica." Isabella glared at her and then turned her attention to the old man in the bed. "Look at him. You've upset him! It isn't good for Michael to get upset like this!"

"He wouldn't get so upset if you'd quit giving him tranquilizers."

Isabella whirled to face Cole. "I know what's best for Michael. I've been here. You haven't. So don't you dare presume to tell me my business!"

Cole caressed his father's forehead, brushing the wisps of hair into place. Then he stood up.

"I'm going to sue you for custody of my father," he declared evenly. "My lawyers are drawing up the papers."

"Well, my lawyer is getting an injunction against you, to keep you from entering this house. And I want you out." She pointed to the door. "Now."

Cole looked down at his father. "Bye, Pop. Don't worry. I'll be back."

"He can't hear you," sneered Isabella. "Now get out!" Cole lurched toward the door, and Jessica ran to catch up with him. "Count yourself out of my good graces, Jessica," Isabella called after her, "if you choose to leave with that troublemaker."

Jessica felt a flush of rage flame in her cheeks. She

paused at the threshold and straightened her shoulders, intending to hurl angry words at Isabella. Then she thought better of it. Her anger was useless against the woman, her energy better spent elsewhere. She took Cole's arm and pulled him into the hall.

They had gone only as far as the main hall near the front door when Shawn breezed into the room and called out to them. Jessica let her hands slide from Cole's elbow.

Shawn sidled up to Cole, slinking and garish in a panne velvet dress that looked like a set of cathouse drapes. Jessica felt embarrassed for her.

Cole gave her a stiff smile. "Hello, Shawn."

"Boring party, isn't it?" she asked, curling her lip. "I've never seen more old fogies in my entire life! I've been thinking of doing something drastic."

"Like what?" Jessica asked.

Shawn gave her a devilish smile. "Like taking charge of the music. I've got some CDs that would blow this party wide open."

"Well, why don't you get them?" Cole suggested smoothly as he slid his hand around Jessica's elbow. "I think it's a great idea."

"Yeah!" Shawn smiled and hurried up the stairs.

Cole retrieved Jessica's coat and then guided her out of the house. They trudged silently down the stairs, both absorbed in thoughts about Michael. When they reached the lawn, Jessica looked up to see a figure approaching them. She stared, and when her eyes adjusted to the darkness, she thought she recognized her father's shambling walk.

"Who's that?" Cole inquired.

Jessica swallowed in dismay, certain now of the drunken gait. "It's my dad."

Robert Ward insisted he wasn't drunk. He intended to go to the Cavanetti Christmas party and was arriving fashionably late as was his custom. Jessica was grateful she had intercepted him and spared him such a public humiliation, but she wished he would quit talking. Every slurred word wounded her. She didn't want even Cole to see him this way.

He was so drunk he couldn't stand up straight.

Cole reached for him to keep him from swaying. "Hold on there, Mr. Ward!"

"Damn driveway!" Robert mumbled. "Why don't they pave the damn thing? A man can lose his damn balance on all the damn gravel."

Jessica was grateful that the darkness hid her flush of shame. She took her father's arm. He had dressed in a tuxedo that was both rumpled and out of style. His bow tie tilted beneath his chin.

"Dad, come on. You're too late. The party's over."

"Is not. Look at the cars."

"Yes, but everybody's getting ready to leave. Let's go back and have a nightcap at the bungalow. You want to, Cole?"

"Cole? Who's Cole?" Robert squinted at Cole's face. "Thought you were Nick. Or are you Greg?"

"No." Cole smiled. "I'm Nick."

"Say, Nick." Robert swayed, and Cole kept him from falling. Robert patted his face. "Say, son, how's your dad?"

"He's okay, Mr. Ward."

"Good. He's eighty, you know."

"I know." Cole glanced at Jessica over her father's head. Jessica looked away, mortified.

"And I'm sixty-eight. Do I look sixty-eight to you, Greg?"

"You look fifty, if you look a day."

Robert guffawed and then stumbled backward. Cole and Jessica caught him and held him between them.

"Come on, Dad. Let's go home."

"The night's young, Jess. Young!" He hiccuped and lurched. Cole and Jessica each took an arm and nearly carried him back to the bungalow.

No one spoke. Robert was suddenly incoherent, and Jessica was tongue-tied with rage and shame. Cole strode forward, his face set with grimness.

Jessica opened the door of the bungalow, and Cole followed her into her father's bedroom. He helped put Robert on the bed but left Jessica to undress him. Jessica bent to the task, damning her father for his sudden interest in socializing. Why had he decided to attend a party this evening of all nights? He hadn't left the bungalow property for years. Surely now Cole would realize the truth: her father was an alcoholic. Bitter and heartbroken, Jessica hung the wrinkled tuxedo in the closet, lined his shoes in a neat row, and shut the closet door.

She made sure her father was well covered and closed the bedroom door behind her. She felt miserable. The entire evening had been an emotional debacle. She would never be able to face Isabella again, Michael Cavanetti was a prisoner in his own home, and Cole had seen her father plastered out of his mind. What could be worse? Jessica planned to fall into bed and cry herself to sleep.

She pulled off her coat, walked to the front closet to hang it up, and was surprised to find Cole standing in the living room. She paused, holding her coat in midair.

"Didn't you mention a nightcap?" he asked, holding up a decanter of wine.

"I thought you had left."

"I did. I got some seventy-seven Merlot from the guest-house."

"Oh." Jessica stuck a hanger in her coat and thrust it onto the rack.

"Do you have some glasses somewhere?"

"In the hutch in the dining room." She stumbled forward, wondering why Cole hadn't left in disgust at her father's behavior.

Cole found two goblets and returned to the living room. Jessica stood between the couch and the fireplace and watched him, numbed by the trauma of the evening. She saw him take the stopper from the decanter and pour the cranberry-colored wine into the goblets. He gave one to her.

"Cole—" she began, prepared to defend her father.

"I want your opinion, Jess," he interrupted. "Tell me what you think of this wine."

"What?" Jessica asked, wondering why he wasn't saying anything about her father.

"I want your opinion. Give it a swirl and a sniff, like I showed Lucy at the open house."

Wine tasting was preferable to discussing her father's alcoholism. Jessica stuck her nose into the glass.

"What do you smell?" Cole asked.

Jessica sniffed. Then she sniffed again.

"Well?"

"This is going to sound funny, but I smell tobacco."

Cole smiled. "Anything else?"

"Vanilla." She took a final sniff. "And some mint."

He sipped his wine and grinned at her over the rim of the goblet. "All right. Now take a swig."

She took a taste and swished it around in her mouth, hoping she remembered all the steps Cole had outlined. She breathed through her nose and analyzed the sensations the wine created on her tongue.

"How's it taste?" Cole inquired.

She swallowed. "It's sweet. Smooth. I like it." She looked at the glass thoughtfully. "It's like drinking claret velvet."

Cole let out a laugh and looked at the ceiling.

"What's so amusing?" she asked.

Cole's gaze sparkled at her, showering her with the glitter of his approval. "You've missed your calling, Jess. You'd make a helluva wine critic!"

"I would?"

"You've got quite a nose. I noticed it right off the other night."

Jessica looked at her glass, oddly gratified by his praise, even though she wished he would notice other features of her anatomy.

"Claret velvet," he mused, holding the goblet up to the light. "I've never thought of it before, but claret velvet describes Merlot perfectly."

"I've always liked the sound of claret velvet."

"Like in 'The Highwayman,'" Cole added. "A coat of the claret velvet, and breeches of brown doe-skin."

"They fitted with never a wrinkle," Jessica put in. "His boots were up to the thigh."

"And who was the highwayman after?" Cole mused, taking a sip of the Merlot. "Tess?"

"Bess, the landlord's daughter." Jessica was pleasantly surprised that Cole knew portions of one of her favorite poems. She had once recited it to him long ago and had assumed he wasn't listening at the time.

"Ah, yes. The landlord's black-eyed daughter, plaiting a dark red love knot into her long black hair." He paused, as if hearing the words for the first time. "Into her long black hair."

Cole's voice trailed off as he looked at Jessica's cloud of ebony hair. Jessica could not tear her gaze away from his face. He had a strange look in his eyes, as if he saw past her and deep within her simultaneously.

"So you remember that silly poem," she declared in an effort to break the spell.

"Sure." He blinked back to his senses. "I remember a lot, Jessica." He sipped his wine. "You'd be surprised."

Jessica fingered the stem of the wineglass, wanting to change the subject. His perusal of her hair had set her heart fluttering haphazardly in her chest. "So you're going to sue for custody of your father?"

"Hell, yes." He reached for the decanter of Merlot and held it out. "A bit more?"

"Please." She offered her glass, and he refilled it. Jessica took a drink, feeling the fingers of warmth spreading through her chest. She liked the Merlot even better than the Cabernet Sauvignon which Cosimo had given her.

"Cole, about my father . . ."

Cole put the decanter on the coffee table.

"He gets depressed during the holidays. Because of my mother, I suppose. Anyway, he always drinks too—"

"Jess." Cole raised his glass and interrupted her. "A toast."

She wondered at his words but raised her glass, thankful that he had curbed her lame explanation. He clinked the rims of their goblets.

"To bullshit," he toasted.

She blushed hotly and yanked her glass from his, but Cole had anticipated her reaction and twined his arm around hers, trapping her elbow with his forearm.

"Drink," he commanded, offering his glass to her lips.

She stared at him.

"Drink, Jessica." He tipped the rim upon her lips and watched as the blood-red wine poured into her mouth. She swallowed and then gazed in fascination as he drained the wine from her glass.

For a moment their arms remained entwined and their gazes locked, as they both realized that a strange form of communion had just occurred. Then Cole bent down and tasted her lips. His mouth was warm and gentle, almost as if he were asking permission to kiss her. Jessica froze. This was the moment she had dreamed of for years, the edge of the fantasy. What would happen if Cole did not like the way she kissed? Or worse yet, what would happen if Cole did not live up to her expectations? Sick with indecision, Jessica pulled away from his mouth.

"No more bullshit, okay?" Cole murmured. "Friends deserve better."

"What do you mean?" she breathed.

"Your father is an alcoholic, isn't he?"

She stepped back, knowing she couldn't avoid the truth any longer.

"Yes."

"That explains a lot of things," Cole replied. "How long has he been like that?"

"Years."

"And you've been hiding it, covering up for him all this time, haven't you?"

"What else could I do?" Jessica rubbed her arms. "There was no one to turn to for help."

"Why didn't you ever tell me, Jess? I'm your friend."

"Friend? You think you're my friend?" She shrank from him.

"Hell, yes."

"People keep in touch over the years if they're truly friends." Cole seemed surprised. "What is that supposed to mean?"

Jessica backed away from him, full of hurt and confusion as the shame of his rejection rushed back to her like a dark wind.

"Jess, what is that supposed to mean!"

"You—you talk of friendship," she blurted. "What about all the time that I—" She broke off, unable to tell him of the years she had carried a torch for him. "That I—"

"That you what?"

"Oh, forget it!" She turned away and hugged her chest. The wine was making her say more than she meant to divulge. Damn Niccolo Cavanetti and his 1977 Merlot. She pressed her lips together and glared at the floor as Cole came up behind her.

"Jess, would you open up a little? You're like a sphinx sometimes." He reached for her shoulders, but she shook him off.

"You can't just breeze into people's lives and expect them to jump into the huddle and play the game your way, Cole." She glared over her shoulder at him. "Am I speaking your language now?"

"Loud and clear."

"You expect to call the plays, throw the passes, and win the game, all on your own terms. And then you think you can just pick up, go to another town, and all your fans will be breathlessly waiting to worship you when you come back!"

Cole surveyed her in silence. Then he narrowed his eyes. "You're really sore about something, aren't you, Jess?"

"Yes! And you're so caught up in yourself and your own problems that you don't even know what it is!"

"So, this is going to be a guessing game, is it?"

"I thought you liked guessing games." She whirled to face him. "I thought you liked mysteries!"

"But I'm not a mind reader. That's the trouble with women. They think men should be able to read their incredibly convoluted minds."

"It's not incredibly convoluted. Anyone with a scrap of sensitivity would know what's bothering me. You just don't have what it takes to understand women."

"Obviously." He put his glass on the coffee table and straightened. "So, I haven't been a good enough friend over the years to merit friendship now. I take it there's some kind of statute of limitations on friendship that I didn't know about. When did my time run out, Jessica? Last year? Five years ago? Ten?"

"How about thirteen years ago, Cole? How about the night of your graduation party?"

He stared at her, and Jessica turned away, unable to face him any longer. Her cheeks burned, and tears scalded her eyes, but she refused to break down in front of him. She dropped her glass onto the table and stumbled out of the living room. Cole came after her, but she ran to her bedroom and slammed the door. She had said more than she ever intended to reveal to him, and she could not face the questions he would surely ask.

Cole knocked on her door. "Jess, come on!"

"Go away!"

"Come out of there and talk to me!"

Jess wiped the tears from her cheeks as she stood in the center of the room and listened to his impatient rapping.

"Jess!"

She covered her ears to block out his entreaties and fell onto her bed, weeping. Unfortunately, while she could plug her ears and close her eyes, there was nothing she could do to block him out of her heart.

Cole finally left the house. For a long while afterward, Jess lay on her bed while hot tears rolled into her pillow. She had no one to confide in, no one to tell her troubles to. She felt so alone that she ached inside.

As she wept, Jessica found herself imagining what she would say to Brother Cosimo if he were to ask her why she was crying. He might have scared her with his spellbinding the other night, but on the whole he had always been easy to talk to, and she felt as if he genuinely cared about her well-being. Then she found herself visualizing what Cosimo would look like sitting in the chair near the window, his robe full of shadows.

Jessica heaved a heavy sigh and rose on her elbow, deciding she might as well dress for bed. It was then she noticed a dark form in the chair, just as she had imagined.

17

Jessica scrambled to her feet, dashing the tears from her cheeks. "What are you doing here?" she demanded.

"I heard you crying." Cosimo rose.

She backed away. "Keep away from me!"

"I promise I will not lay a hand on you." He held his arms away from his body as if to assure her that he would not touch her. "I am sorry if I frightened you last night. It was not my intention."

She stared at him with bleary, burning eyes, wanting to believe him. Slowly his arms lowered.

"How did you get in here?" she questioned, tilting her head.

"Through the door. You were weeping so much, you did not hear me."

Jessica glanced at the door and wondered if someone could have walked into the room without her noticing.

Cosimo took a step toward her. "Tell me now, my lady of the night, what makes you weep?"

Jessica looked at the floor, trying to decide if she should say anything more this evening. What little she had told Cole had turned their nightcap into a fiasco. Still, Jessica felt a great need to spill her troubles out to someone, especially Cosimo. She breathed a heavy sigh and raised her head.

"I've never been able to open up to people, Cosimo. And now, when I want to open up, I can't."

"Why?"

"I guess I don't want people to know what I think, what I feel."

"And why is that?"

"When I was young I had to think twice about everything in relation to my father. I could never be natural or open about anything. Every step I took had to be guarded and thought through." Jessica fingered the tourmaline crystal at her throat. "I guess the lessons learned in childhood have become a habit, because now I can't do a single thing spontaneously."

"I see." Cosimo clasped his hands.

"I've always thought it was foolish and dangerous to open your heart to people."

"Why should it be?"

"Well, suppose they took advantage of your feelings, or thought you were silly or out of line."

"There is always the danger of that. But it would be a strange world, Jessica, if no one knew where the other person stood. If no one opened his heart, we would all live in darkness and fear."

Jessica nodded and looked away, fighting to keep her lips from trembling and the tears from flowing again.

"You are afraid of being thought a fool?" Cosimo asked gently.

Jessica nodded again.

"Then you will live in fear all your days, Jessica."

"I know." She brushed back her hair. "But it is so difficult for me, Cosimo."

"You were surprised by the sweetness of wine," he replied. "So may you be surprised by the sweetness of candor."

"But what if Cole is not what I want him to be? What if he doesn't want me as much as I want him? How will I ever know what he really feels for me?"

"You will not know, Jessica," Cosimo chuckled. "You cannot know these things when you suffer in isolation."

"I suppose you're right."

"You expect too much of yourself." Cosimo put his hands in the sleeves of his habit. "*Amare et sapere vix deo conceditur.*"

"And what does that mean?"

"To love and to be wise at the same time is scarcely possible even for a god."

Jessica could hear the smile in his voice, and the words brought a slight lift to her lips as well as to her spirit. She inclined her head to the monk. "Well said, sir."

"Unfortunately, I cannot take credit for the words. They belong to someone else. But the sentiment is mine."

He reached out for her, and Jessica raised her hand to meet his, unafraid now of what he might do. His hand was warm and strong, tanned and callused, and he squeezed her fingers gently.

"Open your heart to Niccolo," he urged. "What is the worst he can do?"

"Laugh?"

"Is it laughter of which you are truly afraid, Jessica, or something else?"

"I don't follow you."

He looked at her hand and lightly caressed the back of it with the broad plane of his thumb.

"Are you not afraid that he will desert you?"

Jessica froze. She stared at the darkness in the cowl.

"Deep down, my lady of the night, are you not afraid that Niccolo will leave you again?"

The truth struck her like a blow. Her mother had left her. In all the ways that mattered, her father had left her. Cole had left her, too. Dear God, but she had been lonely after Cole had left Moss Cliff. Yet she had never allowed herself to acknowledge her dependence on him. She had gone on as if nothing affected her, had pursued her career with a singleminded intensity born of the need to ignore the deep emotional gap in her life. No wonder she had never found fulfillment with other men. She had left her heart on Moss Cliff thirteen years ago.

Jessica pulled back, but Cosimo did not release her.

"You fear that if Niccolo does not love you, he will surely go away, and you will be alone again."

"No," she breathed.

"And you can't bear your loneliness any longer."

"No—"

"But you can't bring yourself to risk finding out whether you will have love or loneliness."

She shook her lowered head, swamped by the realization that she feared Cole's desertion more than anything else.

"Tell him how you feel, Jessica."

"I can't. It wouldn't be right anyway. He has Lucy."

"Are you certain?"

"No, but it's not something you ask!"

"So you will not fight for Niccolo's heart?"

Jessica raised her head. "What do you mean?"

"If you love him, you will fight for him. And for yourself. I'll wager you have not fought for anything for yourself in your entire life. For your father, certainly, and for other people, but not for Jessica Ward."

Jessica stared at him, speechless. He was right. She had learned never to expect anything from life. And with no expectations, she never made any demands.

"It is time for you to ask something of life, Jessica, to demand something for yourself for a change."

She lowered her head and was silent, too rattled to make a reply.

Cosimo sighed and enclosed her hand in both of his, and for a moment he simply caressed her skin while he stood like a dark tower before her. She was grateful for his presence and his words of advice. In all her years, she had never been able to lean on anyone, to confide in anyone, or to find comfort. His touch gave her hope and strength.

Jessica looked up at him. "Cosimo, how do you know me so well?"

"Oh"—he patted her hand and slowly released it—"I think we are old friends, you and I, Jessica."

"But how?"

"Perhaps beings are meant to cross paths on more than one occasion, and our paths have crossed before."

"Is that what you were getting at last night?"

"Yes. But you do not seem to remember the other path, so I will not press you about it again."

Jessica crossed her arms, unwilling to admit to her flash of knowledge about Cosimo.

"I must go." Cosimo inclined his head. "Good night, Jessica."

"Good night. And thank you, Cosimo. I—I feel much better now, having talked to you."

"I am glad."

"Will I see you tomorrow?"

He paused at the door. "If you so desire."

"Cosimo?"

"Yes?"

"How did you get to be so wise?"

He chuckled. "I have had plenty of time to think, my lady."

Jessica spent the following morning cleaning house and baking cookies, keeping her hands busy so her thoughts would not linger on Cole. She thought about her paper instead, about how she would prove, based on the paintings and frescoes she had studied and on her knowledge of the heavens, that a comet would pass the earth in thirteen years. She had only six days until she left for California, and she had written less than five pages.

She pulled the last pan of molasses crinkles out of the oven and turned off the heat. The chewy brown cookies were a Cavanetti recipe, one she knew Cole particularly liked. She slid the warm cookies off the sheet and took the pan to the sink. After she had tidied the kitchen, she took a plate of cookies to the guesthouse, hoping to explain her behavior of the previous evening.

The cottage was surrounded by cars and reporters beneath a canopy of umbrellas. Jessica weaved through the crowd and the puddles, wondering what was going on. Had

Cole done something rash again? She craned her neck to see over the shoulder of a man with a video camcorder. On the porch of the guesthouse were Cole, Lucy, and a graying man with a florid face. Cole's face was a blank mask, but Jessica saw the telltale flatness that covered the sparkle in his eyes when he was upset. Lucy stood at his side, a worried expression pinching her open face.

"What's going on?" Jessica asked the man with the camcorder.

He turned slightly to see who had addressed him. "Cole Nichols has just been told that he's out of the play-offs."

"What?" Jessica gasped. She knew enough about football to realize that being out of the play-offs would devastate Cole. She lowered the plate of cookies.

"Who's the man with the gray hair?"

"That's Tom McNarren, the Bulls' coach."

Jessica watched the coach wave off further questions and step down from the porch. Reporters swarmed around him, but he shook his head, jammed on a hat, and pushed through the crowd to his car. Jessica tried to get to the porch, but the reporters surging in the opposite direction jostled her backward. Helpless, she watched Cole disappear into the guesthouse.

Once the door slammed, the reporters began straggling out of the yard. Jessica glared at them as she approached to knock on the door.

"Lucy?" she called. "It's Jessica."

After a moment the door opened a crack.

"Oh, Jessica." Lucy opened it wider. "Come in. I thought you were one of those bastards coming to bother Cole."

Jessica slipped into the house, and Lucy quickly closed the door behind her.

"A reporter told me that Cole won't be starting in the play-offs. Is that true?"

Lucy nodded. "He won't be playing at all."

"How is Cole taking the news?"

"Oh, the usual. He flew into a rage." She looked over her shoulder, then back at Jessica, and she lowered her voice.

"At least he didn't have one of his fainting spells. That would have ruined his chances forever. The coach thinks he's too old, that he should retire."

"Retire? He's strong as an ox!"

"Tell that to Coach McNarren, why don't you?" Lucy shook her head and ambled to the couch. She picked up a set of ankle weights and a towel, which she slung over her shoulder. "I just don't see why he can't give Cole one more chance. This will probably be Cole's last year, and here he's going to be on the bench. What a way to end a career."

"Where is he?"

"He went to his room to change. Said he wants to go jogging."

"Do you think he'd mind if I knocked on his door?"

"I'm sure you wouldn't bother him."

Jessica walked down the short hall to the master bedroom and rapped on the door. "Cole?" she said softly.

No one answered. The door was slightly ajar, so she pushed it open and stepped inside. The room was dark, the bed unmade. Jessica stepped around a pile of athletic shoes and sweats. Then she saw Cole slumped in a chair, his head in his hands. He didn't look up when she repeated his name.

She hesitated, unsure whether she should stay or leave him alone. It would certainly be easier to go, for she didn't know what to say to ease his pain. Had the tables been turned, however, she would have wanted comfort at such a time. Still carrying the cookies, she slowly approached him and stood, gazing down at his slumped shoulders.

"Cole, I'm sorry."

He did not look up. His hands were jammed into his hair, forcing up glossy tufts between his fingers.

Jessica felt helpless. What else could she say? Perhaps she should have stayed away. Maybe he was simply sick to death of people bothering him and wanted to be alone.

Lacking words to express her sympathy, she lay her hand upon his shoulder in a gesture of comfort and support. She heard his breathing pause. Slowly she slid her palm to the base of his neck and raised her thumb to touch his jaw in a light caress.

"They're fools, Cole," she murmured. "They just don't understand."

Finally Cole pulled his hands out of his hair and looked up. "My career is over, Jess."

"It can't be."

"It would take a miracle to convince the coach to put me back in." He sighed. "And I don't believe in miracles much anymore."

"I do," she replied. "At least I'm learning to. You must, too."

"Why should I?"

"Because once you lose faith, you lose hope."

"You're certainly singing a different tune than you did last night." He attempted a halfhearted smile.

"I've been doing a lot of thinking." She withdrew her hand and held out the cookies. "Here's a peace offering."

He looked at the plate and raised his eyebrows. "Molasses crinkles?"

"The same."

"You're kidding!" He pulled off the plastic wrap while Jessica sat down on the bed behind her, happy to see his attitude improving.

He offered her a cookie and then stuffed one into his mouth. "Thanks, Jess," he said around the mouthful. "I love these."

"I know. I remember things, too." She nibbled at the cookie in her hand.

Cole sat back in the chair and surveyed her as he ate another from the plate in his lap. "Do you know how long it's been since I had home-baked cookies, Jess? Probably ten years." He put the plate on the nightstand. "These are great. Just like I remember from the old days."

Jessica rose. "Cole, I'm sorry about last night. I—"

"Oh, forget it—"

"No, listen." She held up a hand. "I take back what I said. I was being mean. I want to be friends. I've always wanted to be your friend, Cole." Remembering Cosimo's advice on candor, she took a deep breath and plunged onward. "Ever since I was a little girl, I thought you were the strongest, most handsome, kindest boy I knew."

He stopped chewing and stared at her.

"Even when I was in high school, I thought you were so much better than the boys I dated." She clasped her hands in front of her. "I wish you would have looked at me then, Cole. Just once." Her voice trailed off to a whisper as Cole rose to his full height.

"Goddamn." His voice was husky with surprise. "You never let on."

"You never looked."

"How could I?" He clenched his jaw as if holding back his own flood of frustration. "Who was I, poor Niccolo Cavanetti, to look at rich Miss Jessica Ward?"

"What—what do you mean?"

"I was nothing but a field hand, Jessica. I saw the way you lived, and I knew the way we lived. I never had a decent haircut or the right clothes. Hell, I couldn't even talk the way you talked."

"But I didn't care!"

"I did." He turned away from her and looked up at the ceiling.

She gazed at his broad back, realizing for the first time that his own pride, not disdain for her, had kept him from approaching her.

"Then you did notice me," she murmured.

Cole nodded. "I used to look at the cheerleaders and pick one out who reminded me of you—a snooty, exotic-looking, cool one—and play my heart out to impress her, to change that coolness to admiration."

"Did you?"

"Sometimes. But afterward I'd find out that the coolness was not what it seemed, and neither was the cheerleader."

"Cole, I—" Jessica broke off, stunned by his confessions. Never in her wildest dreams had she considered that the results of candor would be this illuminating.

"And now I'm a disowned, has-been football player, Jess. Not exactly what you'd call a screaming success."

"Cole." She wrapped her arms around him, hugging his big shoulders and pressing her cheek to his back, as she had longed to do ever since he had returned to Moss Cliff. She spread her fingers over the muscles of his chest, closing her eyes against the pleasure she felt in touching him. "Oh, Cole!"

She felt him stiffen, and she squeezed her arms more tightly around his torso. "You're my friend, Cole, regardless of all that. You're my very best friend, and you always will be."

"Don't, Jess!" He pried her hands from his chest and stepped away. "I don't want your Goddamn pity!"

She dropped her arms, flushing with shame. She'd made a mistake. She had spilled out her feelings, and he had refused her. Cosimo's advice hadn't helped at all. "You think I told you all this out of pity?"

"Why else?"

"Maybe because I care about you!"

Slowly he turned to face her. "Listen, Jess, I know you mean well. You want to say something that will make me feel better. But don't give me this crap about friendship. You didn't want my friendship last night. So why now? Nothing's changed since then, except that my life is crumbling around me."

"Cole!"

"I'm not a charity case, Goddammit. You think cookies and kind words will bring my father's health back? My career back?" He turned away. "Why don't you just leave me the hell alone!"

"Okay, I will, you—you—egotistical idiot!" She strode to the door and yanked it open. Then she glared at him over her shoulder. "You think you're the only one with problems? Welcome to the real world, Niccolo!"

Cole grimaced as the door slammed behind her. The real world? What did Jessica Ward know of the real world? She had no idea what it was like for an athlete to face the bitter end of his career, benched for the rest of the season and shamed by the newspapers for something he had never done. Real world. He snorted in disgust. What did she know about life, when all she'd ever seen was from the small end of a telescope in her quiet career at a university? How would she feel if she had to face retirement at the age of thirty-five, never to know the rush of victory again, never to hear his fans screaming his name?

Cole grabbed his robe off the back of a chair and strode to the bathroom. He had tried to fight the blackouts, but they had grown worse. His coach was only doing what was right for the team. Yes, Cole was on a downhill slide—his pride along with his career. And he'd be damned if he'd take Jessica Ward with him.

He knew he shouldn't have yelled at her like that, but her embrace had nearly overpowered his sense of pride. He had almost succumbed to her words, had almost believed that she wanted him. And why would anyone want plain old Niccolo Cavanetti?

He didn't want her pity. He wanted her love and respect. And nobody loved a loser.

18

Cole followed a young lad up a winding stone staircase that led to a bedchamber high in a tower. He climbed ever higher, his legs and hips tired from riding for two days and nights. It had been ten years since he had ridden a horse, his battle days long past. Though he had enjoyed being astride the handsome gelding, he was suffering now and knew that in the morning his muscles would be even more stiff and painful. Before retiring for the evening he would apply one of the liniments in his bag. But first he was to be shown his patient.

He had been working in the winery when he was summoned by the abbot and asked to make this journey. Over the years he had lived at the monastery, Cole had acquired a considerable knowledge of plants and healing, and his talent for treating wounds and sickness was well known in the area. Usually he did not travel more than a few miles from the monastery to treat his patients and was soon back in the safe seclusion of his winery and pharmacy. But this journey had taken him far from the Benedictine brothers to a castle in the Alps, to a land of rock and snow and forbidding cliffs. Cole had never seen the fortress before and did not know the lord who ruled it. Apparently the overlord was a duke who found his southern holdings more to his liking during the fall and winter.

He shivered involuntarily while the boy knocked on a heavy wooden door at the top of the endless stone steps.

The door was opened by an old woman on whose face Cole saw lines of grief. Her eyes were red with weeping.

"Ah, brother, you are too late!"

"Too late?" he repeated, disappointed.

"My lady is gone!" she exclaimed, burying her face in her apron while she hunched away from him.

"When?" Cole followed her into the chamber.

"Moments ago. If only you had come sooner! Oh, Mother of Mary! She is gone!"

Cole strode past the fire blazing at the hearth. He could see a woman lying on a huge bed fashioned of carved walnut spirals hung with green velvet. There were no sewing frames, no trunks of clothes, no pile of cast-off slippers, and no musical instruments in the room, evidence that the chamber was not used often.

He hurried to the woman in the bed and stared down at her. She was middle-aged, gaunt, and pale but still very beautiful. Her head was bound in strips of linen and her delicate white hands lay crossed on the quilt that covered her torso, positioned as if she were prepared for burial. Cole put his hand on her forehead.

"She is still warm."

"But she isn't breathing! I heard her take her last breath! I heard her death rattle!"

Cole's heart beat like a drum in his chest, but his outward movements were calm and deliberate. He drew off his bag of medicinal supplies and put it on the bed. He reached inside for a leather pouch full of crumbled pennyroyal. Taking a pinch from the sack, he rubbed it between his thumb and fingers and held it to the woman's nose. The sharp smell had no effect on her.

"What happened to her?" he demanded of the old woman.

"She fell from a horse. Hit her head. She hasn't opened her eyes since."

"When was the fall?"

"A fortnight ago, good brother."

"That long?"

"Aye."

"And she hasn't eaten or drunk since then?"

"Nay! I tried, but—"

"She's probably died of starvation and thirst!" Cole's voice was sharp with exasperation. Then he turned to his patient, sorry for his sudden burst of temper. The old woman had wilted at his harsh words. She was grieving enough. There was no need to heap guilt upon grief.

He had only one recourse left, a treatment he had seen performed in the Holy Land by an Arab physician. He would try to blow the breath of life back into the dead woman. He opened her mouth and pressed down her tongue with his right thumb, tipping back her head at the same time to open the passage of her throat. Then he pinched her nostrils, took a breath, and bent over her. The old woman stood aside, regarding the process with concern and horror that anyone would kiss the dead.

Cole breathed steadily, careful not to injure the woman. She was delicate and small, and her capacity for air would be much less than his. For minutes on end he breathed into her, worrying that she wouldn't begin to breathe on her own, afraid that he had forgotten a crucial step in the treatment. Sweat broke out on his forehead from sheer concentration, but he refused to give up, knowing he would have to accept her death if the treatment did not work.

Then he felt a weak convulsion, and the woman coughed. Cole hung above her, tense with hope as he watched for further signs of life. His patient coughed again.

"God save us!" the old woman shrieked, running out of the room, her skirts flapping at her feet. She slammed the chamber door behind her.

Cole ignored her outburst and plunged his hand into his bag, locating a glass tube and a small bottle that contained a strong concoction of distilled wine. He drew some of the liquid into the tube and held it to the woman's lips, letting it drizzle down her throat. The shock of the strong spirits was enough to wake anyone from the sleep of death, and the sweetness of the wine would immediately revive her if she had any shred of life left in her. She sputtered and breathed more deeply but still did not open her eyes. Cole followed the strong draught with water from an urn nearby. She gulped down the water like a hungry bird. Cole silently thanked Giovanna for teaching him the technique of feeding someone through a dropper. Her technique might give this woman another chance at life.

Nearly an hour passed as he held her in a sitting position in the circle of his right arm, her head propped against his chest. He had not held a woman to his chest since Giovanna, and the sensation of her slight body was both precious and heartrending to him. Patiently, carefully, he continued to feed her with the tube until she could take no more. Then he simply held her against his body, knowing she should be kept as warm as possible.

Her breathing continued in shallow but steady aspirations. Cole was hopeful that she would survive, though she might never awaken if something had happened to her brain during the fall from the horse.

Curious to see the extent of her head injury, Cole unwound the bandage from her head, which loosed an abundance of wavy black hair. Reminded of Giovanna's soft, raven-black curls, Cole was distracted for an instant while his old heartache flared. He forced his thoughts back to the present and gently lay his patient upon her pillow so he could inspect her skull for the wound. He found a lump behind her right ear, which he checked for festering.

The wound must have been considerable, because even after fourteen days there remained some swelling. But the skin had not been broken, and there was no sign of blood loss or poisoning. For good measure, he ran his sensitive hands down her neck, checking the bones for any injury that might have gone unnoticed by the others. While he felt her neck, he glanced at the woman, his first real perusal of her face since her head had been unbound. How like Giovanna she appeared with her cloud of hair cascading over the pillow. Cole drew back some of the black hair that had fallen over her cheek and stared at the gaunt profile and delicate jawline thus exposed. For a moment he hesitated, not believing his eyes.

Was he seeing visions? Was he in some kind of dream? Had he traveled too long without rest? Sweet Jesus, this sleeping woman *was* Giovanna! The realization struck the strength from his legs. He sank onto the side of the bed, stunned. What was she doing here? What stroke of fate had brought them together after all these years? A cool wave of horror passed over him as he realized he had seen her dead. His mouth went dry. He swallowed and turned to her, knowing something akin to a miracle had just taken place in this tower high in the Alps.

"Giovanna!" he whispered in amazement. With a trembling hand he caressed the side of her face. Ah, God, what if she had died? What if he had not saved her? Then dark dread clutched him as a frightening thought burst inside his head. Good Lord, what if he couldn't keep her alive?

A bolt of determination shot through him, sending him to his feet. He couldn't lose a moment gawking at her. He must use every precious minute to heal her. He wouldn't sleep, he wouldn't rest until he brought Giovanna back to her senses. Just as she had kept a vigil at his side in the Holy Land, so would he remain with her until he brought life back to her limbs and into her eyes. More than anything he wanted to look into her eyes again.

"Giovanna," he whispered, bending near her ear. "Ah, Giovanna, 'tis your baron come to rescue you, to fight for you."

She made no movement, and her silence broke his heart. He caressed her cheek tenderly as tears blurred his vision.

"Giovanna, I am here. And I will not leave until you are well."

He couldn't resist the temptation to kiss her. Lightly, reverently, he touched his mouth upon hers and breathed in the blessed rose-scented perfume that lingered in her hair.

Jessica hurried back to the bungalow, stepping mindlessly through mud puddles, fuming about what had just happened between her and Cole. He had told her to leave him alone. He might as well have slapped her in the face. His damn pride had blinded him to the truth. She didn't pity him. She loved him! Why couldn't he see that? Jessica was so intent on her thoughts that she didn't notice the brown sedan parked in the driveway until she had almost reached the porch steps.

A heavyset man rose from the bannister and met her at the top of the steps.

"Detective Turner," Jessica blurted, taken by surprise.

"Afternoon, Miss Ward."

"Good afternoon. How are you?"

"Could be better. Like to get this case solved before Christmas." He reached into his rumpled trench coat and pulled something out. "Got a search warrant here." He handed it to her for inspection. "Like to look around the grounds some more."

"Why?" Jessica gave a small laugh. What could the Ward property have to do with a murder case?

"Got to check out everything, Miss Ward. Just got done touring the winery." He reached into his jacket again and pulled out a plastic bag, which he held in front of her face.

"Ever see these before, Miss Ward?"

Jessica looked at the contents of the bag—a pair of brown metal-framed glasses. She made no sign that she recognized them as Cole's.

"Where'd you find those?" she asked.

"Just answer the question, Miss Ward."

"No, I don't think I've seen them before."

Detective Turner studied her for a long moment before he replaced the bag in his coat pocket. He pulled out his notebook and stubby pencil.

"What do you know of that quarterback staying in your guesthouse?"

"You mean Cole?" Jessica pulled her jacket more tightly around her torso.

"Yeah."

"He's a friend. I've known him since I was a little girl."

"Then you must know that he wears glasses."

"Well, yes, sometimes, but—"

"Isabella Cavanetti swears the glasses in the bag are his."

"They could be." Jessica shrugged. "He wears contacts most of the time, so I'm not really sure."

Detective Turner wrote something in his notebook and then squinted at Jessica. "You say you know this Cole Nichols. Has he ever acted . . . strange?"

"What do you mean?"

"I've heard he blacks out. Can't remember even fainting."

Jessica felt a sense of dread as she realized the direction of the detective's questioning. Could he be considering Cole as a suspect in the murders? Impossible! Yet why was he questioning her about Cole? And where had the glasses come from?

"Has he ever blacked out in your presence, Miss Ward?"

"Yes, but only for an instant. Then he was as good as new, as if nothing had happened. I think his blackouts have been blown out of proportion by the press."

The detective took more notes. "Do you know where Mr. Nichols was on the evening of Thursday, December nineteenth?"

"Two days ago?" Jessica tried to remember. Between her father, Cosimo, Michael, and Cole, so much had been going on that she had trouble keeping track of time. Yet as she thought back, she remembered that Thursday had been the day she had gone to the Cavanettis to discuss the lease with Isabella and Frank. And that was the evening Cole had roared away in his car, furious at Isabella for bringing the Mafia to St. Benedict. Her feeling of dread deepened. "I—I—don't remember."

Jessica lurched toward the door of the bungalow. Detective Turner's puffy eyes watched her, making her nervous.

"Was he with you?"

"No."

He snapped his notebook shut and stuffed it into his pocket. "Thank you, Miss Ward." He turned to begin his search.

Jessica touched his sleeve. "You don't think Cole has anything to do with that murder in the park, do you? He couldn't possibly be involved!"

"What makes you so sure, Miss Ward?"

"He's—he's just not a murderer!"

"Mrs. Cavanetti thinks otherwise. Says he loses his temper and strikes people. And there's that woman in Philadelphia, claims he assaulted her."

"No, I don't believe it. Not Cole."

"Well, Miss Ward, sometimes folks can surprise you. I've seen it all, and every once in a while I still get surprised."

Detective Turner found nothing during his search, or at least he didn't reveal any findings to Jessica. The minute he left, she ran over to the guesthouse to warn Cole and was told by Lucy that he had gone into town.

Worried, Jessica called Maria, but their conversation did little to ease her fears. Maria wailed a long string of Italian before Jessica calmed her down enough to talk sense. Apparently, Isabella had slandered Cole to the police detective, telling lies, giving the wrong impression of Cole's character. Maria was beside herself with worry. Jessica tried to reassure her, even though her own fears nearly choked her.

Then Maria went on to explain how Michael Cavanetti hadn't stopped calling for Niccolo since the Christmas party. To make things worse, Shawn and Isabella were fighting over something that Shawn had stolen from Isabella. The entire house was in an uproar. Jessica comforted Maria, assuring her that Cole was innocent and that no one was going to pin a murder on him, no matter what Isabella said. Cole would get custody of his father soon, too. All Maria had to do was hold on for a while longer.

Feeling none too confident, Jessica hung up the phone and grabbed her jacket. She needed to get away. She drove through the mist and fog rolling across Moss Cliff and headed down the hill toward the nearest grocery store.

Jessica shopped all afternoon, far longer than she had intended. She bought Christmas presents and some new clothes for her father. Everywhere she went she saw newspaper headlines about Cole Nichols being replaced as quarterback of the hottest football team in the country. One of the papers displayed a picture of him. She had never seen Cole in uniform before, and she peered more closely. Great body, of course, but the shadow of his helmet obscured his features.

She had no desire to face her father's early-evening drunkenness, so she caught a quick dinner and sat through a movie to put off returning home. By the time she drove up to Moss Cliff, it was quite dark and snowing lightly. The road was slick, and she had to take the curves slowly and avoid using the brakes. She rolled to a stop in front of the bungalow and began carrying in her purchases, glad she was wearing sneakers instead of her slick-soled black boots.

She hoisted the last bag out of the trunk and closed the lid. As she straightened, she saw a dark figure slip behind a tree near the guesthouse. Jessica froze. For a moment she stood near the car, the volume of her senses turned up to high, listening for the smallest sound, watching for the slightest movement. She scanned the bushes near the cottage and saw the shadow move down the slope toward the river. The figure was dressed in a long, dark garment. Was it Cosimo? Was it Cole? Was it the escaped prisoner?

Jessica didn't know what to do. She felt an urgent need to follow the person down the hill, to discover what was going on, to try to help clear Cole's name. But it would be stupid for her to go alone. What if the figure was the convict, Rogers? What could she do to defend herself against a murderer? But if she didn't move soon, whoever it was would be so far ahead that she would lose sight of him in the darkness.

Wildly, Jessica glanced around. Cole's Jag wasn't parked nearby, so he wasn't home to help. Her father couldn't help either. He was probably passed out in the family room. There were no guns in the house, no weapons with which to defend herself. But Jessica knew she had to go after the figure, regardless.

As she dropped the groceries on the porch, she noticed the yellow can at the top of the bag. Oven cleaner. Jessica picked up the aerosol can and smiled. One spray of caustic oven cleaner to the face and a man might think twice about assaulting her. It was better than nothing. She popped off the lid and held the slender container in her right hand as she loped over the yard to the guesthouse.

Jessica rounded the corner of the cottage and ran down the trail. She could see the person ahead of her, walking steadily and carrying a bundle in his arms. A wave of fear passed over her, chilling the sheen of perspiration on her skin. Could that bundle contain a body? What was she getting herself into? She could see the garment better now that she was closer, and she was certain the figure wore a monk's habit and cowl. Could it be Cosimo? She wished she could call out to him, but she knew that if the figure was not Cosimo, she would be placing herself in mortal danger. Better to play it safe.

Once or twice she stumbled in the darkness. Luckily, however, she did not make a sound, and the figure was unaware he was being followed. Jessica trailed at a distance of about a hundred feet, picking her way through the vineyard. She was surprised when the robed figure did not pass over the bridge that led to the bog. Instead, he followed a path that turned toward the cliffs above the blue-gray waters of Puget Sound. Jessica shivered, reluctant to continue. The trail ahead was shrouded by rotting alders, impenetrable thickets of crab apple, and blackberry brambles twelve feet high. It was much darker and much more dangerous than the vineyard.

The figure strode on, however, unaware of her presence

or her dilemma. Soon he would vanish in the darkness and mist, and Jessica would never know his destination or his identity. An image of Cole's picture in the newspaper flashed into her thoughts. She had to help him. If the figure ahead of her was the convict, she had to find out where he was hiding. If she didn't help Cole, she knew she would see another article in the paper, an article accusing Cole Nichols of murder. She had to plunge onward. Gripping the oven cleaner even more tightly than before, she stepped forward.

The trail wasn't uphill or the pace hurried, but Jessica's breath came fast and hard by the time they arrived at the edge of the cliff. For nearly a half hour she had trailed the robed figure, concentrating on every step so as not to make a sound. The effort had frayed her nerves and exhausted her. Yet so far she had not been discovered. She crouched near a huge cedar stump while the monk slung his burden over his shoulder and bent slightly near a pile of rocks. Then he disappeared.

Jessica jumped to her feet. Where had he gone?

Carefully she advanced, shaking the can of oven cleaner to prime it for spraying in case the figure accosted her. She held it out like a gun as she stepped toward the pile of rocks. Straining, she peered around the largest boulder and felt a draft in her hair. Air flowed from the rock pile, and she could hear footsteps echoing in the distance. She eased around the boulders and saw a black hole large enough to creep through without having to drop to her hands and knees. A cave!

For a moment she listened to the footfalls inside. They were getting fainter and fainter. How far into the hill did the cave go? Then she smelled smoke and knew a torch or a fire had been lit. She crept forward into the opening, surprised to find steps fashioned from stone. With one hand trailing the passage wall, she descended, gradually realizing the opening was not a cave but a steep stairway leading to the bottom of the cliff. But what was at the bottom?

Each step she took brought her closer to the smell of smoke and the dim light at the bottom of the dark tunnel.

She pressed close to the wall as she arrived at the foot of the stairs, hoping she would not be seen. Fortunately, the light source was not powerful, and most of the stairs were shrouded in shadow. Her jeans and jacket blended in well.

Jessica craned her neck. She had descended to a huge cavern, lit by a single torch burning in a sconce opposite the stairs. The figure was busy lighting another and affixing it to the wall. Jessica turned the other way and saw a shimmer of water. The cavern opened onto the beach. In all the years she had come to Moss Cliff, she had never known about this cave above the beach, probably because the opening was small and at least five feet from the ground. High tide most likely blocked the opening altogether and sent water rushing into the cavern. Torchlight suddenly glimmered in tide pools near her feet, validating her theory.

She turned her gaze back to the figure, who picked up his bundle and walked into another chamber to the right, taking a torch with him. Jessica pushed away from the wall and crept across the cavern floor, careful to step only on stable rocks and to avoid the tide pools, lest she alert the monk with noise.

Just as she had gained the doorway of the second chamber, she put her foot down on something that moved. Jessica scrambled sideways, biting back a scream of alarm as a huge crab reared up and skittered over her other foot. Jessica lost her balance and fell backward, losing her grip on the can of oven cleaner. With a bump and a clang and a splash, it bounced into a pool of water as Jessica fell on her rump.

Jessica froze at the sound. She heard footsteps running toward her and looked up to see the dark figure burst through the passageway.

19

"My lady!"

Jessica wilted. She threw back her head and laughed, shaking with relief, while Cosimo stood above her in surprise. He reached down to help her to her feet.

"Oh, Cosimo!" she exclaimed, welcoming the warmth of his hand. "Thank God it's you!"

"Who did you think it was?"

"That convict—Rogers." She brushed off the seat of her jeans.

"The murderer?"

"Yes!"

"Why would you think I was a murderer?"

Jessica quickly explained what she had seen upon her arrival at the bungalow and her reasons for following him. "I think the police are beginning to suspect Cole in some way," she added.

"Niccolo? Impossible."

"That's what I say. But apparently they found his glasses in the bog. They wouldn't tell me where." She brushed the dirt from her palms. "I'm frightened, Cosimo. Sometimes the press and the police can crucify an innocent person, just to satisfy the public, just to prove that they're doing their jobs. Cole is a prime target for them right now."

"This is very bad," Cosimo mused. "Very bad for St. Benedict."

"Very bad for Cole, for goodness sake! Forget the winery, Cosimo."

"I can't." He turned to her, his voice firm but gentle. "I am the guardian, remember?"

"But what has Cole to do with all of this? What did his father mean the other night when he pointed to Cole and said 'leg'?"

"You spoke to Michael Cavanetti?"

"Briefly. He's very upset about something, but he can't talk very well. He said something about you, too. And then something about Frank not being chosen. What does it all mean?"

"He said that to you?"

"To Cole and to me." She tried to see into the cowl, damning the shadows that hid his face. "If you're the guardian, Cosimo, you must know something. You must know what's going on."

He turned away as if to avoid her questions, but Jessica planted herself in his path.

"Cosimo!"

"Leave this to me, Jessica."

"What do you mean? What can you do?"

"I can do plenty."

"What, put a spell on Detective Turner?" She crossed her arms. "I've been thinking about your sudden appearance here after a long absence, about Cole's arrival, the coinciding dates. I don't know how, but you're connected to Cole, aren't you? You haven't been here since Cole left thirteen years ago, have you?"

Cosimo was silent. Darkly silent. Jessica felt a prick of fear but did not back away. She was too intent on learning the truth.

"I won't have you sacrifice Cole," she declared. "He's not to be a sacrifice, Cosimo!"

"He won't be. It is imperative that he remain at St. Benedict. Why do you think I have urged you to reveal your love to him? So he will stay here at St. Benedict, marry you, and continue the tradition."

Jessica closed her mouth, surprised.

"I am the guardian, Jessica. The guardian. I must place that duty above all else. Even above my own desire."

"What desire?"

"My heart's desire," he replied. Then he hurled the phrase up to the ceiling of the cavern in a wail of want and need. "My heart's desire!"

Desire. Desire. Desire.

Jessica stumbled backward, awed by the raw pain that tore from his breast. She watched him slowly lower his head and then saw his shoulders droop.

"Cosimo . . ." she began, wanting to reach for him but half afraid that he would lash out at her.

"Do you know how I suffer, my lady?" he whispered. "When you speak of your love for Niccolo, when I counsel you in affairs of the heart? Are you aware that I have a heart just as real as yours?"

"As real as mine?" she countered. "How can you? You're a—"

"Yes! What am I, Jessica?" He whirled to face her. "What am I? I am not a spirit. I am not a ghost!" He reached out, and, before she could pull away, he snatched her hand. "Ghosts cannot touch, ghosts are not made of flesh as I am." He raised her hand to the darkness beneath his cowl. Jessica watched in fascinated alarm, afraid of what lay in the shadows. "Ghosts cannot kiss the hands of beautiful women."

Jessica felt warm, tender lips upon the back of her hand. She felt the ridge of his teeth and the moist heat of his breath as he whispered a name against her skin. Jessica swallowed and did not pull away, recognizing the depths of Cosimo's suffering.

"I am a man, Jessica. A man who has loved only one woman in his lifetime. But that woman was never his. And now he knows that she never shall be his. In the great river of time, she shall never be his."

"Cosimo, what are you talking about!"

"I am talking about you, my lady." He released her hand. "You. You who cannot remember her ugly left-handed baron."

Baron. Baron. Baron.

The word seemed to echo through the cavern. Jessica looked around wildly, as if she could see the word swirling in the air. An odd sensation settled over her as the words died in the distance. She did remember a baron. She did remember the touch of Cosimo's lips and the sound of his voice. The vague memory tugged at her thoughts.

"I hoped you would remember me, or at least remember my voice. But, alas, I was wrong. You remember nothing. Perhaps I overrated the depth of a lady's love for me."

"I'm sorry, Cosimo."

He shrugged.

"I wish I could remember. I'm certain whoever this lady was, she loved you."

"The lady was you, Jessica."

"But I am here in the twentieth century. She was in the twelfth."

"She is somewhere within you—a memory, a sensation. You simply do not remember."

"I would if I could, Cosimo. Please believe me. I think you are a wonderful man. You have taught me so much. But my heart belongs to Cole. It has always belonged to Cole. Surely you know that."

He shrugged again and sighed.

"Come." He held out his hand. "I will take you back."

They returned up the stone stairs and walked single file down the path to the vineyard, Cosimo in front and Jessica following. She kept her gaze on his back, worrying about him, her heart aching for him, and wondering what his connection was to Cole. Somehow that connection was important, and she knew she must discover the link between the two men.

They trudged up the hill toward the guesthouse, at a slower pace because of the grade. Jessica's shoes were soaked, her hair was matted with wet snow, and her hands were blocks of ice. She felt miserable, not only because of Cole but because of Cosimo. She should tell him that she had remembered a wisp of the past, but she was afraid to let him know, worried that he would try to hypnotize her again.

As they came up to the guesthouse, a movement caught Jessica's eye. She glanced at the rear of the cottage, where a small veranda had been built outside the master bedroom. Jessica saw the veranda door open and someone slip out of the house—someone with light tips on her dark hair. Stunned, Jessica gaped at Shawn as the young woman buttoned her coat and scampered down the walk and around to the front of the house. Shawn hadn't noticed their presence.

Jessica felt a hand on her shoulder and jumped.

"Pardon, my lady," Cosimo said softly. "I did not mean to startle you."

Jessica couldn't speak. She was too shocked at the sight of Shawn slipping out of Cole's bedroom.

"Jessica, it is not what it seems," Cosimo began.

"Not what it seems?" She turned on him. "Why are you suddenly protecting Cole? To save the winery?"

"It is not that."

"Shawn can have children. Why not let *her* and Cole carry on the grand tradition!"

Cosimo took both her shoulders and held her tightly while she struggled, overcome by the pain of betrayal.

"Jessica, hear me!" he commanded. "Do not doubt Niccolo!"

"I just saw his sister-in-law sneak out of his bedroom. Don't you think that's a bit odd?"

"Nothing happened between them, believe me."

"How do you know? Can you see through walls, too?" She struggled. She wanted to run away. She wanted to fling herself on her bed and cry. How could Cole take Shawn and not her? She tried to wrench free. "Let me go, Cosimo, let me go!"

His hands clenched harder until she stopped struggling

and stared at him in alarm. He had no intention of releasing her. His big hands were strong, and there was no way she could break his hold.

"Jessica, *you* belong to St. Benedict—not Shawn and not Isabella."

"Cosimo!"

"You must trust me, Jessica."

"Trust? I don't trust anyone! Least of all you, with your secrets, with your hidden face! If you want me to believe you, Cosimo, if you want me to help save St. Benedict, you'll have to give me some answers!"

He stared at her.

"Cosimo, I deserve some answers!"

"Yes." His grip relaxed. "You do." He dropped his hands from her shoulders. "Come, I will show you something."

He stepped toward the guesthouse, walked across the veranda, and opened the door. Jessica followed, wondering what Cole would do when the monk appeared in his room. Would Cosimo lecture Cole on his lack of principles in inviting Shawn to his bed? She wiped the wet hair from her forehead as Cosimo held open the door for her.

The house was warm, and Jessica chafed her hands as she glanced at the unmade bed where Cole lay sprawled facedown on the coverlet. He was dressed in a dark blue velour robe and clutched an envelope in his hand. Bags from department stores littered the room. A glass of wine stood on the nightstand next to the phone. Cole was either so drunk or so deep in sleep that he didn't hear the door close.

Cosimo motioned toward Cole. "Wake him."

Jessica shot him a questioning glance, but Cosimo said nothing more and simply put his hands in the sleeves of his habit. Jessica walked to the bed and leaned over to shake Cole's shoulder.

"Cole," she called softly. He didn't stir. "Cole." Her voice was louder this time. Still he made no movement. She shook him harder. He was a dead weight on the bed. Jessica straightened.

"I can't wake him."

"Neither could Shawn."

"How can you be so sure?"

"Because Cole will stay sleeping until I choose to wake him."

"You've hypnotized him!" Jessica put a hand on Cole's shoulder as if to protect him.

"No," Cosimo chuckled. "He has released me."

"What do you mean, released you?"

"When his defenses are down, whenever he is asleep, it is then that I am set free."

"Set free?" Jessica replied. "I don't understand."

"It is all part of the legacy, my lady, the Cavanetti legacy that Michael has been trying to tell you about."

"What is the legacy?"

"Part of it is memory, a collective memory of all the Cavanetti priests who have lived and died through the centuries. Cole has that memory."

"What do you mean by 'collective'?"

"I mean that if Cole chose to remember, he could recall all of us in vivid detail."

"Then you also have this memory."

"No. I am the very first, Jessica. I am the father of the Cavanetti line."

His voice was low, powerful, final. Jessica felt a chill run down her spine.

"Ordinarily my spirit would reside within Cole as part of his memory, as part of the tradition of the winery. But as you know, Cole broke with tradition. And his spirit is so strong and dominating that he has managed to deny the memory within."

Jessica felt another chill as the realization struck her. "And so his blackouts—"

"His blackouts are the result of a battle inside him. He can no longer deny his heritage, Jessica. I, too, am strong. And until he embraces his responsibility I will be forced to continue as guardian and he will suffer more and more blackouts."

"How do you—how do you appear?"

"I manifest this image of myself. I am what you might call an out-of-body experience."

Jessica stared. "But you don't seem like one. You've touched me. You are warm, just like a real person. You're not having an out-of-body experience like any I've ever heard about."

Cosimo shrugged. "I have set no limits on myself. Perhaps that is why."

Jessica tore her gaze off his robed figure and glanced down at Cole. "So what you're saying is that every time Cole has a blackout, you appear."

"Precisely."

"And whenever you appear, Cole cannot move or speak or wake up."

"Exactly. But remember, only a few people ever see me. If Shawn or Lucy came in at this moment, they most likely would see only you."

"And why is that?"

"Why?" Cosimo walked to the door and looked out at the snow falling past the glass. "I've come to the conclusion that it is not you who sees me, but the lady sleeping within you."

"Then I have a collective memory, too?"

"We all do. It is simply more dominant than usual in the Cavanetti males."

Jessica caressed Cole's dark hair. "What must Cole do to prevent the blackouts?"

"He must return to the winery. He must assume his role as owner and wine-maker."

"And then you will be satisfied?"

"Ah, lady of the night"—he glanced at her over his shoulder and slowly turned to face her—"I will find it most difficult to be satisfied, now that I know who you are."

Frank pressed against the wall of the chapel as Shawn walked past, her leather boots clicking on the wet sidewalk. She clutched her coat around her with both arms, hunching against the chill wind that blew damp snowflakes against her face. Frank watched her duck into the chapel and waited until she turned on the lights. Then, with a grimace, he stepped from the shrubbery and followed her.

He let the door slam behind him, and she looked up, startled, her lighter poised at her cigarette. The cigarette drooped in her lips as he approached her. For once he had surprised her, and he savored the look of confusion in her eyes.

"A smoke?" he sneered. "Doesn't Nick permit smoking in bed?"

She ignored his comment and flicked her lighter, concentrating on the flame near her cupped hand. By the time she dropped the lighter into her coat pocket, she had mastered her surprise, and her eyes telegraphed only the usual brassiness. Still, she seemed preoccupied, and her hand shook as she took another drag of her cigarette. Good. Perhaps she knew she had overstepped the bounds once and for all.

"You don't know shit, Frank," she remarked, and blew out the smoke through pursed lips.

Frank watched the movement, slightly distracted by the pink point of her tongue. "I know where you were, Shawn, so don't try to lie."

"You followed me?" she glared at him. "You bastard!"

"Yeah, I followed you. I wanted to see how low you'd go."

"I was just looking for companionship."

"Companionship, my ass! You went there to hop into bed with my brother. My brother! God, Shawn, don't you have *any* decency?"

"Your brother is a hunk, Frank. A real man. Someone who can give me what I need. When I don't get what I need from you, I go where I can find it."

"Slut!"

"Call me all the names you want, Frank. I don't give a shit. I'm sick of your whining little voice and your limp little—"

"Shut up!" he roared, grabbing her arm. "Just shut up!"

She tried to yank out of his grasp, but he clutched her tightly. This was one time she wasn't going to walk away and ignore him.

"You stay away from Nick! Understand?"

She curled her lip at him.

Enraged, Frank shook her. "Understand, Shawn?"

She glared at him, unafraid. "You should see him," she remarked, "He's huge, just—"

"Shut up, Godammit!" Something snapped inside Frank. He couldn't even see Shawn's face anymore. In its place was a blotch of red. He couldn't hear her voice either. A thundering roar filled his ears, drowning out her taunts. Furious and disgusted, he shoved her away from him, and the thunder changed to a crashing metallic sound.

Frank blinked. Shawn had fallen against the altar, knocking two silver candlesticks to the floor and pulling an embroidered cloth with her. She scrambled to her feet and flung away her cigarette.

"Bastard!" she yelled. She swung around to leave, but Frank lunged for her, grabbing her hair. He snapped her neck back until she grimaced in pain, and he held her pinned against him. He could tell she was frightened now, and the smell of her fear aroused him immediately. He bent to her ear.

"Don't ever let me catch you with another man, Shawn. You understand?"

When she didn't respond, he gave her hair a vicious tug. She yelped.

"Understand, Shawn?"

"I understand, all right," she spit through clenched teeth. "You're a bastard!"

He shoved her again, spinning her sideways, hoping to send her sprawling. Then he'd fall upon her and ravish her on the floor of the chapel. He would teach her a lesson in understanding.

But as Shawn lost her balance, her arms flailing to stop her fall, the heel of her boot caught between two flagstones, trapping her foot while she plunged backward. Frank heard a sickening thud as her head hit the side of a pew, and she crumpled to the floor in a heap of leather and lace.

"Slut," Frank muttered. It served her right. Maybe when

she got up in the morning with a splitting headache, she'd think twice about cheating on him again. He probably shouldn't have been so rough, but at least he'd gotten her attention this time.

He walked up to her, but she wouldn't look at him. She was probably hoping he would leave her alone so she could run to Nick and bitch about her husband's abuse. Well, he was going to wait right here until she got up.

"Come on, Shawn," he said tersely.

She lay on the floor without moving. Frank poked her rump with the toe of his shoe. She didn't make a peep.

"Shawn, come on. Get up, you little slut."

When she didn't rise, he sighed in exasperation and reached down to grab her arm. She was limp, unconscious.

A shaft of chilled fear swept away his anger. Frank let go of her arm and straightened as he stared at her. What had he done? He peered at her neck. He could see her pulse. At least he hadn't killed her.

"Come on, Shawn. Wake up!" His words came out in a whine, and he remembered how Shawn had accused him of whining. He rubbed the back of his neck and looked around helplessly. What could he do? Should he call a doctor? He dashed for the chapel door. His mother would know what to do. She'd get him out of this.

Isabella hurried to the chapel while Frank ran off to get a blanket for Shawn. She hadn't even taken time to throw a coat over her shoulders. Frank's blubbering had alarmed her, and she was anxious to determine for herself the extent of her daughter-in-law's injuries. She opened the chapel door and rushed in.

Shawn lay on the floor, unmoving. Isabella called to her but saw no response. As she approached she could see the red bump on Shawn's temple where she had hit the pew. For a moment Isabella stood over her, nearly awed at the unfamiliar image of a quiet, helpless Shawn. It seemed almost a shame to bring the girl to her senses.

Shaking off her daze, Isabella grabbed a prayer cushion and bent down on one knee, intending to put the pillow beneath Shawn's head.

"Bastard . . ." Shawn muttered in a slurred voice.

Isabella frowned. And suddenly she realized that there was a way to keep Shawn quiet and helpless forever. It would be a simple job, and now was the perfect opportunity. Isabella pressed the pillow onto Shawn's face, holding it firmly against her mouth and nose. Shawn struggled briefly, raising her hands in a feeble gesture of defense, but after a few moments she went limp.

Isabella lifted the pillow from her face just as the door opened and Frank ran in.

"Here's the blanket," he called, trotting across the floor.

Isabella rose. "It's too late, Frank." She hugged the cushion to her abdomen while she stared down at Shawn, inspecting her for any sign of life and hoping to find none.

"What do you mean?"

"I got this pillow to put under her head, and when I bent down, I realized she wasn't breathing."

"What?" Frank's face lost its color. He lowered to one knee at Shawn's side.

"She's dead, Frank. The fall must have killed her."

"But she was breathing when I left."

"She probably had a brain hemorrhage or something."

Frank dropped his head into his hand and leaned on his knee. "Oh, God!"

"Frank, it was an accident." Isabella touched his shoulder. "It couldn't be helped."

"I pushed her, Mother. I didn't mean to hurt her. She just made me so damned mad."

"You pushed her?" Isabella took her hand from his shoulder.

Frank nodded. "I killed her, Mother. Don't you see?"

Isabella stood up straight. "As far as I can see, it was an accident. You'd never intentionally hurt anyone, Frank." She put her palm on his head. "I know you must feel terrible, Frank, but she asked for it. Girls like her often come to a violent end. And maybe it's not so bad that she is dead."

Frank stared at her. "How can you say that?"

"She was a troublemaker. She slept around. You said so yourself. And she was blackmailing me, Frank. She claimed she had a letter that proved I had an existing marriage when I married your father. It's better for the both of us that she's dead."

"But—"

"You must do something with her body, Frank. I'll dispose of her things. We can tell everyone that she got angry and left. We've all been arguing these past few days. Surely Maria won't question the fact that Shawn got fed up and left."

"But—"

"I'll clean up the mess in here while you take care of her." Isabella replaced the pillow and bent to pick up a candlestick. She glanced at her son. He hadn't moved from his kneeling position. "Really, Frank, get a grip on yourself!"

20

Cole sat slumped in a chair next to Giovanna. He stared at the fire while his patient slept in the bed a few paces away. He knew she would mend now. She had not yet spoken or opened her eyes, but after a fortnight of his constant nursing, her face had lost its gauntness, and her skin was once more touched with apricot, just as he remembered.

He knew his task was near completion, their days together numbered, and the realization made his heart heavy. He did not want to leave her. But in the end he knew he would. Giovanna was a married woman. He belonged in a monastery miles away, out of sight of human beings who might be offended by his horrible face.

Only Giovanna had not been repulsed by his wounds. He wondered how she had been able to kiss his freakish face and tell him that she loved him—she who was so beautiful.

He propped his cheek upon his palm and gazed at the flames, remembering the Greek fire, the pain, the days and nights spent in the tower with Giovanna. He had loved her so much. He loved her still. But he knew he would carry his love to the grave and never know the sweetness of life with Giovanna.

"My lord?"

Her voice was still fresh in his thoughts, as if he had heard her speak only yesterday. Yet more than ten years had passed since anyone had called him my lord. He sighed.

"My lord baron?"

The voice sounded so real. Cole raised his head, and his fingertips slid down his cheek as he glanced at the bed. For a moment he stared in shock, and then he scrambled to his feet.

"Giovanna!" She was awake! She was looking at him. She was smiling!

Cole dashed to her side. "Giovanna!"

"It *is* you!" She smiled weakly. "Oh, it *is* you!"

"You've come back!" Cole gathered her into his arms and crushed her to him. "Thank God!" Ecstatic with joy, he held her head against his chest, mashing her raven waves with his big hand. "Oh, God, Giovanna!"

She raised her hands to his chest, and he burst with happiness at her touch, forgetting that her face was pressed into the harsh wool of his cowl and habit.

"My lord!" she whispered.

Cole bent down and nuzzled her face, rubbing his cheek against hers as his eyes closed with joy.

"I thought I heard your voice in my dreams."

"Yes." He kissed her cheek and jaw. "I have been here, waiting for you to awaken, Giovanna."

"I have been asleep so long, my lord, so long!"

His mouth found hers, and he kissed her passionately, holding back with considerable effort so as not to hurt her. He longed to push her back to the pillows and cover her with his body and make love to her.

She touched his face. "How did you find me?"

Cole pulled back. "I was summoned to help you. I'm a healer myself now."

"And a monk?"

"A lay brother."

"But what about your lands?"

"I gave them to the church. I had to retire from society. Because of my—my face."

"Your face?" Giovanna ran delicate fingers over his scarred features and gazed at him, love turning her topaz eyes to molten gold. Cole watched her, fighting the urge to kiss her again. "It looks wonderful to me, my beautiful baron."

"You are delirious, my lady!" He urged her back. "Rest now. You have been very ill."

She lay back, exhausted, but still managed a smile. Cole's heart lurched in his chest.

"Would you like anything, Giovanna?"

"Only you, my lord."

"That must wait."

She nodded and sighed. "The tables have turned, have they not?"

"Aye. A twist of fate."

"Tell me." She covered his hand with hers. "Is my husband here?"

"No. He is gone south and is not expected back for some weeks."

"Good." She closed her eyes and breathed in. Cole watched her closely. He had nursed Giovanna, bathed her, surveyed every inch of her. He had not forgotten the scars he had seen or the fading bruises of bodily punishment quite unlike marks of a fall from a horse.

"Tell me, Giovanna," he began, "how came you by the scars on your back?"

Her eyes slowly opened. "He gave them to me."

"Your husband?"

"Yes."

Cole felt a flush of anger. "Why?"

"Because I was disobedient."

"He whipped you?"

She closed her eyes. "Yes."

Cole was silent, thinking of the suffering and abuse she must have endured over the years. Sharing the old count's bed was probably punishment enough for a young woman, but physical abuse went beyond acceptable behavior.

"I have never been obedient to him, my lord. Never once

have I given in to him. He takes me only by force."

"Giovanna—"

"I know that I have wifely duties, but I find it very hard to obey."

Cole saw tears running out of the corners of her eyes. He squeezed her hand.

"All I ever wanted was you, my baron. You."

"Why did you marry him?" Cole's voice cracked.

"I had been betrothed to him since I was ten years old. My father would not break the agreement even though I begged and pleaded. He said I would grow accustomed to Brindisi's attentions. But I never have. He's a vicious pig."

Cole felt something hard and sharp turning in his guts. He didn't want to hear any more, but Giovanna continued to speak.

"I wanted to die. I wanted to be delivered from the misery of being his wife. After he hit me that last time, I had no desire to live anymore. But then I heard your voice. Something inside me responded to the sound of your voice. You brought me back, my lord."

"And I am so glad you have come back." Cole raised her hand to his lips and kissed her fingertips. "But your husband was not at fault this time. They say you fell from your horse."

"I did not fall." She retracted her hand. "My husband beat me senseless. Here in this room. There was no fall from a horse."

"Then I heard only lies," he muttered. "But why did Brindisi beat you in a stranger's home? Was he so certain that no one would hear your cries?"

"He was too angry to consider the consequences." Giovanna put an arm across her eyes.

"Why, Giovanna?"

"Because I gave my son to the church."

"Why would he be angry about that?"

"Because my son is his sole heir." She breathed in and sighed heavily. "But I would not have my Niccolo growing up learning how to be a man from that beast Brindisi. So I have given him to the church. And my esteemed husband will never find him, though he searches to the gates of hell!"

Jessica woke up early the next morning, eager to tell Cole the reasons for his blackouts, to give him hope and maybe talk some sense into him. She ate a quick breakfast and dressed. When she opened the drapes in the study, she noticed a small stack of paper near the typewriter. Curious, she picked up the top page and scanned the opening scene of a play. She flipped through ten pages of the script, then put down the stack, her eyebrows raised. Her father had actually started writing a play.

Heartened, she breezed to the front door just as the doorbell rang. She opened the door and was surprised to see Greg on the porch, holding a pot of poinsettias.

"Seasons greetings!" he exclaimed, handing her the plant.

"Why, thank you, Greg." She glanced at the bright red leaves and then back at Greg. "You're an early bird this morning."

"The early bird catches the worm!" He stomped his feet and blew on his gloved hands as if to inform her that he didn't want to stand out in the cold any longer.

Jessica reluctantly took the hint and showed him in. "Would you like a cup of coffee, Greg?"

"Please." He glanced at his watch. "I've got to be over at the Cavanettis at nine o'clock, though."

"Oh?"

"Business."

He followed her into the kitchen while he pulled off his gloves. She poured a mug of coffee for him and half a cup for herself and then leaned against the counter.

Greg unbuttoned his coat but did not take it off, since he had only a few minutes to spend.

"What business do you have with the Cavanettis?" she asked, trying to keep her tone casual.

"Well, looks like I might swing a deal and become partners with Isabella."

"Partners in the winery?" She sipped her coffee and studied him.

"Not exactly. Moss Cliff is no place for a winery, Jessica. The land is far too valuable."

"But I've heard Michael Cavanetti say a million times that the microclimate here is perfect for a vineyard."

"That may be, Jessica, but not perfect enough to merit the dedication of acres of prime land with a scenic view."

Jessica cradled her cup between her palms. "So what you're saying is that you and Isabella have plans to buy the vineyard property and develop it?"

"Not as such." Greg gulped his coffee. "But I intend to try to convince her."

"Shouldn't take much." Jessica's words were sharp with sarcasm.

"I don't think so either. What a Christmas present this will be! By next year I could own most of Moss Cliff. What a feeling!" He beamed, and Jessica returned a faint echo of a smile.

"Say, Jessica." Greg put down his mug. "Give me a break on this land, and, who knows, you might be doing yourself a favor down the line."

"What do you mean?"

"We'll keep the land and the money in the family."

"You mean your family."

"Yeah, but families can merge, Jessica." He clasped his hands together in front of his coat and tilted his head, waiting for her reaction as his words sank in.

Jessica stared at him, speechless. Was he proposing marriage?

"Ha!" Greg swept forward. "Got you on that one!" He took her shoulders. "You should see the look on your face!"

"I'm not sure I'm following you in all this, Greg."

"I'm making you an offer, Jessica. We could do worse, you and I, than tying the knot after all these years."

He was proposing marriage in his own insensitive, financially motivated way. Jessica stared at his moustache, hoping he wasn't going to kiss her. She backed away.

"This is rather sudden, Greg."

"I know, I know." He held up his hands as if he realized he had rushed her. "Just think it over. We can take it nice and slow. No need to rush into things."

"Greg, I don't want to—"

"Maybe not now, but we can date, see each other more often. Who knows?"

"I'm going back to California in a few days."

"You are?"

"Yes."

"Well, that does make it more difficult. But we can see each other on weekends."

"Greg . . ."

He looked at his watch. "Dammit, it's nine. I have to go, Jessica. Just promise me you'll think it over."

He pecked her on the cheek and hurried out of the house, leaving Jessica in a daze in the doorway. Then she caught a movement out of the corner of her eye. Cole must have been nearby, and when he saw Greg, he turned and loped toward the vineyard. Jessica stared after his retreating form. What had he seen? More important, what had he thought he had seen? Damn that Greg Kessler. The worst thing for her relationship with Cole right now was for Greg to be seen leaving her house early in the morning. She grabbed her jacket and sprinted after Cole.

The only reason she caught up with him was because he was detained at the bridge by a policeman who had cordoned off the span with yellow strips of vinyl.

She puffed to a halt as she heard Cole protesting about being barred from the park.

"No one is allowed in the park, sir," the policeman replied. "One of our decoys was attacked early this morning." He studied Cole's face. "Say, aren't you Cole Nichols?"

Cole was about to answer when a man in a trench coat clumped over the bridge and ducked under the yellow markers. Jessica frowned, recognizing Detective Turner's puffy face.

"Good morning, Miss Ward."

"Good morning. How are you, Detective?"

"Tired. Been up half the night." He scanned Cole's tall figure. "You must be Cole Nichols."

Cole returned the chilly glance with one of his own. "Yes." He held out his hand. "And you are . . ."

"Detective Turner." He shook hands, stuffed his left hand into the pocket of his coat, and retrieved his notebook. He flipped it open. "Mind telling me where you were last night, Mr. Nichols?"

"Why?" Cole crossed his arms in indignation. Jessica took a step toward him.

"Where were you last night between the hours of two and four A.M.?"

"Asleep."

"Any witnesses?"

"How would I know? I was asleep." Cole glared at the bridge and then back at the detective. "And if you have any other questions, you can talk to my lawyer."

"Mr. Nichols, I'm not insinuating—"

"You damn well are, Detective. And I don't like it!"

The younger policeman looked away, as if embarrassed that anyone would speak to Detective Turner in such a fashion. Then Jessica saw his body go rigid with alarm.

"There he is!" The policeman pointed to the park. "There he is!"

Detective Turner whipped around with surprising speed for a man of his age and bulk.

Jessica narrowed her eyes and followed the policeman's line of sight. She glimpsed a flash of light-colored clothing as someone darted into the bog across the river and disappeared behind a clump of dogwood.

Then Jessica noticed Cole. His body had tensed as if he were a big cat that had just caught sight of its prey. She had never seen him on the playing field. She had never seen him perform. And when he vaulted over the barricade, she drew back in surprise and watched him fly across the bridge, barely taking two strides to cover the distance.

"Hold it!" Detective Turner bellowed.

"Cole!" Jessica gasped.

"Nichols, come back here!" Turner trotted to the edge of the bridge and yelled again, but Cole sprinted far ahead, burning up the distance with the effortless grace of a truly gifted athlete.

"Damn him!" Detective Turner threw his notebook to the ground. The younger policeman retrieved the book and shook off the wet leaves that stuck to it.

"Don't worry, Detective. That's Cole Nichols!"

"So what!"

"Well," the policeman sputtered, "Cole Nichols is the fastest quarterback in the country. Faster than Randall Cunningham. No one can outrun him." With a rapt expression and a huge grin, he observed Cole's progress. "God, look at him go!"

Jessica watched Cole run, awed and fascinated herself.

"Rogers could be armed," Detective Turner said. "Nichols is a fool."

"But if Rogers had a gun, why hasn't he shot his victims?"

"Still, he may be dangerous."

"So is Cole Nichols. I'd hate to be the one he tackles!"

Detective Turner jammed his notebook into his pocket and waved to the officer. "Come on. We'd better back the damn fool up." Then he glanced at Jessica. "You stay right here, Miss Ward."

Jessica nodded and hugged her arms around her chest, hoping that Cole would overtake the murderer but at the same time worrying that he might be running to his doom.

The rest of the morning was a kaleidoscope of confusion. As soon as Cole came out to the jogging trail with a cowering figure in front of him, Jessica sprinted across the bridge, heedless of Detective Turner's order to stay put. Cole had not only raced through the bog and tackled the convict, he had also convinced Rogers to admit to his murders in front of a rolling camera. A newsman hoping for exclusive coverage of the mayhem on Moss Cliff—either the murders or more Cole Nichols mischief—had been lurking in the area with his equipment and had hit pay dirt. He was on the scene when Cole brought down the criminal. He filmed everything—the tackle, the brief struggle, and the smooth psychological games Cole had played with Rogers, promising him national news coverage, appealing to the convict's skewed sense of pride in his feats.

Detective Turner fumed at Cole's interference but was as eager as anyone for Rogers's confessions. Jessica was awed by Cole's cool, quick thinking and his knowledge of human nature. She could almost imagine Cosimo reasoning with the convict, prodding his competitiveness with the argument that a renowned quarterback was more famous than any murderer. Rogers had protested, saying he would go down in history as one of the most heinous of serial killers once all his victims were found. He bragged about a murder committed years before he'd gone to prison, the first of a series of murders that had never been solved, going so far as to hint that one of the bodies had been disposed of in this very bog.

Now Rogers stood in Detective Turner's custody, smiling darkly and casting sidelong glances at Jessica. She averted her eyes from him and caught a glimpse of something shining against the light cover of snow. Jessica stepped closer and picked up a shoe, a black shoe with a buckle on one side.

"What's that?" Detective Turner inquired.

"A shoe." Jessica had seen the shoe before, and she suddenly remembered where. Shawn had worn a pair just like this the day they had gone shopping together.

"Odd." Detective Turner took the shoe and turned it over in his hand while he inspected it. Jessica shuddered. The sight of a cast-off shoe always made her feel uneasy, as if the owner had left an appendage behind.

"That looks like the style—" Cole broke off his words.

"Like what style, Nichols?"

Jessica saw Cole's eyes grow flat and dark. "It looks like Shawn Cavanetti's shoe."

"Your brother's wife?"

"Yes."

"But what would Shawn's shoe be doing out here?" Jessica said.

Detective Turner shrugged. "I'll check it out after I take the prisoner downtown." He grabbed the convict by the upper arm. "Come on, Rogers." He pulled the man toward the waiting squad car, but before he had taken more than a few steps, he looked back at Cole. "Thanks for your help, Nichols."

Cole nodded at him and turned to leave.

The journalist followed Cole, begging for an interview. Cole shook his head and headed down the path, but Jessica caught his arm, knowing this was one interview that could have a positive impact on his career and one she was not about to let slip by.

"Cole would be happy to grant an interview," she said with a forced smile. "Why don't you come on up to the house and I'll fix you both some coffee?"

"Say, great!" The journalist beamed. "How about it, Mr. Nichols?"

Cole glared at Jessica and then at the newsman.

"You're going to make the evening news in a big way, Mr. Nichols," the reporter put in, "interview or not."

Jessica squeezed Cole's arm. "Cole, this could be good for—"

"Since when has the press been on my side?" he retorted. "No, thanks. No matter what I do or say, you guys twist it into something rotten."

The newsman hobbled after him, struggling with his equipment. "Wait, Mr. Nichols. I promise, you can have the final say over anything I write!"

"Sure. Until it gets to your editor."

"Cole." Jessica stepped in front of him. "This is the best time to prove that you won't have blackouts anymore, that you're fit to start in the play-offs."

"Oh? Since when can I offer that guarantee?"

"Since today. I'll tell you about it later. But believe me, it's over. And to top it off, you're a hero."

"You sure are, Mr. Nichols! After this story goes on the air, you'll be getting awards from all over the place."

Cole broke away. "I don't want any awards. I just want to be left the hell alone."

"Cole, please—"

He strode away, and Jessica's shoulders wilted. Cole's mistrust of journalists was blinding him to the benefits of this interview. Near her side, the newsman dropped his camera case to the ground and let out a sigh.

"Too bad," he murmured. "He's a great subject. With a face and a body like that, he could go to Hollywood after he retires."

Jessica glanced at the journalist and straightened her shoulders. "You give up too easily, sir. Come on. I'll change his mind."

21

Cole granted the interview, but he was not pleased. After the newsman left the guesthouse, he ducked into the shower, leaving Jessica in the company of Lucy.

"What's with him?" Lucy asked, nodding toward the master bedroom.

"I think he's mad at me," Jessica replied, picking up her jacket. "I foisted that journalist on him."

"Oh, Cole is such an ass sometimes! That reporter seemed like his biggest fan. How could he object to him?"

"Cole doesn't trust the press." Jessica strolled to the front door. "And I can't say I blame him."

Jessica spent the rest of the day in town selecting a Christmas tree and trying to figure out how to convince Cole she had been right about the interview. She drove back to the bungalow in the early evening while more snow fell. Perhaps it would be a white Christmas after all, an unusual event for the area.

She leaned the tree against the porch and went inside. Voices wafted from the study, and she wandered down the hall, wondering who could be visiting. Her father sat at the desk, a tumbler of Scotch in his hand, while Lucy stood in the middle of the room, reading lines from his new play. Jessica retreated unseen, slightly disappointed that her father, though evidently sober, was still drinking.

She decided to bring in the tree, but before she bent to hoist it up, her gaze traveled across the lawn to the guesthouse. No lights shone in the windows, and Cole's car was missing. Her heart sank. Where was he? She wished she could talk to him and settle their differences, but he was such a hothead that he'd probably stay out half the night, driving too fast on the slick roads.

More than anything, Jessica wanted to make everything right with Cole. She wanted to tell him that she loved him, regardless of his quick temper, his career troubles, or his years of absence. But how could she broach the subject when he was so angry with her?

Jessica glared at the Scotch pine she had purchased. Why had she even bothered with a tree? Who cared? She didn't feel like celebrating Christmas anymore, and her father wouldn't know Christmas from any other day, as long as he had his booze.

She sighed and stuffed her hands into her coat pockets. She felt the need to talk to someone, but Cole wasn't home and that meant Cosimo would not be available to her either. Jessica decided to go to the chapel. Maybe a few moments of meditation would settle her nerves.

Quietly she slipped into the small building. She wasn't a Catholic and didn't observe the rituals Maria performed upon entering the sanctuary, yet the chapel gave her the sense of peace she needed.

Jessica sat down in the first row of pews and looked up at the stained glass window, now a dark rectangle. Then her eyes traveled down to the image of Christ in his suffering. She regarded the beautiful wood statue while her thoughts drifted away from her problems. Lastly, she glanced toward the reliquary where Niccolo Cavanetti's robes and rosary were enshrined. Jessica jumped up in alarm. The robe had vanished.

Who had taken it? Cole? Why would he need a disguise now? Was he going to try to get his father out of the house again? He was so upset he might try something foolish. She knew she had to stop him.

Jessica ran to the door and out to the walk. She saw tracks in the snow, which shot a hole in her abduction theory. The tracks didn't lead to the Cavanetti house but down the walk toward the guesthouse and then to the vineyard. Jessica followed the tracks, more curious than concerned for her safety. After all, the murderer had been apprehended, and there was nothing to fear in the night now.

By the time she trotted down the hill into the vineyard, she saw a robed figure crossing the bridge over the Samish Slough. Why would Cole go out to the bog? Jessica increased her speed and sloshed through the thin layer of wet snow on the ground, all the while keeping her expertly trained eye on the figure ahead of her.

She walked off the main jogging path onto a lesser used one that dipped into the swampy darkness. Her father had never let her play in the bog when she was a child because of sinkholes and quicksand. At least the moon was out and she could see where she was stepping. Jessica carefully picked her way through a grove of brittle alders and blackberry canes. Twigs caught at her jacket, and moisture dripped from the branches overhead. The air was heavy and thick with the smell of decaying leaves and damp earth.

The figure was only a few yards away. Jessica watched him turn toward a pond on the left. Though almost certain the figure was Cole, she decided to remain unseen and unheard and let this curious drama play itself out. Noiselessly, she edged behind a huge willow stump and watched.

"Oh, Jesus!" she heard him swear. Then he paced back and forth on the bank of the pond, swearing and sighing, highly agitated. With a tight constriction of fear in her throat, Jessica realized that the voice did not belong to Cole. And if not Cole, then whom had she followed?

Abruptly the figure stopped pacing. Had he seen her? Jessica froze in place, not daring to move or breathe. Then the man reached into a pile of brush and pulled out a thick, gnarled willow limb. He carried it to the water's edge and poked at something.

Jessica moved around the stump, trying to get a better view, and inadvertently stepped into a hole at the base of the stump. Her foot plunged through a rotten root, and a resounding *crack* shattered the stillness of the night.

The robed figure whirled around, still holding the branch. For a moment they faced each other, and then Jessica pulled out her foot and lunged away, slipping and sliding down the twisted path. Behind her she could hear someone running, gaining on her. She pumped harder, fear giving her more speed. But not enough. Before she had reached the river, she was tripped and thrown to the ground.

Frantically, Jessica struggled against the hands that grabbed her wrists, the knee that pinned her thighs. She arched and twisted, but the man held her fast, breathing heavily and staring at her as if deciding what to do with her. She could not see the face shadowed by the hood of the cowl, but she recognized the cologne that wafted around her, heightened by the chase and the heavy wool garment he wore.

"Frank!" she gasped.

"You just had to follow me, didn't you?" he snarled. "You've always got your nose in the Cavanetti affairs, don't you?" He increased the pressure on her wrists, and Jessica winced in pain.

"I thought you were—"

"I didn't mean to kill her. But who'll believe it? I had to do something!"

Jessica stared at him, stunned. Had Frank killed someone? She couldn't believe it. Then she remembered the shoe she had found in the bog. Shawn's shoe. Had Frank killed Shawn and taken her body to the bog? If so, Jessica wondered what Frank would do to her.

"Frank, I didn't see any—"

"Shut up and let me think!" He jumped to his feet and yanked her off the ground, holding her right arm bent behind her back. Any sudden movement sent stabbing pains to her shoulder and elbow.

"You're hurting me, Frank," she gasped as he pushed her ahead of him. She couldn't believe he would actually harm her. Yet his grip was insistent, and he seemed distraught, out of control.

He forced her over the bridge and up the trail toward the cliffs, swearing when she slipped or attempted to reason with him. By the time they reached the woods at the top of Moss Cliff, she was truly afraid. Frank had definite plans for her. Was he going to throw her over the cliff? She dragged her heels.

"Cut it out, Jessica!" he snapped, jerking her arm.

She choked back a yelp of pain and tried to concentrate on a plan of escape. Somehow she must get away from Frank, for there was no one to help her in this deserted place. Jessica forced herself not to cry. Crying wouldn't help. She had to remain clear-headed and rational.

Frank dragged her to the jumble of boulders marking the entrance to the stairway that led to the cavern. Frank went first, pulling her by the wrist while she resisted.

"I'll throw you down these stairs, Jessica, if you do that one more time!" He gripped her arm, and she was surprised at the strength in his slender fingers.

"Frank, let me go. I'm no threat to you."

"Sure. You're just the Easter Bunny." His nervous laugh echoed down the corridor and returned in a maniacal cackle that sent shivers across Jessica's scalp.

When they reached the bottom, Frank stumbled through the darkness, and Jessica fell to her hands and knees on a patch of cold sand. Frank pushed her onto her stomach and sank his knee into the small of her back, immobilizing her. Jessica glanced back at him, her cheek in the rough, cold sand.

"Don't hurt me, Frank. It won't do you any good."

"I don't know *what* to do with you," he retorted. "But I know what I should do. I should even the score."

"What score?"

"Nick had my wife. So I should have you."

Jessica froze. In her wildest dreams, she had never thought Frank would rape her. "Cole didn't sleep with Shawn."

"Yes, he did." He pushed harder into her back. "I caught her sneaking out of Cole's room just last night."

"I saw her, too. But Cole was asleep the whole time. He couldn't wake up."

"You expect me to believe that? What do you think I am, a moron?"

The pressure of his knee suddenly eased. She heard him fiddling with his clothes, then the clink of a belt buckle. She tensed, ready to roll away from him at the first opportunity. He would have to take off the robe and undo his pants, and while he did so she might find a chance to escape. But Frank didn't remove the robe. He pulled Jessica's hands together and secured them with his leather belt.

"Frank . . ." Her voice quavered.

"Don't worry." He forced her to a sitting position with her back against a rock. "You were never quite to my taste, Jessica."

She breathed a sigh of relief. Maybe he was simply going to leave her in the cavern and make an escape, maybe flee to Canada and drop out of sight. That was far more likely than his raping or killing anyone in cold blood.

He stepped beside her and wrapped the rope belt of the monk's robe around her torso, then tied it behind the rock.

"Good luck, Jessica," Frank said, walking back in front of her.

Jessica paled as a sickening realization hit home. At high tide the beach entrance to the cavern was underwater. The sand on which she sat was wet, and the boulder behind her bristled with clusters of mussels and barnacles, creatures that required submersion in water to survive. She was bound to a rock that sat below the tideline. And the tide was coming in.

"Frank, don't do this! Don't leave me here. Please, Frank."

"I have no choice." He paced the sand in front of her outstretched legs. "You know what I did. You saw where I went."

"I wouldn't tell. Honestly, Frank!" Fingers of water flowed into the depression at the heels of her boots, soaking the hem of her slacks. Jessica pulled up her knees. The tide was rising quickly.

"If you hadn't been so snoopy, you wouldn't be here. Think about that!"

Jessica swallowed, wondering how long it would take before the water surrounded her. She would surely suffer hypothermia before drowning. The water was ice cold. She yanked at the rope, trying to break away, but the line held tight.

"Frank, I'll give you the property. I'll sign it off to you—just untie me!"

"Everything is falling apart, Jessica. Don't you see? Even owning the vineyard won't help me now."

Water flowed around the rock, seeping into the seat of Jessica's slacks. She shuddered and sniffed back the moisture at the end of her frozen nose. She heard Frank walking away, leaving her to die in this godforsaken cave.

"Cosimo!" She whispered an anguished prayer. "Cosimo, help me!"

Help me. Help me. Help me.

Her voice echoed in the darkness. Water lapped at her feet and hips, and Jessica struggled once more against the rope, only to scrape her hands on the jagged crowns of the barnacles.

Suddenly a glimmer of light caught her eye. Jessica jerked around to look at the stairway, where a dim flicker lit the corridor. She strained to see, pulling at the cord until her muscles ached. Frank stood transfixed between the stairway and her boulder, the hood drooping around his shoulders.

The light grew stronger, and the ring of approaching footsteps grew louder. Frank stumbled backward, knowing his escape route was blocked by whoever was coming down the stairs. Then a shape materialized in the opening of the corridor, a towering shape in a black robe. Cosimo!

Jessica shouted for joy at the sight of him.

He stepped forward, holding a flaming torch. For every step Cosimo took, Frank retreated a pace, until he stood at the edge of the water next to Jessica.

"Who are you?" he stuttered, his face white with fear.

"I am the guardian." Cosimo's powerful voice thundered through the cavern, adding to the impressive sight of his tall, broad-shouldered figure. The torch threw patches of light over his black robe, and Jessica thought she saw the glitter of an eye deep in the shadow of his hood. "And you—you defiler of that sacred robe—shall burn in hell!"

"Is that you, Nick?" Frank's lips drew back in a sick grin. "Come on. Stop playing games."

"I am not Niccolo. And this is no game." Cosimo stepped closer. "I am Cosimo Cavanetti."

"C-C-Cosimo Cavanetti?" Frank looked back at the opening of the cavern as if to determine his chances at bolting toward the beach. The tide had nearly sealed off the opening. Wildly, he glanced back at the monk in front of him.

Jessica twisted in her bonds. "He killed Shawn. Her body is in the bog."

"I didn't mean to!" Frank pleaded with outstretched arms, his hands shaking. "It was an accident! I didn't mean to!"

"And you planned to kill Jessica as well?"

"Yes. No! I mean, I had to do—"

"Silence!"

Frank cringed at the bellowed command.

"Untie her."

"Sure. Right." Frank fumbled with the knotted cord and then unclasped the belt. Jessica scrambled to her feet and skittered out of the pool of water, running up the slope to the dry ground behind Cosimo.

"Listen, Nick, I didn't intend to leave her—"

"Silence!" Cosimo stepped down the slope. "You cowardly little man. You deserve to suffer the death you had planned for Jessica."

"No, please don't—"

"But I am weary of killing. Killing gives no satisfaction, does it, Franco?"

"Come on, Nick. Quit this monk stuff. I'll give myself up. Just cut it out."

"You think I am Niccolo? I assure you, I am not." He put a hand to his hood. "You see?"

Cosimo pulled back the folds of wool. Jessica, standing behind him, saw only a mane of black hair. But Franco was presented a full frontal view of Cosimo Cavanetti's face.

"My God!" Frank choked. Jessica saw his face drain of all color before he crumpled to the ground. Cosimo pulled the hood back into place and looked down at Frank lying on the sand with his shoes in the water.

"Spineless bastard," he murmured. Then he turned to Jessica while he lay the torch on the boulder to which she had been bound. "Are you all right, Jessica?"

"Oh, Cosimo!" Jessica broke from her trance and threw herself into his arms. She hugged him fiercely, burrowing her nose into the folds of his cowl. He felt solid and warm, a bastion of safety and security. His arms came around her in a hard embrace, pinning her against him. One of his hands plunged into her hair, massaging her scalp as if to make certain she was unharmed. She clung to him, her arms around the breadth of his torso, her palms on the flat planes of his shoulder blades. She could feel the hard rise and fall of his breathing.

"Jessica." His hand slid down the back of her neck, sending a shiver of heat through her while the sound of his voice rumbled into her heart. This powerful, gentle being had just rescued her, had answered her prayer of desperation, and now he pressed into her with the hunger and desire of a mortal. Jessica wanted to kiss him, wanted to reach up and hold his face and kiss him. But the urge confused her. She felt the same desire for Cole. How could she feel the same thing for both men? She backed away, sliding her arms from his torso.

"You are wet," Cosimo began, his voice husky with emotion. "We should go back."

"Yes."

"Take up the torch. I'll follow with Franco."

"What will you do with him?" she asked, trying to distract herself from the sensations she had felt in his arms.

"Do not worry about Franco. I will take care of him. You must call the authorities."

Cosimo bound Frank's feet with the belt and his hands with the rope and then slung him over his shoulder as if he were no heavier than a sack of flour.

"Hurry, Jessica. It is cold, and you are wet."

Cosimo left Jessica at the porch of the bungalow. Her hands shook so much she could barely fit the key in the lock, and her jaw ached with the effort of keeping her teeth from chattering. She hobbled through the doorway on frozen feet that felt brittle inside her shoes.

Lucy saw her in the hallway and let out a small cry.

"Jessica! What happened?"

"Call the police, Lucy. Ask for Detective Turner. Tell him to get out here right away." She was so cold that her words slurred together.

Lucy took her by the arm. "You're frozen! Where have you been?"

"On Moss Cliff with Frank. He's gone crazy, Lucy."

"Did he hurt you?"

"No. Just call the police!"

"First we've got to get you out of those wet clothes." Lucy dragged her to the bathroom. Jessica collapsed on the seat of the toilet, exhausted.

"I can manage," she protested weakly. "Just make the call."

"Okay, okay, but you'd better take a hot bath. Right now!" Lucy pulled on the faucet of the bathtub and left the water running as she hurried out to the phone in the kitchen.

For a moment Jessica stared at the water and remembered how the sea had swirled around her in the cavern. She shuddered again and pulled off a shoe without untying it. She let it fall to the floor with a thud while she removed the other shoe. Then she peeled off her sodden socks with stiff, shaking fingers.

Lucy knocked on the bathroom door. "Jessica? I talked to Detective Turner. He's coming right out."

"Good. Thanks."

"Can I help you with anything?"

"No. I'll be all right, Lucy. Thanks."

"I'm going to get Cole. He'll want to hear what happened. I'll be right back."

Jessica let her go, even though she was quite certain that wherever Cole was, Lucy wouldn't be able to rouse him. She shed the rest of her clothes and stepped into the bath.

At first the hot water burned her toes, but gradually the pain eased and she sat down, stretching out her legs. She breathed in and reclined against the slope of the tub, luxuriating in the blessed heat. She closed her eyes.

A few minutes later, she heard the front door slam and Cole's voice demanding to know where she was. Jessica sat up, surprised that he had come to the house.

"Cole!" Lucy protested on the other side of the door. "You can't go in there. She's in the bathtub!"

Jessica grabbed a towel off the rack in case Cole barged in, but Lucy seemed to have stopped him in time.

"Are you okay in there, Jess?" Cole asked.

"Yes. I'm doing much better."

"Good. I'll make you something hot to drink."

Jessica hurried with her bath, dried off, and grabbed her robe from a hook on the back of the door. As she tied her hair in a haphazard loop on top of her head, she frowned at her pale reflection in the mirror. The episode with Frank had all but drained her. Yet she knew it was a miracle that she was alive. She hung up her towel and washcloth and padded out to the hallway.

Cole had heard the bathroom door open and was standing in the hall when she appeared. "Jess!" he exclaimed. "What's going on?"

"Frank killed Shawn," she answered, taking the cup of

coffee he held out to her. "He's gone off the deep end, Cole. He was going to kill me, too."

"What?"

"But Cosimo saved me." She sipped the coffee.

Cole's brows drew together at her words, and he scrutinized her face. "Cosimo saved you?"

"Yes." She stared at him in earnest. "Cole, I've got to tell you about the connection between you and Cosimo."

"Hold it, Jessica." He clutched her arm. "Are you sure you're all right? Did you fall and hit your head or something?"

"I'm telling you that Cosimo was there! He's as real as you and I, Cole. And he saved my life!" She stepped back. "You don't have to believe the truth if you choose not to!"

"It's just that—"

"Oh, forget it!" She lurched away from him, nearly spilling her coffee, and fled down the hall. She was angry with Cole for not believing her. If he couldn't accept the presence of Cosimo, he would never be free of his blackouts.

Cole followed her to her room and closed the door, turning his back while she dressed.

"Jess, I'm sorry I seem doubtful about the ghost monk."

"He's not a ghost. He's part of your heritage, Cole. He's the founding father of the Cavanetti line. And he's here because he can't let tradition die." She pulled on a sweatshirt and a pair of heavy socks. "Cole, you will keep having those blackouts until you accept your role—your role as a Cavanetti."

"Why?"

"Because the vineyard requires a guardian. And if you aren't there to serve as guardian, then Cosimo has to assume the job. He comes out of your memory, Cole, and he manifests himself when you are sleeping or unconscious!"

"Out of my memory when I'm asleep?" Cole whirled around and stared at her. "What a bunch of bullshit!"

In sweatshirt and socks, Jessica glared at him, heedless that she hadn't pulled on her jeans. His stubborn disbelief infuriated her. "If it's just my imagination, why didn't you wake up last night when I came to your room?"

"You came to my room?"

"Yes. You were asleep. I couldn't even wake you up. I shook you, called your name—you were completely oblivious to me." She yanked on her jeans, satisfied that he believed her on one count. "Cosimo and I stood by your bed and talked, and you slept on, unaware."

Cole ran a hand through his hair and gazed at her, perplexed.

"Cosimo says you Cavanettis have a collective memory, that you can remember every ancestor in vivid detail. Don't you recall anything about the past, Cole?"

"Nothing." He shrugged. "I just have crazy dreams when I'm unconscious."

"What kind of dreams?"

"Oh, dreams where I'm some sort of knight. A crusader. Then I'm some kind of—" He broke off and looked at Jessica, a strange expression darkening his eyes.

"Some kind of what, Cole?"

He ran his hand through his hair again. "Some kind of monk."

"That's Cosimo! You do remember him after all!"

"I've never been called Cosimo in the dream."

"What's he like, this monk?"

"Well, he's big. Kind of like me, I guess. And he's got something wrong with his face. Terrible scars from being burned."

"Yes!" Jessica exclaimed.

"And he's got something going with a countess, this beautiful dark-haired woman who—" Cole broke off and stared at Jessica. "Goddamn, Jessica. The countess—I just realized—Giovanna looks just like you!"

"Giovanna? Her name is Giovanna?"

"Yes. Giovanna di Montalcino." Cole sank to the bed, his head in his hands. "What's going on, Jessica? What's happening to us? How do you figure into all of this?"

Jessica longed to lay her hand on his shoulder, but she

wasn't about to open herself up to another rejection. "It all has to do with the river of time, Cole, and paths that cross more than once."

"What in the hell is that supposed to mean?"

At that moment the doorbell rang.

"It's probably the police," Jessica said. "Come on, Cole. We'll talk about this later."

"You bet we will. I want to know everything this Cosimo has told you."

Before she could respond, someone rapped on the bedroom door.

"Hey, you two," Lucy called, "break it up. Detective Turner's here."

22

"*Isn't it a little late for social calls?*" Isabella Cavanetti swept into the drawing room, attired in a magenta velvet dressing gown with a ruffle around the high neckline. Detective Turner stood as she entered. Jessica remained seated. Cole turned from his stance near the fireplace and regarded her coolly.

"You!" she gasped, catching sight of Cole. "I thought I told you—"

"Please, Mrs. Cavanetti. I asked him to come," Detective Turner interrupted. "I've just been informed by Miss Ward here that there's been another murder."

"Another murder?" Isabella's fingers spread across the plush fabric at the base of her throat.

"Miss Ward claims that your son Frank killed his wife, Shawn Cavanetti."

Isabella stared at Jessica in shock. "Impossible!"

"He admitted to killing her, Isabella." Jessica leaned forward in her chair.

"No, no, that's quite impossible. Shawn left here last night. They had a big fight and—"

"Did she leave?" Detective Turner put in. "Or did Frank

kill her and take her body to the bog, hoping the murder would be attributed to the serial killer? We did find that shoe in the bog this afternoon, you know."

"And as I told you this afternoon, that shoe could belong to anyone. Lots of people wear those shoes."

"Maybe if we spoke to your son, ma'am, he could clear this up for us."

"Frank is not at home, Mr. Turner."

"Do you know where he is?"

"I'm afraid not." Isabella clasped her hands in front of her and gave him an imperious stare. "Now, if you will excuse me, Detective, it is late, and it has been a busy day."

Cole leaned on the mantel and surveyed Isabella with dispassion as he drew an envelope from the pocket of his jeans.

"Before you retire, Isabella," he said, opening the envelope, "perhaps you can shed some light on this."

Isabella glanced at the paper in his hand, then leveled her stare at Cole. Her eyes were hard, her expression cruel. Jessica felt a stab of compassion for Cole. This heartless woman should have been his mother, yet she was the person responsible for nearly all of his problems.

"And what is that?" she asked in an icy tone.

"Something Shawn gave me for safekeeping. She was afraid you'd lay your hands on it."

"Nick, I'm tired. I've spent the day trying to calm your father. I'm in no mood for any games."

Cole strolled forward, holding the paper he had slipped out of the envelope.

"Have you read this letter, Isabella?"

Before she could answer, the front door burst open, and Maria cried out in the hall. Jessica jumped to her feet as Frank lunged into the drawing room, still dressed in the black robes of Niccolo Cavanetti, his hair disheveled and his eyes wild as he glanced frantically from face to face as if he didn't recognize a single person in the room.

"Frank!" Isabella said, horrified by his appearance.

"Help me!" he choked, running to his mother and falling

to his knees before her. He flung his arms around her legs. "Help me, Mother!"

"Frank!" Isabella stared at him, appalled. "Get a hold of yourself!"

"Don't let him get me, Mother!"

"Who?"

"Cosimo Cavanetti!"

Isabella glanced at Jessica and then at Detective Turner. "What are you talking about, Frank?" She tried to get him to let go of her, but he held her fast.

"He'll kill me! He said he'd kill me!"

"Frank, you're talking nonsense!"

"No! He's out there! He—he—knows all about Shawn! He told me that he'd kill me if I didn't confess! He told me I'd burn in hell!"

"Frank!" Isabella clutched his shoulders. "Frank, you're not making any sense." She looked up at the detective. "Shawn's disappearance has really affected him, Detective."

"So it seems," drawled Turner.

"He's hideous, Mother! You should see him! He looks like a monster. And he's seven feet tall. And I'm sure he'll kill me!"

"Oh, Frank." She patted his back. "You've been drinking, haven't you?" She flashed a smile at the detective.

"I haven't, Mother! I swear!" He sank his face into the space above her knees. "Tell them it was an accident, Mother! I didn't mean to kill Shawn! Tell them it was just an accident! God, tell them I never meant to hurt her!"

Isabella struggled out of his grip and staggered backward, leaving Frank to huddle on the floor. "Frank! Get a hold of yourself!"

"Tell them, Mother!"

"I don't know what you're talking about!"

"Yes, you do! You were there! You said it was a good thing that she was dead. Tell them!"

Isabella's eyes grew round with disbelief. She took a few steps back, shaking her head in futile denial.

"Tell us, Mrs. Cavanetti," said Detective Turner. "You were there?"

Jessica saw Isabella pale.

"She was blackmailing you, Mother! And she was cheating on me!" Frank glanced up at the accusing faces that surrounded him. "She was a slut! She was a slut! She made a fool out of me!"

"Frank, just be quiet!"

Detective Turner spoke up. "I suggest you dress, Mrs. Cavanetti. And you too, Frank."

Isabella turned on him. "Whatever for?"

"You're coming down to the station for questioning."

"Tonight? You must be out of your mind!"

Detective Turner only smiled, as if to imply that his sanity was not in question. Isabella stared at him for a moment, then turned on her heel and stormed out of the room.

The detective suffered her behavior with bland indifference, then held out his hand to Jessica. "Thank you for your help, Miss Ward. I hope we can count on you tomorrow to show us where the body is buried."

She shook his hand and nodded.

Turner glanced at Cole. "Sorry that I doubted you, Mr. Nichols. That was some tackle you made this morning."

"Thanks."

"See yourself on the evening news?"

Cole shook his head.

"You're the all-American hero now—you can count on that!"

Cole smiled shallowly and glanced to the side as Maria hobbled toward him, holding out her pudgy arms.

"Oh, Niccolo!" She hugged him around his waist, and Cole bent down to her. "Thank God! Thank God!"

"Everything will be all right, Maria. Just you wait and see."

"I know it is terrible of me to say this, Nick, but I hope we never see that Mrs. Cavanetti again!"

"There might be a chance of that, *cara mia*." Cole patted her back. "She may be charged with being an accessory to murder. And if not, she still faces a bigamy charge for already being a Mrs. when she married Pop."

Maria nodded and pulled back to put her hands on either side of his face and gaze up at him with eyes full of glistening adoration. "I'm so glad you have come home, Niccolo! Now everything will be like old times again!"

"I hope so." Cole glanced at Jessica, his gaze locking with hers over Maria's white hair.

Cole felt an inordinate amount of relief as he watched the police car pull away, taking Isabella and Frank to the station downtown. He prayed he would never see the poisonous Isabella again, at least not in the Cavanetti house. With her gone, his father might have a chance to recover, a chance to regain his old spirit. Cole sighed. At least one part of his life was improving.

One glance at Jessica, however, and his relief faded. She lstood near the front door, looking more drawn and worn than he had ever seen her. Her beautiful skin was bereft of color, her eyes had shadows under them, and her lips were unusually pale. He longed to take her in his arms and kiss away the troubled look in her eyes. But after his outburst of the day before, he could hardly blame her for keeping her distance.

"Jess," he ventured, "you look beat. Let me take you home."

"All right." Her voice was flat.

Cole got their coats and walked with her down the lane to the bungalow. She didn't say a word. She just ambled toward the house with her hands stuffed in her pockets. She stumbled once, and Cole reached out to keep her from falling, using the incident as an excuse to wrap his arm around her shoulders. She fit perfectly tucked against his torso.

Jessica didn't object to his closeness, probably because she was too tired to protest. Cole smiled wryly at the thought as he opened the bungalow door. Lucy was still there and met them in the hallway. Cole filled her in on the new developments as he guided Jessica to her room. He closed the bedroom door while Jessica pulled off her coat and gave it an uncharacteristic toss toward the nearest chair.

"Sit down and I'll take off your shoes," Cole said, surprised when she sank to the mattress immediately.

"Thanks, Cole," she muttered.

He untied the skinny laces and pulled off her boots. "If you lie back, Jess, I'll take off your jeans."

His suggestion was made innocently and received innocently, but the instant Jessica sank back upon the comforter, Cole flushed hot with desire at the thought of disrobing her and had to struggle to get control of himself.

Fortunately, Jessica closed her eyes and flung an arm over her face. "I don't know why I'm so tired," she murmured.

"Trauma is exhausting," he replied.

Cole wondered how he would ever keep himself in check once he touched her. He wanted nothing more than to sink upon her and make love to her. He'd wanted to make love to Jessica ever since they danced together at the Falls Winery open house. And having held it back only made his desire more acute. He was still looking at her, trying to decide what to do, when she stirred.

"Cole?" she asked, as if wondering what was taking him so long.

He straddled her legs and unbuttoned her jeans. She didn't move. Cole could see the bud of her navel, and he swelled as hard as a rock. He should have let Lucy tuck Jessica into bed. He was a madman for doing this.

With two hard tugs, Cole pulled down her jeans, trying to ignore the way her hips arched off the bed as he slid the fabric down her thighs. Then he pulled the pants over her knees and feet and stood up. He occupied his hands and attention with folding the jeans into an uncharacteristically neat bundle, and set them on the chair with her coat. Then he turned back to her, hoping she had burrowed out of sight under the covers.

Jessica had only managed to roll onto her side with her knees drawn up. Her thighs were long and slender, milky white, her knees and shins graceful and sleek as a dancer's.

The arc of lace where her panties curved high on her hip sent blood racing to Cole's loins. He tore his glance away from her, swearing at himself for his sheer stupidity. With an oath, he dragged the bedcovers out from under her and carefully draped them over her slender form. She snuggled under the bulky covering and sighed.

"Good night, Jessica," he said between gritted teeth.

"Good night, Cole. Thanks."

"No problem." He lurched toward the door.

"And, Cole?"

"Yes?"

"Your father . . ." Her voice was slurred. "He'll be in good hands now."

"I only hope it isn't too late," he replied. "See you, Jess."

Cole rolled out of bed at the sound of distant footsteps and the faint clank of metal. He had not donned the arms of a warrior for the past ten years, but his senses were still keenly honed, and he could tell that someone was mounting the stone stairs with a sword strapped to his side.

Cole wriggled into his habit while Giovanna stirred sleepily in the bed still warm from their recent lovemaking. Spending the past few nights with her in his arms had been glorious, heavenly, almost enough to satisfy him should he be banished to some future hell without her.

But Cole had no time to dwell on the future, for the tower door slammed against the stone wall, and a squat, heavyset man burst into the chamber, sword in hand. Rondolfo di Brindisi had returned to the castle unannounced and in a foul temper.

"Giovanna!" the count barked.

Giovanna sat up in alarm, her naked breasts luminous against the dark fur coverlet.

"Whore!" Brindisi shouted.

Cole's left hand ached for a sword of his own. He felt no shame for having been in Giovanna's bed; Brindisi had relinquished any claim he may have had on his wife the day he had beaten her senseless and left her to die. Cole had brought her back to life. She was his now, as she was meant to be. And he wanted nothing more than to kill this swine who had literally beaten his Giovanna to death.

"How dare you!" Giovanna spat, tossing back her hair in a gesture of defiance. Obviously she was not ashamed of her actions either.

"Cover yourself, you besotted whore!" He flung a discarded robe at her. "I leave you for a month, and what is the first thing I hear? You are bedding a priest! Whore!" He raised a gloved hand to strike her.

"Hold!" Cole thundered.

"You!" Rondolfo turned on him. "You shall die, priest! No man makes a cuckold of me! Not even a man of God!"

He lunged for Cole, swinging his heavy sword with both hands. Cole jumped aside. He threw a stool into Rondolfo's path, but Rondolfo viciously kicked it aside. His eyes were red with anger, and his yellowed, uneven teeth were bared.

"Die for your sin, you hideous bastard!" Rondolfo swung again, nearly catching Cole's robe with the point of the blade.

Cole looked around for a weapon, but nothing in the chamber could match the deadly advantage of a sword. He grabbed the only item within reach—his hooded cowl—and this he threw upon Rondolfo's head. The count staggered in momentary darkness before he yanked the garment off, giving Cole the chance to bring his clasped hands down upon Rondolfo's sword arm in a bone-shattering blow. Rondolfo howled in pain and dropped his weapon, which clanked to the stone floor.

"For Giovanna!" Cole cried, pummeling Rondolfo's face and paunch until the man stumbled backward, battered senseless, no match for the strength of Cole's rage.

"Cosimo!" Giovanna screamed. "He has a knife!"

The name Giovanna shouted caught Cole off guard, and he glanced away for a fraction of a second—time enough for Rondolfo to lash out with the blade. Cosimo grunted in pain as the dirk found purchase in his shoulder, but he did not retreat. Instead, the baron roared his battle cry and, in an unbelievable show of strength, hauled Rondolfo off his feet and hurled him across the room.

With a look of astonishment on his face, Rondolfo sailed through the air, hit the wall, and fell forward, impaling himself on his own knife. He stiffened, and his eyes widened in horrified surprise as he realized he had caused his own death. Then he slumped over his folded arm and lay still.

Before Cosimo could act, he heard more footsteps in the tower stairwell. Rondolfo's men-at-arms swarmed into the chamber, followed by the old woman Cosimo had frightened with his powers of healing.

"There he is! Murderer!" she screeched. "Sorcerer!"

Cole stared at her, heedless of his bleeding shoulder and his hideous face bared for all to see.

"Count Rondolfo is dead!" a sergeant said, drawing his sword. "Seize the priest!"

The other men grabbed Cosimo's arms and wrestled him toward the chamber door while Giovanna jumped out of bed, dragging the coverlet with her.

"Cosimo!" she screamed.

He struggled, but they dragged him past her. He strained to look at her over his shoulder.

"Cosimo!" Her topaz eyes were on fire with fear.

"I'll be back, Giovanna!" he cried. "Giovanna! I'll be back for you!"

Cole woke up, his heart pounding, his face covered with sweat. Gingerly he touched his shoulder. It ached from the position he had assumed in the chair by his father's bed. He rolled his shoulder back and forth to ease the cramp while the vision replayed in his thoughts. He had dreamed of Cosimo Cavanetti. In the dream he had *been* Cosimo Cavanetti. And he had made a promise to a woman who loved him—a promise that he doubted twelfth-century Cosimo had been able to keep.

In spite of the warmth of the room, Cole shivered. Maybe

the things Jessica had been trying to tell him were true. Maybe Cosimo did exist in his mind somewhere. Perhaps what he thought were mere dreams were actual events playing through his memory. Cole frowned and shifted in the chair. The thought that he might be part twelfth-century monk was damned unsettling.

He looked down at his father, who slept peacefully in his bed without the aid of tranquilizers or sleeping tablets. Did his father dream of Cosimo Cavanetti, too? Is that what his father had tried to tell him so many years ago, when all he could think about was football? His father had tried to talk about the Cavanetti legacy the night of Cole's graduation party, tried to induct his son in some kind of weird ritual, but Cole had laughed off such old-country nonsense. Now that he was coming to grips with his Italian background, however, Cole found the legacy neither amusing nor nonsensical.

He leaned down and put his hand over his father's wrist. "Pop, I'm ready to listen now," he declared softly. "Ready when you are."

23

Jessica woke up at four o'clock in the morning. She squinted at the glowing radio alarm and sank back onto the pillow, wide awake. For a few minutes she tossed and turned, trying to force herself to sleep, but sleep would not come. She had a vague feeling of unease, as if she had forgotten to do something important. Finally, she threw off the covers and got up. Maybe her barely started paper had something to do with her insomnia. In four days she would fly back to California with nothing but a wild tale of murder and mayhem to show for her time at Moss Cliff.

She pulled on her robe, brushed her teeth, and padded down the hall to the study. The stack of paper by her father's typewriter was thicker this time. He had actually continued to work on his play. Jessica felt a flicker of hope but instantly smothered it with her usual caution. Better not to expect anything.

She pulled out the manila folder that held the few pages of her presentation. Quickly she scanned the text, shaking her head over the rocky introduction. She grabbed a pen and crossed out the opening sentence, scribbling in a replacement, but her hand was cold, her writing crabbed. A fire might improve both her penmanship and her state of mind.

Jessica piled kindling and logs on the fireplace grate, and soon a healthy fire crackled upon the hearth. She rose and ambled out to the kitchen to get a cup of tea while the room warmed up. While water heated in the teakettle, Jessica sniffed, detecting a crisp pine scent, and she ventured toward the source of the smell.

There in the family room stood her Scotch pine, decorated with ornaments and tinsel and twinkling lights. Jessica stared at the tree in wonder as a lump swelled in her throat. She thought of all the years she had been responsible for the Christmas decorations, all the while longing for a magic that had never come. At six, she had learned the truth: there was no Santa Claus. At seven, she had learned not to expect anyone else to visit her house on Christmas Eve either. At ten, she had learned to create her own Christmas. And at twelve she had learned to invent her own life and that of her alcoholic father.

The whistle of the teakettle roused her from her memories. Jessica hurried back to the kitchen, fighting an overwhelming urge to cry. She pressed her lips together as she doused the tea bag in the cup. What elf had decorated the tree? Lucy? Surely not her father.

Whoever had decorated the tree, Jessica was grateful. Maybe this year things would change. Maybe her life would turn around. Maybe her father would turn over the proverbial new leaf. Could she dare hope? And how would Cole figure in her life? She squeezed out the tea bag and threw it into the trash, trying hard to restrain the flame of hope that flickered inside her.

She carried the cup and saucer to the study and was surprised to see a dark figure standing before the fire.

"Good morning, Miss Ward."

"Cosimo!" Jessica swept into the room. "What are you doing about at this hour?"

"Niccolo sleeps. You do not. I take my chances when they occur."

Jessica put her teacup on the desk. "Would you like some tea?"

"No, thank you."

She sat on the edge of the desk and gazed at the monk, who stood silhouetted against the firelight.

"Cosimo, I didn't tell you earlier, but I was so thankful that you came to me in the cavern. You saved my life."

"I have always tried to come when you had need of me, my lady of the night."

"Yes, you have, haven't you?" No one had watched over her since she could remember, not even her father. Cosimo alone had been a constant source of support for her.

Yet she had kept the truth from him. She knew they were linked in a way that was important to Cosimo, but she had never admitted it, and she felt wretchedly dishonest for keeping silent out of fear. There was nothing to fear from him. Jessica hung her head, overcome with guilt.

"But soon you will have no need of me." Cosimo stepped toward her. "And I shall not be here."

"What do you mean?" She felt a stab of panic.

"I am here to bid you good-bye, Jessica." He put his hands into the sleeves of his habit.

"Good-bye?" Her voice cracked. What was he saying?

"Niccolo is accepting the Cavanetti legacy, thanks to you. Soon there will be no need of my presence here at St. Benedict."

"No need of your presence!" Jessica stared at him. "What about me?"

The hood shifted as he tilted his head. "What about you, Jessica?"

"What will I do without you, Cosimo? I need you!"

He said nothing. He merely stood before her as her words came back at her. She heard them repeat in her ears and felt a flush of surprise at her outburst. She had never needed anyone, or at least had never admitted to needing anyone. She raised her chin, blinking back the sheen of tears that burned her eyes.

"You will have Niccolo," he replied at last.

She bit her lip, trying to contain her tears and the painful constriction in her chest. "But Cole is not you."

"Yes, he is."

"But, Cosimo, what about our talks, our—"

"Jessica." He held up one hand to quiet her protests. "I cannot stay. Once Niccolo accepts his heritage, there will be no more need of a guardian. And if I try to fight Niccolo to remain in the present, I will only do harm to us both. Besides"—his voice softened—"I must admit that it is somewhat painful for me to remain."

"No . . ." Jessica shook her head in disbelief as she stared at him. How could he abandon her like this? What would she do when he was gone? Who would counsel her, comfort her? The prospect of never seeing Cosimo again hit her like a blow. Granted, she had planned to go back to Stanford, but she hadn't thought she would be giving up Cosimo's companionship forever.

"No!" Frantic, Jessica bolted to him, flinging herself against the great wall of blackness that towered before the fire. She threw her arms around his neck and embraced him with all the strength she possessed. "Oh, Cosimo!" She breathed in the scent of him, the musky smell of woolen cloth and the fresh odor of sun and soil. "Cosimo!" She closed her eyes and clutched the back of his hood, drawing his head to her as if to trap him in the present. "Cosimo, you're a part of me! You can't leave me!"

For a moment he remained silent, his hands at his sides, his neck straight, his head thrown back—as hard and uncompromising as a tower of stone.

"Cosimo! Don't leave me!"

"I must." He put his hands on her wrists as if to pull her arms from around his neck. "That is my fate. I must always leave."

"No. You have a choice this time."

"I have no choice. You are Jessica Ward. You belong to Niccolo Cavanetti. You have no memory of what you once were to me."

"Yes, I do. I just never told you that—"

Cosimo's grip tightened. "What haven't you told me?"

"That I am—" Jessica swallowed. "I think that I am Giovanna di Montalcino."

"Giovanna?" Cosimo whispered.

"I was afraid before, Cosimo, afraid that you would hypnotize me, practice your sorcery on me."

"I am no sorcerer."

"When you asked me to think back that night, to listen to your voice, I had a weird feeling that I did know you. And that night in the cavern, when you said I did not remember my ugly left-handed baron? Well, I did!"

"Sweet Jesus!" Cosimo clutched her head between his hands, his thumbs splaying beneath her cheekbones. "Ah, lady, you did wound me!"

"I'm sorry! I was afraid—"

"I would never hurt you." His fingers gripped her tightly. "Never."

"I know that now." She stared into the darkness of his cowl. "Cosimo, you said once that Giovanna was never yours, that she never would be yours."

"Yes. I promised to come back for her, but death kept me from my vow. I never knew what became of her." He paused, and she felt his hand stroke her cheek. "I have never been able to rest, thinking what might have befallen her. And all the years, Jessica, all the centuries, I have searched and waited for our paths to cross again."

"And so they have," she breathed. She touched his hand. "Cosimo, I can't tell you what happened to Giovanna. But if you wish to put me in a trance, perhaps you might find your answer."

"You would agree to that?" he asked, barely suppressing his astonishment.

"I would do anything for you, my lord," she replied, lowering her head.

He crushed her to his chest in an iron hold of joy. And then he smoothed her hair and led her to the chair by the fire. She sank onto the cushion.

"Look at the flames, Jessica."

She obeyed and draped her hands on the upholstered arms of the wing chair.

"Listen to the sound of my voice." He stepped behind her. "Just listen to the sound of my voice. Do not think of who I am, or what I am . . ."

Giovanna looked down the narrow mountain valley at the green plain in the distance. She was exhausted, her belly was heavy with child, and it hurt to ride. Yet she had to press onward. She had to reach the monastery that loomed on the far horizon. At the Benedictine monastery she would find Cosimo, and there she would give birth to his child. She would lay the babe in his arms and then tell him of his eleven-year-old son, whom he had never seen. Giovanna winced and lay a hand on her bloated abdomen as her horse picked its way over a jumble of rocks on the trail.

She had fled from one hamlet to another since Epiphany, trying to hide her identity, trying to find her baron. He had been taken from one monastery to another, and her quest had been long and arduous. Traveling while pregnant had taken its toll, too. She was quite certain that Cosimo wouldn't recognize the pale, scrawny creature she had become. She feared for the child growing inside her, knowing the difficulties she had endured along the way must have affected its development. And how weary she felt. Her money had run out days ago, and she knew hunger and thirst for the first time in her life. Only the hope of finally joining her baron kept her riding when all she wanted was to lay by the roadside and sleep.

The horse sauntered onward, rocking her into a trance. She dozed on and off while the trail leveled out and followed a river that led to the buildings of the church. The August heat played tricks on her eyes, turning the surrounding vineyard to a shimmering sea of green. Giovanna wiped away the sweat that ran down her face and tried to breathe while her stomach cramped against hunger and the life inside her. The air was so hot she could almost hear it. How long could she last? She squeezed her eyes against a knot of pain in her womb. How long could she keep to her horse when her head felt so heavy, her belly so hard?

Presently, her mount passed under a stone arch into a courtyard, clopping on the cobblestones. The noise brought her to her senses, and she raised her head. Men in black robes issued from the shade of a building ahead of her. She had made it to the monastery, and the sight of the monks made her sob with joy.

Hands reached up for her. Her senses swirled. She tried to struggle from her horse, but her limbs would not obey her. She tried to speak, to tell them she had no more strength, but even her mouth would not obey her. Something hot and moist trickled down her bare leg under her gown. Ah, Lord, her babe was coming! She must rally the last of her strength. Yet she had no more in reserve. And childbirth was the hardest task a woman could undertake. She swooned.

Giovanna awakened in a sparse, cool chamber. The first thing she saw was a crucifix on the wall at the foot of her cot. Her glance darted to the small window on the other side of the room. Stars twinkled in a black sky, and a cool breeze wafted above her face.

Giovanna grimaced. Her head pounded, and she could feel her skin glowing with a fever—a bad sign for a woman who had just birthed a child. And where was her baby? She moved her head to view the entire chamber, but it was empty except for a chair near the door. She lay back and closed her eyes, her flaccid belly a riot of agony.

"Please, God," she whispered as hot tears rolled out of the corners of her eyes. "Please!" But Giovanna didn't have enough strength to form the remaining words of supplication. She fell asleep, praying for her child, for Cosimo, for understanding from her Creator.

In the morning she felt even worse. She could no longer lift her head. When a young priest came into the chamber, carrying a child swathed in a blanket, she didn't have the power to reach for her baby. Giovanna wept as the priest held her black-haired child before her.

"Your son," he said, smiling. His eyes were sad, however. Both of them were well aware of her fever and her lack of strength to fight it. Many women died from such fevers.

"Ah!" Giovanna's lips quivered into a tremulous smile. "He's beautiful."

"He's quite healthy. He will do well."

"Thank you, Brother." Giovanna swallowed and licked her lips against the pain that wrenched the lilt from her voice.

"Tell me, is there a lay brother here named Cosimo Cavanetti?"

"Cosimo?" The priest looked at her sharply and then straightened, fumbling with the baby's coverlet.

"I was told he would be here."

"He was, but—"

"Please. I must see him."

"I am sorry, my lady. That would be impossible."

"It is very important. I have been searching for him for—"

The priest shook his head. "Brother Cosimo is dead."

"What?"

"Did you not know that he was a sorcerer? He brought a woman back from the dead. And it is no troubadour's tale, either, my lady. There was a witness to his sorcery, an old woman who saw him raise a woman from the dead! Imagine it!"

Giovanna stared at the ceiling. Her vision clouded. Cosimo was dead? It was unthinkable. She had to tell him of his sons, she had to tell him that she loved him, that she would be his, that she was finally free to be his wife. Sobs shook her, and each one sent her spiraling into a dark void of pain.

"I thought everyone had heard the tale of Cosimo Cavanetti," the priest put in, seeing he had caused her such a shock.

"Not I."

"They walled him up alive. That's what they do to sorcerers, you know."

Giovanna forgave his eager thoughtlessness. He was a young man, unversed in heartache and grief, which might have stilled a wiser tongue. She closed her eyes, tired beyond belief.

"What will you name your son?" he asked in an effort to raise her spirits.

She opened her eyes. "Cosimo."

"You can't mean it!" He crossed himself, his eyes wide with horror.

"Yes. Promise me, Brother. You will name him Cosimo!" She lurched to a sitting position, defying her body's scream of protest. "Name him Cosimo—I beg you!"

He stepped backward, clutching the baby to his narrow chest. "You're mad!"

"He was no sorcerer!" she cried in anguish. "Why did they kill him? Why did they have to kill him!"

For a moment the priest stared at her. Giovanna wept while his form wavered from black to white before her bleary eyes. Then her vision suddenly went dark. She collapsed, falling to one side. The last thing she felt was the stone floor, so cool against her burning cheek.

Jessica opened her eyes to find Cosimo on his knees before her, both hands clutching the arms of her chair. Her own hands were clenched into white fists in her lap. She glanced at Cosimo, startled to see him so close to her.

"She died," he said softly. "She died, just like that."

"I think so."

"She gave me two sons." He shook his head in wonder. "I had two sons."

"How else could you have started the Cavanetti line?"

"True." He nodded. "I had not given much thought to it." His hood moved as he looked down. He lay a hand over her tight fists, and she tried to relax them.

"It seems Giovanna has been searching for you as well, Cosimo. She must have loved you very much."

"Aye." He rubbed the back of her hand but still did not rise to his feet. "But why didn't she tell me that Niccolo was my son? She should have told me!"

"Maybe she was afraid to take the risk. Afraid you would challenge Rondolfo di Brindisi and come to harm. And after Rondolfo was dead, she could not find you."

"If only she had told me sooner, I would have stolen her away from that beast of a husband. I loved her."

The wistfulness of his voice sent a stabbing sensation through Jessica's heart. Such love, to last for centuries like this! She knew with sudden clarity how to help him, how to give Cosimo what he needed so desperately. And she must not be afraid.

"Cosimo?" She reached for the hood of his cowl. "Let me look at you."

"No." He tensed and pulled back his head. "No, Jessica."

"Yes. I want to see you."

She grasped both edges of the hood and slowly drew them back from his face. She steeled herself for the sight that would be revealed in the firelight. Frank had collapsed after seeing Cosimo's face, so Jessica knew she would be facing a hideous visage. But she was certain her love for Cosimo's inner beauty would give her the strength to face his outer deformity.

"No," Cosimo protested. But the hood fell around his shoulders, revealing his wounded countenance.

His mouth was twisted on one side, pulled into an eternal sardonic smile against a cheek full of raspberry-colored bumps. Jagged lines and spots of white led to a ragged patch of raven-colored curls near his ear. His left eyelid drooped over a milky eyeball that stared blindly into oblivion beneath a shredded brow. His forehead was a pitted and puckered expanse that stretched under his uneven hairline. But his right eye was black and glistening, full of intelligence and kindness, hinting at the man beneath the scars. He must have been handsome once, as good-looking as Cole. Jessica felt her heart lurch with compassion as he covered his face with his hands.

"No," he protested, his voice thick.

"Yes," she answered. She drew his hands away and leaned forward to kiss his scarred cheek. With trembling hands, she drew his head toward her so that she could kiss his forehead, his brow, his eyelid, and his jaw. Jessica felt the tenseness ease in his body, and then his hands encircled her waist.

"Don't, Jessica," he murmured. "Giovanna was the only—"

"You forget, my lord." She ran her hand over his thick black hair. "I am Giovanna."

"You are Jessica."

"No." She cradled his face in her hands and met his gaze. "I am Giovanna di Montalcino. And you are Cosimo Cavanetti. And we have found each other at last and forever."

Then she leaned forward, slanting her head to place her mouth on his. Slowly, deliberately, she kissed his lips, marveling that she felt no twisted scars upon them. He squeezed her torso with his big hands and pulled her halfway out of the chair, sighing raggedly as her lips lingered upon his and accepted him in all his wounded ugliness.

She felt no fear, no revulsion at his touch, only an overwhelming sense of love and happiness. She slipped down against him until they knelt thigh to thigh on the floor. He kissed her sweetly, then passionately, then wildly, bunching her ebony hair to his face and reveling in the touch of its silkiness upon his skin. Jessica bent her head back, and he pressed kisses upon her neck, arching her backward until her hips pressed into his. His lips made her forget who she was, and soon she was slipping into a strange physical plane where all she could feel was his mouth and hands and all she could hear was their breath coming fast and hard. Cosimo pushed the robe off her shoulders and slid his hands over her breasts, caressing her as he murmured her name. Jessica closed her eyes, swept from reality.

"I am yours, my lord," she murmured, "and you are mine."

When Jessica woke up hours later, she found herself on the sofa in front of the hearth. The fire was nearly out, and her legs were cold, her hip joints cramped. She sat up, shocked that she was lying naked beneath the robe that had been tucked around her. What time was it? Where was Cosimo?

She remembered their hours of lovemaking and flushed, scrambling to her feet as if to outdistance the memory. She glanced around the room, looking for a sign of him. Had he left her for good?

Then her eye caught sight of an unfamiliar book sitting on the desk next to her research paper. She stumbled across the floor, drawing her robe on at the same time. There on the desk was an ancient manuscript with a tattered leather cover. Jessica knew just by looking at it that it should be in a museum. She reached out a trembling hand and gently opened the book.

Inside was a record of observations of the heavens. Each page bore a date. May 5, 1101. May 6, 1101. Her heart pounded in her chest. Where had this volume come from? Then she noticed a parchment marker slid between two pages. Carefully she turned to the indicated spot and looked down at the star map. There was her comet, sailing through the twelfth-century sky, just as she had theorized but had been unable to prove with existing documents.

"Yes!" she whispered, a grin of victory on her lips.

Then she noticed that the parchment marker bore a scrawled note. She raised it closer to her face, squinting in the faint morning light at the tiny writing.

My lady, as the stars in the heavens, my love for you shall last forever, it read. *Cosimo Cavanetti, 1074–1991.*

She gazed at the marker for a long time while her grin faded to a sad smile. Then she carefully tucked the parchment away at the back of the book.

24

Jessica stood in the Cavanetti kitchen and curled her fingers around the steaming mug of coffee Maria had put on the counter beside her. "Thanks, Maria," she said. "It was cold out there."

"So you found the place all right?" Maria poured coffee for Cole and herself.

Jessica nodded. The morning had been a gruesome exercise. She was glad Cole had insisted on accompanying her to the bog when she had shown the police the spot where Frank had dumped Shawn's body.

Cole had stood beside her the whole time, his arm around her shoulders, and had insisted that she leave when the dredging began. She was thankful to have been spared the sight of Shawn being pulled from the pond.

"They're dredging now," Cole put in. "It might be a while before they find anything. All we can do is wait."

"Poor Shawn." Maria shook her head while she sipped her coffee. "She didn't deserve to die."

The doorbell rang, and Maria set down her mug to hobble out of the kitchen. Jessica watched her go, feeling numb. The events of the past few days had drained her. The early hours spent with Cosimo hadn't done her energy level much good, either. She sighed, and Cole caressed her hair.

Without a word he ran his hand down the back of her neck. Jessica closed her eyes and let herself be pulled to his chest. She loved Cole but pride was an invisible barrier between them. How she longed to say the words that would break down the wall and let them be to each other what Cosimo and Giovanna had been. But her own pride and fear kept her lips silent, her heart in check.

Only four days remained until her return to California, not nearly enough time to develop a lasting relationship with Cole. They had wasted valuable time bickering and fighting, and now the hours were slipping through her fingers.

Jessica sighed again, knowing it was too late for them. Maybe she would have to repeat Cosimo's pattern, forced to wait centuries until she crossed paths with Niccolo Cavanetti again. She leaned her forehead against the placket of his sweater while his arms came around her. He bent his head, and she felt his nose in her hair while his hands slid up and down her back.

"Cole," she whispered in anguish.

"It'll be all right, Jess," he murmured, obviously thinking she was upset about Shawn. "It'll be over soon."

He was still holding her when she heard Maria head back to the kitchen, Lucy in tow. Jessica pulled away from Cole and found her mug, which she lifted to her mouth.

Lucy bustled into the room, and the look on her face told Jessica that something was up. Lucy held up a newspaper. "Cole, did you see this?" she asked.

"No."

"Look!" Lucy strode forward, folding the paper to display the front-page story. "Read this!"

Cole raised his eyebrows at Jessica and then turned his attention to the article. Lucy grinned at him, impatient for him to finish.

"How do you like that!" Cole exclaimed.

"What is it?" Jessica asked, trying to peer around his shoulder.

"That woman in Philadelphia?" Lucy pointed to the news photo. "She lied about Cole assaulting her. Seems she cooked up the story to make her boyfriend jealous."

"What?" Jessica sputtered in disbelief.

"I knew it!" Maria crowed.

"She admitted to lying. She saw the news story on television about Cole catching that serial killer, and she decided to come clean about him."

Jessica squeezed Cole's arm. "Oh, Cole, that's great!"

"This calls for a celebration!" Maria exclaimed. "I'm going to get some champagne!"

They were sipping the last of the champagne when Greg Kessler arrived at the Cavanetti mansion. Jessica smiled as he handed his coat to Maria. She wasn't especially happy to see him, just feeling giddy from Cole's news and the champagne. Besides that, Cole stood next to her with his arm around her waist, and she liked the feeling of his body close to hers.

"To what do we owe the pleasure?" Cole asked, his voice crisp and cool.

"I hear there's been some trouble," Greg replied. "Anything I can do to help?"

"Not a thing." Cole's arm tightened around Jessica. "We have everything under control."

Greg looked at Cole and then at Jessica, as if confused by their familiarity. Jessica gazed back at him, content to let him wonder.

"What's this I hear about Isabella being in jail?"

"It seems Isabella and Frank have run afoul of the law," Cole answered simply.

"Oh." Greg licked his lips. "I was concerned about the lease. Doesn't it have to be signed by Christmas Eve?"

"Yes. But I don't think Isabella will be available to make arrangements." Cole grinned. "Looks like you're out of luck, Kessler."

"Maybe I can sign in her stead," he suggested. "After all, we're practically partners already."

"No." Jessica shook her head. "A Cavanetti must sign."

"Well, how about if I take the documents to Isabella? I'd be happy to facilitate the deal."

"I'm sure you would, Greg. But Isabella isn't exactly the best candidate right now." No need to spread gossip, Jessica decided. A murder charge was quite enough for one family, without questioning the woman's legitimacy to the Cavanetti name. "Besides," she added, "I've got a Cavanetti right here who can do the signing."

"But, Jessica, I thought we had an understanding," Greg protested.

"You thought wrong, Greg."

Greg stared at Jessica and then at Cole, obviously frustrated that he could do nothing more to gain control of the property.

"How about it, Cole?" Jessica asked, knowing her words would needle Greg. "Would you like to sign the papers?"

"I'll do better than that. I'll sign a check as well." He squeezed her against him while Greg watched in dismay. "I've always wanted to own a vineyard. Especially St. Benedict."

Greg left the Cavanetti house soon afterward, and Jessica decided to go to the bungalow to get the lease for Cole to sign at the guesthouse a few minutes later. Lucy followed her out the door.

"Just look at this snow!" Lucy exclaimed. "Isn't it pretty?"

Jessica nodded. The entire grounds were covered with a light dusting, transforming them to a fairyland of crystal and whipped cream.

"I just love it up here," Lucy went on. "I've never spent any time in the Northwest before. And I just love it."

"It is beautiful. Especially up here at Moss Cliff."

"How could anyone ever leave it?"

"I don't know, Lucy." Jessica stared straight ahead, a lump in her throat. "I don't know."

She could tell Lucy was looking at her as they walked, but she couldn't seem to make conversation. Somehow the scenery didn't hold her interest while her heart was slowly breaking.

"Say, Jessica, I was wondering . . ." Lucy began. "Well, I don't mean to be rude or anything, but would you mind if I spent Christmas Eve with you and Robert?"

Jessica glanced at her. What a strange request. What about Cole?

"What with Cole leaving, I'll be all alone. And I hate spending Christmas Eve alone, don't you?"

Cole was leaving? Jessica stared at her in shock, then tore her glance away so Lucy wouldn't see her stricken look. She felt a hand on her sleeve.

"Jessica, didn't you know Cole was leaving?"

"He didn't mention it."

"Well, he just got called this morning, and then things got kind of hectic, what with the police and all. He's flying out after lunch. There's a big meeting concerning his place on the team. The development in the Philadelphia story must have done him some good."

"So he's going to St. Louis?"

Lucy nodded. "His teammates nearly rioted when they found out he was being replaced. Then with Cole catching that murderer, his coach probably thought better of his decision. How could he possibly bench a hero?"

"So Cole might be reinstated?"

"That's what this meeting is all about."

Jessica tried to be happy. It would mean the world to Cole to be reinstated. But why hadn't he told her himself? And why hadn't he let her know he was going? Was she so unimportant to him? She stumbled up the stairs to the bungalow porch. Cole was leaving, deserting her once again. Football would take him away from her, just as it had thirteen years ago.

"I hope you don't mind that I decorated the tree," Lucy said, trailing her into the house. "Your dad helped—he thought you'd like the surprise."

"He did?"

"Yes. And it was fun. I haven't decorated a tree for years! I've always been on the road at Christmas time."

"With Cole?"

"Not always. I've got more clients than him, you know."

"Of course."

Lucy crossed her arms and looked at Jessica, pursing her lips. "You didn't think that I—" she touched her chest, "that Cole and I—"

Jessica blinked, flustered, and fumbled with her jacket zipper. "Of course not."

Lucy stepped toward her. "Listen, Jessica. Cole is crazy about you—don't you know that?"

Jessica felt her ears flame. She raised her head. "He's never said anything."

"That man!" Lucy shook her head and put her hands on her hips. "I told you he's an ass sometimes."

"How do you know anyway? Has he said something to you?"

"He doesn't have to! God, haven't you seen the way he looks at you?"

"No, I—"

"I've known Cole for years, Jessica. He's had his women—don't think he hasn't. But they've been more like part of his image than part of his life. You know what I mean?"

"I think I understand what you're saying." Jessica's heart surged in her chest.

"They flutter on his arm like exotic birds. He's always good to them, but kind of detached. Not like he is with you. You two seem to go together, like bookends or something. And the way he looks at you. God, if a man looked at me like that, I'd melt in my socks!"

"We're just old friends," Jessica stammered, stunned by Lucy's disclosure.

"Friends, my foot!" Lucy laughed. "Now you get those papers, Jessica, and get over to that guesthouse right now. I'll stay here and make lunch for your dad."

Jessica stared at her. "All right."

"Get!"

◆ ◆ ◆

Jessica let herself into the guesthouse and found Cole in his room, throwing clothes into a suitcase. He glanced over his shoulder when he heard her step in the doorway. He had taken off his sweater and was dressed in a knit polo shirt that revealed his well-formed biceps.

"Hi, Jess."

"Hi." The sight of his clothes in the suitcase dampened her spirits, but she forced a smile.

He dropped a sweater on top of the pile of shirts.

"You know, you should fold those," she commented. "They're going to get all wrinkled if you pack that way."

"I'll get them ironed at the hotel, Mother Superior." He winked at her. "Okay?"

She tried to ignore the way the wink tugged at her heart. She reminded herself he was leaving her. "So you're going to St. Louis this afternoon?"

"Yes. How did you know?"

"Lucy just told me." She followed the movement of his long fingers as he folded a silk tie. She had always thought his hands were among his most attractive features.

"I hope it won't upset any plans," he added.

"Not at all." She never had Christmas plans. She usually spent it alone while her father slept most of the day. Yet, Christmas might be different this year with Lucy sharing part of it. She liked Lucy and would be grateful for the companionship. But no one could substitute for Cole.

"You didn't tell me you were leaving," she ventured, trying to keep her tone casual.

"It was so busy this morning. I wanted to tell you when we were by ourselves."

"Oh. Well, I've got the papers here, if you want to sign them before you go."

"Sure." Cole shut the suitcase and pulled if off the bed. He set it on the floor and then walked up to her.

She held out the envelope, careful not to let her fingers brush his. Cole scanned the documents and then flattened them against the nightstand. He got a pen out of the drawer and signed his name at the bottom of the agreement. He retained his copy and then folded the papers and returned them to her.

"I suppose you want a check now," he teased.

"Right now."

"Afraid the plane will crash and you won't get your money?"

"No. I just don't trust you, sir." She smiled at him.

He grinned and pulled a checkbook from the drawer. He filled out a check, ripped it off, and gave it to her.

"Do you have any ID for that?" She raised her eyebrows.

A slow smile blossomed on his lips, and his eyes filled with sparkling lights. "Now, ma'am, just what kind of ID do you want?"

"Driver's license? Major credit card?"

Cole slipped out his license and gave it to her, playing along while the grin hovered on his lips.

She surveyed his picture and then shook her head. "I'm going to have to have something else for a check this big."

"How about this for ID?" He grasped her shoulders, and his mouth sank over hers. Jessica gasped in surprise and pulled back before his kiss could deepen.

"Don't!" She pushed against his chest. The check curled in her hand.

"Why?"

"You're toying with me."

"No, I'm not."

"You're going away. Let's just say good-bye and leave it at that."

"Jess, what I said the other night—"

"You told me to leave you alone, and that's what I'm trying to do!" She broke from his grip.

"Let me explain what—"

"You don't have to, Cole. Every time I've tried to reach out to you, you've pushed me away!"

"But—"

"I can't take it anymore! I never know where I stand with you!"

"Well, welcome to the club, Jessica!" he retorted. "I don't know where I stand either!"

Jessica stared at him, impatiently brushing away the dampness trickling down her cheeks. Suddenly Cosimo's image came to mind, and with it his advice to be candid, to take a risk, to demand something for herself. This was her last chance to make Cole understand. She wouldn't let him go this time without at least telling him how she felt. She wouldn't repeat the mistake Giovanna had made.

"Can't you see, Cole? All these years . . ." She straightened her shoulders, determined to reveal her feelings. "All these years, I've been in love with you!"

"What?"

"I've loved you ever since I was a girl! I don't pity you! I don't care whether you make touchdowns or not. I just love you—"

There. She had told him. Now when he went away, at least he would know the truth.

But, to her chagrin, she broke into tears. She quickly turned away from him, stumbling toward the bedroom door.

"Jess!" Cole lunged after her, grabbing her arm, urging her around to face him. "Ah, Jess." His voice was like a caress. He touched her cheek with a tender gesture that nearly melted her resolve.

She closed the lids of her burning eyes, trying to keep her lips from trembling.

"Just go, Cole. You've never wanted me."

"Never wanted you?" His fingers dug into her arms. "The hell I didn't!"

"Just leave and—"

He smothered her words against her lips in a sudden swooping kiss that sucked her heart up into her throat. His hands slid around her as he gathered her into his arms, clutching her slight frame against his as if he were a giant bird of prey about to bolt into the sky with her.

"Cole . . ." Jessica clung to his neck as he parted her lips with his strong, warm tongue. She felt something inside her break apart and rush free, taking away her fears, her pride, and the damnable wall between her and Cole. With a gasp of joy, she opened her mouth to him, suddenly so fierce with hunger that she burrowed against him and growled like a savage beast. Her hands slid up the sides of his neck, over the taut ridges of his face, and into his glossy hair.

The kiss was a nuclear blast, mushroom cloud of heat that imploded from her mouth to somewhere deep inside her belly. She arched into Cole, a hard blow of alabaster in his great raven wings. She crushed her breasts against his chest as his thumbs found every feminine curve of her—under her arms, around the base of her breasts, down the small of her waist, and over the sleek line of her buttocks. His hands took possession of her as if she were warm clay and he a sculptor. She raised her leg and drew it alongside his hard thigh, aching for him. Cole sucked in his breath and clutched her to his loins.

"Jessica," he breathed. "I love you, too. Ah God, I do love you!"

She threw back her head as Cole played the ivory flute of her throat, moaning her name into her skin as if to brand her with the heat of his voice. She closed her eyes as Cole bent her over his arm and caressed her breasts.

This was what she had waited a lifetime for: to surrender to Cole, to feel his beautiful body against her, to feel his strong, capable hands imprint her skin and soul with his desire. No man had touched her exactly this way, no man had made her feel this utterly possessed, because no man had ever held her heart. Jessica melted onto his arm as his mouth sank over the fabric covering her breast.

He urged her backward onto the bed and knelt above her, his chest heaving with desire.

"You've got to initiate me now, Mother Superior," he gasped, lowering his mouth to her lips. "I'm a desperate man!"

"You're ready to take your vows?" she whispered with a smile. She closed her eyes in delight as he kissed her ear.

"I'll even propose properly on the plane." He unbuttoned her blouse. She thought her breasts would burst from the need to feel his mouth upon her.

"Oh?" Her smile grew wider as hope flared inside her.

"Thought you might like to spend Christmas Eve in St. Louis with your favorite quarterback."

"Oh, Cole!" She wrapped her arms around his neck. Spending Christmas with Cole would be a dream come true. She didn't care about finishing her paper or flying halfway across the country in holiday traffic. She would be with Cole, where she belonged, where she had always belonged. She hugged him with all her strength. "Oh, Cole! That would be lovely!"

"Merry Christmas, Mother Sup."

Epilogue

Jessica stood at the window of the Cavanetti mansion, looking out at the party in progress on the piazza. She held a small box in her hand, a last-minute gift she had forgotten to put on the table with the other gaily wrapped presents for her son.

She smiled as she saw his dark little head bobbing around the table as he blew a noisemaker in the face of his father and then his grandfather. She heard Maria shoo him away from the cake with a good-natured reprimand.

Jessica smiled. Her heart overflowed with love for her five-year old son, for the wonderful family that was finally hers. Never in her wildest dreams had she thought she could be this happy. Little Niccolo had changed her life forever.

Jessica reached up, unconsciously wrapping her fingers around the Super Bowl ring she wore on a chain around her neck. Cole had given it to her the year he had been asked back to his team for the play-offs and led the St. Louis Bulls to victory, telling her he never could have done it without her. She wore the ring with pride, and all the world knew she was the wife of Cole Nichols. But she was more proud of the simple band upon her finger that told the world she was the wife of Niccolo Cavanetti.

Jessica opened the door and breezed out to the warm summer evening. Soon the grapes would be ready for harvest, and the vineyard and winery would be swarming with activity. She had to admit she loved it all, even the busy end of summer.

Niccolo ran up to her.

"Mama! What's that?" he squealed.

"Something for my favorite Cavanetti!" she replied, gathering him up for a kiss.

Cole grabbed her from behind. "I thought *I* was your favorite Cavanetti!" he protested, nuzzling her hair.

"I thought *I* was!" Michael Cavanetti put in, stamping the end of his cane on the flagstones.

She grinned at her father-in-law. "I've got you all fooled, haven't I?"

Maria clucked and shook her head. "When is that father of yours going to get here?" she demanded. "Didn't I tell him eight o'clock? He said he and Lucy would be here by eight o'clock!"

"Oh, he's just being fashionably late," Cole said, patting Maria's cheek. "Don't worry. Have another glass of Riesling."

Jessica's smile wavered for a moment as she thought of her father. He had changed, too. The day the police had found the skeletal remains of her mother next to Shawn Cavanetti in the bog, her father had turned his life around.

For twenty-five years he had succumbed to alcohol, believing his glamorous wife had left him for another man. But she had not left him or her child. She had been murdered.

The truth had shocked Robert Ward out of his alcoholism. He had checked into a detox center, quit drinking for good, and now he had a new wife and a new play on Broadway. Jessica shook her head in wonder that his life—and hers—had finally moved foward.

Still, she sometimes wondered about the past and wished she could call upon Cosimo for answers and wisdom. She missed him. Though she never spoke of him to anyone, deep in her heart was a secret place where Cosimo still dwelled.

Sometimes she thought she saw a dark figure by the monkey puzzle tree near the guesthouse. But usually when she looked again she saw nothing, and she chided herself for imagining things. And sometimes, when she looked at her son—

"Mama! Mama!" Niccolo called, yanking her hand.

She looked down at his dark eyes, his glossy black hair. "What, Niccolo?"

"Look, Mama! A shooting star!"

She followed his pointing finger and saw the arcing light plunging toward the earth.

"Make a wish!" Maria cried. "Quick, before it disappears!"

Niccolo shut his eyes, grinned, and then opened them.

"I did it!" he squealed, jumping up and down. "I get my wish! I get my wish!"

"What did you wish for, Nicky?" asked Michael Cavanetti, leaning over the top of his cane.

"To be a knight. To have a big, big horse and a big, big sword! This big!"

While everyone else chuckled at his enthusiasm, Jessica stared at her son. Then she wrapped her arms around him and, squeezing him tightly, smiled a secret smile.

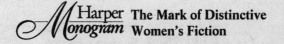

AVAILABLE NOW

FOR ALL TIME by Parris Afton Bonds

A time-travel romance for today's women. Stacie Branningan, a modern woman, is transported back to Fort Clark, Texas, in the 1870s. There, embodied as her own grandmother, she meets her soulmate, the man she's been yearning for all her life.

WINGS OF THE STORM by Susan Sizemore

When a time-travel experiment goes wrong, Dr. Jane Florian finds herself in the Middle Ages. There, she vows to make the best of things. Unfortunately, she hasn't counted on her attraction to her neighbor—the magnetic Sir Daffyd. An award-winning first novel told with humor and sizzle.

SEASONS OF THE HEART by Marilyn Cunningham

In this bittersweet novel of enduring love, Jessica, an idealistic young woman, falls in love with Mark Hardy, a bright but desperately poor young man. Not realizing Jessica is pregnant, he leaves her to seek his fortune. Years later he returns to find Jessica married to another man.

ALL MY DREAMS by Victoria Chancellor

Set in colonial Virginia in the year before the American Revolution, ALL MY DREAMS is the story of a woman who will stop at nothing to save her plantation—even if it means buying a bondsman to give her an heir. But her plan backfires when the bondsman she purchases is a wrongfully transported English lord.

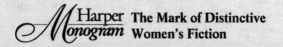

Harper Monogram The Mark of Distinctive Women's Fiction

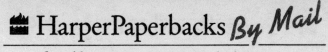

If you would like to receive a HarperPaperbacks catalog, fill out the coupon below and send $1.00 postage/handling to:

HarperPaperbacks Catalog Request
10 East 53rd St.
New York, NY 10022

Name _____

Address _____

State _____ Zip _____